BEYOND THE RIFT

ALANA ANKH

Dreamspinner Press

Published by
DREAMSPINNER PRESS

5032 Capital Circle SW, Suite 2, PMB# 279, Tallahassee, FL 32305-7886 USA
http://www.dreamspinnerpress.com/

Beyond the Rift
© 2014 Alana Ankh.

Cover Art
© 2014 Anne Cain.
annecain.art@gmail.com
Cover content is for illustrative purposes only and any person depicted on the cover is a model.

ISBN: 978-1-63216-173-4
Digital ISBN: 978-1-63216-174-1
Library of Congress Control Number: 2014948399
First Edition October 2014

Printed in the United States of America
(∞)
This paper meets the requirements of
ANSI/NISO Z39.48-1992 (Permanence of Paper).

Glossary of Terms and Locations

Species

Andari (native land, Anderra)—Race of mages gifted in defensive and summoning magic. Andari are fair-skinned, their faces soft, heart-shaped. With few exceptions, all Andari wear their hair long in traditional hairstyles that identify their relationship status. They are of lighter build, not prone to physical combat. A specific feature of Andari physiology is their heat, a period of extreme sexual desire. Considered shameful by Andari, it is the reason for their restrictive rules on sexuality.

Aranken (native land, A'rankin)—Race of powerful elemental mages. While they are originally from the Eastern Realm, a group of Aranken traveled to find a new home and became the ancestors of the Nikari.

Ndara—Extinct race distantly related with the Andari; no magic abilities but strong in physical combat, agility, and speed.

Nikari—Powerful species born from the union of the Aranken and the Ndara. Nikari are gifted in elemental offensive spells as well as physical combat. Despite being a relatively new species, through this unique blend of abilities, they managed to defeat the other races on their continent. Dusky-skinned, with sharp, angular features, they retain some Ndara traditions (specifically hair-braiding very similar to Andari). Their eyes are always black but rimmed with different colors (gold, bronze, silver, etc.). Like the Andari, they also have powerful impulses. However, theirs are not sexual, but violent. When they are particularly dangerous, their eyes glow. Many Nikari bond with interdimensional creatures called nightwolves.

Nikari-Andari Half Blood—Half-breeds between the two species, Half Bloods are weaker in magic than both Nikari and Andari, although their abilities vary greatly from individual to individual. Certain provinces in Anderra treat Half Bloods dismissively, whereas in others there are Half Bloods with an acknowledged

Nikari ancestry and wealth and land that compensates for their less potent magic.

SPECIFIC TERMS

Andari-related

Awaye—Dance of Andari origins, very sensual, specific to couples

Father (Andari family)—male who contributes additional magic to the offspring; involved in anal penetration with a female *odale*. Through the magic caused by the process of conception, both the sire and the father have direct bloodline connection to the offspring.

Malynsa—a sweet fruit native to Anderra

Odale—Temporary concubine used by a couple (usually same-sex) for procreation. Odale organize in guilds and abide by contracts that give them no rights over the resulting offspring. Female odale are used by homosexual (male-male) couples. Male odale are used by both lesbian couples and heterosexual couples. In the case of heterosexual couples, male odale are sought out for the purpose of improving the magical proficiency of the offspring.

Reysen—the deity most species believe in, also known as the Creator

Sire (Andari family)—male who is the genetic parent of the offspring, involved in vaginal penetration with a female odale

Wave-wayfaring—method of long-distance travel used by the Andari, involving creating a corridor through the fabric of time and space. It is more stable than dimensional rifts and not as dangerous but is less time-efficient.

Nikari-related

A'Mora—consort of the former Morai, mother of the current Morai (equivalent of the queen mother)

Darach—a long, curved dagger, the traditional weapon of the Nikari

Morai—the Emperor of the Nikari Empire

Moris—the male consort of the Morai

Mora—the female consort of the Morai

Moraistele—from *stele*, concubine; concubine of the Morai

Nightwolf—large interdimensional beast in the shape of a huge, mount-sized wolf. Nightwolves bond with certain Nikari, creating a unique telepathic connection between them. The color of a nightwolf's eyes is usually the same as the rim of a Nikari's pupil.

Reada wine—a Nikari drink, very spicy and potent, allowed only to Nikari past their age of majority

Rift—method of long-distance travel used by the Nikari, involving cutting a hole in dimensional space. Dimensional travel is instantaneous but can be very dangerous for untrained users and often causes physical pain.

Sharani—endearment, Nikari for beautiful one.

Stele—concubine of a Nikari, officially considered part of the household of the Nikari in question. The existence of a concubine does not contradict the possibility of marriage, and a Nikari with a concubine can take a spouse. This is an unusual arrangement, as Nikari are possessive of their mates and are rarely willing to share intimate affections. The institution of concubinage nonetheless persists, and is most common among high-ranking Nikari nobles and the imperial family.

ARANKEN MAGIC

Aranken magic is based on a combination of elements. Different types of mages are as follows:

Fire Starter: mage with powers over fire and air

Destroyers: mage with powers over earth and fire

Nurturer: mage with powers over water and earth; usually has potent healing abilities

Storm Caller: mage with powers over water and air

PROLOGUE
ARRIVAL

SEVERAL HOODED figures walked through the forest, the heavy mist settling over them like a physical barrier. The group rode forward, always forward, following their relentless leader, ignoring the less-than-pleasant weather that had plagued them since they'd come to this distant land. Not that it mattered. The elements couldn't harm the Aranken. Their magic was too potent for that.

Of course, those very same abilities had guided them to abandon their home and come here instead. Their group was only the first to ride out in search of a haven from their increasingly chaotic and dangerous land.

A tall man rode up to his ruler's side and whispered, "We're being followed."

Lord Seyan'Kel'Fezenda shot him a smile. "I know. They've been trailing us for a while. Don't worry. We can take them."

His second-in-command gave him a discreet nod and continued to ride by his side. It could have been due to the simple fact that he meant to protect his leader or maybe to prevent additional conspicuous behavior. Either way, Seyan felt thankful for the other man's proximity. He had faith in his own abilities, but he knew that no man, no matter how powerful, was unbeatable. In strange lands, facing strange foes, it paid to be cautious.

When their enemies struck, the Aranken group was more than ready for it. Deadly arrows came at them from every direction, blocking the distant rays of the sun. Seyan quickly cast a wind spell, deflecting the projectiles, while his second-in-command formed an ice shield around the two of them. Behind them, their companions summoned their own magic.

The clouds responded to the call of the Aranken soldiers, and hail fell from the skies, accompanied by angry bolts of lightning. The magic weeded their foes from their hiding places, but the battle was just beginning.

They were quick, these strange people, fast on their feet, moving like shadows, hard to aim at. The Aranken were powerful, but the time it took to cast their spells left them vulnerable to the well-aimed daggers thrown by their opponents. A Storm Caller and a Nurturer fell to their attack, before the Fire Starter by their side surrounded his group in a wide circle of flames so bright and hot it melted the blades.

With swift, efficient orders, the Aranken leader guided his men to go on the offensive. It wasn't easy for him to find the weak spots in his opponents' defenses, but he did it nonetheless. His second-in-command created ice under the feet of their enemies, canceling the physical advantage the other group had over the Aranken. Several of their attackers fell almost instantly, struck by lightning or fire bolts they could no longer dodge.

Finally, one of their Destroyers summoned his earth abilities. Soon, their surviving opponents were trapped in inescapable stone cages.

Seyan checked up on his soldiers and saw that the other Nurturers from their group were already tending to injuries. There were a few dead, and that dulled the glow of victory into something more sedate.

Nevertheless, all of them had known this endeavor would be risky since they'd left A'rankin. The question was—would the death of his men be for naught?

Seyan peered closer to the cages. The dark blue skin of the warriors intrigued him, but their physical prowess gave him an idea he couldn't shake.

One of the men clutched the stone bars, testing their solidity. It would be futile to attempt escape, but the fact that his captives seemed strong-willed appealed to the Aranken lord.

That part of him that was attuned to the elements knew what he had to do. They'd come here for a reason—to make sure what had happened in A'rankin never would again. These people had advantages and strengths Aranken soldiers simply didn't have.

Seyan smiled. "This is where we'll build our new home," he told his second-in-command. "Send word to the other groups. This will be the birthplace of the Nikari."

Never again would his people suffer like he had. Never again would they be at the mercy of monsters. He would weed out the weakness of the Aranken from his veins, and in the process, he'd build a stronger future for all of them. If the past ever came knocking at their door, they would be ready. Seyan would make sure of it.

CHAPTER ONE
MASKS

A thousand years later

"THIS IS a terrible idea, Your Lordship. Please. We should go back."

Ignoring his manservant's protests, Ivy sneaked through the garden, hiding behind a statue and scanning his environs for any sign of guards. He spotted several silhouettes patrolling the edges of the garden and grimaced. Oh well. He had been ready for that.

"Come along, Akolo," he whispered to his manservant, "or I'll leave you behind."

With a frustrated huff, Akolo fell silent and followed Ivy out of his hiding place. Ivy took a deep breath and murmured a cloaking spell, wrapping his magic tightly around him and Akolo. As quietly as possible, they slipped past the guards and headed toward the back gate of the property.

As a rule, the service entrance was always open, but not tonight. Tonight, a heavy lock blocked the access to the road beyond. Fortunately, Ivy had known about it, and in fact, had counted on his father's habit of shutting down the manse every solstice. Sweeping his fingers over the lock, he murmured another spell, willing the lock to open for him.

Mercifully, it worked. The gate swung open far more violently than Ivy had expected, but by some sort of miracle, he managed to catch it before it hit the fence and drew entirely unwanted attention.

"Your Lordship," Akolo tried again.

Ivy shushed him and stepped outside. As his manservant followed, Ivy shut the gate behind them. His father believed him to have retreated to his quarters, so, if all went well, the older Andari would never know about Ivy's little rebellion.

It took a while, but at last Ivy and Akolo managed to make their way outside his father's territory and enter downtown Seanda. Ivy's efforts were rewarded since the solstice carnival was already well underway.

As the capital city of the province of Reptatte, Seanda usually bustled with activity. However, at late hours, the Andari tended to retreat to their homes or to indoor establishments. Tonight, this had changed. The quiet Seanda evening had exploded in a display of color, diversity, and joy. The streets were lined with stalls and tents offering all sorts of products, from meals to toys or jewelry. Wreaths of flowers and symbols of the Creator adorned each home in sight, the decorations in tune with the lively carnival.

The smell of candied *malynsa* permeated the air, beckoning partygoers to approach and usually finding an adequate target in the throng of children already demanding the treat. The scent of burning torches and smoked meats added to the bouquet of aromas, while laughter, merriment, and song bubbled all around.

Ivy made his way through the crowd, taking in the sights with a mix of anxiety and happiness. Behind him, his manservant kept muttering imprecations and pleas. "Your father will figure out that you escaped, and then he'll punish both of us."

Ivy settled his mask more carefully on his face. He knew that, in all likelihood, Akolo was right, but he couldn't turn back, not now. "I'm sorry, Akolo, but this is my last chance. I need to feel alive just once. Will you truly begrudge me that?"

Akolo sighed heavily but said nothing more. Perhaps he realized that Ivy hadn't escaped tonight just for the purpose of upsetting his overbearing father. Sure, that could have been a very good reason, but Ivy prided himself on not choosing such childish, petty ways of revenge.

No, tonight he had another goal. In cities like Seanda—ruled by Full-Blooded Andari—the summer solstice was celebrated by encouraging openness toward the rest of the settlements of Anderra. It was the one time when Full Bloods came together with their Half-Blood cousins and, sometimes, even their less pleasant Nikari leaders. The masquerade balls brought all sorts of people together, blurring the well-defined lines of their social structure for a single night. Seanda opened its gates to all, and within the enjoyment and laughter of the carnival, they found togetherness and the hope for understanding.

Ivy was accustomed to Half Bloods, as most of the servants in his household—Akolo included—came from such families. However, the rich, powerful Half Bloods who now formed part of the landed gentry were an entirely differently matter. Their magic was not as potent as his own, but that didn't make them any less intriguing. And then, there were the Nikari. How was Ivy supposed to fear and loathe someone he didn't even know?

Of course, everyone knew the general history of the Nikari. Ironically, the ancestors of the Nikari, the Ndara, had been distant cousins of the Andari, which was why, to this day, some customs of the two species bore slight resemblances. However, after the Ndara had been taken over by the foreign Aranken force, countless things had changed.

Now the Nikari occupied the entire Western Realm and were regularly a reason for Ivy's father's rants. Ivy didn't want to borrow the opinions of others. Like he'd told Akolo, this was his last chance to figure things out for himself. And maybe, just maybe, he'd actually experience what it was like to live before the gilded cage of his parents' desires snapped shut around him.

Ivy shook off his glum musings, refusing to let his impending betrothal ruin tonight. He caught sight of a stall that sold *reada* wine and quickly made his way there, ignoring Akolo's protests. Traditionally a Nikari drink, it had spread all throughout Anderra after the Great Wars and had become quite popular, especially in the northern regions.

"First time?" the merchant asked with a grin.

Ivy nodded, not bothering to deny the obvious. Even with the mask, he couldn't hide his Andari Full Blood nature. His fine, fair complexion and heart-shaped face contrasted with the dusky skin and sharper, more angular features of the Nikari. At most, people might mistake him for a particularly exotic-looking Half Blood, but even that was doubtful. Nikari blood guaranteed that Half Bloods were never as slender as Andari tended to be, and their skin tone was very distinctive, far darker than Ivy's.

The merchant gave him a long look, probably realizing the truth. Still, he didn't turn Ivy away. He poured Ivy a generous portion of the brew and said, "Careful now. Just take a sip. It might be too strong for you."

Ivy arched a brow. He knew all too well the Nikari didn't drink their wine by sips, and he could identify the challenge in the merchant's voice. Drinking reada wine was only allowed after a Nikari—and naturally, an Andari—reached his age of majority. Coincidentally, Ivy had just come of age a fortnight back. He refused to step back from the challenge as if he were some child.

Taking a deep breath, Ivy gripped the offered glass and analyzed the bubbling crimson liquid. Without allowing himself to hesitate, he drank down the entire contents.

For a few seconds, nothing happened—or maybe it just seemed that way to Ivy. Then the world came crashing down, the scents, lights, and music becoming sharper, hotter, brighter. Ivy's eyes watered as the heavily spiced brew scorched his taste buds. He swayed and distantly berated himself for his recklessness. It was a good thing Akolo manifested behind him and supported him because otherwise, he might have collapsed right then and there. Ivy didn't think he could have survived the embarrassment.

Ivy leaned against Akolo and managed to gather his wits. Sweet Reysen, the brew must have been more potent than Ivy had thought. He suddenly had the impression that Akolo smelled very good and seemed far taller and more muscular than Ivy knew him to be.

"Are you well?" a male voice asked behind him.

Ivy froze as the smooth baritone cleared the lingering fogginess from his mind. No wonder Akolo's hold on him had felt different. It hadn't been the manservant who'd kept him from falling.

As quickly as possible, he straightened himself and pulled away from the stranger. Turning on his heel, he instinctively checked his mask. Once he ascertained it remained in place, he faced the other man, only to blink in shock at the sight that met his eyes.

It didn't take a genius to figure out the stranger was Nikari. His piercing black gaze was sharpened by gold-rimmed irises that appeared to glow in the light of the torches. He was easily a head taller than Ivy, but twice as bulky, with the difference being all muscle. His traditional Nikari garb did nothing to hide his warrior's build, the tight tunic and breeches instead emphasizing his barely leashed virile strength. Twin braids of dark hair framed his cheeks, marking him as a seasoned warrior. A black mask hid part of his dusky-skinned face, adding an edge of mystery and danger—as if that had been necessary.

Ivy's mouth went dry, and for a few moments, he couldn't remember how to speak. He tried to fall back on his deeply ingrained manners, or maybe to remember his lessons on Nikari mores, but it was all a blur in his mind.

The stranger frowned, and Ivy realized he hadn't replied to his question. Snapping out of his trance, he stammered, "F-Fine." Frustrated with himself, he straightened his back and added, "My apologies. I should have known better than to take him up on the offer."

The stranger threw a dark glare toward the merchant. "Sometimes, people like that enjoy teasing Full Bloods. I doubt he expected you would actually do it."

Ivy took his cue and glanced in the direction of the stall. Indeed, the merchant seemed alarmed by Ivy's brief fainting spell, or perhaps by Ivy's unexpected savior. He had paled and was wringing his hands, the very picture of anxiousness. "Can I get you anything? Water? Tea, perhaps?"

Ivy shook his head, although the gesture made him a bit dizzy. He'd have liked to blame the wine, but he highly suspected the Nikari's proximity affected him more than his people's brew. "I'll be fine. My own fault for not knowing my limits. How much for the wine?"

"No charge," the merchant said, already recovered from his shock. "Thank you for the patronage."

Ivy stepped away from the stall, avoiding looking at his unlikely companion. "I probably earned him twice as many sales for the night," he told the stranger.

"Probably," the Nikari replied. A brief pause followed, and Ivy dared to glance at his companion. Unsurprisingly, he found the stranger scrutinizing him with those deep gold-rimmed eyes. "Am I making you uncomfortable?"

A denial was on Ivy's lips, but he stopped himself before he could utter it. The question seemed more rhetorical than anything else, and going against the obvious would just insult the other man's intelligence.

"Maybe a little," he admitted with a sheepish smile. "I don't mean any offense. It's just that I've never met a Nikari before."

Much to his relief, the stranger didn't seem upset. His eyes glittered with something that Ivy could have sworn was amusement, or perhaps interest. "Well, you have now. Or, wait. You haven't."

Pulling Ivy away from the crowd, he sketched a courteous Nikari bow. "I am Kris."

Something inside Ivy eased, and he answered the Nikari's bow with an Andari one of his own. "Ivy. It's a pleasure to make your acquaintance."

"Ivy," Kris repeated the name as if tasting it. "You have a beautiful name. It suits you."

Ivy's face flamed. It was quite stupid. He'd had other Full Bloods complimenting him on all sorts of things, but it had never impressed him or given him much confidence in his appeal. To be true, he suspected his only worth as a spouse lay in his ancestry. But Kris had no reason to shower him with sweet lies, and that meant something.

He wanted to say something in turn, but he didn't get the chance. His manservant suddenly made his appearance, breathing hard and scanning Ivy's face with wide, startled eyes. "Your Lordship…. Thank Reysen. We should return home. I spotted Nikari in the crowd."

Embarrassment and dread collided inside Ivy. Obviously, Akolo hadn't spotted Kris, which was perhaps unsurprising, given that Nikari tended to blend in with the shadows when they chose to do so. Ivy could still feel him there, watching, though. He debated introducing Kris to Akolo, but that would only make Akolo panic. Despite being a Half Blood, he'd never been comfortable with Nikari. Ivy suspected that stemmed from the fact that Akolo had never known his Nikari father. Many Half Bloods who occupied positions like Akolo had a history of abandonment.

Then again, if Ivy's father or his sire found out that Akolo had allowed Ivy anywhere near a Nikari, his history would be the last thing he'd have to worry about. Nothing Ivy could say would save him from their wrath.

Well, it couldn't be helped. He didn't want to leave the carnival yet, especially not now when he'd met such an interesting man. "I know," he told Akolo. "Akolo, I'd like you to meet Kris."

On cue, the Nikari stepped forward, drawing a gasp from the Half-Blood manservant. "Kris, this is my friend, Akolo," Ivy added.

This time, Kris didn't bow, but he did sketch a small smile. "Greetings, Master Akolo. You mustn't worry. Nikari aren't as dangerous as you seem to think, at least not at carnivals. I'll keep Ivy company and make sure he is safe from any dangers."

He didn't say it, but his tone implied Akolo hadn't been doing such a good job so far. To top it off, his mannerisms and his use of the word "master" suggested he'd guessed Akolo's position in Ivy's household and, naturally, Ivy's background. Akolo winced and tried to stammer a protest, obviously realizing he'd committed a serious mistake by using Ivy's title even if they'd come here in disguise.

The conversation might have descended into something nasty, but the cheerful tones of a melody reached Ivy's ears. Kris seemed to lose interest in Akolo and arched a brow at Ivy. "A dance?"

"I'd love to," Ivy replied with a wide smile.

Kris took his hand and pulled him back into the crowd. Ivy couldn't suppress a gasp at the shock of pleasure that coursed through him at the simple touch, and he felt thankful that the sounds of the lively carnival hid his loss of composure.

His embarrassment became irrelevant when Kris guided him to the city square where dozens of minstrels had gathered, their lutes and melodic voices bringing age-old Anderran melodies to life. Couples were already swaying in front of them, and Ivy was encouraged by the sight of several other Nikari dancing with Andari. Granted, most—if not all—of the Nikari's dance partners were probably Half Bloods, but who would care if Ivy joined?

The current song was a lively *treska*, a style of dance that hailed from the beginnings of Anderra and which Nikari had adopted as well. Ivy and Kris bowed to each other again, and then Kris twined his fingers with Ivy's. As the music flowed over them, they moved together on the cobblestone of the square. Two steps forward, one step back, Kris twirling him around, over and over, leaps and jumps in complete synch—they danced like longtime partners, and it was full of energy and the joy of a new beginning. Ivy found himself laughing harder than he ever had, especially when Kris spun him around so fast all the other dancers blurred.

When the *treska* finally wound down, Ivy was breathing hard and feeling so happy he could fly. Mercifully, his hair had stayed put in its tight braid, because otherwise, he'd have been forced to leave to fix it—and he didn't want to go, not yet, not ever. Kris was smiling too, widely, openly, the expression of joy softening the sharp features of his face. "You're an amazing dancer," he said over the last dying tunes of the song.

"Thank you," Ivy replied. "I'm only as good at dancing as my partner is."

Kris chuckled and opened his mouth to say something else, but the minstrels started a new song, keeping him from speaking. Ivy's eyes widened as he recognized the new melody.

The *treska* didn't allow for much bodily contact other than their hands and arms, but the *awaye* was different. Only couples ever danced it—couples involved in a deep romantic relationship. Whereas the *treska* was a party dance and illustrated mirth and merriment, the *awaye* meant seduction. For an Andari, especially a Full Blood, it would only be allowed with a betrothed or someone who would soon become one.

Kris didn't immediately move. He stood there, still holding onto Ivy's hands. "Would you like to stand this one out?"

Ivy should have taken him up on his offer. It wouldn't be appropriate for him to dance the *awaye* with Kris. But Kris's eyes were so hot on him, and his hold on Ivy's hand felt so warm and comforting.

His words weren't a challenge, not like those of the merchant. They held an honesty and a gentleness that acknowledged the true meaning of an *awaye* dance. And Ivy couldn't deny his heart's desire.

He took a step closer to Kris, his heart racing. When Kris's hands landed on his waist, Ivy's breath caught, and he looked up into Kris's eyes, wondering what it was about the Nikari that drew him in so much.

The song's mellifluous tones guided their bodies flush against one another. Ivy could feel every inch of Kris now, from his powerful chest to his muscled thighs, and sweet Reysen, everything in between. He could now say for certain that the stories of the generous endowment of the Nikari were true—as the hard member nudging Ivy's hip eloquently proved.

"I apologize," Kris whispered in his ear as he slowly tilted Ivy back. "I'm afraid I can't control my body's response around you."

Ivy wrapped his arms Kris's neck and replied, "There's nothing to apologize for. You flatter me."

He didn't know whether he was trying to be honest, or flirtatious, or coy. He'd never been good at broadcasting a particular emotion, and Kris awoke so many things inside him that Ivy couldn't even distinguish them all. Fortunately, he didn't have to, because the *awaye* did it in his stead.

Smiling, he followed the steps of the dance, lifting his leg almost all the way to Kris's hip. For a few seconds, Kris swept his palms over Ivy's thigh, and then the dance went into its next motion. As Ivy set his leg down, Kris pulled him so close not even air could make its way between them. Ivy pivoted on his heel, and Kris hugged his back, which brought Ivy's ass in contact with Kris's erect dick. Ivy dropped his head on Kris's shoulder—not a motion of the dance, but his own response to Kris, to the other man's addicting scent. To his credit, Kris released a nigh-tortured groan, which told Ivy his dance partner was as affected by the dance as Ivy himself. Encouraged, Ivy sinuously ground against Kris, more aware than ever of the intimacy of the dance, but reveling in it just the same.

Kris's arms tightened around his chest, and he bit Ivy's ear—another thing not usually present in the dance. Still, he followed the next steps, twirling Ivy and bringing them face-to-face again.

As the *awaye* exploded into passionate, almost harsh notes, Kris lifted Ivy into his arms and tossed him into the air. Ivy landed safely into Kris's embrace, and it occurred to him that he could never have danced the *awaye* with anyone else. His imminent betrothal seemed so distant now and so wrong. After tonight, Ivy knew he could never go through with it, no matter what his father said.

Kris set Ivy back down on the ground. They swayed together, following the music, their bodies never once separating. It was amazing, but Ivy felt more at home in Kris's arms than he ever had in his father's manse.

At last, the dance ended, with both of them still wrapped in a tight embrace. Ivy never wanted to let go, but he did nonetheless, aware of the fact that, at this point, they were drawing a lot of attention.

Another song was starting, but Kris pulled Ivy away from the dancers. Ivy supposed that, after the intense *awaye*, another dance would have felt wrong. Still, he couldn't help but feel a pang of loss when Kris released his hand.

"Your manservant is probably furious," he commented.

"If he saw us, yes," Ivy replied. "But it doesn't matter." Blushing, he added, "It felt right."

Kris swept his fingers over Ivy's lower lip and his cheek. "It did, didn't it?" he murmured.

Ivy stared at the other man, hypnotized by the golden glow of Kris's eyes. Kris was so close to him now, as close as he'd been during the dance. Their lips were within a hair's breadth of each other, and Ivy knew that any moment now, he'd get his first kiss.

As it turned out, he was mistaken, because at the last possible moment, Kris pulled away. He shook his head, as if physically trying to dispel whatever thoughts were running through his mind. Ivy cursed himself for his foolishness. He could only imagine what Kris must think about him. A Full-Blood Andari, supposedly untouched but dancing the *awaye* and willing to kiss a man he'd just met?

"I should go," he told the other man. "Akolo... Akolo is likely looking for me."

Much to his surprise, Kris stopped him. "No, don't go. You should enjoy the carnival. It's your first time here, is it not?"

Ivy blinked in surprise, not knowing what to make of his companion's words. "How did you know that?"

Kris chuckled. "It's written in your eyes, and you are an open book to me, Ivy. But never mind that. Come. The carnival can offer you many pleasures."

Taken aback by Kris's mercurial behavior, Ivy nevertheless followed the Nikari. Soon he forgot all about his misgivings as Kris introduced him to all sorts of diversions that Ivy had never experienced. He taught Ivy how to walk on stilts, or at least made the attempt. Of course, Ivy failed to learn and kept falling, but he couldn't bring himself to mind, because Kris was always there to catch him. Together, they tested a million other treats and watched the parade, chuckling at the occasionally peculiar costumes. They laughed and danced and held each other, and Ivy forgot to berate himself for his inappropriate openness toward a stranger. He made it his business to wave at Akolo whenever he saw his manservant in the crowd, but Kris always pulled him away before Akolo could reach him.

Finally, they retreated to the shade of a large tree and sat down. Ivy leaned against Kris's shoulder, finding the closeness natural and the silence comfortable. When Kris's hand landed in his hair, though, it occurred to Ivy this was his chance to finally have a few of his questions answered. "Can I ask you a serious question?" he blurted out.

"Oh, that sounds scary," Kris replied, caressing Ivy's hair. "What's on your mind?"

For a few seconds, Ivy hesitated. He didn't want to ruin tonight by pushing for information. But he hadn't come here solely because he wanted to have fun. He hated learning only what his father wanted him to know. What good did his magic do if he didn't have the discerning knowledge to use it appropriately?

"I want to understand," he said. "What's it like to be Nikari? Why did the Nikari take over Anderra in the first place?"

Kris tensed and pulled away from him. "Why are you asking me this?"

"Because I've never been given true reasons during my lessons," Ivy replied. "There are so many things I don't know, and my mother once told me that there are two sides to every story."

A pang of loss coursed through Ivy even as he said the words. He hadn't seen his mother in over two decades. How he wished things had been different, that she'd stayed with him—but the ways of the Andari didn't allow it.

Doing his best to shake off the memory, he gave Kris an earnest look. "Won't you tell me?"

Kris scanned Ivy's face with his deep, gold-rimmed eyes, seeking his own answers to questions Ivy couldn't hear. Whatever he found must have satisfied him, because he visibly relaxed and leaned against the tree trunk. "Your mother was a wise woman indeed," he commented, "but you must be more careful. Technically speaking, you and your friend are Nikari too, or at least Nikari citizens. You would do well to remember that in public. Even here, your words might reach unfriendly ears, and certain figures might attempt to make a name for themselves by arresting you for dissent."

Ivy gaped. He had not expected Kris to tell him that. Of course, he realized the other man had a point, but he was so used to the ways of the Full Bloods that he'd forgotten to be cautious.

"Don't be afraid," Kris said with a slight chuckle, cupping his cheek. "I'm not going to allow anything to happen to you. But you must promise me to be a little more cautious in the future."

"I promise," Ivy replied sedately. "It's just…. Things are so different here. Sometimes, it truly doesn't feel like…."

"Like you're part of the empire at all?" Kris guessed when Ivy trailed off. "Well, you must understand, Ivy, that Anderra earned certain privileges that other territories don't have. As for why that war happened…. What can I tell you? It's not easy to point fingers, especially not after all this time. Kings and emperors can often forget their own limitations, and neither your people nor mine are immune to that rule. Perhaps you've been told that the Nikari indiscriminately conquer every land they set their eye on, and to a certain extent that's true."

"But Anderra was an ally of the empire before the war," Ivy offered tentatively.

"Indeed," Kris replied approvingly. "And they would have continued to be allies if the two leaders had been more open to compromise and less prone to warmongering and manipulation. But it was a long time ago. Why does it matter to you?"

Ivy sighed. He wished he could have said his interest was completely selfless, but that would have been a lie. "Because our history defines my present." He laughed self-deprecatingly, aware of how ridiculous he sounded. "To put it bluntly, I'm one of the lucky few who has to help perpetuate our culture and our bloodline."

"Ivy…." Kris started to say.

Ivy quickly silenced Kris, squeezing the other man's hand. "Leave it. I should not have brought it up. It's too beautiful a night for morose musings."

"That it is," Kris said. His expression sobered, and his eyes fixed Ivy with an intensity that took his breath away. "Ivy, would you do me one favor?"

Kris's tone told Ivy that whatever request the Nikari had, it meant a lot to him. He nodded and waited for Kris to elaborate.

"Take your mask off," Kris finally said.

Ivy would have expected anything but that. The solstice carnival employed masks for a reason—so that Nikari, Full Bloods, and Half Bloods could mingle without fear of reprisal. Even if they'd found a fairly private spot, the fact remained that Ivy had risked coming here and letting go simply because he'd had the safety net of secrecy.

Then again, Kris had guessed Ivy's identity hours before, in which case the mask was largely meaningless. Ivy almost laughed when he realized that even if he'd known Kris had figured out his secret, he hadn't panicked in the slightest. His heart told him he could trust the Nikari.

He would have immediately complied with Kris's request, but something held him back. It wasn't distrust but rather the desire for full disclosure.

"Only if you take it off too," he told the Nikari.

Kris's full lips twisted into a sharp smile. "Agreed."

Both of them sat back and looked at each other. It was only a simple motion, but for Ivy, it meant something. When Ivy reached for his mask, so did Kris. Ivy would have liked to drink in every single moment of the scene, but for one instant, as he was removing his mask, his vision became obscured. And then, when he set aside the item, he could only stare at the sight that met his eyes.

Kris was by no means classically handsome, not by Andari standards. Indeed, his cheekbones were a little too sharp, and his eyebrows seemed drawn together, as if in a perpetual frown. And yet, Ivy thought he'd never seen a more attractive man in his life. Without his mask, the light blue of Kris's skin came clearly into focus, and Ivy couldn't help but reach for his face, marveling at the color so unlike his own.

He had been drawn to Kris before he'd seen the Nikari's face, but now, he could barely breathe. Maybe he shouldn't have asked—he'd just gotten used to the Nikari's proximity, and now he'd been reduced to a puddle again.

Thankfully, Kris was too focused on Ivy's face to begrudge him his embarrassing behavior. "You're beautiful," Kris said, his fingers traveling over his cheek, then exploring the curve of his nose. Ivy wanted to say that his looks couldn't compare to Kris's virile handsomeness, but he found himself leaning into Kris's caress instead. Kris trailed his callused digits over Ivy's forehead and eyebrows with a gentleness that should have been out of place in such a strong warrior. Was he as fascinated with the differences between their skin tones as Ivy? What thoughts could be going through his mind right now?

Ivy got the answer to his mental question moments later, when all of a sudden, Kris pulled him into his lap and pressed their mouths together. Ivy didn't immediately register the kiss. It came as a complete surprise, especially after Kris's earlier behavior. Ivy panicked, not knowing how to respond and at the same time, fearing his lack of enthusiasm would cause Kris to change his mind. Just as he'd suspected, Kris did pull away without taking things any further.

Ivy could have kicked himself for his stupidity. He might have been an innocent in bed, but that didn't absolve him of complete idiocy when it came to taking what he wanted. And he did want Kris. That much had been obvious from the beginning.

Unlike the time before, though, Kris didn't retreat into more harmless territory. His hold on Ivy tightened, and it didn't seem like he had any intention of letting go. "Relax," Kris whispered in his ear. "Just let me in."

The Nikari's dick throbbed against Ivy's ass, and his voice was like honeyed steel, slashing through Ivy's doubts with the same efficiency he probably used during combat. His fingers trailed over the ends of Ivy's braid, and the forbidden caress made Ivy shiver in Kris's arms and melt against the Nikari's chest.

"That's it, Ivy," Kris encouraged. "Surrender to me."

That was the only warning Ivy got before Kris kissed him once more. This time, when Kris's tongue traced the seam of his lips, Ivy granted the Nikari entrance. He didn't even have to think about it. An instinct as old as time guided him, crystallizing his lust for Kris into a fog that clouded all else save the two of them. His submission earned him a muffled groan from Kris. The world shifted as Kris pushed him down on the grass, never once separating their mouths.

His larger body landed on Ivy, pinning him to the ground. The gentle exploration from before exploded into a passionate onslaught of sensation. Kris devoured Ivy, his tongue tangling with Ivy's, tasting him with a ferocity that should have been frightening but wasn't. He clutched Ivy's clothing convulsively while he ground against him, his erect member nudging Ivy's own arousal.

Ivy lost himself in Kris's scent and touch. He felt so hot, his skin scratchy where it came in contact with his garments. Why was he wearing clothes again? He couldn't remember. It was such a waste when both he and Kris could be nude, their naked bodies sliding against one another on the grass.

He moaned into their kiss as the images he summoned fueled the fire burning inside him. Unable to hold back, he clung to Kris, exploring every inch of the Nikari he could reach. The material of Kris's garb frustrated him, but the muscles underneath still tempted him, and the feel of all that barely leashed strength under his fingertips inflamed him beyond belief.

Kris bit his lower lip, as if chastising him for his daring. He didn't quite draw blood, however, and the dangerous edge the slight pain added to the kiss made Ivy cling to Kris more savagely, clawing at Kris's back through his shirt.

Their desire for each other would have likely guided them into perilously intimate territory had another presence not interrupted them. Ivy didn't even notice it at first, too lost in his passion to care about anything else. But then Kris tensed and broke their kiss, his body going as taut as a bowstring as he reached for a dagger strapped to his boot—a weapon Ivy hadn't even noticed until now. Ivy blinked, trying to understand why the lethal grace with which Kris moved made him want to pounce on the Nikari. There had to be something wrong with him, because weapons were made for destruction, not for seductive purposes.

Before Ivy could figure out the answer to his dilemma, Akolo slid into their haven, breathing hard. He paled and froze upon seeing Kris's threatening position. When Kris relaxed and released his grip on his weapon, Akolo finally found his voice. "Your Lordship," he said. "Thank Reysen that I found you. We must go. Your father... I saw him in the square."

Ivy felt like Akolo had dumped a bucket of water on top of him, quenching his ardor. If his father found him in the embrace of a Nikari, blood would flow. His father had a temper, and sometimes he forgot that they only maintained their nobility privileges due to the benevolence of the Nikari Morai.

He turned toward Kris, struggling to find the right words to explain the situation to the Nikari. He didn't want this beautiful experience to end here. He was so afraid that if he left now, he'd never see Kris again and he'd spend his entire life wondering what could have been. Sweet Reysen, he didn't even know Kris's full name or if the Nikari even had any interest in him beyond this night.

"Your Lordship," Akolo prodded when Ivy continued to hesitate.

Kris didn't acknowledge Akolo's insistence in any way, but much to Ivy's surprise, he smiled. "Go," he murmured in Ivy's ear. "I'll find you. I promise."

Ivy's breath caught. He met Kris's eyes, and the decision he saw shining in those surreally beautiful orbs gave him the courage to pull away. He got up on shaky legs and said, "I'll wait for you."

Akolo released a sound of distress, and Ivy knew he could expect a lecture later. He couldn't worry about that right now, though. He arranged his clothing, hoping he'd be able to bypass his father's scrutiny by blaming the less than perfect condition of his outfit on a particularly energetic *treska*. He couldn't do anything about his hair but hope it had stayed in its braid. Finally, he pulled his mask back on, and with one last look toward Kris, he fled his sanctuary and lost himself in the crowd.

KRIS WATCHED Ivy go, forcing himself to remain calm even if he was anything but. There was nothing he'd have liked more than to follow Ivy, drag him off, and destroy anyone who got in the way.

Ironically, that impulse kept him in check because Kris refused to surrender to his baser nature. He was no inexperienced youth, and he had more satisfying ways of claiming his prey, in a manner that no one would be able to question.

Kris got up and put his mask back on. In hindsight, the protectiveness of Ivy's parents might have been a good thing. Ivy had not recognized his face, but if they'd gone any further, Kris would have had to reveal his identity. Kris didn't want that, not just yet.

By the time he returned to the carnival, the joyfulness of the partygoers had decreased significantly. Kris heard murmurs of Earl Titexe Erethe having scoured the crowd with his golems. If he'd had any doubt about Ivy's identity, that would have made the matter crystal clear.

Lingering in Seanda would obviously draw unnecessary attention. He caught sight of his second-in-command waiting in the shadow of a stall and gave the other Nikari a barely perceptible nod. *We're leaving,* he sent out.

Just like Kris expected, Sai heard him. Retreating from his hiding place, he started to make his way toward the city gates. The rest of their group followed, slowly and surreptitiously so as not to draw the attention of the Andari.

Kris let them go and spent a few more minutes entertaining the thought of following Ivy to his father's manse. Even if the lavish structure hadn't been an obvious target, Kris could still track Ivy down anywhere the young Andari went. In spite of all the smells permeating the air, Kris could still scent Ivy's perfume, fresh, sweet, yet with a hint of wildness hiding underneath. Just like the man himself. Creator, just the memory of how Ivy had moved against him threatened to fray Kris's control. The innocent heat in those emerald eyes would have felled a lesser man. His slender body fit so right against Kris, and Kris had been moments away from ignoring Andari mores and undoing the tight hairstyle that kept him from burying his fingers in Ivy's white-blond hair. He could too easily imagine himself doing so now.

Deciding not to tempt fate for much longer, Kris followed his men out of Seanda. A great deal of people were leaving, wary of Earl Erethe's interference with the night's entertainment. That was a mixed blessing, because anxious people tended to pay heed to the Nikari who mingled amongst them.

Unfortunately, Nikari weren't that good at illusion spells, but Kris had faith that his disguise would keep him from being too conspicuous. Whoever looked too closely would just see another Nikari come to enjoy the carnival, nothing more. It wasn't all that hard, given that Seanda seemed quite popular with Kris's kin. Kris certainly couldn't blame them, not after he'd seen its attractions.

His men waited for him by their mounts, a good distance from the city. Kris's nightwolf greeted him with a pleased growl, and Kris patted the beast's large head. "Well?" he asked Sai. "Have you gathered information of any significance?"

"It seems that our sources were correct," Sai replied. "I've heard several Andari, mostly Half Bloods, complaining about an increase in taxes. Supposedly, Earl Titexe Erethe blames it on the Morai."

Kris smiled without humor. "It's easy to blame the empire for everything that's not right. Wouldn't it be interesting if they learned the gold Titexe is gathering isn't being siphoned into Nikari coffers?"

"What would you like us to do, Your Majesty?" Sai inquired.

Kris remembered Ivy, his innocent smile and his sweet lips. He probably shouldn't allow their meeting to influence his decisions as a sovereign. The Nikari Morai had responsibilities he couldn't shove aside for the sake of his libido.

Even as he thought this, though, Kris faltered. He couldn't dismiss Ivy's effect on him. Truth be told, he'd forgotten the last time anyone had made him smile and drove him wild with such intense lust. With all the beautiful courtesans who'd warmed his bed throughout the years, Kris had always been able to keep his naturally predatory instinct in check. Not so with Ivy, and if he let the matter go, he would regret it.

Why was he even debating it? He'd promised Ivy they'd be together again. An impulse oath, no doubt about it, but it didn't make it less valid and didn't change the fact that Kris didn't regret it. He knew full well that Ivy was betrothed to someone else, but that wouldn't stop him.

"For the moment, keep watching Erethe and his family," he instructed Sai. "I want to know every move they make."

Sai frowned. Kris didn't provide any explanation to his order, but he could only guess what Sai was thinking. The only times Kris went to check up on potential rebels was before he made the unavoidable decision to eradicate the problem before it could fully form. Sai had been waiting for the order to arrest the Erethe family, or at the very least Titexe and his bond mate.

Nevertheless, Sai didn't protest. "I'll stay behind to watch them," he said with a military salute.

Satisfied that his orders would be fulfilled, Kris mounted his nightwolf. As his men followed his example, Kris fixed his gaze straight ahead of him and slashed his hand straight down. The dimensional rift appeared a few feet away from him, swirling wildly.

"Keep me posted, Sai," Kris told the other Nikari. "I want every single detail on the family, as soon as possible. By tomorrow."

If Sai was surprised that Kris had repeated the command, he didn't show it. To be fair, he didn't get much of a chance. Holding onto his nightwolf's fur, Kris guided the beast forward into the rift.

For a single, barely identifiable moment, the unraveled force of time and space struck Kris, but Kris contained it, keeping himself and his mount safe. That second passed, and then he was in his palace, in the barren room that served as a rift gateway.

Kris held the rift open until his men came out safely. Once he made sure there had been no injuries throughout the less-than-safe transport process, he dismounted and guided his nightwolf to the dens.

A thought drifted into Kris's mind—but this time, not his own. *Pack?*

Kris chuckled at his nightwolf's inquiry. He supposed he couldn't be surprised Attcha had smelled Ivy on him. *Soon, my friend. Soon.*

CHAPTER TWO
PREPARATIONS

"THIS IS all your fault! I told you it wasn't a good idea to teach him elaborate magic."

Ivy's sire scoffed and crossed his arms over his chest, glaring at Ivy's father. "Forgive me for pointing out the obvious, but an Andari of Behnivyr's talent needs training to achieve his full potential. Besides, whether I'd tutored him or not, he'd still have figured out things on his own."

"That doesn't change the fact that you facilitated his escape," Ivy's father fumed. Just like Ivy had known, the Andari noble had been furious that Ivy had dared to go to the carnival. Thankfully, he didn't know about Ivy's little tryst with Kris. And sweet Reysen, Ivy really had to stop thinking about that while he was in his parents' company.

As if on cue, his father turned toward him, narrowing his eyes at Ivy. "Look at him, Rasami. He's all flushed. Reysen only knows what he was doing out there."

His sire hummed thoughtfully as he scanned Ivy from head to toe. Ivy knew better than to believe his sire would defend him against his father's fury. They weren't close—they never had been. In fact, his sire spent three-quarters of his time away from Seanda, tutoring others on the magic arts, and even if he had the ability of wave-wayfaring, he rarely bothered to use it when it came to visiting Ivy.

It was a testament to the seriousness of the situation that Rasami had come here now, and so Ivy braced himself for the unavoidable explosion. "Speak, Behnivyr," his sire said, reproach thick in his voice. "Is there anything we should know? I trust you didn't do anything to bring dishonor upon us."

Ivy thanked Reysen that the partygoers had been too focused on themselves to register the less-than-chaste *awaye* Ivy had danced with

Kris, and especially the kiss that could have built up to so much more. Clearing his throat, he said, "I merely drank some of that awful Nikari wine. It didn't agree with me."

The beauty of his response was that he'd managed to tell the truth without revealing his true transgression. He didn't know if his sire was completely convinced, but Ivy's talents protected him from Rasami's considerable mind-reading skills. He doubted his parents would risk breaking through his mental shields to find out what he was hiding.

"Very well," Rasami said after a small pause. "But I can't imagine you wasted your little visit to the carnival on sloshing yourself with drink."

"There were a lot of activities," Ivy answered. "I got into the occasional dance, although it was difficult because I didn't have a partner. I watched the parade and tasted some treats I hadn't eaten before."

His father scowled fiercely. "Just the same, your disobedience isn't as harmless as you might want to make it seem. I can't imagine what Marquis Torildy will think if he finds out about this."

"I suspect he never would have found out if you'd been more discreet in your quest for our errant son," his sire said reproachfully. "Truly, Titexe, was it necessary to bring an entire battalion of golems to find him?"

"It wouldn't have been necessary, Rasami, if you'd stayed here where you belong," his father replied bitingly.

Ivy plopped down on the settee in his father's office and stared off into the distance, already accustomed to the argument. His parents were both very powerful, but their magic couldn't have been more different if they tried. Whereas Titexe held significant abilities in invocation, Rasami was more inclined toward divination and illusion magic. This was the main reason they'd bonded—to create an Andari with abilities in all three branches—but it also meant that they didn't get along at all.

As always, his father ranted and raved whereas his sire just stood there, watching him with a sneer. When he did speak, his biting comments could have flayed the skin off a lesser man. Ivy closed his eyes and tuned them out, his mind returning to his memory of Kris. It had felt so right to be in the Nikari's arms. That was where he belonged; he knew it beyond any shadow of a doubt. Kris's touch, his warmth, his scent, his passion, and his gentleness—everything about him drew Ivy like a moth to the flame.

His parents must have noticed his distraction, because they stopped arguing and focused on him once more. "Listen closely," his sire told him. "Your bonding is in a few weeks. You are absolutely forbidden to do anything that would jeopardize it."

Ivy debated his response and recalled Kris's promise to him. In the past, he'd attempted to free himself from the burden of this union, but unfortunately, his betrothal to Marquis Torildy went back a decade now. The marquis had been painstakingly chosen from a long line of suitors impressed with Ivy's pedigree and his abilities, and the betrothal agreement had already been signed. If Ivy refused the bonding now, the penalties involved would not only fall on his family, but also on his people, especially since Torildy was a marquis, and Ivy's father just an earl.

Being stubborn now wouldn't help him, but he could find a way to stall. "I'm so sorry, Sire," he told Rasami. "I made a mistake. I realize that now, and I understand how important the bonding is." He hesitated slightly. "I just thought… I know so little of the world. How can I be an adequate spouse for His Lordship when I rarely even leave the manse?"

Ivy held his breath, waiting for a reaction from his sire. That was the one weak point Rasami had—the pursuit of culture. He was well-known and appreciated for his extensive knowledge on the magical arts and his ability to sway an Andari with one twist of tongue. In all likelihood, he'd see Ivy's lack of experience as potentially harmful, not just for his reputation but for Ivy himself and his future bonding.

"He has a point," his sire said. "The marquis is a well-traveled, cultured individual. He will not appreciate ignorance."

"Rasami, we've discussed this before. It is not safe for Ivy to leave Seanda."

So apparently, his sire had brought the matter up in the past. It surprised Ivy, because he'd never gotten the chance to mention it, what with Rasami being gone most of the time. It also gave him some hope that he'd manage to stall the bonding.

"I'll leave Seanda anyway once I am wed," he said. "At the very least, I would like to know my own land, my own people."

"We don't have a lot of time at our disposal," his father reminded him. "Even if I did agree to this—which I haven't—you'd be forced to come back after a few days at the latest. There are still a great many preparations to be made for the ceremony."

"The ceremony can be delayed if need be," Ivy offered, trying not to sound too eager.

Judging by his father's expression, he failed.

"Your bonding with Marquis Torildy will happen just as we planned it. Don't think you can elude the bonding through your sudden need for knowledge."

Ivy didn't bother to say he'd always wanted to know more. It was a moot point, since right now he did have a side interest, which his parents had guessed. To top it off, the smile on his sire's face didn't bode well for his future.

"Now, my dear Tex, let's not be so hasty," he said.

Tex? His sire never called anyone the short forms of their names unless he had something suspicious planned, something Ivy usually disliked. "Here is what we're going to do, Behnivyr. We'll take a week to travel. I will come with you, and we'll invite Marquis Torildy along. I'm sure he'll appreciate spending some time with you."

Ivy's heart fell. The only good thing that had come from his father's overprotectiveness was that he hadn't been forced to spend too much time with the lecherous Torildy. He'd been actively trying not to think too much about what would be required of him during their bonding night, and while, as a rule, that worked, it didn't help him now.

He had no hope of outsmarting his sire. Just like Kris had said, he was an open book to anyone who cared enough to read him.

Biting the inside of his cheek so hard he tasted blood, Ivy forced a smile of his own. "Thank you, Sire. That sounds wonderful."

His sire smirked and patted his head as if Ivy was a particularly well-trained pet. Ivy let it slide. His parents couldn't possibly mistake his words for enthusiasm, but they would take them as surrender. They didn't know the secret in his heart and didn't realize that he had every intention of fighting for what he'd found tonight. He'd made a promise, and he planned on keeping it. There had to be a way. But how?

A few days later

KRIS LUNGED forward, his *darach* ruthlessly slashing through the air, aimed at his opponent's throat. At the last moment, the other Nikari managed to block Kris's attack with his own dagger, while trying to use the second blade to incapacitate Kris.

He was too slow, too slow by far. Kris dodged the attack, dropping to the ground and kicking the other Nikari's legs from underneath him with one simple maneuver. His opponent tried to get up, but Kris was already on him, his dagger nudging the soldier's throat.

"You need more training," he told the other Nikari. "You're ridiculously lax on your right side. In real combat, I could have taken you out in ten seconds."

He pulled away and sheathed his dagger, giving the other Nikari time to gather his wits. The soldier instantly shot to his feet. "Thank you, Your Majesty," he said with a salute. "I will remember."

He departed the sparring grounds, his stiff stance telling Kris he must have been a little harsher than he'd intended. Well, it couldn't be helped. These new recruits had to learn to fight, and he might as well teach them himself. At the very least, it released some of his accumulating frustration.

Kris was just considering whom to select as his next sparring partner when a familiar figure entered the training room. He hadn't seen Sai since the day of the solstice. He'd given the other Nikari time since he knew some missions couldn't be rushed, but the delay put him in a foul mood.

Wiping his face with a cloth, he left the sparring field. *Do you have any news?* he sent to his second-in-command.

Some, yes, Sai replied.

Kris waved for the remaining Nikari to continue training without him and guided Sai outside. As always, the courtyard of the palace teemed with activity, ranging from soldiers heading toward the barracks, to servants carrying supplies and den masters checking on the nightwolves. They all bowed and murmured greetings as Kris passed but didn't actually stop what they were doing.

Of course, the actual palace was a little harder to cross without interruptions, as there were always countless nobles, governors, and diplomats begging for a meeting with the Morai. Hailing from all the provinces of the Nikari Empire, they came to lobby for better positions for their respective lands, fewer taxes, budget increases, or additional security.

One look from Kris told them all to wait until he was unoccupied. He retreated to his private quarters, where he could be sure no one would overhear the conversation between him and Sai. Not for the first time, he wished Sai could report to him using the mind arts, but Sai had only limited mental powers, and straining them was never wise. Not to mention that telepathic communication worked best between family or close friends and not so much with underlings.

Once they were behind closed doors, Kris gestured for Sai to speak. "Well? Tell me. What did you learn?"

"The son of Earl Titexe Erethe, Behnivyr, is set to marry Marquis Torildy Dekar."

Something ugly and angry stirred in Kris's chest at Sai's words. He'd already known about Ivy's betrothal, but that didn't make it any easier to hear. "Sai, this isn't news. The Erethe have been preparing for that wedding for years now."

He tried to keep his voice level and calm, but he must have failed, because Sai tensed. Still, the other Nikari was too well trained to show fear, even when it came to Kris. "Yes, Your Majesty, but there's more. Rumor has it that Dekar has already chosen an *odale* for the two of them. Furthermore, they have been traveling throughout the Reptatte district for the past couple of days."

Kris scowled. "To what purpose?"

"It is unclear," Sai answered. "From what I managed to gather, the young Behnivyr requested to learn more about his people before the bonding ceremony, although his reasons are debatable."

"But you believe them to be connected to the rebellion brewing in Reptatte."

Sai nodded. "I deem it very likely, yes. Originally, I wouldn't have said Behnivyr had any information with regard to his parents' plans, but in light of recent events, I've changed my opinion."

Kris ignored him. He could already guess what had caused Ivy to make the request. If he'd insisted, it must have been because he was trying to delay the wedding, to give his would-be suitor time to come for him.

Well, Kris had waited long enough. He'd been musing over how to proceed ever since he'd returned to Nikaret, and while he couldn't say he'd found the best possible solution, he didn't have much choice but to go through with it. There was a time and place for subtlety, but sometimes the easiest, most straightforward path was the only way to go.

Ivy might be horrified once he figured out Kris's true identity, but Kris had to take that risk. At the very least, he'd help Ivy out of an unwanted betrothal. If, in the process, he'd end up claiming Ivy as his own.... Well, Kris had no intention of complaining.

"Sai, listen closely. Here's what we're going to do."

One week later

"AND TOMORROW, we're scheduled to meet the future mother of our children. I took the liberty of picking a candidate myself, but of course, if you have other preferences, we can change our minds."

Ivy listened to his betrothed drone on and suppressed a grimace of distaste. "Isn't it a little too soon to think about having children?" he asked as he scanned the village square for any sign of his sire.

The marquis released a frustrated huff. "Of course not. I've been waiting a long time for you."

Ivy didn't bother pointing out that the other Andari's desires were none of his responsibility. "I've just come of age. I'm not ready to be a parent."

Torildy's hand landed on his arm, squeezing too tightly for comfort. Ivy found himself forced to face the other Andari, whether he wanted to or not. "Between the two of us," the marquis said, "I'm sure we can manage."

Ivy knew he should choose his battles and that, for the moment, he was better off holding his tongue. However, the past few days had been far more difficult for him than he'd expected, and it certainly didn't help that his sire kept stalling and leaving him alone with Torildy whenever he got the chance.

"Marquis Torildy, here is how I see the situation. You're probably aware that my mother was an odale. I respect the guild a great deal, and I appreciate the service they provide. But it is too soon for us to resort to them. Perhaps sometime in the future we will find someone else, a second bond mate that will be a suitable mother for the child. It is always best for a babe to grow up with all of his parents, not just two of them."

Never mind that so far Ivy had yet to meet any woman who appealed to him in a romantic or even sexual way. Since he'd lived all his life in Seanda, without much contact with the outside world, he hadn't deemed this lack of attraction toward females strange. Apparently, he'd been mistaken.

A memory of Kris popped up in his mind, sudden and unbidden. Ivy barely managed to suppress a whimper as his member hardened, and his body clenched in need. Torildy took a step closer to him, peering closer at his face. "Are you well, my dear? You've been behaving quite oddly."

The other Andari's scent repulsed Ivy so much that he nearly threw up right then and there. He might have done exactly that had his sire not deigned to show up at last. "Behnivyr? You look terrible. Perhaps we should return to Seanda."

Ivy nodded. He wished he could explore more of the villages and towns where his sire had taken him, but not even the quaint beauty of the locales could distract him from the burden of Torildy's presence and the recollection of Kris's touch.

"Yes, Sire," he told Rasami. "We should go back. I'd like to share midmeal with Father anyway."

His sire nodded in approval. "You're quite correct. We need to check up on the preparations for the bonding."

Ivy didn't acknowledge that in any way. He just followed his sire as the older Andari proceeded to thank the village elders for their hospitality. The villagers led them to the outskirts of their settlement, whereupon Ivy and his companions mounted their horses.

Ivy managed to muster a modicum of interest for watching his sire summon their way home. Wave-wayfaring was a skill he hadn't managed to master yet, so he couldn't help but marvel as his sire's chants created a tunnel of pure energy out of thin air.

"Remember to follow me closely," his sire reminded him as the tunnel stabilized. "It's quite safe even for young folk such as yourself, but we don't want you to get sick."

Rasami told him that every time they waved anywhere. In fact, it had given Ivy the one idea he had that would help him delay the bonding. Some sort of sickness on his part—one that he could actually create, not simulate. Simulation would never work because his parents would see straight through the lie. Sadly, that plan had a very clear hole—the fact that Ivy healed with striking rapidity from any sickness or injury, something he blamed on his talent with the healing arts. But it was the last idea he had, and he felt fairly certain he could find some sort of potion that would be able to circumvent his magic.

He was still musing over this when his sire guided his mount into the portal. Ivy did the same, only to be struck by the strange sensation that always assaulted him when wave-wayfaring. Truth be told, it wouldn't have been too different from riding on a regular road, except it felt an awful lot like they were being guided along by a powerful current. The temperature always changed—sometimes dropping, other times increasing—as did the intensity of the light.

Today, the wave was hot but dark, like a particularly uncomfortable summer night. Sweat trickled over his spine and nape, and his mouth dried with thirst. His mount released a small neigh of protest, but kept going, used to the stress of wave-wayfaring.

At last, the tunnel ended, and they emerged on the other side, back in Seanda. Much to Ivy's surprise, his father was already waiting for them. It was unusual, as the Andari lord never greeted them outside of the manse and definitely not before Ivy and his companions had recovered from their journey through the wave.

The reasons for the change became obvious when Ivy's father frantically approached. "Thank Reysen you've returned," he said. "We've just received a message from Nikaret."

"From the empire capital?" Ivy asked. "Why? What's happened?"

"Apparently, the Morai has decided to host a celebration with all the important figures from every province of the empire," his father said, sounding none too pleased. "The reason isn't stated, but we've all been invited."

Judging by the way his father stressed the latter word, Ivy guessed the invitation was more of a command than anything else. Ivy frowned. The Nikari rarely did things for no reason. Could this have anything to do with Ivy's conversation with Kris? He should have been a little more careful when it came to revealing details of his family life. True, he hadn't actually told the Nikari his parents were guilty of sedition, but he might have given Kris a clue that they needed to be analyzed more carefully.

Ivy dismounted, struggling to keep his breathing even and not display his panic. His parents posed no danger for the empire, and whatever comments they made in the privacy of their own home wouldn't affect their long-standing respected position in Anderra.

Even as stable boys came forth to take care of his horse, Ivy closed his eyes and thought about dark, gold-rimmed eyes. He couldn't believe Kris had betrayed him, not after the earnestness of Kris's promise. No, there was something more going on. Then again, he might even be jumping at shadows. This could be entirely unrelated to Ivy. Reysen only knew what the Nikari Morai had on his agenda.

"This is a disaster," his father went on to say. "How are we supposed to continue the preparations for the bonding if we're not even here?"

"Let's not worry just yet," Ivy's sire said. "The Nikari are regularly quite expedient in any of their proceedings. I can't imagine we'll be delayed."

"In any case, I must return to my home." The marquis didn't seem pleased with the prospect or with this development. "My dear Behnivyr, it is with great sorrow that I part from you. We will discuss our future odale more when next we meet."

Ivy muttered something suitably polite, or at least he tried to. Judging by the dark look his father threw his way, he wasn't wholly successful. His sire covered his almost-gaffe by offering, "I'll lead you home, Your Lordship."

"You have my thanks," the marquis replied. He looked toward Ivy, and something in his stance told Ivy that the older Andari had planned to kiss him good-bye. Thankfully, that would have entailed Torildy dismounting, which would have been awkward and inappropriate given the timing. And so, Torildy just smiled and said, "I will count the moments until our reunion."

Aware of his father's furious glower, Ivy forced a more enthusiastic good-bye. "As always, Your Lordship, you flatter me. I trust you will have a smooth journey on the wave."

Uttering the friendly response felt like pulling teeth, but it did nudge things along. His sire started to chant again, and the wave-wayfaring tunnel manifested in front of them for the second time. It couldn't have been easy for Rasami to summon a second portal so soon, but perhaps he meant to pacify Torildy and compensate for Ivy's ill temper.

For his part, Ivy didn't feel in the least bit guilty. In fact, he breathed a sigh of relief when his sire and his betrothed disappeared into the tunnel. Alas, as the doorway closed behind them, his father immediately proceeded to point out his displeasure with Ivy.

"You promised you'd show some respect and openness toward the marquis. Is it truly so difficult for you to understand the importance of this bonding?"

"I apologize, Father," Ivy said. "I just haven't been myself the past few days."

He didn't confess that the reason for his behavior lay in his body's sudden decision to respond to the mere memory of a Nikari he'd only spent a few hours with. Thinking of it that way, it was truly alarming, and it opened up possibilities Ivy didn't dare to consider yet.

His words must have convinced his father, though, because the older Andari sighed and said, "I see. Well, try to get some rest tonight. We'll leave next morn, at daybreak. Hopefully, the Morai won't demand too much of us, and we'll be able to return soon."

Ivy didn't look forward to a long journey through the wave, but it couldn't be helped. "You're probably correct, Father," he said. "Now, with your permission, may I go to my room?"

"Yes, of course. I will see you at evening-meal."

He wasn't listening to Ivy anymore, so Ivy took advantage of it and retreated into the manse. He badly needed a wash and some sleep. And if a certain Nikari came to him in his dreams, Ivy wasn't about to complain.

CHAPTER THREE
REUNION

"I STILL don't understand why you've decided to go through with this ball." Kris's mother released a delicate huff as she guided her nightwolf through the undergrowth. "It's not like you."

From his position on his own mount, Kris arched a brow at her. "Why, isn't it obvious? I did it for you. You thrive on intrigue and gossip, and balls are the only way I can get you to court."

The A'Mora laughed heartily, causing her mount, Fegala, to release a sound of animalistic amusement. "And now you're teasing me. Oh, my dear, do not play me for a fool. I can tell when you're hiding something. I'm your mother, after all."

Kris couldn't help but smile and regretted it a second later when her eyes widened. "Creator…. An actual smile? Now I know you're keeping a secret from me. You truly must tell me."

And Kris would have told her, except he wasn't quite sure he had anything to tell. A meeting at a masquerade ball with a mysterious Full-Blood Andari meant nothing, at least not to an outsider. It was only today that he'd find out whether he and Ivy could build a more concrete relationship based on those moments they had shared.

"Everything will be revealed in time," he told his mother. "And don't point out my smiles. The servants are already giving me suspicious looks."

"Well, can you blame them? It's not like you smile all that often or without just cause."

She sounded concerned now, which Kris both hated and appreciated. She was the only one—other than his nightwolf, of course—who had never, not once, displayed fear or subservience to him. Even in public, she remained as affectionate as ever, a scandalous change from the regular behavior of a Morai's mother. But then, her lighthearted demeanor was one of the reasons why, to this day, they remained so close.

Kris guided Attcha onward, considering whether he should reveal the summer solstice events. "Kris?" his mother asked him. "Is there anything wrong?"

Her nightwolf growled, displaying her own nervousness and concern for Kris. Attcha nipped Fegala's ear, playfully letting her know that he could handle the situation.

In turn, Kris replied, "I'm fine, Mother. Come sit with me."

He guided his nightwolf toward a small stream that lazily made its way through the forest, only to meld with the Endana River further on. As Kris dismounted, Attcha went ahead to drink from the clear water. In the distance, the mountains rumbled, as if in response to Kris's inner turmoil.

His mother eventually joined him—without her mount, as well— and waited in silence as Kris gathered his thoughts. "I met someone," he finally said.

Judging by his mother's expression, she'd expected something more along the line of him deciding to start a new war. "Someone?" she repeated. "You mean…. A romantic interest?"

Kris laughed. "You seem shocked."

"Well… I am. I'd next to abandoned all hope of having grandchildren and had started to get used to the idea of having to be acting Mora forever. But never mind me. Tell me more. Who is this mysterious 'someone'?"

"He is a Full-Blooded Andari. I met him during the solstice, when I went to one of the Andari carnivals."

"Creator…. You're serious about this. That's why you summoned representatives from all the provinces here. For his sake."

"Quite." Kris shot his mother a serious look. "Mother, if things happen the way I want them to, if he's willing to be with me in spite of my being the Nikari emperor…. The court won't be happy. I will need your help."

"And you have it," she replied without a moment of hesitation. "You know, Kris, that my most fervent need is for you to be happy. If this Andari is the reason behind your smile, he will find a friend in me."

They lingered for a while longer in the forest, although they didn't speak of Ivy again. Finally, as the sun hit its apex, Kris could no longer bear the impatience and summoned Attcha to his side. His mother smirked at him. "He's probably in Nikaret already, isn't he? No wonder you've been trying to distract yourself."

Kris grunted. "I decided it would be for the best if we met at the ball. He'll probably be exhausted after the journey through the wave, and who knows how he'll react to seeing me?"

His mother's smile faded. "I must admit that I'm anxious about this secrecy, but I do understand. What's his name? I'll keep an eye open and make sure everything is in order for him."

"Behnivyr Erethe," Kris replied, waiting for the unavoidable explosion.

"The son of the would-be rebels?" his mother inquired. "Oh dear. Are you sure about him?"

"Yes, Mother. Just wait until you meet him, and you'll see I'm right."

She nodded, but she remained quiet as she waited for Kris to create the dimensional rift. Both of them mounted their nightwolves, and Kris opened the portal, his skin vibrating with the need to see Ivy. He leaped into the rift and landed safely on the other side, with his mother following mere seconds later.

I will go look into the arrival of your suitor, his mother whispered in his mind. *Be at ease, my son.*

Kris nodded in thanks, feeling more grateful than ever that he had her by his side. They parted ways at the nightwolf dens, since Attcha and Fegala were assigned separate private spaces. Once alone, Kris headed inside.

If the palace was busy on a regular basis, now it had become simply chaotic. Nevertheless, Kris sensed without needing to be told that Ivy had arrived. The distant scent of his perfume lingered in the air, the fragrance tempting Kris to follow it toward the guest chambers.

Not all guests would fit in the palace, but Kris had made sure each invitation held the location of where every individual party of visitors would be accommodated. Naturally, the Erethe would stay on palace grounds. Ivy had received an individual room Kris could have easy access to.

It was probably a good thing that Kris ran into his uncle Phura. "Your Majesty," the older Nikari greeted him. "You look well. Thank you for your kind invitation."

"You know you are always welcome in Nikaret," Kris replied neutrally. "And Shuri? Did he stay behind in Tarkquin?"

Phura's lips twisted in a rare smile. "He jumped at the chance of visiting. Apparently, he's quite eager to test out his new blades, and no one else but the Morai will do."

Kris caught himself before he could grin back. "I'm sure I'll find time for at least one sparring match with my dear brother."

His uncle's pleasant expression dissipated at Kris's words. Undoubtedly, he must have taken them as a dig to the fact that Shuri wasn't his real son. Kris mentally sighed and, not for the first time, wished Phura's hatred had died along with Kris's father. Unfortunately, he knew better than to think that would happen. Even if Kris and Shuri were just half brothers, they looked too alike to mistake them for cousins—as the official story claimed. The fact remained that the former Morai had no qualms about bedding his own brother's wife, which had left them all with perpetually awkward family reunions.

Just the same, Kris cared deeply for Shuri. For political reasons they couldn't spend enough time together, so he doubted the sentiment was reciprocated, but even so, he liked knowing he had a sibling. But it wouldn't be wise to tempt fate, not with Ivy in the palace and close to him.

"In any case," he said, "I will see you and Shuri later. Have an excellent day."

"Thank you, Your Majesty," the older Nikari replied. "I look forward to tonight's ball."

Something in Phura's tone told Kris the man meant it but not in a good way. It was as he'd told his mother. His future with Ivy—if it existed—would involve a great deal of difficulty and risk. But Kris had always liked challenges, and should this gamble pay off, Kris stood to win more than Phura could ever imagine.

This time, he no longer smothered his smile. "So do I, Uncle," he said. "So do I."

He left the older Nikari standing there, gaping after him, and headed toward his quarters. He had a ball to get ready for.

IVY WAS no stranger to grand balls and official ceremonies. His father often hosted such fetes in Seanda, and more than once, Ivy had been the center of attention there. But none of those parties, however lavish they had been, had prepared him for the one the Nikari Morai had thrown.

The first moment he entered the ballroom, he was struck by the number of people mingling in the cavernous space. Dressed to impress in formal outfits according to their own cultures, they formed a kaleidoscopic display of beauty and style.

Julisse women wrapped in brightly colored togas mingled with the more sedate Tarkquinian ladies, dressed in loose, flowing garbs that covered them from head to toe. Similarly, eccentric nigh-nude Tarkquin males were engaged in conversation with robe-clad Andari. And among all of them were the stoic Nikari, male and female warriors unerringly boasting full military regalia.

The room itself had been prepared to match its distinguished guests. The light emanating from the glittering magical torches struck the large blue crystals that peppered the room in a tight geometric pattern. From his lessons, Ivy remembered they were called *nektra* crystals and were solely native to the area around Nikaret. The reflected rays danced over the walls and ceiling in an abstract display of pure magic. But when Ivy peered closer, he could see the blue light depicting scenes of combat and conquest, images of the proud Nikari leaders building their empire. There were no woven tapestries like in Andari households, just banners bearing the mark of the Morai. The cold beauty of it made Ivy shiver in a mix of awe and apprehension.

So far, the only familiar type of decoration he'd seen was a portrait, one of the very first Nikari emperor, Seyan'Kel'Fezenda. But even the brushstrokes in the image seemed odd and unfamiliar. Now more than ever, Ivy felt impossibly young and lost among things alien to him. It certainly didn't help that ever since they'd come out from the wave, the strange feelings that had appeared after the solstice had returned with a vengeance.

However, Ivy refused to let his anxiety show. Clinging to the lessons his sire had hammered into his mind—thank Reysen for that— he followed his parents into the room. They were soon intercepted by an Andari count who'd shown interest in Ivy before his betrothal to the marquis had been arranged.

"Greetings, my lords," the count said. "It's such a pleasure to see you again."

Ivy's parents greeted the count in turn. "How have you been, Count Allevios?" his father asked. "I've heard good things about your new policies with regard to the Half-Blood populace."

His words were ambiguous enough to tell Ivy that those policies probably didn't benefit Half Bloods. Ivy had a headache just thinking about the political clashes that would ensue. But Andari aristocracy was still very set in their ways, especially in certain provinces like the ones led by Ivy's father and Count Allevios. They tried to cling to tradition where they could, since the Nikari had already claimed Anderra's independence. They didn't realize such conflicts made things worse for everyone.

Allevios laughed lightly, oblivious to Ivy's silent fuming. "I try. I would love to hear your ideas on it later on." Turning toward Ivy, he added, "In the meantime, I have to say, Behnivyr, you're even lovelier than I remembered."

"You are too kind, My Lord," Ivy murmured.

"Simply being honest." The count smiled, and a tinge of bitterness slipped into his voice when he continued, "I hear congratulations are in order for your upcoming nuptials."

"You have my thanks," Ivy replied. His anxiousness melted into frustration, and with a touch of sadistic glee, he added, "You are, of course, invited. I'm sure my betrothed would be happy to have you there."

His father's mien of dismay was satisfying to notice. Even better, they couldn't chastise him for the jab—because the count would be invited. He wouldn't attend—it would be considered gauche since any Andari in their circle of friends knew about the count's almost embarrassing insistence to bond with Ivy.

In the end, courtesy of Ivy's so-called gaffe, Allevios departed after numerous reassurances that he would, indeed, visit Seanda soon. No sooner had the count taken his leave than Ivy's sire dragged him aside behind a large banner. "Son, I beg you to watch your tongue. We need the assistance of these people. Offending them isn't in our best interest."

"I meant no offense," Ivy argued. "You and Father would have invited him to the ceremony anyway."

His sire glowered at him. "The illusion of stupidity doesn't become you, Behnivyr. You would do well to remember that you are not a child and neither am I."

Ivy could easily stomach his sire's disappointment but not his cool disdain. He took a deep breath and struggled against the feeling of humiliation. His sire was right. The comment had been petty and out of place, and he shouldn't have said it.

He had to remember that they were at an important celebration, and his private problems needed to be at least temporarily discarded. "You're right, Sire," he said. "I promise I'll make you proud of me."

The next hour or so passed in a blur of meaningless smiles, introductions, and conversation. Ivy put forth his best possible performance, and that pacified his parents. Still, he was once more distracted from his resolve when he caught sight of a tall Nikari, somewhere to his right.

For a few seconds, Ivy froze, breathlessly staring in that direction. The Nikari's back was to Ivy, but Ivy could still identify him. Kris. Of course Kris would be here. Ivy should have expected it. He should have been ready for it, but he wasn't, not in the slightest. Reysen, what would he say? What would he do?

He shook off his incipient panic attack when he realized something didn't feel right. This Nikari seemed slightly shorter and more slender than Kris. Indeed, when the stranger turned, Ivy's suspicion crystallized into certainty. The Nikari certainly resembled Kris but nothing more.

A crushing feeling of disappointment filled him. He must have made a sound, because his sire nudged him inquiringly. "What is it?"

Ivy knew he should probably drop the entire matter, but he couldn't help but use the offered opportunity to his full advantage. "Who is that?" he inquired.

Rasami followed his gaze and went rigid. "Don't ever approach that man, Behnivyr. Don't you even dare to look at him. You're liable to stir offense."

Ivy averted his eyes, waiting for his sire to elaborate. No explanation followed, so Ivy resigned himself to living with the not knowing. Still, the sight of the mysterious man convinced Ivy that Kris must be a guest at the ball too. In all likelihood, the two of them were related.

He scanned the crowd, surreptitiously trying to find Kris. He was fairly certain that, in spite of the throng surrounding him, he could still spot the Nikari he sought. Alas, there seemed to be no sign of Kris, and he couldn't risk running off in hopes of encountering the other man. His parents had told him from the very beginning that he was forbidden to be on his own even for a minute—which, given the number of people here, was understandable.

And then the time for mingling finally ended as the moment they'd all been waiting for arrived. The sound of a gong silenced every person in the room, and a liveried Nikari called out, "His Imperial Majesty, Morai Kristelien Fezenda, and Her Imperial Majesty, A'Mora Katara Fezenda."

On cue, everyone dropped to their knees and bowed lowly, their eyes fixed on the marble floor. Ivy knelt as well, but he couldn't *not* look. Like a man in a dream, he watched as the large, ornate doors of the ballroom opened, allowing entrance to the man who had haunted Ivy's nights and days from the first moment they'd met.

He was just as handsome as Ivy remembered, or perhaps even more so. Ivy didn't know how he could have mistaken him for the Nikari from before, because there couldn't be any comparison. The simple garb he'd worn the night of the solstice had been replaced by a similarly styled but far more elegant uniform. The black of the material was complimented by supine curves of silver that arched over his chest and shoulders, framing his powerful muscles. A black fur cloak lay over his shoulders, bound together by a crystal brooch in the shape of a nightwolf, and a solid crown of adamant adorned his head. In the bright lights shed by the magical torches, he looked like a majestic warrior of old, like a figure from the surreal images displayed through the crystals. Kris. Short for Kristelien. Ivy had fallen for the Nikari Morai.

Kristelien Fezenda. The youngest Morai ever to take the throne after his father, Spatha, had died. Sweet Reysen, how could Ivy have been so stupid? Sure, he could have never guessed the emperor would deign to come to Seanda. To top it off, he'd never seen a portrait of the Morai or anyone in the imperial family. Nevertheless, Kris's behavior hadn't been that of a regular Nikari. Ivy realized that now, and he realized Kris's answer to his question should have clued him in to the truth.

By Kris's side, a stunning Nikari woman approached, wearing the female and somewhat more elaborate version of Kris's garments. She was so beautiful that Ivy would have been jealous had he not known her to be the A'Mora—the Nikari emperor's mother.

He must have been gaping at them for quite some time, because his parents noticed his less than discreet attitude. His father pulled on his sleeve, and Ivy quickly stared down at the floor. What now? Why had Kris engineered this entire ball? Was it connected to Ivy, or had Kris already forgotten about him, about their promise? Had the moments they'd shared been all a lie, a sham to make fun of the foolish young Andari willing to jump into the arms of the first Nikari who crossed his path?

Ivy clenched his fists and forced himself to even out his breathing. It was too soon to judge, far too soon. Thinking rationally, the Nikari Morai was too important a man to stoop to humiliating Ivy—who, in the big picture, was quite insignificant.

Something more must be going on. Why had the Morai been there that night in the first place? Why had he approached Ivy? His previous doubts returned, and he berated himself for his naïveté. Could the matter have anything to do with his parents? If so, where did Ivy stand? Had he only been a plaything for the powerful Nikari emperor?

It looked like he wouldn't receive the answers to his questions anytime soon. Kris and his mother did take position on the throne, but alas, Ivy and his parents needed to wait for their turn to proceed with the formalities of their introductions. And that was liable to last a long time, given that the Morai spoke to his guests in order of rank, with the nobles belonging to the earlier conquered lands taking precedence.

Since Anderra had maintained its independence the longest, Ivy had to be very patient, indeed.

He distracted himself by trying to catch the murmurs of the people around them. "I wonder what this is all about," someone—perhaps the governor of one of the largest provinces in Julissa—was saying.

"Another war," a second voice replied. "I can already imagine more taxes being imposed to subsidize the campaigns."

"Why summon all the nobles, then?" a third one inquired. "For a discussion on the war effort, only governors would be necessary, if that. Besides, a war on whom? The Nikari have already conquered the entire Western Realm."

The argument seemed to stump them all, which Ivy could definitely understand. He kept his mouth shut and lingered around his parents, doing his best not to stare at Kris. Oddly enough, it didn't take too long for Kris to dismiss each individual group of guests. Most people didn't seem surprised, which Ivy surmised meant that it was the Morai's way to be time efficient when it came to such formalities. Still, he couldn't help but be grateful for it, and his foolish heart started to race faster and faster as the moment of their reunion approached.

At last, his parents walked to the throne and knelt, and Ivy followed their example. "Rise," the Morai said magnanimously. "Welcome to Nikaret. Too many moons have passed since the noble Andari have graced these halls."

"You honor us, great Morai," Ivy's father replied. "We truly must apologize for our error. I am afraid the distance between Seanda and Nikaret conspires against us."

"Indeed," Kris replied. "I do believe your son has never visited Nikaret before."

Taking his cue, Ivy's sire gestured for Ivy to step forward. Ivy complied, although he politely held his eyes down as his parents spoke to the Morai. "You are correct, Your Majesty. This is our son, Behnivyr. He's just recently come of age, and he will soon be bonded to Marquis Torildy Dekar."

"Is that a fact? I assume congratulations are in order. Am I right, Behnivyr?"

Upon being directly addressed, Ivy looked up and faced Kris. He opened his mouth to answer, but his words died when he took in Kris's expression. Kris's gaze was hot as it landed on him, just like it had been that night, and suddenly, Ivy knew that, no, none of it had been a lie. He just stood there, staring and aching for a man beyond his reach.

Kris arched a brow—and it was all exactly like the moment they'd first met, when Ivy had been tongue-tied and reeling from a far too spicy drink. The familiarity steadied him, and he found his voice and his manners. "Thank you, Your Majesty. You are most kind."

He ached to drop a comment on a certain promise that someone other than his betrothed had made, but that would have been unwise, to say the least. In the end, it didn't matter, because something dark and teasing glittered in Kris's gold-rimmed eyes. "I trust you'll enjoy your stay here," he said. "Perhaps you'd be interested in seeing the nightwolf dens. They are quite remarkable to behold, especially for a young Andari such as yourself."

Ivy's sire made a noise, although Ivy had trouble interpreting the emotions that had caused it. There must have been a hefty dose of wariness involved, but also intellectual jealousy. Nightwolves were notoriously territorial, and Andari scholars had been struggling for decades to get firsthand information on them. All requests to approach the dens had been denied, so Andari—as well as all other races in the empire—had little information on the legendary beasts. However, nightwolves were also very dangerous, and any unfortunate individual who annoyed one of the animals might find themselves becoming dinner. The fact that Ivy had been invited to see the dens spoke volumes of Kris's interest in Ivy and also implied that Ivy was under his protection.

"I'd be honored," Ivy said, not bothering to suppress a smile. "They are fascinating creatures."

"They are, indeed, although some people deem them monsters. But…. As a wise woman once said, there are two sides to every story."

Ivy's heart nearly stopped. If he'd wanted evidence of the fact that Kris remembered their conversation, and his promise, he'd received it. He knew he should acknowledge the words in some way, but his vocal cords refused to obey him.

Fortunately, Kris must have decided their conversation had already lasted too long and was liable to draw more attention than would be wise. "Meanwhile, My Lords, I trust you will enjoy the festivities. It is so rare for the empire's representatives to get together like this. Perhaps it will foster togetherness within us all."

Ivy's parents tensed, and Ivy guessed this remark had been addressed to them. So there was something going on, something he hadn't known about. He wished he could ask, but his parents were already thanking the Morai. Kris dismissed them, and Ivy was pulled aside, to a more private corner. "What was that all about?" his sire inquired. "Why did he act that way?"

Ivy was still reeling from his conversation with Kris, so he didn't even have to fake his shock. "I have no idea."

His dazed voice let his lie pass unnoticed, or perhaps his parents were too concerned with their own affairs to worry about Ivy's deception. Then again, it would have been hard for them to imagine that Ivy had already met Kris during the one night he'd dared to escape the manse and go anywhere without his parents' supervision. What were the odds?

His parents kept watching the Morai while Kris met with the rest of the Andari. Once the official introductions ended, both Kris and his mother left their thrones. To Ivy's surprise, Kris made a beeline for the Nikari Ivy had confused him for earlier in the night. Meanwhile, Kris's mother approached Ivy and his parents.

The three of them greeted the A'Mora with a low bow, as deserving of her station. She acknowledged their gesture with a nod, then inquired, "Would you like to go to the dens now, Your Lordship?"

Her question took Ivy aback, but he recovered his composure. "Certainly. I'd love to."

He offered her his arm—although the differences in their ranks and ages made the gesture somewhat superfluous. Nevertheless, she took it with an approving smile. "Lord Titexe, Lord Rasami, I trust you'll enjoy the ball in spite of me whisking away your beloved son."

Ivy's parents smiled tightly. "Naturally. We must thank you for giving Behnivyr a chance to see something so rare."

"Oh, the merits are not mine," Katara said enigmatically. "In any case, I will endeavor not to keep him for too long. Have an excellent evening."

With that, the A'Mora started to guide Ivy away. They left the ballroom through a pair of glass side doors that led into the gardens. As soon as the noise coming from the ball melted into a distant hum, Katara addressed Ivy. "You look disappointed," she said. "Perhaps you expected someone else to be your guide?"

Ivy couldn't tell what answer she was waiting for and didn't know what would be wise to reveal. Had Kris told her about the night of the solstice? He must have. Otherwise, she wouldn't be here with Ivy. Still, until Ivy spoke to Kris, it would be best to act prudently in terms of what he said and did. After all, discretion was the better part of valor.

"I'm still in awe with the hospitality and generosity you've showered me with," he answered. "Very few Andari are granted the honor to be personally attended by Your Majesty, and even fewer get to see the nightwolves."

The A'Mora burst into strikingly cheerful laughter. "You're very good at half-truths. I wonder if that should worry me or give me a measure of relief."

It didn't surprise Ivy that she had called him up on his vagueness, but at least she didn't seem offended. Still, he didn't know how to answer, and when she didn't say anything else, he feared he might be reading her wrong and he'd made the worst possible impression on her.

They left the gardens and entered a large courtyard. In the distance, Ivy thought he could hear the howls and growls of the nightwolves. "I must remind you to stay out of the dens unless told otherwise," Katara said. "I would hate to have to explain to my son why you lost a limb."

"I understand," Ivy replied. "I will respect their space."

Ivy couldn't be sure, but he thought his phrasing had pleased her. Once more, she subsided into silence as they followed the howls to a large area that must have been at least ten times the size of the huge ballroom. Ivy had imagined the dens to be somewhat similar to horse paddocks, but they weren't, not at all. Each individual nightwolf was assigned a barred-off space wherein constructions similar to natural caves had been erected. In fact, they almost looked like actual dens taken from the forest and dropped there in the courtyard. There was to be no real symmetry with regard to the size and location of the caves, which, taking into account the Nikari culture, seemed somewhat unusual.

The dens were guarded by Nikari armed to the teeth. They didn't react to his presence and instead saluted in acknowledgment of the A'Mora. If they found it peculiar that she had chosen to give a random Andari a tour, they didn't show it. The moment he stepped beyond the guards, a chill wind assaulted Ivy, coming from the dens. Ivy blinked in surprise, but when Katara didn't comment on it, he didn't ask either.

She led him to one of the first stalls, where a huge nightwolf— easily as big as any horse Ivy had seen and at least twice as bulky—lay in wait. The beast greeted Katara with an enthusiastic growl, and Katara smiled at it. "Is this your nightwolf, Majesty?" Ivy inquired. He didn't know why, but somehow, he doubted it. The gold of the creature's eyes reminded him of someone else entirely.

Katara shook her head, still looking at the large beast. "This is Kris's mount, Attcha. He's more liable to be friendly to you than mine, under certain circumstances, of course." Abruptly, she turned toward him and pinned him with a strikingly familiar gaze. "Lord Behnivyr, I will be blunt. When my son told me about you, I was both happy and wary. If I'd had to pick a romantic interest for Kris, it wouldn't have been you—for reasons that are largely independent to yourself, for that matter. But back in the ballroom, I saw the way you were looking at my son. Tell me something. Do you think that you, as a Full-Blooded Andari, can carry the burden of the Morai's affection?"

Her words would have taken him aback and shocked him into speechlessness, if not for the way she'd phrased the latter question. As it was, he followed his heart and repeated, "Burden? It's never a burden to be with people you care about."

Too late did he realize what he'd said and what he must have admitted to. He might have been vague again, but the truth behind his words couldn't be hidden. Katara eyed him speculatively, a knowing glint in her dark, gold-rimmed eyes. "And do you? Do you care about my son?"

Ivy looked away, unable to withstand the weight of her scrutiny. "We've only just met," he said. "I don't understand any of this, and I don't know what he's thinking."

Katara hummed thoughtfully. "Another half-truth. Well, my dear Behnivyr, I might let you get away with it, but you can't expect that from my son."

All of a sudden, Ivy's skin heated and a lustful awareness filled him, just like in the ballroom. Katara must have felt something too— although naturally, in a different way—because she said, "This is my cue to take my leave. Have a wonderful evening, Lord Behnivyr, and do care about my son. As long as you have that courage, you and I will be great friends."

Without further ado, Katara turned on her heel and departed, disappearing in the direction of more distant dens. Ivy would have tried to thank her, but his attention had been drawn to the nightwolf's den, where, against all odds, a familiar figure had appeared.

"Hello, Ivy," Kris said as he patted his nightwolf's large head. "I do believe the two of us have a conversation pending."

CHAPTER FOUR
DECISION

KRIS MET Ivy's gaze, taking in the play of emotion in the Andari's lovely green eyes. "Wouldn't you agree with me?" he prodded.

Ivy still didn't answer, although the way he bit his pink lips and clenched his small fists was pretty eloquent in itself. Kris hid a smile. The past few hours had been among the most torturous of Kris's life, but it had been worth it, simply to see the expression on Ivy's beautiful face.

Creator, he was even lovelier than Kris remembered. His white-blond braid had been adorned with tiny Andari gemstones, and his emerald robes hugged his slender body to perfection and made the color of his eyes stand out even more. In the bright light of the Nikaret moon, he seemed to glow, his pale skin almost translucent, giving the impression of an ethereal creature torn from the pages of a particularly seductive story.

When Ivy spoke, though, he managed to surprise Kris. "How did you end up in the den?" Kris decided it wouldn't hurt to set Ivy's mind at ease a bit before they tackled the most obvious matter that concerned them both. With a wave of his hand, he unlocked the barrier of Attcha's den and gestured for Ivy to enter the enclosure. "Come. I'll show you. And don't worry. Attcha won't hurt you."

In spite of the tension between them—or perhaps, partially, because of it—Ivy took him up on his offer. He bypassed the barrier and didn't even acknowledge the sound it made when Kris locked it up again.

"Am I allowed to touch him?" he asked, scanning Attcha's large form with open interest.

Kris already knew the answer, but he waited for Attcha to make the first move. The nightwolf didn't delay in doing exactly that. He couldn't communicate with Ivy like he did with Kris, but he did take a step forward and lay down, much like a less dangerous canine pet would have.

Ivy released a sound of awe. "He understands me."

"Of course," Kris replied. "Nightwolves are actually far more intelligent than non-Nikari realize."

Ivy knelt next to Attcha and gently buried his fingers in the nightwolf's fur. A rumble of pleasure echoed through Kris's connection to the beast. His mind translated it into several main concepts. *Soft. Warm. Pack.*

Attcha's approval pleased Kris, but then he hadn't doubted the beast would like Ivy. "He's friendly," Ivy noted.

Kris chuckled. "No, he really isn't. No nightwolf is friendly."

Attcha decided to add to Ivy's confusion by displaying his belly to the Andari and waiting to be scratched. Kris shook his head at his nightwolf's shameless display. "He's taking advantage of you. Be careful, lest you spoil him beyond belief."

"I don't think I would mind." Ivy smiled. "He's a magnificent creature. I consider myself privileged for his acceptance."

Kris dropped down next to Attcha and leaned against his nightwolf's big body. "Just remember that not all nightwolves are like this. They won't hurt you because they'll be able to smell Attcha on you, but it wouldn't be wise to approach them just the same. They're not pets. In fact, he's more liable to consider you his pet."

Attcha huffed and got up, giving Kris the cold shoulder and proceeding to nuzzle Ivy's face. Ivy laughed and hugged the creature's neck, not seeming all that bothered by the razor-sharp fangs inches away from his throat or the slobber that would likely destroy his carefully chosen outfit.

"It's all right," he told Kris. "I can feel it—the fact that he likes me—in my heart. I suppose it's because of my mixed affinity, but it's very... nice. Warm. Safe. He's... protective of me and happy."

Kris had no idea how Ivy had identified Attcha's feelings so well. In fact, Ivy himself seemed surprised. It pleased Kris, but it also made him feel slightly jealous. He'd never expected to be jealous of his own nightwolf, but there it was.

Attcha snorted, obviously guessing Kris's thoughts. He freed himself from Ivy's grip and nudged Kris with his large paw. *Go. Claim.*

Kris didn't have to be told twice. He shot to his feet and offered Ivy his hand. After a small moment of hesitation, the young Andari took it. As Ivy got up, Kris removed his cloak and wrapped it around Ivy's shoulders. "I promised I'd show you how I got here. For the moment, keep that on."

Ivy eyed him with obvious skepticism but didn't pull away or refuse Kris's present. In fact, Kris noticed that he took a deep breath, as if inhaling the cloak's scent. Whatever doubts Ivy had with regard to their relationship, the Andari was just as attracted to Kris as he'd been before he'd found out about Kris's true identity.

Kris was not above using their obvious chemistry to his advantage, especially not when his body already responded to Ivy's proximity. He took Ivy's hand, suppressing a shiver at its softness. Creator, he could already imagine how good it would feel to have all of Ivy's skin against his, or better yet, to bury his cock into Ivy's tight ass.

Swiftly reining in the lustful beast that rose within him, Kris guided Ivy to Attcha's cave. The wind picked up as they approached the structure. "Where are we going?" Ivy asked, his voice shaking ever so slightly.

"You'll see," Kris promised. "Just trust me on this, all right?"

In response, Ivy held onto Kris's hand even tighter. The show of faith simply fueled Kris's desire for Ivy, and he once more experienced the temptation of pulling Ivy into his arms and ravishing him right then and there. But as close as he might be to his nightwolf, he had no intention of initiating any romantic overture in Attcha's den.

When they entered the cave, Ivy released a soft gasp. "Is that…. Is that a dimensional rift?"

Kris knew the portal waiting in Attcha's cave must have been quite a sight for anyone who hadn't expected it, and especially a young Andari with no experience with rifts. He made sure the cloak was safely wrapped around Ivy and started to explain. "Yes. You see, Ivy, this isn't common knowledge, but nightwolves aren't beings of this dimension. When a Nikari first opens a dimensional rift, there is a chance that a nightwolf pup will emerge from inside. They pick us, not the other way around, and they only come to those they deem worthy. Just the same, they remain wild creatures. That first rift always stays open, protected through a magically enforced barrier. That way, the nightwolf can always return to his or her home."

"Aren't rifts unstable, though?" Ivy inquired. "Isn't it dangerous to have so many in the same place?"

There was no judgment in Ivy's voice and no fear, simply curiosity and interest. Here he was, in front of a portal that, from what he knew, could easily tear him limb from limb, but he didn't seem afraid at all. Kris wondered what he'd done to deserve that. Then again, he already knew the answer. Ivy's faith in him was largely unjustified, and Kris vowed to fix that very soon.

"No," he answered, "because these aren't regular rifts. It's quite difficult to explain, as everything you know about rifts was taught to you by Andari scholars, but to be brief, the portals are stabilized by the magic of the union between a Nikari and a nightwolf. It's actually quite safe to travel through, as long as its Nikari owner is with you. It shouldn't even hurt. Just the same, keep the cloak on. It will protect you."

Ivy nodded, and Kris wrapped his arm tightly around the young Andari's waist. Together, they stepped through the rift. Kris willed the portal to obey his instructions, and in the blink of an eye, they were back in the palace, in his quarters.

Ivy swayed a bit, and Kris caught the Andari before Ivy could fall. "That was… quite strange," Ivy said.

"Did it hurt?" Kris inquired, already kicking himself for taking a useless chance when they could have easily walked back to the palace.

Ivy shook his head. "No, not at all. It's just…. The transition is so sudden."

Ah, yes. Ivy was used to wave-wayfaring, so dimensional rifts naturally took him aback. "The first journey is a little confusing for everyone. Don't worry. It will pass, and you'll get used to it in time."

He guided Ivy to a low settee, now thankful that he'd chosen Attcha's portal to initiate Ivy to dimensional rifts. Truly, he should have known better than to worry. Their landing hadn't even disturbed any of the furniture and ornaments in the room, and with the protection of the cloak, Ivy had probably not experienced any real discomfort.

For a few seconds, Ivy just sat here, breathing steadily. Kris joined him on the settee and waited for the unavoidable inquiry. When it came, the question itself shocked Kris through its simplicity. "Why?" Ivy asked, turning bright and confusion-filled eyes on him.

Why. There were so many things Ivy could mean with that simple word. Why had they met? Why had Kris been in Seanda? Why had Kris invited him here to this particular ball? Kris could almost hear all those questions as if Ivy had spoken them out loud. He saw them in Ivy's earnest, green gaze, and he wondered how the Andari would react to the reply.

In the end, he decided to explain everything, in logical order. "I visited Seanda for official reasons, and no, I had no intention of approaching you. It was complete happenstance—believe it or not—and I didn't even know who you were, at least not immediately."

He very much doubted Ivy would be satisfied with his vague explanation of "official reasons," and indeed, that seemed to be the case. "It's something to do with my parents, isn't it?" Ivy asked quietly. "That's why you spoke to them the way you did, back in the ballroom."

Kris sighed. It would have been better if Ivy hadn't asked, but he'd known better than to truly hope for it. "The Morai isn't a popular man, especially not among Andari. Many people resent the leadership of the Nikari, and unfortunately, your parents are among them. I was there to investigate them, and the results of my inquiries proved to be quite unfortunate for them. As unpleasant as the entire matter is, I've decided to set it aside. Because of you."

It hadn't been an easy choice to make, and the balance between his own desire for Ivy and the stability of the empire was a delicate one. Ivy's eyes widened as the young Andari realized exactly what he was saying. "I…. Should you even be telling me this?"

"Probably not," Kris agreed. "But then, I'm not just the Morai with you, am I?"

"To me, you're Kris," Ivy answered, "the man I met at the carnival solstice and I shared my first kiss with. But…. What can I be to you? Why did you bring me here?"

Even as he spoke, Ivy was leaning closer to Kris, and his pupils dilated. His breath began to come in pants, and he bit his lower lip, much like he had the night of the solstice.

Kris tried to remember what Ivy had asked, but whatever he might have intended to reply was dissipating in a cloud of lust. Clinging to the last remnants of his control, he said, "Ivy, I—"

Before he could even finish the phrase, he ended up with a lapful of Ivy. The young Andari wrapped his arms around Kris and pressed their mouths together. His inexperience still showed, but he made up for it in enthusiasm, rubbing his ass against Kris's crotch even as he attempted to deepen the kiss.

Kris knew enough about the Andari to realize that taking what Ivy offered wouldn't be fair to him. But for all of Kris's good intentions, he was only a man, and in the end, the instincts of the Nikari were just as strong as those of the Andari.

And so Kris plunged his tongue into Ivy's wet cavern. He devoured Ivy's mouth, growling when the Andari's flavor exploded on his taste buds. Creator, Ivy was even sweeter than Kris remembered, his innocent passion more intoxicating than the strongest reada wine. And when Ivy moaned and eagerly surrendered to him, Kris forgot about all the scruples that had held him in check until tonight.

He broke their kiss long enough to steady Ivy in his arms. He removed the bulky cloak on Ivy's shoulders, since it had served its purpose and would only be cumbersome now. At last, still carrying Ivy, he left the couch. Undeterred by Kris's motion, Ivy licked his neck and nibbled on his collarbone, apparently intent on driving Kris crazy. Kris was highly tempted to summon a dimensional rift just so that they could reach his bedchambers faster, but even if that had been necessary, he couldn't have mustered the concentration.

By the time he succeeded in carrying Ivy into the bedroom the traditional way, his cock throbbed in his breeches so hard he ached. He deposited Ivy on the mattress, his mouth watering at the sinful sight Ivy made. Ivy extended his hands, reaching for him, his green eyes having gone almost black with passion. Lost in it, lost in Ivy, Kris joined Ivy on the bed and covered Ivy's body with his own, fusing their mouths together once more.

The moment reminded him of what they'd shared the night of the solstice. This time, however, there was no manservant to interrupt them. Ivy's parents couldn't reach him here, even if they did realize Ivy was with him. Right then and there, Ivy belonged to Kris.

That knowledge just stoked the fire inside Kris, making the kiss inadequate to sate his thirst for Ivy. When he separated their mouths for the second time, he did so only because he had other plans. Ivy released a moan of protest, but the sound turned into a gasp when Kris reached for the bindings of his robes.

Acknowledging Ivy's enduring innocence, Kris forced himself to slow down. "You can still say no," he murmured.

"I…." Ivy took a deep breath and shook his head. "I don't think I can. I don't want to. I've been waiting for this since that night."

Kris could certainly understand what Ivy meant, because he felt the same. His duties and his role aside, he craved Ivy more than he did his next breath. As he slowly parted the material of Ivy's elegant garb, he knew he could never let Ivy go. It was too late to go back now, far too late for both of them.

Fortunately, Ivy didn't seem to have any intention of changing his mind. In fact, at one point, he grew impatient and tried to rush things along, to help Kris undress him faster. But his hands were trembling, and he couldn't quite get a grip on the intricate laces and buttons, so he ended up making things worse. Kris smiled down at him and brushed a ghost of a kiss over Ivy's mouth. "Let me," he said simply. "There's no rush. We have all night."

His words must have convinced Ivy, because he relaxed on the bed, allowing Kris to continue with his self-appointed task. Kris eagerly did so, now pressing kisses to every inch of silken skin he revealed. His efforts received more than adequate compensation when Ivy arched against him, whimpering, wordlessly begging for more.

In spite of his own urgency, Kris took things slow. Even when he set Ivy's garments aside, he didn't remove his own, using them as the last barrier keeping his impulses in check. Flimsy as it was, it kept the frayed thread of Kris's control from unraveling altogether, and it allowed him to lavish each and every inch of Ivy with attention, just like the beautiful Andari deserved.

He started out by tracing Ivy's slender form with his tongue. Ivy's plump nipples immediately drew his attention and Kris zeroed in on them, taking one of the erect buds in his mouth. In reaction, Ivy released a nearly agonized cry. "Sweet Reysen…. Please, Kris. Oh…. Please!"

Kris would have hazarded a guess that Ivy himself didn't know what he was asking for. The Andari buried his fingers in Kris's hair, but he seemed undecided on whether he wanted Kris to continue sucking on his nipples or to advance on to more daring caresses. Ivy's responsiveness awed Kris, and he continued to test it by rubbing Ivy's free nipple with his fingers. The volume of Ivy's cries increased, as did the intensity of his frantic writhing.

Distantly, it occurred to Kris that he could make Ivy climax just through this simple foreplay, without even getting involved in genital contact. If he'd had any scruples left, he would have done it. But at the end of the day, Kris was not that selfless. Even if he could have controlled his own libido, he refused to lose the chance to bind Ivy to him.

And so, wicked as it might have been, Kris released Ivy's nipple from his mouth and licked down Ivy's chest. He couldn't resist stabbing his slick muscle into the tiny hole of Ivy's belly button. By now, Ivy had definitely decided where he wanted Kris's mouth, and his hands insistently tried to guide Kris onward. The last threads of Kris's guilt vanished, and he went for the gold, taking Ivy's dick into his mouth.

Ivy screamed, and if Kris hadn't known any better, he could have mistaken the shout as one of pain. However, the scent and taste of Ivy's passion left no room for doubt, and he sucked Ivy's cock all the way into his throat, devouring the rigid shaft much like he had Ivy's sweet lips.

Some Nikari considered the act of performing fellatio as a surrender of control, but Kris knew better. There was nothing quite like guiding the pleasure of your lover as the other man tried and failed to set the pace. Sucking Ivy's dick was even more satisfying. The open passion which Ivy displayed felt so natural, so unlike the reluctant surrender most Nikari put up for the purpose of pleasing their Morai in bed. Not so with Ivy. For Ivy, it seemed so honest and not just something that Ivy agreed to for Kris's benefit. Whether Ivy realized it or not, he craved Kris's overpowering passion, every inch of him practically emanating that need.

The addicting taste of Ivy's precum made Kris's head spin, and he released a growl of lust. In turn, the vibration caused by the sound ushered Ivy into a renewed bout of thrashing and writhing. Drunk on Ivy's desire for him, Kris reached down to rub his fingers over Ivy's taint. He rolled Ivy's balls in his palm, exploring the wrinkled sac with his digits. When it became obvious that Ivy was moments away from coming, he released Ivy's dick and took the perfect spheres of Ivy's testicles in his mouth, laving them with his tongue and noting additional differences in their physiology. Unlike Kris's, Ivy's body felt completely smooth to the touch, hairless even in the genital area. Kris hadn't deemed himself picky with regard to body hair, but he changed his mind now as he reveled in pleasuring Ivy with his mouth.

As it turned out, Ivy seemed to enjoy Kris's new discovery even more than Kris did. All of a sudden, his body convulsed and went rigid. He cried out Kris's name as he found his peak, his dick spurting creamy jets of pinkish semen. Most of Ivy's offering landed on his chest and abdomen, but Kris gathered his wits at the last moment and managed to catch the last few waves in his mouth.

Even Ivy's essence tasted sweet, and Kris couldn't help but crave more. As Ivy rode the last waves of his climax, Kris licked Ivy's dick clean, then went on to hunt for every errant drop. Ivy reacted beautifully to his thoroughness. Even if he'd just come, his dick hardened once more.

However, instead of reaching for Kris, Ivy pulled away from him, evading Kris's caresses. He took a couple of deep breaths, scanning Kris's face with a mix of awe, need, and uncertainty. Kris didn't move, knowing he'd already pushed Ivy more than he should have. Through one simple act, he'd made Ivy his lover, and Ivy couldn't hide anymore or turn back, even if he wanted to.

Still, something ached inside Kris when Ivy reached for his braid, his hands trembling. Before he could stop himself, he gripped Ivy's wrists and shook his head. "You don't have to. We can end things here. No one need ever know."

In truth, he should have known better than to offer, and even as he said the words, he regretted them. "Do you really think I would do that?" Ivy asked quietly.

He didn't have to say it, because they both knew that, for an Andari, intercourse couldn't just be swept under the rug. It wasn't their way, and a lie like Kris had suggested would dishonor Ivy more than extramarital sex ever could.

"No," Kris admitted, "and I was selfish enough not to care. You…. You deserve better than this."

Ivy's scowl melted into a sweet, affectionate smile. "I've already given myself to you," Ivy said, "and I don't regret it. This doesn't matter anymore."

He freed his hands from Kris's grip and undid his braid, the mark of his innocence in front of any Andari. Now free, his hair came tumbling over his shoulders in waves of white-gold, the gemstones that had previously adorned it falling onto the pillows. Ivy shivered, but whatever apprehension or distress he must have experienced was overcome by lust. "Touch me," he whispered. "Take me. I'm yours, Kris."

It would have taken a man stronger than Kris to refuse that offer. That last phrase destroyed the lingering remnants of Kris's control. Through a handful of words, Ivy managed to shatter Kris's mind.

No sooner had Ivy finished speaking than Kris reached for him, crushing their mouths together. *Yours.* It was a heady thought, because Kris wanted exactly that—to own Ivy, to possess him in every possible way, to claim him and brand him as his. He bit Ivy's lower lip and growled as the metallic, yet sweet taste filled his mouth. Combined with the flavor of Ivy's spunk, it made for a particularly decadent kiss.

Ivy wrapped his arms around Kris's neck, enthusiastically responding to his ministrations. It almost seemed like freeing his hair had given him that extra nudge he'd needed to throw all caution to the wind. While he still surrendered to Kris's domination, he did some touching of his own, fumbling with Kris's clothing as he tried to remove the last barrier between their bodies. Unlike the night of the solstice, he refused to be deterred and actually managed to free a few buttons and maybe even tear some seams. Kris didn't have the patience to take his clothes off the regular way. He just shredded the outfit he'd worn for the ball, at the same time discarding his boots. Ivy moaned into the kiss as Kris's magic buzzed against his skin. It couldn't have hurt him—Kris was far too experienced at such spells—but the distinctive feel of Kris's energies obviously excited him.

Kris decided that interesting tidbit needed to be explored, and he had just the way to do it. Unlike the Andari, Nikari didn't have different types of magic. Their abilities largely involved some type of offensive spell, even when it came to the rifts they used for long-distance travel. However, Kris was fortunate enough to know that he could use his talents to tease and tantalize as much as he could use them to hurt.

His new plan gave Kris the incentive to break their kiss. Ivy moaned in protest, but Kris didn't grant his lover the chance to vocalize that complaint any further. Once again, he took Ivy's nipple in his mouth while he slid his hand between their bodies to grip Ivy's shaft. As he did so, he tamed the natural magic inside him and sent a shock of electricity through Ivy through the two direct points where he was touching the Andari.

This time, Ivy didn't even scream. The sound that escaped his lips was more like a choked incoherent plea than anything else. Encouraged, Kris continued to flood Ivy with energy, always keeping a tight rein on the magic so as not to hurt him.

He needn't have worried about that, because judging by the throb of Ivy's dick, the young Andari was more than enjoying Kris's ministrations. And Kris would have liked to watch him writhe and hear him whimper for hours on end, to make Ivy come just like this, through his powers. There were a million other things they could do, a million sensations Kris could summon in Ivy's body. But alas, Kris's use of his magic in their sex play had the added effect that Ivy's arousal echoed into him in a deeper way, rocking him to the very core. His own cock demanded to join in on the fun. Releasing his tormenting hold on Ivy, he flipped the young Andari on all fours. Ivy yelped, having obviously not expected the change in positions. Kris wrapped his arm around Ivy's waist, keeping him from falling face first on the bed.

"I'm sorry," he whispered in Ivy's ear. "I wanted to take my time with you, but I can't wait anymore."

In response, Ivy pushed his ass out, wiggling it invitingly. Through his advanced senses, Kris could hear the pounding of Ivy's heart, scent the aroma of his surrender. There was no fear, no doubt, only heat, only need—a need they both shared.

Kris reached for the nightstand, where a vial of translucent oil discreetly waited. He uncapped the lid and poured a generous amount in his palm. After spreading the twin globes of Ivy's ass, he rubbed the liquid over Ivy's pink, clenching opening.

He expected Ivy to tense, but instead, Ivy threw his head back, abandoning himself to Kris's touch. Kris didn't know what was more intoxicating, Ivy's beauty, his trust, or his innocent passion.

In the end, he didn't choose, because he could have it all. As he slid one finger into Ivy's body, he buried his nose in Ivy's hair, inhaling deeply. Ivy's sweet perfume combined with the scent of sweat, lust, man, and a hefty dose of magic. Struck by the realization that Ivy's powers responded to his, maddened by the tight feel of Ivy's muscles squeezing his fingers, Kris groaned. Right then and there, he would have given up his crown just so he could bury his dick in Ivy's body and claim him as his own.

By some miracle, he held back and added another finger to Ivy's channel. Scissoring his digits, he stretched his lover, preparing him for penetration. As Ivy's flesh accommodated him, Kris crooked his fingers inside him and found Ivy's special spot. With a gasp, Ivy pushed back, demanding more.

Kris couldn't have denied Ivy if he wanted to. At last, he deemed Ivy as ready as he was going to get. He pulled his fingers out of Ivy and slicked his dick with the oil, hissing as the touch of his own hand nearly made him come before he could take Ivy. Only his burning need for Ivy kept the nearly unavoidable from happening.

Kris added more oil to Ivy's hole in the hope of minimizing Ivy's discomfort. Finally, he positioned his cock at Ivy's opening and slowly, ever so slowly, pushed inside.

ALL OF his life Ivy had been told that for any respectable Andari, intercourse could only happen after a bonding ceremony—with the odale guilds being the exception that confirmed the rule. He'd taken it to heart and accepted it as true, until the moment he'd met Kris.

Against all odds, Kris had made Ivy go into heat. Ivy had realized it long ago, but he'd been too afraid to accept it. He was no longer afraid. In fact, the rapture he experienced at Kris's hands had banished all of his fears and doubts.

Kris entered him, the Nikari's dick popping past the ring of guardian muscle and taking Ivy's virginity. Even if Kris didn't rush, it hurt. Ivy couldn't deny that. Yes, Kris had prepared him, but the Nikari's cock was probably far more generous in girth than three fingers.

It should have frightened Ivy, but instead, the burn cleared his mind of the haze of his heat. In that moment, just like when he'd loosened his hair, he felt the rightness of this union, and he knew that nothing, not societal mores nor politics or racial prejudice, could change that.

Kris continued to feed his dick into Ivy's ass, inch by excruciating inch. It seemed like too much, far too much. Just when Ivy thought his body couldn't take any more of the relentless pressure, Kris proved him wrong. He felt so full, full of Kris in every possible way, and still Kris kept going. Ivy clenched his fists into the sheets, struggling to breathe, to make sense of feelings too intense for one man to process.

At last, after what seemed like forever, Kris's prick fully impaled Ivy, his balls flush against Ivy's asscheeks. For a few seconds, Kris stilled inside him. He pressed a kiss to Ivy's naked shoulder, and the gentleness of the gesture transformed the passion between them into so much more. But then Ivy had already known that what united them was more than simple lust, and he could easily tell Kris realized that too.

"All right?" he asked quietly.

Ivy nodded. He wished he could have told Kris he was more than all right, that he felt happier than ever before. Since he couldn't make his vocal cords work, he let his body speak for him.

Supporting himself on all fours as well as he could, he clenched his ass muscles around Kris in a wordless plea for more. Fortunately, Kris understood, and judging by the growl he responded with, he had every plan to pay Ivy back for what he might have seen as teasing. Ivy held his breath, anticipating a hard round of fucking. To his surprise, it didn't happen. Kris pulled out of Ivy, then pushed back inside, just as smoothly and gently as before. The spongy head of his shaft nudged Ivy's special spot, and he whimpered as renewed ecstasy exploded over him.

Kris rocked in and out of him, maintaining a relentlessly steady pace that felt far too pleasurable to deny but didn't satisfy the burning ache in Ivy's gut. Kris was holding back, Ivy realized, and he didn't want that. He wanted to belong to Kris, to be Kris's haven in a world in which, for everyone else, his affection was a burden.

Perhaps it was the memory of the A'Mora's words that gave him enough strength to say, "Kris.... Please...."

He had no idea how to express all the thoughts and emotions gripping him, but he didn't get the chance to try. A dry chuckle escaped Kris. "It seems that I'm displeasing you."

The next thing Ivy knew, Kris slid out of him altogether. The feeling of emptiness left Ivy bereft and confused, but also more at Kris's mercy than ever. Kris rolled Ivy on his back, and Ivy blinked, trying to figure out what his lover had in mind.

Kris brushed a lock of hair out of his face and smirked. "I want to see your eyes when I make you truly mine."

Just like that, Kris lifted Ivy's legs, practically bending him in half. In one single thrust, he buried his erect dick inside Ivy so hard his teeth rattled. Ivy almost came right then and there as Kris unerringly struck his special spot. If he didn't, it must have been because of the look in Kris's eyes.

The gold around Kris's pupils began to glow, and Ivy couldn't have looked away if he wanted to. In a fascinating twist, the gold began to consume the black of Kris's eyes, until the darkness disappeared altogether in a deceptively dazzling and hypnotizing array of light and color.

Somewhere at the back of his mind, Ivy remembered Nikari were at their most dangerous when their eyes were glowing. He didn't care. In fact, he was elated because he could feel it now, the truth hiding behind the carefully constructed façade of the Morai, the reality only he could see. His Kris: the man who was so much more than the ruthless emperor of a nation of deadly warrior mages, the man who'd awakened Ivy's heart and body, but also his trust and loyalty.

And so, Ivy met Kris's gaze without fear and opened his heart to Kris. He felt the moment Kris slid into his mind. *That's it, Ivy. Let me in.*

Ivy couldn't have said if Kris spoke out loud or through his apparently considerable mental powers. The latter was probably the case, because he hadn't seen Kris's lips move. The intrusion in his mind should have shocked him, but the touch was nothing like what Ivy had experienced throughout his lessons into the mind arts. It felt like the brush of a butterfly's wings, so soft, barely there.

Then again, how could Ivy focus on even analyzing Kris's mental powers when he finally had what he wanted, the full unrestrained passion of his lover? That first thrust was only a sample of what Kris planned, because he set a punishing pace, impaling Ivy over and over with his erect prick. With every second that passed, he moved faster, his thrusts harder and harder, until they grew almost violent, just on the right side of pain.

Ivy could do nothing but surrender to it. Trapped in Kris's passion, enthralled by Kris's gaze, he became a willing slave of the Morai. He was aware of the butterfly wings crystallizing into gentle fingers that began to peel away Ivy's mental shields. Ivy hadn't known his agreement to come to Kris's bed might entail that, and he hadn't been ready for it, not really. He trembled, the unfamiliarity of the sensation startling him.

Kris must have realized that, because his mental voice drifted into Ivy's mind. *Shh.... Don't be afraid,* sharani. *I won't ever hurt you.*

Ivy believed Kris, but it was the endearment that gave him pause. *Sharani.* The Nikari word for "my beautiful one." Hearing it, knowing what it meant distracted him so much that he almost missed the moment Kris retreated from his mind.

The change shocked Ivy, and he instinctively reached out, trying to keep Kris from pulling away. Pure magic burst from him, melting into a call toward Kris, a voiceless cry of need and desire. Kris's mental touch returned, but so did the electric power that the Nikari had displayed earlier.

Kris didn't try to remove Ivy's shields again. Instead, they fell together into a dance as old as time, with Kris continuing to ravage Ivy's body. He steadied Ivy's legs on his shoulders, his lips twisting into a near snarl, his motions becoming wild, almost savage.

It was hot, rough, and perfect, a dream, an electric storm and a whirlpool of carnality which threatened to sweep Ivy's sanity away. And all throughout it, Kris's gaze stuck to his face, never faltering, a golden sea in which Ivy could easily drown.

When Ivy's orgasm came, it exploded through him like the death of a star, his magic entwined with Kris's as deeply and intimately as their bodies. Every inch of Ivy flared to bright, brilliant life, and he clung to Kris as he fell over the edge, spurting hot cream that painted his chest and Kris's blush pink. Kris thrust inside him one more time, and then wet heat filled Ivy, signaling the other man's climax.

As both of them shuddered through the waves of their orgasms, they held onto each other, their united forms the only thing keeping reality from shattering. And even as the pleasure started to settle and the magic swirled back in its place, that profound feeling of togetherness didn't fade.

At last, Kris slid out of Ivy's channel, and they collapsed together on the bed. For a few moments, neither of them spoke. Ivy was still reeling from the incredible pleasure he'd experienced at Kris's touch, in awe of the perfect way they'd come together.

When he could think, however, he remembered the way Kris had tested his shields. "About earlier," he whispered. "You didn't go through with removing my shields."

He really wanted to ask why Kris hadn't done so, why he hadn't claimed Ivy in the way of the Nikari. True, what Ivy knew of it, he'd learned from his sire, and Rasami's descriptions hadn't been very flattering. Had his reluctance offended Kris?

Obviously guessing his thoughts, Kris smiled at him and brushed a kiss over Ivy's temple. "It's too soon," he replied. "Be patient, *sharani*. Everything will come in time."

The affection in Kris's voice settled most of the niggling uncertainty in Ivy's heart, and the rest was swept away by fatigue. Distantly, he remembered they should be returning to the party, but he couldn't muster enough energy for socialization. When Kris pulled him close, Ivy curled against his lover's chest. Kris buried his fingers in his now-loose hair and whispered, "Sleep, *sharani*. I'll take care of everything. I promise."

Safe in Kris's hold, Ivy complied. He closed his eyes and surrendered to slumber, and when he drifted into the embrace of oblivion, he did so with a contented smile and a peaceful heart.

WHEN IVY fell asleep, Kris didn't immediately pull away. He allowed himself the privilege to cling to Ivy for a while longer, reveling in Ivy's scent, his warmth, and the softness of his hair.

Finally, though, Kris surrendered to the inevitable. As stealthily as possible, he extracted himself from Ivy's embrace. Ivy mumbled his name in his sleep but didn't wake. Their intercourse and the aftermath of his heat would probably keep him in deep slumber all night.

Kris made a brief trip to the bathing chamber and washed up, eliminating the traces of their spent passion. He returned to his bedroom with a wet, warm washcloth and gently cleaned Ivy, making sure he wouldn't wake his lover in the process. Once he was done, he tucked Ivy in under a thick quilt.

He hated leaving Ivy alone after what they'd shared, but the Morai still had duties to attend. He'd already been gone too long, and since Ivy had disappeared about the same time he had, there would already be whispers of the reasons behind it.

Of course, what had happened between him and Ivy would become obvious in the morning, but Kris preferred the revelation to come on his own terms. Besides, his private life aside, it always paid to keep an eye on certain nobles and diplomats.

He dressed quickly, finding an outfit identical to the one he'd destroyed. Once he finished his preparations, he left his bedchamber and headed back to the living room. He wrapped the cloak of nightwolf fur around his shoulders, all the while staring at his bedroom door.

Intellectually, he knew Ivy was safe here—safer than anywhere else in the city, in fact. His quarters were warded against rifts created by anyone except him, and there were guards posted outside. Nevertheless, some additional protection wouldn't hurt.

With a motion of his hand, Kris opened a rift, mentally summoning his nightwolf. Attcha promptly leaped out of the portal and sniffed him with interest. He tilted his head and eyed him with obvious disapproval. *No claim. Why? Claim soft one.*

Kris wondered what Ivy would think if he knew Attcha identified him as the "soft one." Then again, he couldn't exactly argue with Attcha's point, since minutes ago, he'd been busy exploring Ivy's soft, silken skin. He did, however, need to explain the situation to his nightwolf.

I can't. He needs to get used to me first, to understand life here.

When he'd touched Ivy's mind, Kris had realized that, in spite of Ivy's natural openness toward him, Ivy shied away from that kind of intimacy. It wasn't a bad thing. In fact, Kris counted himself lucky for it, because he shouldn't have rushed into it to begin with. A claiming by Nikari standards would involve the claimed person having all of their mental shields removed. That could be very frightening and even traumatic if both people weren't perfectly certain of what they were doing.

At some level, Attcha seemed to understand this. He rumbled, the sound one of approval. *Tame.*

It wasn't exactly taming, but Kris couldn't be uncomfortable with the term. He'd spent the better part of his life at Attcha's side, and he knew nightwolves didn't think like people did. Likely, Attcha's idea had been different from the way Kris had understood it. Attcha's thoughts didn't always translate with complete exactitude into Kris's consciousness.

In any case, the nightwolf was here now, and Kris couldn't linger any longer. *I need you to watch over him in my stead for a while. I have to return to the celebration.*

In response, Attcha nudged him with his big muzzle. *Protect soft one. Yes.*

Kris guided Attcha to his bedchamber, although he didn't actually have to. The big nightwolf settled down at the foot of the bed and Kris knew that anyone who tried anything against Ivy would find themselves facing a very nasty surprise.

Since he was here, Kris couldn't resist the temptation of kissing Ivy one last time. His lover's lips were as soft as usual but this time unresponsive. Reining in the instincts that still told him to claim Ivy, Kris turned on his heel and left the room.

He didn't bother using another rift. Instead, he exited through the door. The guards outside didn't seem surprised at his appearance— undoubtedly, they'd heard him and Ivy.

"Make sure Lord Erethe isn't disturbed," he ordered. "Oh, and my nightwolf is inside, so don't step in his territory."

The guards saluted. "Yes, Your Imperial Majesty."

Satisfied Ivy would be safe, Kris headed back toward the ballroom. By now, his mother had returned as well and was deep in conversation with Ivy's parents.

Yet another problem that needed to be dealt with as soon as possible. The Andari couple probably didn't realize how close they'd come to being arrested. Most of the Full Bloods took their privileges for granted, and while Kris had no intention of depriving anyone of that, he hated it when these people made him look like a despot.

The crowd parted for him as he made his way to the small group. He kissed his mother's hand and nodded in greeting at the two Andari nobles. "Lord Titexe, Lord Rasami. I trust you're having a pleasant evening."

"Your hospitality is, as always, of prodigious quality," Rasami replied. "However, we are concerned. It seems our son is missing."

His mother discreetly took her leave and focused on distracting the people around them. Kris pulled the two men aside from the main party, making sure they wouldn't be overheard. "I assure you your son is quite safe," he finally replied, not bothering to suppress his smirk. Leaning in closer to the two Andari lords, he whispered, "In my bed."

Rasami's eyes widened, and Titexe released an outraged gasp. "You can't…. You can't do this."

"Can't I?" Kris asked. "You'd best remember who you're talking to, My Lord. You seem to have forgotten, and there's a price to be paid for poor memory."

Titexe's jaw clenched, and he might have done something stupid had his mate not grabbed his arm, holding him back. "Your Majesty," Rasami said, "you must understand. Our culture is very specific with regard to such matters. And Behnivyr is already set to bond to someone else."

"Lord Rasami, nothing moves in this empire if I don't will it. Do you truly think your marquis will ever be able to touch Ivy?"

Had they realized that Ivy's betrothed had oh-so-conveniently skipped attending the first night of the ball? If they hadn't, they would eventually. Rasami Erethe was very intelligent, and he'd figure out that Kris wouldn't have zeroed in on Ivy without knowing him beforehand.

However, they didn't know what Kris felt for Ivy, and Kris didn't intend to enlighten them. "Your son is my *moraistele* now," he said. "He belongs to me. I realize you had entirely different plans for him and his very strong magic, but it's a moot point."

Rasami took a deep breath, obviously realizing there was nothing he could do about the situation. "Your Majesty, if you'd excuse us," he said at last, "I do believe my bond mate and I are indisposed."

"Of course," Kris replied. "I hope you'll feel better in the morning. I look forward to seeing you at breakfast. You'll be able to speak to your son then."

Titexe twitched satisfyingly at the image Kris conjured with his words. Still, he said nothing more. Rasami muttered a curt good night, and together, the two Andari departed, leaving the ballroom.

Kris watched them go for a few moments, then turned toward the figure leaning against a nearby column. "You like eavesdropping too much, Shuri."

"And you like making enemies, Your Majesty," his brother replied.

Kris snorted. "I made enemies of three quarters of the people in the empire when I took the crown." And that included Shuri and their uncle, for that matter.

"Nevertheless, is it really safe to take an Andari Full Blood for a moraistele?"

Kris laughed. "Oh, my dear brother. You shouldn't believe everything you hear. Why would I want to do that?"

He left a glowering Shuri in the shadow of the column and went to invite his mother to dance. *It's starting already,* she whispered in his mind.

Yes, Kris said. *But good things are worth taking a chance on.*

His mother smiled at him, and Kris knew she agreed. How could she not? Because in all this confusing, complicated situation, one thing remained crystal clear and certain. Ivy was definitely worth it.

Chapter Five
Concubine

WHEN IVY stirred into wakefulness, he didn't immediately know where he was. He blinked, trying to identify the peculiar furniture and the far too vast doorway. He didn't really have any success with it, at least not until he realized his body ached in unfamiliar places. Ivy's face flamed. The twinges were more than enough to remind him what had happened last night. He'd given his innocence to Kris.

In truth, he should have expected this would happen. He should have been ready for it from the moment he'd realized he was in heat. But the Andari heat was treated like something shameful, since Ivy's people considered it disgraceful to allow one's lusts to get the better of him. His father used to say that if he did go into heat, it should only be over his intended—and even then he shouldn't reveal its existence, lest his bond mate think ill of him.

Well, things definitely hadn't happened the way Ivy's parents had expected. The heat had faded now that Ivy's immediate need had been sated, but he found he didn't regret pursuing the impulse at all. Kris was the only man whom he could have willingly given his virginity to.

The Morai must have left sometime during the night because there was no sign of him now. When Ivy swept his hand over the sheets, he found them cold. Of course, in the process, he did note that the material bore the traces of spent passion. If he'd had any doubt about what he and Kris had shared, that would have clearly settled it.

The memories stirred renewed heat inside him, and he might have gotten himself worked up had a low growl not sounded somewhere in front of him. The big head of a familiar nightwolf appeared from beyond the foot of the bed. Ivy blinked in surprise. "Attcha? What are you doing here?"

The nightwolf couldn't answer through words, but he did get up and make his way to Ivy's side. Since Ivy still lay in bed, the looming form of the beast seemed quite threatening, but Attcha fixed that by dropping back down onto the floor and placing his head on the mattress next to Ivy. He flicked his ear and eyed Ivy with interest.

Chuckling, Ivy scratched the nightwolf's ear. "Did Kris leave you here to watch over me?" Attcha released a low rumble, which could have been an affirmative response or a reaction of pleasure at Ivy's touch. Just the same, Ivy was fairly certain he must have guessed right. It was nice to know Kris hadn't left him alone even when duty had forced them apart, and he realized Kris couldn't have abandoned the ball altogether just so Ivy could sleep in his arms. Still, the entire thing made him wonder about his situation.

Kris's absence might be frustrating, but it also allowed him to think. He slid out of the bed—causing a grumble of protest from Attcha—and plopped down on the chair in front of the mirror.

He stared at his reflection and at the loose hair he could no longer bind. The tiny gems his sire had so painstakingly pinned to his braid were gone, lost among the sheets. Symbolic, perhaps. His old life might be over, but it hadn't been one he'd wanted to begin with. After this, his parents would no longer be able to trap him in a gilded cage. The betrothal with Torildy would undoubtedly be canceled.

It occurred to him that he hadn't seen the marquis at all last night, but that didn't mean anything. Besides, he had more pressing concerns, such as what position he'd occupy in Kris's life.

He didn't dawdle too long on these questions, because the sound of the opening door startled him from his musings. Mindful of his nudity, Ivy slid back into the bed and covered himself with the blankets.

He should have known better than to worry, since Kris was the one who entered the bedroom, looking as handsome and unruffled as the day before at the ball. "Good morning," he said, smiling at Ivy. "I'm sorry I couldn't be here when you woke up. It seems that three-quarters of the empire required my attention last night, and the remainder of them decided to approach me this morning."

As he spoke, Kris sat down on the edge of the bed, sending his nightwolf away. Ivy berated himself for focusing on his own fears, when it was so obvious Kris had to carry a far heavier burden. "You must be exhausted," he said. "Come to bed."

Kris's gold-rimmed eyes began to gain that lustful look as he scanned Ivy from head to toe. However, he shook his head. "As tempted as I am, you need to recover your strength. Besides, we're going to have to make an appearance at breakfast. I already told your parents we would meet them there."

Ivy grimaced, not really eager for that meeting. But he couldn't hide under the bed, and he had to face the consequences of his actions. He wasn't ashamed of giving his virginity to Kris. If his parents, or anyone else, deemed him dishonorable for going against Andari customs, Ivy would face them without fear. "I suppose you're right, although I must admit I'd rather spend the morning with you."

"Me too," Kris replied, "and we will. Soon. In the meantime, I have a gift for you."

"A gift?" Ivy repeated in surprise.

Kris's expression sobered. "You probably realize that your departure from the ball had tongues wagging. I admit it was partially my own mistake for showing such interest in you when I first greeted you. In any case, there are certain parties that have already caught wind of it, and it would be best to make your position at my side clear."

Kris reached into his pocket and retrieved a small object. It was a gemmed hairpin, very similar in style to what Ivy regularly used. This one bore the marking of the nightwolf, just like Kris's cloak, and was crafted out of the same nektra crystal that had adorned the ballroom.

Ivy gasped as he took in the sight of the present. "Why are you giving me this?" he asked, as if it wasn't obvious.

"I want you to be my moraistele, Ivy. I know it's not an ideal position for an Andari, but—"

Ivy cut him off with an impulsive kiss. As he brushed his mouth against that of his lover, he hugged the Nikari tightly, his heart pounding with excitement.

"I don't care about what other people think or say," he whispered against Kris's lips. "All I want is to be by your side."

Even as he said the words, he realized they were true. He might have come to Kris's bed following a lustful instinct he'd been unable to resist, but this thing between them seemed far stronger than one night of spent passion. In his heart, Ivy had feared Kris would discard him, that he would lose interest now that Ivy had surrendered to him. If Kris made him his official concubine, he didn't have to worry about that.

"That's where you belong," Kris told him, burying his fingers into Ivy's hair as if hypnotized by the white-gold mass. "With me."

Ivy broke their embrace and turned around, giving Kris access to his hair. "Put it on."

He experienced a moment of doubt in which he wondered if Kris would even know how to do it, but his concerns turned out to be unjustified. Kris's strikingly nimble fingers combed through his hair, freeing it from potential tangles and expertly arranging it in a traditional Andari fashion.

Unlike the pleated style that had marked him as a virgin, this particular braid was looser. Two small but elaborate pleats framed the rest of his locks, and the pin completed the picture, all the way down, at the bottom of his hair. Had Ivy been unattached but sexually available, he would have had to leave his hair loose, but this hairstyle suggested he was in a sexual, committed relationship. In this case, the crystal nightwolf of the hair adornment would clearly illustrate whom he belonged to.

A mate bond would add an additional binding at his nape, but Ivy wouldn't think about that. He and Kris had already leapt into intercourse without knowing each other all that well, and while Ivy didn't regret giving his virginity to the other man, he wanted to take his time and understand everything about Kris, to learn what he liked and what he hated, to figure out their similarities and differences.

It did occur to Ivy that Kris was oddly adept at binding hair. When he turned toward Kris again, he arched a brow and said, "I didn't know you had such skills." In a way, it made sense due to Kris's Ndara ancestry, but it still surprised Ivy.

"When I was a child, Mother taught me how to tie braids," Kris said with a light chuckle. "I used to practice on her hair, and by the time I actually earned mine, I got very good at it. They might mean something different than yours, and the style we wear it in isn't the same either, but the actual technique is a lot alike."

The fondness in Kris's tone made Ivy's heart twist. "You're very close to your mother, aren't you?" he asked, unable to keep the yearning from his voice. He knew he shouldn't be jealous that Kris had a mother who loved him, and in a way, he wasn't. Even so, seeing such emotion in Kris just made his own desires sharper.

Kris nodded. "She's the only one other than you who's ever been fully comfortable with me. Well, and Attcha, but he's a nightwolf." He reached for Ivy's hand and squeezed it. "Your mother was an odale, right? I could find her for you, if you'd like."

For a few seconds, Ivy actually considered the offer. It surprised him so much that he couldn't help but imagine his reunion with his mother. It was tempting, and he knew Kris would go through with it if Ivy agreed. Even so, Ivy ended up shaking his head. "No. I haven't seen her since I was five. For all I know, she has many other children, and she won't want one of us to appear on her doorstep seeking familial affection. I don't think I'd be able to withstand that. At least this way, I have beautiful memories of her."

Kris pressed a soft, gentle kiss to his forehead. "The offer still stands if you change your mind. In the meantime, my mother would love to spend some time with you."

Ivy remembered his conversation with the A'Mora from the day before and didn't doubt Kris's mother would keep an eye on him. "She's very protective of you."

"So is Attcha, but you've already received his seal of approval."

Obviously taking heed of Kris's words, the nightwolf made his appearance once again, releasing a low growl. "And now, he's hungry," Kris said with a snicker, "and frustrated that I'm keeping you to myself. Come on. We should go to breakfast. That should put him in a better mood. He enjoys making people uncomfortable."

Pointing to the wardrobe, he said, "I took the liberty of providing you with some basic items of clothing. Go ahead and get dressed. I'll wait for you in the living room."

Judging by the hot look in Kris's eye, Ivy could easily guess why Kris decided to give him space for the preparations. In all likelihood, if

Kris stayed, they would miss not only breakfast, but also lunch. Ivy bit his lower lip, wanting nothing more than to reach out for Kris and touch him. But without the heat to nudge him past his natural shyness, he hesitated and lost his chance.

With one last smile, Kris left the bedchamber, and his nightwolf followed. Ivy pushed off the sheets and headed to the massive wardrobe Kris had indicated. He'd expected to see some of his own garments, perhaps taken from his bags. Instead, he found completely different outfits, some Andari in style, others with a distinctive Nikari feel.

Ivy simply didn't know what to pick. Anything he wore this morning would make a statement. Did he want to point out further that he was Kris's moraistele, or would it be better to illustrate that he'd maintain his own culture and individuality?

As he mused over this dilemma, he caught sight of a suit of elegant robes. Originally, the cut seemed Andari, flowing to the ground like all Andari formal wear. However, upon closer inspection, Ivy realized the seams were less ornate, and the robes themselves would be far tighter on him than anything he'd worn before, like Nikari clothing. Furthermore, the robes were studded with a myriad of blue crystals, just like the one in his hair.

Ivy fell in love with the clothes at once. Of course, he knew he couldn't wear it for breakfast, but it helped him choose a Nikari-style garment. He soon realized that every item in the wardrobe was designed to combine the various styles of fashion. Ivy wouldn't have normally worn breeches and a tunic at a formal function like breakfast with the imperial family, but the material they'd been crafted of provided it a quality Andari casual wear didn't have.

With that decision made, Ivy quickly got dressed, paying close attention not to mess up his hair. Once ready, he headed out of the bedroom and into the main living area. He found Kris sitting down on the couch, absently rubbing Attcha's big head.

When Ivy entered the room, Kris got up and unashamedly scanned him from head to toe. "You look breathtaking, *sharani*. I will be the envy of the entire empire."

Ivy blushed at the praise and at the realization that Kris had no intention of letting him go. All the facts pointed in that direction—the pin, the clothes, the attitude of the nightwolf and the A'Mora. Kris had obviously already decided to make Ivy his concubine even before last night. In the end, that had been the whole purpose of the ball. For him. For Ivy.

As the weight of that settled in, Ivy kissed his lover's cheek. "I don't know if that's true, but allow me to be satisfied with your words just the same."

Kris chuckled and wrapped his cloak around Ivy's shoulders. "All right. Now, we're ready."

Ivy hadn't gotten the chance to ask Kris about the garment the day before. At the ball, he'd deemed it purely ceremonial, but that didn't seem to be the case.

As if guessing his thoughts, Kris proceeded to explain, "This garb is made of nightwolf fur. It's an heirloom from the first Morai. Right now, the technique needed to craft it is no longer used, and it is, in fact, banned. There are only three cloaks like this in existence, mine, my mother's and, that of the Moris, currently in storage. For the moment, you'll wear mine. Since you'll be staying in Nikaret, you never know when a rift might be opened."

"But don't you need it?" Ivy asked, trying hard not to think about the Moris's cloak.

Kris shook his head. "At this point, I'm largely immune to dimensional rifts. I still feel some pain in long-distance portals, but it's not incapacitating or even too bothersome. On the other hand, the type of journey that I'd actually be affected by could send you into shock, even with me there, and at worst, kill you. It's very different from wave-wayfaring."

"I can see that," Ivy replied. "I'll keep the cloak close."

"Thank you." Kris's hand landed on his arm, and the Morai guided him to the door, the traditional way. Attcha followed them like a humongous guardian dog, and as the nightwolf stepped through the doorway, Ivy finally understood why everything was built big here. The Nikari needed things to be big so they could accommodate their interdimensional companions.

The guards outside Kris's door saluted him and greeted Ivy with just as much respect. They didn't even blink when they saw the pin in

Ivy's hair. Ivy guessed they must have been instructed beforehand about his future role in Kris's household. Ivy himself hadn't gotten too used to his new life, but thankfully, the idea of his impending betrothal had already accustomed him to his imminent departure from Seanda.

Kris's voice drifted into his mind, startling him from his thoughts. *You'll meet several people at breakfast,* he said. *You'll need to be wary of my uncle Phura. He's quite resentful of my family, especially of my father, and he'll be willing to do a great deal to upset me. There's also my half brother Shuri. Officially, he's my cousin and Phura's son, but he was actually born from my father's union with Phura's wife.*

Ivy winced. That sounded like a recipe for disaster if he'd ever heard one. He couldn't understand why the former Morai would have looked for coitus elsewhere when he'd had the lovely Katara in his bed, but that was beside the point.

He also made a mental note to ask Kris how he'd learned telepathic communication. That sort of thing could come in handy in a palace where one needed to watch his every word. For the moment, he contented himself with providing a neutral reply. "I understand. Thank you."

As Kris's mental touch retreated from his mind, he and Ivy left the imperial wing and entered a public area of the palace. Instantly, Ivy felt the change in atmosphere. The guards were as respectful and disciplined as before, but the reactions of the guests didn't match those of the Nikari soldiers.

Even as the representatives of the various provinces bowed in front of Kris, Ivy felt disapproving stares aimed at his back. No one dared to say anything, lest they risk insulting Kris, but Ivy had no doubt that once they were gone, the name-calling would begin. Ivy smothered the part of him that would have liked their approval. He stared forward, acknowledging the guests with nods and smiles but otherwise not reacting to their proximity. The solidity of Kris's arm and his familiar warmth told him he'd made the right choice.

Kris led him to a huge dining room that adjoined yesterday's ballroom. What seemed like hundreds of tables had been arranged around the area, presumably waiting for the guests. Kris didn't occupy any of them and instead went outside, into the gardens, where an ornate table already waited for them.

Kris and Ivy were the last to arrive, their seats the only ones free. Other than the two of them, Ivy's parents were present, as well as Kris's mother and two men Ivy didn't immediately recognize. Ivy identified one of them as the man whom he'd yesterday mistaken as Kris. That was probably Kris's half brother. By power of elimination, Ivy decided the last Nikari, an older, bulkier male, had to be Kris's uncle.

"Good morning," Kris said.

When no one said anything, Ivy echoed Kris's greeting, hoping he wasn't committing a breach of protocol. In official situations, the people with highest ranks started the conversation, and Ivy hardly thought he ranked above the A'Mora or the Morai's half brother. But if the Nikari were insulted, they didn't show it.

In fact, the A'Mora got up and greeted them with enthusiasm. "Greetings," she said. "I'm so glad you could join us at breakfast."

Ivy realized the rest of the people at the table had been taking their cues from her, because Kris's uncle uttered a tight "good morning" too. Meanwhile, Kris's half brother said, "I see you have a surprise for us, cousin."

"Not exactly a surprise given the presence of Their Lordships," Kris replied, acknowledging Ivy's parents.

"You honor us through your invitation," Ivy's father replied calmly.

His gaze went to Ivy's hair, and his hold on his glass tightened. Nevertheless, he made no note of it. Likely, he'd already been prepared for it.

Kris and Ivy sat down at the front of the table. Ivy ended up facing Kris's mother but next to his sire. It wasn't an ideal situation, since he could practically feel the tension emanating off the other Andari. Still, it was something he had to accept and would continue to be confronted with even after today, sometimes without the buffer of Kris or Katara's presence.

Meanwhile, Attcha settled down behind Kris's seat, although he seemed to be eyeing Kris's uncle with alarming interest. The Nikari must have been aware of it, because he fidgeted, apparently ill at ease with Attcha's scrutiny. So this was what Kris had meant when he'd said Attcha enjoyed making people uncomfortable.

If Attcha's presence startled Phura into silence, Kris's half brother didn't have the same problem. "You look different this morning, Lord Behnivyr," he said as the servants began to bring in dishes laden with food.

Ivy had expected the blow, and he wasn't surprised it had come from Shuri. One look at Shuri told him Kris's half brother probably despised Kris as much as his uncle did. He would see Ivy's innocence and the Andari mores as a vulnerable point on Kris's side, one he wouldn't delay in exploiting.

Well, Ivy had no intention of being an easy target. He faced Shuri without flinching and flipped his braid over his shoulder, carelessly displaying it. "I'm flattered that you've noticed, Your Highness," he said. "I did indeed decide to comb my hair differently."

Ivy's father choked on his drink, but Ivy's sire seemed unaffected. "It looks good on you, son," he said, his voice level. "I'm quite partial to the hairpin."

"Beautiful, isn't it?" Ivy asked. He hadn't expected the opening to come from his sire, and while he couldn't believe the other Andari had accepted the situation so easily, he appreciated it. "It was a gift from His Majesty," he added with a smile.

"The crystal flatters your coloring," Katara remarked. "Kris, you simply have to get him a necklace to match."

Kris chuckled. "There's plenty of time, Mother." He turned toward Ivy and explained, "My mother has always been displeased with my more traditional Nikari tastes. Expect to be lavished with half the jewelry in the royal treasury."

"Now you're teasing me," Katara commented. "You know I believe that Nikari fashion doesn't have to remain minimalistic, at least not outside combat. We're a prosperous, powerful people, and you practically control the entire continent. We need to display it. And since you're too stubborn for it, I'm sure Ivy will indulge me."

It would have sounded like a familiar, casual debate, except Ivy suspected it wasn't casual in the slightest. Katara had chosen to point out

Kris's power, but she'd also used the short form of Ivy's name. "I'm more than flattered to be included, Your Majesty," he replied. On instinct, he added, "I have to say your taste is impeccable, and you are very talented. I saw some of your work earlier, and I fell in love with it."

Katara blinked in surprise. "Kris told you," she said accusingly. "I wanted it to be a surprise."

"I didn't tell him," Kris argued, his lips twisting into a satisfied and proud smile. "He simply guessed."

Truth be told, Ivy didn't know at which point he'd realized that the clothing he wore had been designed by the A'Mora, but Katara seemed pleased that he had noticed. "It is so rare for me to actually indulge, since Kris only uses such garments in official meetings. I enjoyed the challenge of designing something you would deem suitable."

"Suitable is too small a word," Ivy said. "I only hope I'll do them justice."

"Oh, you already are," Katara replied.

The conversation appeared to irritate Phura, who opened his mouth, as if intending to say something. Before he could do so, Attcha growled from his place behind Kris's seat. In turn, Kris arched a brow at his uncle. Phura remained silent, although Ivy did wonder what the older Nikari had intended to say.

As it turned out, Attcha's intervention changed the course of the discussion. "Your nightwolf is quite remarkable," Ivy's sire observed. "I've never seen one up close before, but I believe him to be an extraordinary specimen."

Ivy suppressed a wince, since he suspected Attcha wouldn't like being called a specimen. Indeed, Attcha turned his fierce gold eyes—so much like Kris's—toward Ivy's sire. Ivy hastened to defuse the situation. "I've found that nightwolves are quite fascinating and far more intelligent than I'd have even dared to dream."

"So you're not afraid of Attcha?" Shuri inquired, his slight sneer clearly illustrating his disbelief.

Ivy shrugged. "I have no reason to be. He's been more than nice to me."

On cue, Attcha got up and padded to Ivy's side. Once there, he dropped down, giving Ivy access to his large head. Like in the bedroom, the nightwolf flicked his ear, and Ivy couldn't help a small fond smile. He buried his hand in Attcha's luxurious, black fur, petting the beautiful creature.

"He seems to have welcomed you in his pack," Katara commented, her gold-rimmed eyes glittering with satisfaction.

"Pack?" Ivy repeated. He'd never heard the term in connection to nightwolves.

"Nightwolves are very protective of their Nikari charge," Kris explained. "They allow close family to come into contact with the Nikari and can even become fond of an outsider, if that person is very close to the nightwolf's Nikari. Such is the case of my mother, for example. But they do have something that is called a pack, which as a rule is reserved for the Nikari's spouse and children."

Ivy froze. He had suspected the extent of Attcha's protectiveness of him must be unusual, but it hadn't occurred to him to make the connection with the Moris. The new information shocked him into silence, but it also caused Phura to finally explode. "With all due respect, Your Majesty, I deem it unwise to compare your moraistele with your future lawful spouse."

"And you know I always take your opinion into account, Lord Phura," Kris replied, "but I was merely explaining Attcha's train of thought. As for the rest, I am perfectly capable of making decisions with regard to my own personal life."

"I never thought you weren't, Your Majesty," Phura said with tight smile.

Shuri cleared his throat, drawing the attention away from his uncle. "Well, in any case, Lord Behnivyr, even if Attcha seems fond of you, don't go thinking you can run around with nightwolves. Not all of them will appreciate it."

Ivy could hear a challenge in Shuri's voice, and he decided to make things clear once for all. "I think nightwolves are like the Nikari," he said. "They are dangerous, yes, but that doesn't mean they can't form bonds of love and fellowship outside their own spheres."

He rubbed the nightwolf crest on his cloak and smiled. "I have no doubt that not every nightwolf will like me, but that's all right. I only need one to be happy. And while I'll respect the space and opinion of the others, I won't let anger or disapproval change that."

Silence fell over the breakfast table. Everyone must have guessed that by the end of his little speech, he'd stopped talking about Attcha and other nightwolves. After all, the most dangerous beasts were sitting with him at this table, pleasantly sharing a meal.

"Fair enough," Shuri said with a smile. He looked like he wanted to add something more, but he changed his mind at the last moment, likely because of Kris's presence. Or maybe it was the way Attcha growled, insisting for Ivy to continue with his caresses. The end result remained the same, and they all succumbed to silence.

It was Kris who restarted the conversation, this time addressing Ivy's father. "Your Lordship, I want to assure you that Ivy will have everything he needs here. I realize that there are certain technicalities that must be dealt with due to the specifics of Ivy's previous situation, but you mustn't worry about that."

"Indeed, the betrothal agreement with Marquis Torildy was on my mind," Ivy's father admitted.

"Again, I assure you there will be no repercussions for you breaking the agreement," Kris said. "After all, who could have denied the Morai?"

"Who, indeed," Phura whispered at the other side of the table.

The fading tension returned with a vengeance, but Kris didn't let his uncle's words deter him. "As I understand it," he said, "His Lordship was delayed by an accident with his carriage. But I will speak to him tonight at the ball. I do hope you'll attend and you'll be able to stay longer this time."

"Of course, Your Majesty," Ivy's sire replied.

After that, the conversation turned to more sedate topics, and Ivy did his best to focus on his more-than-delicious meal. He ended up passing half of it to Attcha and watching the nightwolf chomp with obvious enjoyment. He thought about what Kris had said about a nightwolf's pack and wondered what his life would be like from now on.

THAT EVENING, Kris sat on the throne and struggled not to sulk like a child. He was moderately successful, as everyone seemed to deem his attitude as the normal brooding of the mirthless Morai. However, his mother knew better.

Stop worrying, she said in his mind. *He'll be fine.*

Kris knew that, but it didn't mean he couldn't be impatient. *This is an important evening. I should be with him.*

I understand you're protective of him, but some things he'll have to handle on his own, his mother said. *If you baby him, he'll find it harder to acclimate to Nikaret. Come now. Stop being so glum. He's very intelligent and braver than I expected. He faced Shuri at breakfast. Learn to have faith in him.*

It wasn't that Kris didn't have faith in Ivy. On the contrary, he intellectually knew that, in spite of his delicate exterior, Ivy was far stronger than anyone gave him credit for. It wasn't solely Ivy's conversation with Shuri but the fact that Ivy had been willing to risk his parents' displeasure to find out for himself the truth about Nikari. Ivy's openness, the respect he showed toward Attcha, his interest in the Nikari culture, and most of all, the fact that he'd flaunted convention to be with Kris—those were the most remarkable things about him. Still, Ivy remained so very young, and Kris's instincts didn't care that Ivy could protect himself.

This is his night, he told his mother. *He shouldn't have to begin it alone.*

The argument didn't help him with anything because they both knew he couldn't have accompanied Ivy here. *Sai is with him,* his mother soothed him. *They'll be here any moment now.*

As if on cue, the sound of the gong echoed through the ballroom. "His Lordship, Behnivyr Erethe," the liveried Nikari guard announced.

The main ballroom doors opened, and Ivy stepped into the room. Kris's breath caught. Ivy had been beautiful the previous evening, but tonight he was, plainly put, a vision. The garment created by Kris's mother fit him like a second skin, emphasizing every line of his slender, beautiful body. The light from the torches hit the small crystals on his robes, making him shine like a star. Unavoidably, everyone stared at him, but Ivy fixed his gaze on Kris, his back completely straight, his gait steady and elegant as he walked into the room. The crowd parted for him, like it usually did for Kris and his mother.

Kris's cock went rock hard, and he was thankful for having the foresight of wearing a tunic with a longer cut. He wanted nothing more than to meet Ivy halfway, but respecting the regular protocol would smooth Ivy's entrance into court, and Kris wouldn't do anything to jeopardize that.

Of course, when Ivy knelt in front of him, Kris found the position summoned entirely inappropriate—for this company—images in his mind. He could far too easily see Ivy's lips wrapping around his cock, sucking lightly, then taking him deeper still. Ivy's mouth would be hot and wet but willing, just like his ass had been the night before. He would moan eagerly, begging for Kris to fuck his mouth.

Kris shook his head, trying to dispel the effect of his far-too-vivid imagination. "Rise and approach," he told his lover.

Ivy complied, lifting his beautiful green-eyed gaze to Kris's face. This time, Kris dropped all pretense of formality and added, "You take my breath away, *sharani*."

Ivy blushed and smiled, a hint of charming shyness making its appearance. "You should praise Her Majesty. The merits are hers."

"A garment is only as beautiful as the one who wears it," Kris's mother told him. "I'm glad to see you here, Ivy. I trust you will enjoy your evening."

"Thank you, Your Majesty," Ivy replied, bowing to her.

Losing patience with the exchange, Kris left his throne. He felt very tempted to ask Ivy to dance with him, perhaps even the *awaye*. However, starting the night with an Andari song would be unwise to say the least. Even if news had spread that the Morai had taken a concubine, Kris didn't want to make Ivy more uncomfortable than he already must be feeling.

The decision was taken out of his hands when one particular individual made his appearance. Kris had been waiting for him, and he kept an eye on the Andari noble even as he held Ivy closer to him.

Ivy must have noticed the change in him, because he whispered, "It's the marquis, right? He's here."

Yes, Kris replied in Ivy's mind. *I must admit that a part of me is very eager to confront him for daring to believe that he could have you. On the other hand, I'd prefer it if you didn't have to face the unpleasantness.*

"I knew it was unavoidable," Ivy replied. "Besides, he and I clashed on several matters before. I'm not afraid of him."

Just because he could, Kris brushed his lips over Ivy's in a ghost of a kiss. Taking Ivy's arm, he guided the young Andari to the side. A fuming Lord Torildy lay in wait, although he had been intercepted by Ivy's parents.

Kris knew better than to believe he could rely on the two Erethe lords. Ivy's parents were only mindful of their own interests, and they were biding their time until they could act against him again. In the meantime, though, they could be useful.

"What is the meaning of this?" the marquis was currently asking. "We had an agreement. Why is my betrothed sharing kisses with the Morai?"

"Because he isn't your betrothed anymore," Kris replied, even if the question hadn't been directed at him. The marquis turned to face him, and Kris shot him an unpleasant smile. "Greetings, Marquis. I'm so pleased to see you could make it to my little celebration."

"Thank you, Your Majesty," Torildy said between gritted teeth. "I apologize for the delay."

"That's quite all right," Kris replied. "I'm sure it was caused by circumstances beyond your control."

He himself had arranged it, since he'd known he'd be tempted to create a dimensional rift within the marquis's entrails if the man showed up at his ball with Ivy as his partner. It wouldn't have been too great a loss, but Kris didn't want Ivy to see him like that. Not just yet and preferably not ever.

Marquis Torildy, however, seemed inclined to test Kris's patience. "Now that I'm here, Your Majesty, I must point out that my absence appears to have created a misunderstanding. Lord Behnivyr and I—"

"Are no longer an item," Kris interrupted him. "He's my moraistele now."

For the first time, the marquis noticed Ivy's new hairstyle. He went crimson with rage. "This is an outrage. You can't do this."

"So I'm told," Kris commented idly. "It seems to be a common misconception on behalf of Andari nobles. First Earl Titexe and his bond mate, now you. But you see, Marquis, the fact remains that I *can* do it. In fact, I already have."

Torildy opened his mouth, obviously not willing to give up just like that. Kris could see the insult forming on Torildy's lips, and he awaited it with far more eagerness than he should have.

Ivy intervened before Torildy could give Kris a cause to throw him in the dungeons. "Please, Marquis Torildy. You must understand that my family and I never meant to deceive you. Things just happened this way. Besides, I believe the two of us were never fully compatible. I'm sure that you'll find another bond mate to interest you."

"There were provisions in our agreement," the marquis said. "I'm entitled to take over a portion of the land that is assigned to Seanda."

"That would be the case had Their Lordships reneged on their part of the deal," Kris argued. "However, the fault for this situation lies on my shoulders." And he didn't have to say that Torildy couldn't push him into redrawing any lines on the map. "Nevertheless, I am not an absurd man. Speak to my second-in-command, Sai. I will make every possible attempt to compensate you, although we're probably in agreement if I say that my prize is worth more than anything I could give you."

"Indeed." Torildy smiled bitterly. "Well, I trust you'll enjoy it. No Full-Blood Andari would touch your moraistele now, anyway."

Ivy tensed but held onto his composure. "It's a moot point," he said. "I wouldn't want anyone but His Majesty to touch me anyway."

To emphasize his point, Ivy leaned against Kris in an obviously intimate posture. Even if Ivy was doing it just to twist the knife, possessiveness reared inside Kris. He wrapped his arm around Ivy's waist and kissed Ivy's temple. "I believe we can all agree that it wouldn't be wise. In any case, that aside, I hope you will enjoy the ball. Have an excellent evening, and do contact Sai about what we discussed. He can also ensure a safer means of transportation for when you need to travel back to your home."

"You are very gracious, Your Majesty," Torildy said. He paused, like he'd just realized the possible implications of Kris's words. "I appreciate your offer," he finished in a tense voice.

Kris acknowledged Torildy's words with a nod. Dismissing the marquis from his attention, he focused on Ivy once more. "Dance with me, *sharani*?"

"I'd love to, Your Majesty," Ivy replied with a smile.

He swept Ivy into his arms, and the rest of the world faded into the background as they lost themselves in the flow of the songs, and most of all, in their togetherness.

CHAPTER SIX
DUTY

THE DAYS passed in a whirlwind of intrigue and gossip. Soon the ball ended, and most of the guests departed. Ivy took his leave of his parents, a bittersweet good-bye that had left him emotionally raw.

After that, things settled down—insofar as they could in a place like Nikaret. Ivy didn't always get much time alone with his lover. Kris spent hours on end in his office or his throne room, reviewing reports, receiving news, and generally doing whatever the Morai did on a regular basis.

By now, the servants had moved Ivy's things—including the ones that had been in Kris's wardrobe—to a different room, one in the imperial wing, a few doors down from Kris's. The quarters were similar in structure to Kris's, although slightly less spacious. They were also very different from Ivy's former rooms, and it took a while for Ivy to grow accustomed to them. Even so, it helped that, more often than not, Kris came to spend the night with him.

Those were the moments that made everything worth it, during which Ivy forgot every strange, unfamiliar thing and could lose himself in the rightness of his union with Kris. Kris still hadn't claimed him, but that didn't mean it wouldn't happen. Ivy was just getting used to the proficiency of the Nikari in the mind arts, and he hoped that soon his efforts would pay off.

Kris's mother had proven to be an inexhaustible resource in that regard. She'd taken to training Ivy, teaching him how to communicate telepathically. According to her, Ivy had the raw magic required, but he needed to tame his talent. Most users of the mental arts never managed or only had limited success, which was why telepathic communication was so rare.

It was during one of these lessons that Ivy's regular routine came to an abrupt halt. The A'Mora had been busy teaching him how to open his mind when all of a sudden, she tensed and faltered. Ivy immediately noticed the difference. "Is something wrong?" he asked the A'Mora.

"It's Kris," Katara replied. "He needs me to do something for him."

Katara's tone alarmed Ivy. "What is it? Is he hurt?"

They had traveled to the neighboring forest for the purpose of their lesson, but surely, if Kris had been attacked, they'd have figured it out sooner.

Katara blinked, and her expression cleared. "No, nothing like that. It's just that he's temporarily leaving Nikaret, and he needs me to watch over you."

Ivy's heart fell even as crushing relief filled him. It was strange to experience such paradoxical emotions at the same time, but Kris often had that effect on him. "Where is he going?" he asked the A'Mora.

Katara eyed him speculatively, as if considering whether to tell him or not. She gestured for him to sit down in the shade of a large tree. "This is extremely sensitive information. I wish I could trust you with the details, but until Kris returns, I'm afraid I can't do that."

"But surely you can tell me something," Ivy insisted.

"There's been a rebellion," Katara finally told him. "It's not that serious. On occasion, these things happen. Kris makes it his business to always handle it himself. That way, there's less of a chance of a recurring incident."

"But who would rebel against the empire?" Even as he asked the question, he knew he'd phrased it poorly. There were plenty of people who didn't agree with the way things were run, including his parents. But what he actually wanted to know was who had faced the forces of the Nikari. Was Kris in any danger?

Katara seemed to realize his train of thought. "You needn't worry," she said. "You'll find out everything soon. Just be patient, and stay by Kris's side when the time comes."

Ivy bit his lower lip so hard it bled. "But... I want to be by his side *now*."

He realized he sounded childish, but he couldn't help it or keep the yearning in check. Still, it didn't surprise him that as soon as he finished the phrase, Katara shook her head adamantly. "No. Absolutely not. He's already gone anyway."

"But you can take me to him, can't you?" Ivy insisted. "Through a rift. Please, Your Majesty. I just want to make sure it's safe. I won't even intervene in any way. We can be back in a minute, before he even realizes we're there."

Katara chuckled, but the sound held no humor. "He'll realize it, and so will Attcha. I understand that you're concerned, but you being there won't help him. He needs to be the Morai now, not Kris."

Except Kris was the Morai, and trying to separate the two would be folly. Ivy had realized that from the very beginning, when he'd looked into the gold of Kris's eyes, had seen danger and embraced it.

"I'm not fooling myself, Your Majesty," he replied. "I know who's sleeping in my bed almost every night, and I understand what I agreed to. Whatever my people say of me, I wouldn't have spread my legs for just anyone."

The crudeness of his statement seemed to take her aback, perhaps because Ivy so rarely made any reference to what he and Kris did in private. "Kris won't be happy," she warned him, "with either of us. He doesn't want you to see him like that."

"Things like this won't go away," Ivy said. "Closing my eyes to it won't make it less real."

"Perhaps," Katara said, scowling fiercely. "What is it that you're trying to prove, Behnivyr? Believe me when I say that Kris is just fine. Surely you realize I wouldn't lie to you with regard to that."

Of course she wouldn't. In fact, she wouldn't even be sitting here with him if she'd feared for her son's safety. Was he simply being stubborn and impatient? "If I go there, I'd be a burden for him, wouldn't I?" he asked.

"Probably, yes," Katara answered. "He would feel compelled to ensure your well-being and comfort, and your presence would just draw the eye unnecessarily." Her harsh expression softened. "Come on. Let's go back to the palace. Receive him well tonight. That's what he needs from you."

Ivy said nothing else. She had a point, but for the first time since he'd come here, Ivy felt like an outsider.

He remained quiet as she got up and summoned a rift. By now, Ivy was used to both the sight and feel of the dimensional portals. They were, indeed, very different from the waves his sire summoned, but the imperial family always kept a tight rein on the chaotic energies stemming from inside them.

Still, he wrapped himself tightly in Kris's cloak, just like he'd promised his lover. He held Katara's hand as he stepped through the portal. A heartbeat later, they were back in the palace, in the familiar empty room used as a destination for regular rifts.

The sudden change in environments made Ivy a little woozy. The sensation passed with reasonable ease, but that didn't ease the weight on his heart.

"I think I'll retreat to my quarters," he said. "As always, thank you for the time you've dedicated to instructing me in the mind arts."

Katara nodded. "I do wish I could help you more with regard to the other matter, but you need to be patient. Duty always comes first for the Morai."

She might have been trying to help, but this time, she didn't succeed. Ivy still thanked her, but when he went back to his room, he buried himself in his bed, struggling not to cry. Did none of them realize that duty shouldn't be valued above the feelings in one's heart? Didn't it matter that he had foregone his own obligations to be with Kris?

Then again, how could he compare with Kris? He didn't carry the burden of an entire empire on his shoulders.

No, he was looking at this all wrong. Kris might be the Morai, and Ivy couldn't begrudge him the necessity of his position. However, Katara didn't realize one very simple thing. Ivy hadn't come here to be an ornament. He could help Kris. He didn't know how just yet, but he'd find a way to ease Kris's burden. He just had to.

"I HOPE this won't happen again," Kris told Phura tightly. "I trusted you to watch over an important area in the empire. Whatever differences might be between us, I need you to do your duty for the Nikari."

"Certainly," Phura replied. "And as you know, Shuri and I are always mindful of the welfare of the empire. But you realize, Your Majesty, that certain more remote areas in Tarkquin remain somewhat unstable. They tend to react accordingly to unsettling news from Nikaret."

Kris wanted to put his fist through his uncle's face. Yes, he knew that, but he also suspected that Phura was the one who funded the entire debacle. Something like this always happened when Kris argued with Phura, although never quite to this extent. Sai had gathered more than enough evidence on the matter to make Phura's dealings at the very least suspect. If the other Nikari hadn't been his uncle, Kris would have long ago thrown him in the deepest, darkest dungeon.

"Perhaps you should be the unsettled one, Uncle," he said instead. "I won't always look away from the mistakes you make. And you stand to lose more than me from the instability in Tarkquin."

Phura scowled at him. "You can't possibly blame me for this situation, Your Majesty. I made sure the rebellion was quickly squashed."

"I don't want useless bloodshed—I want prevention," Kris said. "Tarkquin is one of the oldest regions in the empire. Such cores of conflict should have been dealt with a long time ago. But even if that hadn't been the case, I expect my governors to handle the incipient problems before they ever get to me. You might be my blood, Your Lordship, but if you are inept at this task, I will remove you from this position."

"Tarkquin has been under my rule since before you were born," Phura argued. "And I might be the governor here, but it is the duty of the Morai to check in on the provinces of the empire. You would do well to remember that, nephew."

Phura never called him "nephew," and he never talked back to him. It seemed that whatever folly had pushed him into staging this rebellion, it extended into this conversation.

Was Phura testing him? Did he think that because Kris had taken a moraistele, he would be less likely to deal with any threat that came his way with the same ruthless efficiency he'd employed in the past?

Kris supposed he should have expected it. His uncle must have known Ivy's parents were notoriously dismissive of the empire, and yet they had shared his table.

But what his uncle didn't realize was that Kris wouldn't allow anyone—not the Andari nobles nor Phura himself—to disrespect him. He didn't lose his temper. Instead, he turned on his heel and stalked out of Phura's office.

The sound of his uncle's laughter followed him down the corridor and then abruptly cut off. Had the fool finally realized that Kris had no intention of leaving the city of Quintera before he handled this abysmal lack of respect?

Perhaps, but there was nothing he could do about Kris's plan. He created a rift in the center of the corridor, one that sucked in several ornamental tables and rugs. He barely felt the shift of matter as he walked through it—the distance was negligible at best.

Still, he did enjoy the look of shock on the faces of the guards manning the dungeons of the governor's citadel.

Officially, rift usage was forbidden within dwellings, as anyone who came too close to an uncontrolled rift could say good-bye to this plane of existence and surrender to the hands of the Creator. Special rooms existed for the purpose of long-distance travel, both in the Nikaret palace and in any other Nikari residence, like the Quinteran governor's home.

The fact that Kris hadn't bothered to obey that law spoke volumes about his mood. The guards backed away from him, giving him space while murmuring respectful greetings. Kris ignored them. He knew this was where the leader of the rebellion had been taken after Shuri had captured him, and in spite of the labyrinthine nature of the location, he had no trouble finding his destination.

Like all Nikari cells, this particular one boasted only the barest of necessities—a hard cot that provided just about as much comfort as the barren floor, a chamber pot, and a washbasin. The Tarkquinian lay on the cot, bound and gagged. His eyes widened when the door opened and Kris approached. Obviously he knew who Kris was, and it scared him. That always helped smooth things along when it came to getting information out of someone.

Kris crouched next to the prisoner and removed his gag. "Hello, Firaz. I see you recognize me, don't you?"

"Y-Yes, Your Majesty," the Tarkquinian stammered.

"Good. So you must know why I'm here. You're guilty of treason against the empire, but today is your lucky day. I believe someone must be pulling the strings of your little operation, and you're going to tell me who that is."

The prisoner shook his head, but Kris continued to speak, undeterred. "We can do this the easy way or the hard way. Here's your first choice. You'll tell me who is behind this rebellion, and I will let you off with ten years in the palace dungeons. I'll even make sure your family is safe from harm."

"I won't betray my people," the prisoner insisted.

Kris was unimpressed, but then he hadn't expected much of Firaz Madele. According to his information, the man was a mere blacksmith dissatisfied with the pressure put on craftsmen and the difficulty of trade with other provinces. He seemed to believe non-Nikari craftsmen were the only ones who needed to pay taxes to proceed with their businesses. That was obviously false—but Kris hadn't come here to discuss politics.

"You didn't let me finish," he said blandly. "Your second alternative is to just sit there while I break your mind and take the information I want."

The Tarkquinian paled. "Y-You can't do that. You wouldn't do it."

Kris hadn't done it in the past because he'd known what he would find. He'd treated his uncle's little outbursts of temper as nothing more than minor annoyances, insignificant in the greater scheme of things. And to be fair, the previous incidents had been minor, hardly noteworthy at all. Not to mention that he disliked turning people into vegetables. But obviously, he'd been wrong to dismiss the situation so easily, and his uncle would regret forcing his hand.

Kris smirked at the prisoner, knowing that by now, his eyes had turned gold. "Is that right? I assume you're well-informed on why I might want to turn a blind eye to your deeds. Well, even the most trustworthy source can be mistaken at times. And in this case, both of you made a serious error."

He was just about to unleash his mental abilities on the terrified Tarkquinian when the cell door opened. Kris didn't turn, already knowing who'd interrupted the interrogation. "Yes? What is it, Shuri?

"A word with you, Your Majesty?" Shuri asked.

"Of course, cousin," Kris said. "As soon I finish interrogating the prisoner."

He wouldn't put it past his uncle to distract him through a conversation with Shuri and take the Tarkquinian out before the rebellion leader could give them any real information. Shuri hesitated for a few moments, then walked into the cell, joining Kris by the prisoner's side.

"It's somewhat urgent," he insisted. Gritting his teeth, he added, "Please."

Kris knew how much it must have cost Shuri to say that, but while he cared for his half brother, this time around he wouldn't let things slide. "I would be at your disposal, Shuri, if you could guarantee me this man will remain alive until the two of us finish our conversation."

The Tarkquinian released a frightened sound. "No. Look. I'll tell you everything. He forced me. The governor. I was told—"

"Be silent," Shuri cut him off. "You've said enough."

Kris didn't like this new development. He might not hold any real affection for Phura, but he would deeply regret it if Shuri placed himself in the same situation as their uncle. "Stay out of this, Shuri. Implicating yourself won't help him. He's gone too far."

"I know," Shuri said. "I heard."

His mental voice drifted into Kris's mind. *Kris, please. I've never once asked anything of you. I know Uncle Phura committed a serious mistake. No, two mistakes. But he hasn't been himself lately.*

Kris was taken aback by the fact that Shuri had chosen to contact him telepathically. It bespoke of a closeness they didn't share and of talents Kris hadn't been fully aware of with regard to his brother.

Still, the seriousness of their conversation wouldn't let him dwell on his surprise. *Then you'd do well to concern yourself more with controlling him, rather than with my private life,* he said, narrowing his eyes at his half brother. *It's very convenient for you to use the blood-bond between us now that you need it.*

And you know I'd much rather not do it, but I hope my half brother would be more merciful than the Morai.

Kris sighed heavily. *Mercy means weakness for the Morai. You know this.*

Yes, I do, Shuri replied. *The mistake is mine. I let this go on for too long even if I knew that you'd eventually tire of casting a blind eye on his actions. One last chance, that's the only thing I'm asking for. In exchange, I honor bind myself to you.*

Kris didn't want Shuri's servitude. He wanted the man's loyalty. But he was too much of a realist not to understand that such a goal would be nigh-impossible to achieve. He scanned his half brother's face and finally nodded. *Very well. I will not refuse your request or your offer. But I want you to commit that this will never happen again. It is ridiculous to have people from my own house working to stab me in the back.*

Out loud, he said, "We have an agreement, then. In the meantime, I'll have the prisoner transported to Nikaret. Make sure his family is looked after." In the end, Kris would have bet his crown that the blacksmith had been truthful about Phura pushing him into the rebellion. "I'm making you governor in his stead, Shuri. You'll receive the official appointment within two days."

He couldn't imagine what his uncle stood to gain with this childish, irritating behavior, but he'd grown weary of such games. At the very least, Shuri seemed more aware of their position.

Shuri blinked, perhaps surprised at the offer. Still, he bowed, acknowledging his sudden advancement in a traditional manner. "I'm honored by your trust in me, Your Majesty."

I'm relying on you to keep your word, brother. Kris sent through his mental powers. *Resent me if you must but realize that the empire is bigger than both of us, and our duty goes beyond whims and personal desires.*

Does your moraistele know that? Shuri suddenly asked. He was back to his regular, sarcastic and belligerent self—which for some reason soothed Kris. Or would have, if Shuri hadn't brought up Ivy.

He has nothing to do with you or with this. You know what you have to do. Do it, and I won't have to come back here for another even more unpleasant visit.

Judging by Shuri's expression, the other Nikari really didn't want to imagine a visit he'd enjoy even less. Kris could empathize. He took no pleasure in making threats against his family and even less in going through with those threats.

Feeling suddenly very tired, Kris stepped out of the room and made sure he had enough space to make a rift without risking anyone's safety. Sliding his hand through the air, he created the portal, taming the chaotic energies into a gateway to Nikaret.

He stepped through the rift without bothering to say good-bye to his brother or, even less, to his foolish uncle. An instant later, he was back in the palace.

The change in locations didn't miraculously alter what had happened, though. His uncle's actions stumped him. However much hate Phura felt toward Kris's father—and toward Kris, by extension—the man had always respected Kris's title and had refrained from going too far. Was it Ivy's presence that had triggered the change or something else entirely?

He was still musing over Phura's behavior when he ran into his mother outside the rift room. "Ah, son, you're home," she said, like she hadn't already sensed him the moment he'd entered Nikaret. "Good. I trust everything went well."

"As well as it could go, under the circumstances. I made Shuri governor."

A brief scowl crossed his mother's face, before she quickly smoothed it into an approving smile. "He's probably a better choice than your uncle."

So she said, but if there was one thing they'd never agreed on, it was Shuri. Kris's instinctive affection toward his half brother was actually the main reason why his mother no longer resided in Nikaret on a permanent basis. Kris could still remember the argument they'd had that had led to that decision, and it wasn't something he cared to repeat.

"He said he'd honor bind to me," he explained.

"Oh dear. Whatever determined him to do so must have been serious."

Kris expected her to prod further into the details of his visit, so he prevented that by saying, "I'll tell you everything later. I think I need to see Ivy."

Surprisingly, his mother agreed. "That's probably a good idea. He wanted to go after you, and he wasn't happy when I refused to help him."

Kris mentally sighed. The last thing he wanted now was to have a confrontation with Ivy, but he supposed it couldn't be helped. Shuri had been right in telling him that Ivy couldn't have been ready for the difficulties inherent to his position as moraistele. Leaving aside the perfection of their sex life, their relationship wasn't developing as smoothly as Kris would have liked.

"I'll speak to him," he said, kissing his mother's cheek. "Thank you for watching over him in my absence. We'll talk more about Phura and Shuri later on."

"Of course," his mother replied. "I'll be by the nightwolf dens if you need me."

As they went their separate ways, Kris debated how to approach this conversation with Ivy. In the end, it was all about what Kris had pointed out to his uncle and half brother. Duty.

But Ivy had tossed his own duty aside when he'd come to live with Kris instead of bonding with the marquis. Sometimes Kris still couldn't believe Ivy had been willing to brave such censure just for him, and he wondered what he'd have done if Ivy hadn't disregarded the betrothal agreement.

His scattered thoughts didn't help him reach a decision, and he wished he'd taken the time to talk to Attcha. His nightwolf always saw the world in a simpler way, and that usually helped clear Kris's mind as well.

Then again, if he wanted to be perfectly honest, he could have gone to the dens to begin with. The fact remained that it wasn't Attcha he wanted to see, but Ivy.

Whatever he and Ivy would discuss, being around the Andari always lightened Kris's heart. The Creator only knew he needed it.

The moment he entered Ivy's quarters, his lover stepped out of the bedchamber and smiled at him. "Greetings, Your Majesty," he said. "I trust everything went well with your task?"

Kris frowned. "Don't call me by my title when we're alone."

Ivy's smile faded. "You're upset. What happened?"

Kris rubbed his eyes tiredly. The last thing he wanted was to vent his frustrations on Ivy. "Nothing. No, that's not true. A lot of things happened. I just don't want to think about them."

Ivy didn't prod further. "Fair enough." He took Kris's hand and guided him into his bedchamber. "Lie on the bed. An idea occurred to me while I was waiting for you."

Kris complied, his libido stirring as he wondered what Ivy had come up with. Usually, he was the one who initiated intimacies between them, and he found the change quite intriguing.

"On your stomach," Ivy guided him. "Take your shirt off."

"Bossy today, aren't you?" Kris couldn't help but chuckle as he obeyed Ivy. He lay on his stomach, naked from the waist up, and waited.

Ivy straddled him and reached for the nightstand. "Just close your eyes and relax," he said.

It wasn't an easy thing for Kris to do because his instincts demanded that he take Ivy. It would be so easy to forget about his problems, lose them in the comfort of Ivy's welcoming body.

And maybe he'd have done exactly that, but Ivy's hands landed on the naked skin of his back. They were so warm, slick with what Kris decided must be massage oil, and they emanated some sort of magical energy. Distantly, Kris recalled that at one point Ivy had mentioned having healing magic. Or maybe Sai had said it back when he'd been researching Ivy's family. It hardly mattered, anyway, because somehow, that magic reached into Kris's body, smoothing out knots of tension he hadn't even been aware of.

Ivy's clever fingers rubbed and massaged, spreading the oil over Kris's back while tendrils of energy pooled into his body. The familiar feel of that magic made Kris's dick throb in his breeches, but his urgency to take Ivy melted into something lazier, more relaxed—the knowledge that, eventually, their togetherness would progress into further intimacy, but he didn't need to rush.

He didn't know how much time Ivy spent working the knots and kinks from his back. All throughout the massage, he remained silent, but Kris didn't mind. Ivy's magic spoke for him and told Kris just how much Ivy cared for him.

When he did speak, though, Ivy's voice sounded thoughtful, almost sad. "I talked to your mother when you left. Something she said keeps bothering me."

Kris released an inquiring hum, still floating on his daze of relaxation and enjoying the feel of Ivy's hands on him. "What is it?"

"More or less, she said that the Morai isn't my Kris."

Kris tensed, wondering what in the world had possessed his mother to bring that up. He didn't know if Ivy had initiated this entire process to try to draw him into a conversation about the rebellion, but the idea that Ivy would manipulate him like that angered him.

Ivy shushed him and kissed Kris's nape. He didn't seem to expect a reply to his words, not like Kris had thought. "She's wrong," Ivy said. "I can tell that even when you are with me, you're still the Morai. Even when you shrug off your title to come to my bed, your concerns always follow you."

He spoke slowly and steadily, like he'd already accepted this reality without Kris even having to tell him about it. "You can't separate two parts of you and expect to feel whole," Ivy said. "I'm not afraid to accept who you really are. Just remember that, all right?"

As much as he enjoyed the massage, Kris extracted himself from Ivy's gentle grip. He faced his lover and met his gaze. "What would you have me do, Ivy?"

Ivy cupped his face, his hands still warm and slick but his caress gentle and familiar. "I would have you be happy. I can't do much to support you, but I want you to realize that no matter what happens, you'll always have me." He smiled shyly. "To be perfectly honest, I feel quite helpless knowing that the only thing I can give you is forgetfulness."

"It's not just forgetfulness, *sharani*," Kris said quietly. "You give me peace."

Ivy smiled sadly. "Yes, but it's only temporary. I want to make a difference in your life, to help you carry your burden."

"You do help, more than you know," Kris replied. "You give me something to look forward to, something to fight for other than my duty."

He faltered even as the words escaped his lips. Duty was the most important thing for Nikari nobility. It was a lesson he'd learned the hard way. The empire, above all else. The empire's stability, above one's own feelings.

Wasn't that why his mother had set aside her humiliation at being second in her own bond mate's bed? Wasn't it why Shuri still pretended to be Kris's cousin, and Kris allowed it? Wasn't it why Kris turned a blind eye to his uncle's deeds?

The Morai himself meant duty, at least according to the Nikari culture. Kris had never realized how limiting that view could be.

He must have fallen silent for too long, because Ivy leaned closer to him, his green eyes growing concerned. "Kris? What is it?"

"It's… nothing. It just occurred to me that I never used to be Kris at all, not even with my mother. There was always a barrier between us. But…. Since you arrived, it's different."

He couldn't explain it, but he knew now that Ivy was right. His position as the Morai was too engrained in the fabric of his being for him to completely abandon this persona, even with Ivy. Proof in point—the fact that Kris doubted he'd even have allowed Ivy to refuse him. But it worked both ways. Kris didn't have to exist outside the political sphere. The power of the Morai needed to be tempered by heart. Without it, he was exactly what he dreaded to be—a despot.

"You know where I went today, Ivy?" he asked. "I had to travel to Tarkquin. My uncle staged a rebellion simply to test my patience. I almost threw him in the dungeon."

Ivy gasped. "Oh no. What happened?"

"Shuri got in the way. He asked me to give Phura another chance and honor bound himself to me in exchange."

"I can't imagine that was easy for him," Ivy replied softly. "He strikes me as someone who prides himself on his independence."

"You read him well," Kris said, wondering if it was another of Ivy's powers. "Unfortunately, he was brought up in hatred of me and my family. I can't imagine his mother's death helped."

"He blames it on you?" Ivy asked.

Kris grimaced. He didn't know why he'd brought up his family's less-than-pleasant past, but he supposed Ivy needed to know. "Probably. She killed herself after my father died." He cleared his throat, trying to dispel the images that popped into his brain at his recollection of the former Morai's demise. "In any case, I decided he would be a better choice for governor than my uncle. He's done things just to cross me before, but I can't imagine what he thought he'd accomplish by taking it so far."

"If he truly did support the rebellion for his own pettiness, he doesn't deserve to be governor. I can't imagine he didn't know that he'd get people killed through his actions."

The weight of Ivy's words settled between them, and Kris scanned his lover's face, wondering if Ivy realized Kris had killed his fair share of men and women throughout his life. He took no pleasure in it—killing was wasteful, and it never brought about anything good. But at war, it was kill or be killed.

"You're right," he confessed. "Shuri's forces had already contained the rebellion by the time I even got there, and most of the people involved suffered serious injuries or died."

Ivy stared at his hands, obviously not happy but struggling to process the new information. Finally, he looked at Kris once more and squeezed his hands. "I believe in you, Kris," he said. "You're a good man and a good leader. And I know you'll do your best to prevent things like this from ever happening again."

"You don't blame me?" Kris asked, dumbfounded.

"We are all the products of our circumstances," Ivy replied. "How could you have stopped it? You might be the Morai, but you're not omnipotent." He paused, as if considering something. "Some people would say that the root cause of all of this is the empire. Maybe they'd say that no one would've had to rebel to begin with had the Nikari not invaded their lands. But there's no use dwelling on what used to be. The empire itself is only as good or as bad as the people who live in it and who lead it. You can make it so much greater than just a union of territories. I know you can."

The show of trust almost seemed too good to be true, especially since Kris knew the people Ivy mentioned might be Ivy's parents. "Ivy, why do you always show such faith in me?" he couldn't help but ask.

Ivy just wrapped his arms around Kris's neck and kissed his cheek. "Perhaps I just see something in you that no one else does. Then again, it's easy to trust a person when you love them."

Kris held Ivy close as the meaning of Ivy's words penetrated his consciousness. He and Ivy never spoke of love. Such deep emotions between the Morai and his concubine could only lead to disaster. Ivy himself had never said the word, not even in the conversation with Kris's mother which Kris had overheard the night of the ball.

Ivy seemed to remember this as well, because he suddenly went rigid. He released Kris and started to move away. "I'm sorry. I shouldn't have said that."

Before he could stop himself, Kris reached for Ivy, pulling him into his lap. "Don't. Don't apologize. Just stay like this. In my arms."

At first, Ivy remained tense, but slowly, he relaxed in Kris's embrace. As Ivy set his head on Kris's shoulder, Kris inhaled deeply, taking in the familiar scent of his lover. He wanted to say so many things, but the words got stuck in his throat. Perhaps he wasn't as brave as Ivy deemed him to be.

In the end, Kris decided that if he couldn't vocalize his gratitude, he'd show it to Ivy—through his actions. And, all right, it might not have been a solely emotional response. How could it, with Ivy in his lap and his ass straight over Kris's crotch? Not to mention the libido-stirring massage from earlier. No conversation, no matter how serious, could completely put a damper on Kris's desire for Ivy.

It might not be the perfect answer for their situation, but Kris pulled the pin from Ivy's hair and buried his fingers in the silky locks. In response, Ivy released a small aroused gasp. Kris took the sound as encouragement and melded his lips against Ivy's.

As always, Ivy eagerly granted him entrance. Even so, Kris didn't rush things. He explored Ivy's mouth like he had all the time in the world, allowing his regular plundering to melt into slow seduction. Ivy's hands roamed over his naked back, but with an entirely different purpose. His nails raked over Kris's skin ever so slightly, just enough to awaken his nerve endings without actually testing the limits of pain.

His tongue tangled with Kris's own, and as they kissed, Kris summoned his magic and focused on shredding their garments. Ivy moaned into their lip-lock, as attuned to Kris's magic as Kris was to his. Kris felt tempted to tease Ivy with his abilities, but it didn't feel right.

He wanted this to be just about the two of them, he realized, only their touches, only their kisses. His magic was as much a part of him as his heart, but for some reason, making use of it now would seem alienating.

Instead, he lowered Ivy onto the bed, never once breaking their kiss. Ivy's body was silken perfection against his, and Kris had never been more grateful for his ability to get rid of garments with a mere thought. Given access to all of Ivy's beautiful form, he couldn't wait to explore every single inch of it.

That was the only reason why he broke the kiss—because the rest of Ivy just waited to be discovered and lavished with Kris's attentions. And Kris went on to do exactly that. He peppered Ivy's face with gentle kisses, lingering over Ivy's cute nose and also over his eyelids and smooth forehead. Once again, he marveled at the softness of Ivy's skin, over his long eyelashes, and the picture Ivy and Kris made when they were together. They were so different, and yet they fit together just right.

That thought urged him on, and as he progressed over Ivy's collarbone, he explored every perfect line and swirled his tongue in the hollow of Ivy's neck. Ivy threaded his fingers through Kris's hair, although he made no attempt to guide Kris elsewhere. He just held on, clinging to Kris, as if he needed Kris's presence for an anchor.

Lower down Kris went, his attention drawn by the pointed peaks of Ivy's nipples. When he took one of the buds in his mouth, Ivy whispered his name, the sound managing to be both reverent and pleading.

After weeks of being together—and a very healthy sex life throughout that time—one would have thought there could be no real surprises between them. As Kris learned, that wasn't true. Ivy's responses to him might have become familiar, but their lovemaking was different today, and the time he took sucking and nibbling on every inch of silken skin paid off. When Ivy clung to him, his regularly musical cries melted into soft sighs. The writhing Kris usually summoned within his lover morphed into slight tremors, and it was just as beautiful—or even more so—than their previous lovemaking sessions. Or perhaps the comparison was flawed from the beginning. Not that it mattered. Kris just went with what felt right, and he knew now that today needed to be special.

He continued to mouth one of Ivy's nipples while he tweaked the other with his fingers, rubbing lightly, keeping the caress gentle when he could have easily succumbed to the teasing pain both he and Ivy enjoyed so much.

By now, his dick throbbed between his legs, and Ivy's own erection nudged him impatiently, slick with precum. In spite of the sinful temptation Ivy provided, Kris continued with his plan. He released Ivy's nipples with a wet pop and freed his hair from Ivy's hold.

Ivy blinked at him, his green eyes hazy with lust and confusion. Holding Ivy's gaze, Kris kissed Ivy's arm, all the way up, then down, until he reached Ivy's hand. He took each individual finger in his mouth, fellating it like he would have Ivy's dick. Ivy's mouth opened in a soundless cry, and his trembling increased. His free hand clenched into the sheets, and he began to grind against Kris, seeking friction.

Kris gripped Ivy's hip, keeping Ivy in check but also attempting to soothe him. Even as he kissed Ivy's palm, he reached out into Ivy's mind and whispered, *Don't worry,* sharani. *I'll take care of you. I'll give you what you need.*

Much to his surprise, Ivy reached back. *Kris.... Please. I... I want you so badly.*

The slide of Ivy's mental powers over his consciousness made Kris shudder in lust. He hadn't known Ivy had learned how to talk telepathically, but it seemed his lover hadn't even given it much thought. It often happened like this, when one didn't try to force the communication and instead, let it flow. Ivy didn't appear to realize he'd spoken into Kris's mind, so Kris made no note of it.

He didn't even try to rein in his lust but pursued the natural course of their lovemaking, just like he'd intended to. Kissing back up Ivy's arm, he sucked lightly on the inside of his elbow. He buried his nose in Ivy's armpit, making his lover squirm in the process. Ivy's natural scent was even more potent here, strong with sweat and male musk, making Kris's head spin.

Suddenly hungry for everything about Ivy, Kris went to Ivy's other arm and repeated the process. He trailed his tongue over Ivy's skin, tasting every inch of the slender limb. When he focused on Ivy's hand, he traced the lines of Ivy's palm with the slick muscle, all the while watching Ivy's reactions.

For all his urgency, Ivy didn't try to rush Kris along again. Keeping his eyes tightly shut, he took deep breaths as if pacing himself, struggling to take in every sensation. Kris counted that as a win, then mentally laughed at his own tally. This wasn't a battle, and if it had been, Ivy would have long ago won it. He'd definitely destroyed everything Kris had thought to be true—in mere weeks, at that.

Ivy. His *sharani*. His moraistele, and so much more than that. Taking in Ivy's beautiful flushed face, Kris couldn't help but steal a kiss from Ivy's sweet lips. Ivy opened his eyes, and for a few seconds, Kris fell into the emerald depths. Whether Ivy had said those words or not, Kris could still have seen the emotion in those green orbs. He highly suspected his own eyes echoed Ivy's expression.

For once, he didn't bother to hide or mask the fact that he had a heart. He let Ivy see, and Ivy released a soft gasp. "Kris...."

Kris just smiled and continued his journey over Ivy's body. He licked down Ivy's chest but this time didn't linger over Ivy's nipples. Instead, he traced the taut lines on Ivy's abdomen, then stabbed his tongue into Ivy's belly button. Ivy arched his back, the scent of his arousal becoming impossibly strong.

It would have been so easy for Kris to make Ivy come. He knew Ivy's body well, and he could tell the young Andari was close to climax. But he also realized that if Ivy found his peak, Kris's own control would break, and he didn't want to end this, not just yet.

He allowed himself to tease the tiny hole for a while longer, then pulled away. Ivy undoubtedly thought Kris planned to suck his dick, because he moaned and jerked on the bed, working his hips and his crotch against Kris.

However, Kris had other ideas. He bypassed Ivy's groin entirely, focusing on Ivy's hipbone instead. He kissed down, over Ivy's leg, his knee, and finally down to his ankle. He massaged Ivy's skin, sweeping his fingers over the arch of Ivy's foot. All the while, he swirled his tongue around Ivy's toes, much like he had before with Ivy's fingers.

Ivy had never experienced such play, and judging by the sounds he was making, that was a mistake on Kris's part. Kris had been remiss in pursuing these kinds of caresses, but that would stop now. Since he had a lot of time to make up for, he lavished Ivy's leg with his attentions, then went ahead to do the same for its mate. At one point, Ivy started twitching, his limbs moving jerkily and almost hitting Kris in the face. Kris managed to prevent it, and if he wanted to be perfectly honest, he enjoyed seeing it, seeing Ivy so close and so lost in him even if Kris had yet to touch his genitals.

It stirred that part of him he couldn't deny, the beast that wanted to see how far he could take this, just how much Ivy could withstand before he broke. These were instincts Kris usually tried to smother, only to fail when he at last entered Ivy. The part of him that was closely linked to his Ndara ancestors responded to Ivy's passion more intensely than anything else, and Kris followed its urges.

He flipped Ivy on all fours, and his mouth watered at the sight of the twin globes of Ivy's ass. As if planning to wreck Kris's mind completely, Ivy wiggled his bottom, wordlessly demanding what both of them craved. Creator, Kris ached to go through with it, to bury his aching dick inside Ivy's body. And yet he didn't.

Instead, he kneaded and caressed the smooth cheeks, giving Ivy just enough tantalizing pleasure to let the young Andari know he had every intention of taking what Ivy offered. As he did so, he pressed a kiss to the small of Ivy's back, then went up, tracing Ivy's spine with his tongue.

He'd never done this before with Ivy and was surprised when Ivy's moans escalated in volume the higher Kris went. In fact, Ivy almost seemed to have gone in heat again—which should have been, at the very least, unlikely given the frequency with which they had sex. Apparently, Kris had found a very interesting erogenous zone.

He continued exploring Ivy's body, acquainting himself with every inch of his lover. Arms, legs, feet, then back to his upper body, unerringly drawn to it. He kissed Ivy's sweaty nape and buried his face in Ivy's white-blond hair, addicted to his perfume.

It was useless to ask what Ivy wanted, because Ivy's entire body screamed it. And so Kris didn't speak, not even through his mental abilities. For a few moments, he allowed himself the luxury of holding Ivy, so close, so warm, so his.

Finally, when he could wait no longer, he released Ivy and returned to his lover's ass. Spreading the twin globes, he thrust his tongue inside.

It was another thing they hadn't tried, largely because Kris hadn't known how Ivy would react. In some ways, Ivy remained very innocent, and Kris had feared Ivy would see this as dirty or even unpleasant.

In a way, he was proven right, because Ivy tried to pull away. "Kris!" he screamed. "Sweet Reysen.... Kris, stop!"

Kris would have followed Ivy's plea, but he realized that in spite of his words, Ivy craved the pleasure the taboo caress provided. Kris's mind became invaded with a litany of "yeses" which Ivy couldn't have even realized he was broadcasting.

Encouraged, he held on to Ivy's hips and wiggled the slick muscle inside, using it as a tiny cock to stretch his lover. Soon Ivy's vocalized denials melted into pleas for more, which Kris eagerly complied with. He swirled his tongue around the rim, then tongued Ivy deep, groaning as he took in Ivy's most intimate taste.

Much to his surprise, Kris realized that even if he hadn't touched himself at all, his own climax was building up. The pleasure of knowing and understanding Ivy in a way no one ever had and the anticipation of the complete union that would surely follow fueled the natural sexual satisfaction he always felt in echo of Ivy's lust for him.

He was tempted to finish this, to make Ivy come already, but in the end, exactly that temptation kept him from pursuing the goal within his reach. He would do this right, just like he'd intended to from the beginning.

Kris lifted his head, drawing a disheartened moan from Ivy. He changed their positions once again, flipping Ivy onto his back. Aware that intercourse without regular lubrication wouldn't be a very good idea, he reached for the nightstand and retrieved the familiar vial of oil. He slicked up his dick in brisk, harsh motions, struggling not to come at the touch of his own hand. Finally, he added the remaining liquid to Ivy's hole and lifted his lover's legs onto his shoulders.

As Kris positioned his cock at Ivy's entrance, Ivy held his breath in obvious anticipation. Kris's dick ached to be sunk into Ivy's tight heat, but he held back.

"Listen to me, *sharani*," he said. "You've brought more joy into my life than you probably realize. I want to claim you. I want to make you mine."

As he spoke, he reached out into Ivy's mind, but not just with his voice. He tentatively nudged Ivy's shields, reminding his lover what this claiming would entail. If Ivy didn't want it, if he was still afraid, Kris would back off.

Ivy simply smiled up at him. The haze of lust in his eyes cleared for a few moments, replaced by bliss and certainty. He took Kris's hand and settled it over his heart, and just like that, Kris knew the answer.

He saw it in Ivy's gaze, heard it in the rhythm of Ivy's heartbeat under his palm, felt it in the warmth of his skin. He became aware of an acceptance and an understanding he'd never found elsewhere and hadn't expected to encounter in an Andari. But then, Ivy was special. Kris had known that from the moment he'd seen a young Full Blood try to drink reada wine at a carnival.

Still holding Ivy's gaze, Kris prodded deeper into Ivy's mind. One by one, Ivy's shields fell, surrendering to Kris's mental touch. But when the last of Ivy's protection collapsed, so did Kris's. It wasn't something he did on purpose—it just happened, in response to Ivy's trust in him. The barriers that kept everyone else in check could not withstand Ivy's feelings and openness. And when their minds were completely exposed to one another, Kris finally pushed inside Ivy. *Mine,* he repeated. *Mine.*

KRIS'S VOICE and presence in his mind. Kris's dick piercing his body. Kris's heat and strength above him. Kris's scent surrounding him and those deep golden eyes glowing like twin stars. It was everything Ivy craved and more, the closeness he had yearned for from the very moment he'd become Kris's concubine.

He hadn't expected Kris to do this now, to claim him in this way. In fact, when he'd dared to approach the topic of his conversation with the A'Mora, he'd known there was a possibility Kris might get angry, but the more he'd thought about it, the more he'd wanted the other man to know Ivy would always support him.

And now here he was, beneath Kris, with him but somehow also inside him. It seemed that the moment his shields had fallen, so had Kris's. Ivy could understand that for the gift it was, and he would have cried if his eyes hadn't been in Kris's thrall.

As it was, he clung to Kris's neck, surrendering to the sensations and emotions Kris stirred within him. His body buzzed with sexual tension, the build-up from Kris's attentions already having him on the edge of orgasm. And when Kris's dick fully slid inside him, a wave of pleasure rushed over him, so strong Ivy almost choked. He should have come right then and there, but the ecstasy was too intense for his mind to even process it.

A sense of disconnection rose up like a mist in his consciousness, what Ivy felt and what was actually happening two entirely different things. He could experience emotions not his own, see himself through Kris's eyes. He could feel the heat of Kris's dick piercing him but also his own muscles tightening around the erect shaft.

It was disconcerting, to say the least, and something a rational mind hadn't been built to endure. It would have scared Ivy, but Kris's presence cleared the strange fog. That one word popped into Ivy's mind again. *Mine.*

Yes, Ivy belonged to Kris, so utterly and completely that he didn't care about his own identity anymore. A link snapped into place between him and Kris, glowing like the gold of Kris's eyes, soft, warm, yet so dangerous.

The surreal quality of the moment almost made Ivy wonder if he'd fallen into a dream. But he hadn't. This was actually happening, and that knowledge just made it all better, impossibly perfect. Ivy did feel the burn of Kris's entry—he couldn't *not* feel it, given Kris's generous girth. But that feeling coalesced into something greater, into a hotter fire, a pulsing bright energy that swallowed him whole. Tongues of flame licked over his skin, while waves of bliss shook him to the core.

Kris started to rock in and out of him, moving slowly, keeping a tortuously gentle pace. His dick brushed Ivy's special spot with every single motion, adding layer after layer of sensation. Ivy's own member brushed against Kris's abdomen, and between the maddening friction, Kris's cock filling him to the brim, and their minds bonded so intimately, Ivy lost all sense of space and time. The only thing he remained aware of was Kris, the sound of flesh slapping against flesh, his own cries and Kris's grunts, mingling with the mental litany of his name. Deeply carnal and deeply emotional, their union surpassed anything Ivy had ever thought could exist.

Ivy didn't know how long it lasted. He didn't even know what finally made him come. In fact, when his climax rushed over him, he wasn't even sure what had happened, at least not immediately. Pleasure swamped him, over and over, stronger and stronger, until he fell over the edge, unable to withstand the onslaught of sensations. And when Kris thrust inside him one last time and found his peak, Ivy's mind simply exploded, overcome by the flood of Kris's rapture.

It was like being in heat but ten times stronger, so intense it skirted the edges of pain. For a few moments, Ivy blacked out, floating in a haze of unbridled, absolute bliss. Even when he began to recover, the feeling didn't completely fade. Kris's thoughts did vanish from his mind, but the knowledge of the depth of Kris's emotions for Ivy lingered, crystallizing into a rapturous contentment.

As he came to, he found himself still on the bed, with Kris hovering over him, swiping a wet washcloth over Ivy's skin. In spite of everything they had shared, the gentleness of the gesture struck Ivy hard.

Kris always did this, Ivy realized. He might have only claimed him now, but from the very beginning, he'd showed Ivy such affection that Ivy should have never doubted his role in Kris's life.

He wanted to vocalize the feeling, but he didn't. Instead, he reached for his lover again. As Kris lay down next to him, Ivy curled by Kris's side. He set his hand over Kris's heart in an echo of what he'd done earlier. A moraistele's duty was to provide comfort for his Morai. But for Ivy, it wouldn't be duty. It would be love.

CHAPTER SEVEN
FAMILY

DINNER THAT evening was a private affair, made awkward by the tension lingering from the events earlier that day. Kris had yet to explain everything to his mother, and he anticipated a difficult conversation.

Once the meal was served, Kris sent the servants away. When only the three of them were present, Kris took a sip of reada wine and broached the topic at hand. "I have reason to believe Uncle was behind the rebellion."

His mother's eyes widened. "I knew something serious had happened when you said you put your half brother as governor instead, but I couldn't imagine.... Are you certain?"

"As certain as I can be," Kris said. "You know as well as I do that he's done similar things in the past."

"Never like this, though." His mother was shaking her head. "It just doesn't seem like something Phura would do."

Kris had expected disbelief from his mother, but her defense of Phura startled him. Then again, he himself had noticed the strangeness of his uncle's behavior.

"You're right, of course," he said, "but the leader of the rebellion admitted to it. I was just about to look into his mind when Shuri interrupted me and practically begged me to bury the whole thing."

"It could be because of me," Ivy said, speaking for the first time. "He seemed to dislike me, and I poured fuel on the fire when we spoke at breakfast."

"Your presence might be a factor," Kris admitted, "but it's unlikely that he'd go against and disrespect me just because of you."

He related the entire course of the conversation to Ivy and his mother. "What you're telling me boggles the mind," his mother said. "You are his Morai. Above all else, he's always been very aware of that."

"Perhaps…. Well, I could try to look into the matter discreetly," Ivy said. "Although I'm not as skilled at divination as my father, I have been studying hard during my stay here and I think I'd be able to watch him without him noticing."

That was actually not a bad plan. Phura's magic wasn't as strong as Kris's, so he wouldn't be sensitive to Andari divination. Watching him from afar, without involving Sai or any of Kris's intelligence agents, seemed the ideal option. On the other hand, Kris felt reluctant to risk involving Ivy in anything. He believed in Ivy's abilities, but would it be safe for him to use them in such a delicate situation?

Before he could come up with an answer, his mother intervened. "Are you sure you can handle that sort of task?" she asked, frowning. "Not to be dismissive of your efforts, Ivy, but you've been studying telepathic communication, and while you've made progress, you haven't yet managed to complete this task. What makes you think you'll have more success in divination?"

Ivy's face flamed with what Kris recognized as embarrassment. Even if he himself had been thinking along the same line—for different reasons—the last thing he wanted was for Ivy to lose confidence in his own strength as an individual.

"Actually, Mother, Ivy did manage to speak to me telepathically, and that was before I even claimed him. I think he must have been trying too hard with you, because between us, it happened quite normally. Ivy is very talented."

Ivy threw him a shy smile, the redness of his face now a blush of pleasure. Meanwhile, Kris's mother seemed gobsmacked. "You claimed him? He spoke to you? When?"

"Earlier today, when I went to see him." Kris arched a brow. "Surely you must have expected that I'd claim Ivy sooner or later."

"Yes, of course." His mother's shocked expression slowly melted into a pleased smile. "I suppose congratulations are in order and maybe apologies on my side."

"Not at all," Ivy replied. "You're right that in many things I'm still a novice. It's true that I haven't used my divination skills for anything but my lessons, but I have a strong enough feel for Kris's uncle to pursue his presence. Even if I might have been unable to do it before, my bond with Kris provides me with additional support."

"I see." Kris's mother smiled. "Well, I must admit I don't know too much about divination. Perhaps you're right. I would caution you to be very careful. Phura remains a dangerous man, and undoubtedly, he isn't happy with Kris giving Shuri the governor position."

"I actually suspect he'll be more furious about Shuri being honor bound to me," Kris replied. "In any case, we'll give it more thought before we go through with anything."

"If there's anything I can do to help, just let me know," his mother offered.

Kris shook his head. He didn't want her involved in his problems with Phura. It was unfortunate enough that she'd forever have to endure the evidence of her bond mate's infidelity by seeing Shuri. To force her into contributing to the investigation would be cruel.

"That's all right, Mother. Perhaps it would be best if you retreated to your estate for now." He smiled to soften the blow of his words. "I will miss you enormously, and I know Ivy will too, but if something happens, I'd prefer it if you were out of the blast radius."

"My place is by your side, Kris," his mother said, adamantly shaking her head. "I made a mistake in staying away for so long because of my own pride. So this time around, I'll go against my Morai's orders and remain in Nikaret."

Kris couldn't say he was surprised by his mother's reply, but it still pleased him. "Well, this time around, the Morai will allow you to follow your own heart," he said with a smile.

"Good." His mother grinned. "Otherwise, I might have had to show him that I can still turn him over my knee."

As they all laughed, the tension in the room lifted. Kris shared a look with Ivy and reached out into Ivy's mind. *We'll figure it out together,* sharani. *I know we will.*

Ivy nodded. *And don't worry about me. I promise I'll be careful.*

Kris tried not to analyze that statement too closely. Unless he explicitly forbade Ivy to get involved, Ivy would likely want to help him somehow. *Don't put yourself at risk, Ivy. You're far more important to me than my uncle's machinations.*

In response, Ivy squeezed his hand under the table. Out loud, he said, "For the moment, I'll continue my studies. It always pays to learn, even if I don't use divination for this specific purpose."

"I'll drink to that," Kris's mother said with a wide smile. "And to you and Kris. It's so nice to finally see my son smile. I don't think I've ever truly told you how much I appreciate that."

"You don't have to thank me," Ivy said. "I'm not exactly selfless in the endeavor."

Selfless or not, Ivy had brought Kris light in his life, and Kris would always be thankful for that. Perhaps soon he could show Ivy just how far that gratitude went.

A FEW days later, Kris received an unexpected and not wholly wanted visit from Shuri. He'd already sent Shuri his new orders as governor and hadn't expected—or particularly wanted—his brother to drop by so soon. As it happened with these things, the rebellion in Tarkquin had triggered a wave of restlessness throughout the empire, which made him busier than ever, and in a poor mood.

Nevertheless, it was his own fault this had happened, since he'd instructed Shuri to keep him well-informed with regard to developments in Tarkquin. And so he received Shuri in his office as soon as he was notified of the other man's arrival. "Anything new to report?" he asked without preamble.

"We've spoken with the families of the deceased and are providing assistance for them," Shuri replied. "Things seem to have settled down for the moment, although people are still wary."

Kris suppressed a groan of frustration. He hated it when the power struggles of irresponsible politicians caused unnecessary deaths. Unfortunately, as the Morai, he had no choice but to authorize use of force in such cases.

"I suppose it's understandable," he said. Pinning Shuri with a fierce look, he added, "Make sure this doesn't happen again."

"I assure you I'm not happy about it either." Shuri grimaced. "I was the one forced to shed blood."

"And yet, you honor bound yourself to me so that I wouldn't punish Uncle," Kris shot back bitingly.

Shuri didn't acknowledge that comment. Instead, he asked, "Is there anything specific you'd like me to keep you posted on, Your Majesty?"

"Everything. No more secrets, specifically with regard to Uncle Phura."

Shuri glowered at him. "You want me to spy on him?"

"You made a promise. Remember it."

The conversation would have doubtlessly escalated into further unpleasantness had a knock not sounded at the door. Pleasure swelled inside Kris as he identified the new presence. "Come in, *sharani*," he called out.

The door opened, and Ivy shyly entered the room. "I apologize," he said. "I didn't mean to interrupt your conversation." He paused and looked from Kris to Shuri, having obviously noticed the tension. "Is everything all right?"

Kris couldn't resist the concern in those emerald eyes, but neither did he want to get Ivy tangled in messy political affairs. "Yes," he answered. "Shuri and I were just clarifying a small matter with regard to his recent role as governor."

"Oh," Ivy said. He didn't seem convinced, but he didn't prod. "Well, when you finish your meeting...." He paused and bit his lip nervously. "I was hoping we could go to lunch?"

The inquiring tone of Ivy's suggestion made Kris's heart clench. "I'm afraid I'll have to skip lunch today," he replied. There was nothing he'd have liked more than to accept the offer, but right now, he couldn't afford to drop his guard.

Ivy's face fell, but the sad expression vanished in the blink of an eye. "I understand, of course. Perhaps later. I won't keep you further."

"Thank you, *sharani*," Kris replied. "I'll see you tonight." Turning toward his brother, he arched a brow. "Was there something else?"

"No, Your Imperial Majesty," Shuri replied between gritted teeth.

"Speak to Sai and leave a detailed report on the matters we discussed. You're dismissed."

Shuri's nostrils flared, but the scathing imprecation he undoubtedly wanted to utter remained unsaid. He just bowed in typical Nikari fashion and left the office.

Ivy watched him go, then focused on Kris once more. "Are you sure you're all right?" he asked hesitantly.

"More than sure," Kris replied. He didn't like arguing with his brother, but sometimes it couldn't be helped. "Don't worry about me, *sharani*."

Ivy looked like he wanted to say or perhaps do something else, but in the end, he didn't. For his part, Kris wanted to reach for him and kiss those full lips, but he knew that if he did so, he'd never get back to work. He might be able to withstand starvation, but the lure of Ivy's warmth and affection tempted him more than sustenance ever would.

It was perhaps fortunate that Ivy at last broke eye contact. He bowed to Kris and said, "I'll send someone in with a meal for you. And… I'll be waiting for you tonight."

With that promise, Ivy took his leave. Even as the door closed behind Ivy, Kris cursed himself for a fool. Now he was as hard as a rock, and he couldn't expect relief until this evening. Fuck.

IVY DIDN'T know Shuri very well, and their few exchanges hadn't been all that pleasant. However, Shuri was Kris's brother, one Kris cared deeply about. Ivy couldn't expect to be able to do much about their fractured relationship, but he needed to try.

He ran after Shuri and, against all odds, caught up with the Nikari. "Your Highness, wait. Can I have a word?"

Shuri pivoted on his heel so fast Ivy had to force himself not to take a step back. "What do you want?" Ivy hesitated, not knowing how to approach this obviously delicate matter. At some level, he wondered if he was even qualified to handle such a long-term problem, especially since Kris had told him to stay out of Shuri's way. But Reysen help him, he wanted to do something for the two brothers.

"I merely wished to ask you to give His Imperial Majesty a chance. I know that the two of you don't always see eye to eye, but he's a good man."

"It's none of your business," Shuri snarled at him. "You're just Kris's concubine. Don't go thinking you can tell other people what to do because you spread your legs for the Morai."

Ivy went rigid. "And you should not think you're entitled to insult others just because you yourself feel wronged. But the mistake was mine. I shouldn't have approached you."

As he stalked away, Ivy wondered how he could have been so foolish and arrogant. What could he do that Kris hadn't already tried? He could only hope the entire embarrassing exchange wouldn't reach Kris's ears, because it might make things worse.

He was so distracted by his self-berating thoughts that he nearly yelped when a hand landed on his shoulder. "Wait, please," Shuri said. "Don't go."

The hint of vulnerability in Shuri's voice made Ivy turn toward the Nikari. Instantly, Shuri released him, perhaps realizing the inappropriate nature of his touch. "I apologize, Your Lordship. I just…. It's a very difficult situation for me."

The part of Ivy that was pure healer hated to see a soul in pain. "I see," he said softly. Even if Shuri's words had angered him, he smiled. "Well, if you ever need to talk to anyone…."

Shuri blinked at him, obviously surprised Ivy had offered. For a few moments, Ivy thought the Nikari would take him up on his suggestion, but Shuri shook his head. "Thank you, but no. I don't want to put you in that position with Kris."

"You're too kind," Ivy replied, "but I think you should trust His Majesty more."

He half expected Shuri to snap at him like before, but the Nikari didn't. Instead, he changed the subject. "I can't help but realize you don't have a lunch companion. Would you mind terribly if I intruded on your time and asked you to share a meal with me?"

"Oh, of course I wouldn't mind," Ivy replied. "It would be my absolute pleasure."

They ended up in the garden, exactly where Ivy had intended to go with Kris. It kind of embarrassed Ivy, but this wasn't a romantic meal, not in the slightest. It didn't even feel all that comfortable, and not solely because of the insults Shuri had spat at him.

"I didn't mean to take my anger out on you," Shuri said softly. "I just… I realize you have a certain opinion of Kris that I don't share. He somehow manages to bring out the worst in me, but that doesn't excuse my behavior."

For all his elaborate lessons in courtly manners, Ivy didn't know how to deal with such a situation. In the end, he followed his heart and said, "Perhaps you weren't the only one at fault. I shouldn't have presumed to interfere."

"You were merely concerned, and that's understandable."

"Well, as unpleasant as the episode was, it did get us to share this lunch. So in the end, it might not be all bad."

Shuri gave him a look Ivy couldn't quite interpret. Ivy arched a brow. "What? Is there something on my face?"

"No," Shuri replied with a chuckle. "I was merely wondering what someone like you could be doing at Kris's side."

Ivy narrowed his eyes at Shuri. "I'm not sure how I should interpret that."

"Leave it for now," his companion told him. "Don't analyze it in any way. I'm lucky enough to steal His Imperial Majesty's moraistele for an afternoon. Let's enjoy this meal."

Brushing the problem under the rug would help no one, but pushing Shuri could be even more counterproductive. And so Ivy nodded. "I couldn't agree more."

As they ate, Ivy surreptitiously watched Shuri, wondering what to make of this strange change of heart. At one point, Shuri caught him looking and much to Ivy's surprise, grinned at him. "Don't look so surprised. I may not trust His Imperial Majesty, but I have to admit that this time around he was right, and I was wrong." He lifted his glass and added, "To new friendships."

Ivy's bemused apprehension melted into joy. "To new friendships," he echoed.

Throughout the meal, Ivy found himself relaxing in Shuri's company. They didn't approach more delicate topics, but it still seemed like they'd made progress. By the time the lunch ended, Ivy thought he had a better, if not perfect, understanding of Shuri.

Of course, that didn't mean he wasn't surprised when, just before his departure, Shuri smiled with striking warmth. "I look forward to seeing you again soon, Your Lordship. You've given me a great deal to think about."

"I'm glad," Ivy replied, "and I look forward to our next meeting."

Shuri's smile melted into a more sedate expression. "Just.... I... Remember you don't have to listen to Kris all the time. You're better than that."

Ivy didn't know what to make of those words, so he just nodded. "I will remember."

That evening, Kris didn't come to have dinner with him. He arrived at midnight and fell upon Ivy like a starving man would upon a feast. Ivy welcomed Kris's passion, but later, when they cuddled in each other's embrace, a thought drifted into his mind unbidden. Was he truly settling down in the comfort of obeying Kris to the letter? Hadn't he told himself he would do more for Kris? He'd promised Kris and Katara he'd look into learning more about his powers, but so far, he hadn't done anything of the sort.

Kris hugged his waist and kissed his nape. "What are you thinking so hard about?" he asked sleepily.

Ivy turned in his lover's embrace and brushed his lips over Kris's. "Nothing. Just get some rest. It's late."

Kris's eyes drifted closed, and it occurred to Ivy that he might have dismissed Kris's concerns just like his lover had done to him earlier. He pushed the thought aside with a silent scoff. Kris didn't need more worries. Ivy would do his best to train and become a true support for Kris. And until he succeeded in his task, until he was strong enough to share Kris's burdens, it would all have to be his little secret.

CHAPTER EIGHT
CONFLICT

One month later

IVY WALKED through the courtyard of the palace, his head held high, his back straight. He caught the eye of the occasional courtier he knew and nodded in acknowledgment when they greeted him. It was nigh unbelievable that he'd grown so used to living in Nikaret and that the people here were used to him too, but it couldn't be denied.

Under different circumstances, Ivy would have even stopped to talk to some of the Nikari he knew, although now, he didn't do so. He had a particular destination in mind, one that couldn't wait.

In the past weeks, he'd learned some basic facts remained the same no matter what nation Ivy dealt with. Proof in point, the most important thing about accessing a location he shouldn't be allowed in was hiding in plain sight. If one could look self-assured and pretend he actually had permission to be in a particular place, success was almost guaranteed.

Of course, he could argue that he wasn't entirely breaking the rules by coming to the nightwolf dens, since his friend always welcomed his visits. Indeed, the first time he'd attempted this, Ivy hadn't felt quite so certain of his course of action, but he shouldn't have worried at all.

The moment he stepped beyond the guards and into the den area, he caught sight of Attcha lying on the ground, already waiting for him. They'd settled into a sort of schedule, and whenever Kris was busy with his Morai duties—which was pretty often—Ivy visited the nightwolf. He still had lessons with Katara, but for some reason, after that conversation the evening of his claiming, things between them had grown awkward.

And so Ivy had turned to Attcha, and the nightwolf had welcomed him. Even if Ivy couldn't open the barrier of the den—apparently only Kris could do that—Ivy treasured the time he spent with the large creature, more so since Attcha proved quite helpful with regard to Ivy's self-imposed lessons on divination.

Today was no different. *Hello, Attcha,* he greeted the nightwolf through his new mental communication skills.

Attcha padded to the edge of the barrier and released a welcoming woof. *Soft one. Here. Come.*

It never failed to amuse Ivy that Attcha called him "soft one," and it always exhilarated him to hear Attcha's voice in his mind. Unfortunately, he had to shake his head at Attcha's plea. *You know I can't. The barrier won't let me.*

Attcha grumbled in dissatisfaction, but he seemed prepared for the response. His large ears slumped comically. Ivy had never thought such a large, dangerous creature could look cute, but somehow Attcha managed, especially when he gave Ivy a wide-eyed, pleading look.

Snickering, Ivy sneaked his hand past the barrier and pet Attcha's head. *Kris was right. I'm spoiling you.*

He didn't mind, though, especially since it had helped him and Attcha bond so much. Even now, Attcha almost seemed to read his thoughts. *Train?* the nightwolf asked. *See?*

Ivy nodded. *We should go a little further today.*

Attcha growled lightly. *Not safe. Hurt soft one.*

It's all right, Ivy reassured the nightwolf. *I'm not as soft as I look.*

Ivy suspected that if Attcha could have frowned, he would have done so and quite fiercely indeed. *Not very far,* Attcha agreed at last. *Soft one pack. Black fur keep safe.*

Ivy understood and respected Attcha's decision. In the end, Attcha was right. If he pushed himself too far, it could be detrimental to his abilities. Not to mention that he couldn't imagine how angry Kris would be if he found out. So far, Ivy had managed to keep it from him, although, to be fair, Ivy couldn't imagine Kris hadn't been informed about his visits. Stealthy as Ivy might try to be, he was still the moraistele. Kris hadn't addressed it, but often times Ivy noticed the guards watching him. Likely, even if the barrier had opened, they wouldn't have allowed him to go into Attcha's den.

But Ivy wouldn't think about that now. He plopped down on the ground, making himself as comfortable as possible. Meanwhile, Attcha retreated into the cave that served as a hiding place for the dimensional rift.

Ivy closed his eyes and reached out to that part of him he'd inherited from his sire, the magic he used for divination. The purpose of this exercise was fixing himself on Attcha's presence while the nightwolf traveled through the rift. It wasn't easy, and the first time Ivy had done it, he'd only been able to endure the mental strain for a few seconds. Now, he'd gotten much better at it, and with every day that passed, he became more and more skilled in the arts of divination.

He both saw and felt the moment Attcha stepped into the rift. A piercing pulse of agony stabbed into Ivy's skull. Ivy took a deep breath, taming the pain, wrapping his energy around it, using it as a guideline. He continued to track Attcha as the nightwolf expertly navigated through the rift.

It was very different from what Ivy experienced when he used rifts with Kris. Nightwolves were interdimensional beings, so Attcha could exist within the rift for as long as he wanted without feeling any strain. Knowing Attcha so well steadied Ivy in spite of the chaotic impulses the rift fed into his mind's eye.

And then Ivy saw a bright light up ahead and felt like he was on the edge of something momentous. But he didn't get the chance to identify the strange glow. Attcha reeled away from the light and shot back out of the rift at a dizzying speed.

At first, Ivy didn't realize what had happened, but he released his mental hold on Attcha's presence. When he came to, his head was spinning and his heart racing, so he didn't realize someone was standing behind him until a familiar voice asked, "Are you all right?"

"Fine," Ivy lied. "I was just resting my eyes."

He gave himself a few moments to draw his breath, then struggled to his feet. Even if he realized he probably wasn't very convincing, he felt fairly certain his unexpected companion couldn't figure out what he'd been doing. "Greetings," he told Shuri. "I didn't know you were in Nikaret, Your Highness."

"I'm here on formal business," Shuri replied. "You know that since His Majesty made me governor, I've been assigned to periodically report the situation in Tarkquin to him. But in any case, it is, as always, very nice to see you."

Ivy smiled. Throughout the past weeks, he'd forged a tentative friendship with Shuri. They weren't exactly close, but Ivy liked Shuri, and he hoped that one day Shuri and Kris would be able to build a real relationship with each other.

Attcha, on the other hand, displayed no such optimism. As Shuri spoke, Attcha emerged from the cave and padded to their side. Ivy buried his fingers in Attcha's fur, half to steady himself and half to keep Attcha's anger in check. Shuri's eyes instantly went to their point of contact. "You're very brave to be here and touch Attcha, especially when you're on your own," he commented.

"Brave?" Ivy repeated. "What do you mean?"

"I told you once before," Shuri said. "Nightwolves are dangerous."

Ivy didn't know whether to be disappointed by the reply or not. "I'm not afraid of Attcha. He wouldn't hurt me."

Shuri scoffed. "Are you absolutely sure of that? Would you stake your life on it?"

Beyond the barrier, Attcha growled. Ivy continued to pet the beast, undeterred. "I don't know what you're getting at, but Attcha is my friend. I trust him."

Shuri stared at him like he couldn't believe what Ivy was saying. "Do you know how my father died, Lord Behnivyr?"

The apparent non sequitur took Ivy by surprise. From what Ivy had been told, Shuri very rarely acknowledged the fraternal bond between him and Kris and talked about their father even less. Yes, he and Shuri had become friends in past weeks, but Ivy was still nowhere near close to truly understanding Shuri.

Not knowing how to answer, Ivy stayed silent. But Shuri seemed intent on going through with whatever he had in mind. "My father. The previous Morai. I know you're aware that I'm your lover's half brother. He can't have kept it from you, so you needn't worry about saying something that will break his confidence."

Finally, Ivy found his voice. "I admit you've taken me by surprise. I didn't expect you to bring that matter up, especially not here."

"It's important." Shuri peered closer at Ivy's face, and yet again, Ivy couldn't help but notice how alike yet how very different Shuri and Kris were. "I was honest that day, when I told you I wouldn't want you to get hurt."

"And I am thankful for your concern," Ivy said, "but—"

"Please, let me finish," Shuri said, his voice lowering into a near whisper. "I'm sure you're aware that the previous Morai conceived me with Uncle Phura's wife, Yoroshi. Well, you can imagine that his indiscretion made for very unpleasant family dynamics. In the last year of his life, my father attempted to include me more in empire-related dealings.

"That day, we were all out hunting—my mother and I on regular mounts, Kris, his mother, and our father on their nightwolves. I wanted a nightwolf of my own, but I was too young to venture into summoning rifts." Shuri smiled bitterly. "I can still remember the tension, the anger between us. Pushing my mother and Kris's together wasn't the best decision my father made. In any case, it didn't matter, not in the long run, because none of us could do anything when it happened."

Ivy couldn't help it. "What?" he asked. "What happened?"

"My father's nightwolf suddenly went crazy. It threw him off and lunged at him, just like that. We were all so shocked, and the creature moved so impossibly fast... I don't think I'm ever going to forget it." He cleared his throat, as if trying to dispel the unpleasant memory. "Kris snapped out of it first, but by the time he sent a spell at the beast, it had already ripped off two of my father's limbs. And even Kris's magic couldn't take it out. It kept going. In the end, it was your friend Attcha who kept it in check while we tried to help my father. Suffice to say, it didn't work. Not even Nikari can recover from some injuries. He died right there, in Katara's arms."

"I…. That's horrible," Ivy said. He hadn't known Kris's father, but Shuri's words were raw enough to create a vivid image in his mind.

"Indeed," Shuri said. "The beast died, or at least, so Kris claims. I never saw it again because Attcha pushed it into a dimensional rift. You can ask your friend if you don't believe me."

Ivy was tempted, but he didn't want to reveal the extent of his connection with Attcha to Shuri. Tightening his hold on Attcha's fur, he said, "I can't talk to him like that. Only Kris can do it."

He hated the lie, especially since Shuri had trusted him with his own private affairs. In fact, he might have taken it back had he not treasured his connection to Attcha so much.

For his part, Shuri scoffed. "Convenient. In any case, I knew then how dangerous nightwolves were, but Kris refused to ban summonings. He called the whole thing a freak accident. He did institute additional safety measures in the dens, like these barriers you see here. But I don't think it's enough."

"Thank you for telling me," Ivy whispered. "I… I admit it doesn't make much sense to me, but I'm sure Kris had his reasons for what he did."

"I don't know what you see in Kris that's so important to you that you would risk your life." Much to Ivy's surprise, Shuri cupped his cheek gently. "I am honor bound to him, so I couldn't do anything about it even if I did attempt to free you from him. So just be careful."

Ivy's eyes widened. He couldn't believe what Shuri was saying and doing. Shuri's touch froze him in place, because he simply couldn't make any sense of the Nikari's actions. Shuri might have been nice to him, but he'd never touched Ivy or hinted at anything like he seemed to be suggesting now.

Attcha growled, sounding so furious that Ivy could easily imagine him tearing Shuri's hand off. In the end, the nightwolf didn't have to intervene because Kris did it in his stead. He appeared out of nowhere, not even bothering to use the den rift but emerging behind Shuri. "I would take my hand off him if I were you," he said threateningly.

Shuri complied, although he did so slowly, his fingers lingering over Ivy's cheek for a little longer than was appropriate. "Not to worry, Your Majesty. I have no intention of poaching on your territory."

Kris didn't even deign Shuri with a glance. "Wait for me in the throne room, Shuri," he ordered.

His tone was enough to make even Ivy wince. Shuri made no further comment and saluted. He threw one last look toward Ivy, which Ivy couldn't quite interpret, then walked away, leaving Ivy and Kris alone in front of Attcha's den.

"I…. Nothing happened between us," Ivy told Kris, realizing how pathetic the words sounded but unable to help himself. Why did he feel so embarrassed when, in terms of sensuality, Shuri's touch had been insignificant? Kris had done much more within minutes of their first meeting.

It felt different because Shuri was not Kris. Thankfully, Kris didn't seem mad at him. "I know," Kris said. "I realize you'd never betray me like that. It's Shuri who seems intent on breaking his word to me."

The last thing Ivy wanted was for the rift between the brothers to widen because of him. "We merely spoke. He was worried that…. Well, that I was endangering myself by coming to visit Attcha."

"As if I would have ever allowed you to be in his proximity if he'd been a risk to you." Kris snorted, but then his expression sobered. "I take it he told you about my father."

Ivy nodded, and Kris wrapped his arms around him. "I didn't want to bring it up. It's such a painful story, and not solely for me, but also for my mother and even for Attcha." He kissed Ivy's temple and broke the embrace, likely because of the guards who were still watching. "I can't imagine it was pleasant for you to hear."

"It was quite upsetting, yes. But it did answer some questions— like why your brother never got a nightwolf."

"Quite," Kris said. "For my uncle, it simply didn't happen, but I think Shuri could have gotten one if he'd wanted to. But after my father's death…. Well, suffice to say that to this day, he doesn't use rifts much." His distant expression melted into a scowl. "But that doesn't give him the right to try to turn you against me and even less, to touch you. Oh, and for the record, I did know you were visiting Attcha, although he refuses to tell me the reason. It seems you've managed to earn his loyalty."

Ivy heard the question in Kris's words, and he knew he couldn't hide the truth for much longer. "Attcha's been helping me train in divination," he admitted.

Kris shot him a narrow-eyed look. "I won't ever be the one to belittle a nightwolf's talents, but I'm pretty sure they don't extend to divination."

"He's acting as my moving target, of sorts," Ivy said. "I've been tracking him when he goes through the rift."

Silence. Kris just stared at him, unblinking. Ivy braced himself for the unavoidable explosion, but he still reeled a little when it came. "Are you mad?" Kris snarled. "Seeing the inside of a rift can tear apart your mind. What were you thinking?"

"I was never in any danger," Ivy argued. "Attcha anchored me."

"Ah, yes, my beloved nightwolf. It seems I might have had more faith in his rational abilities than was warranted."

"Kris," Ivy tried to say, "I—"

"Don't, just don't," Kris interrupted him. "I'll talk to you later. I need time to cool my head. Wait here."

Turning on his heel, Kris stalked away. Ivy watched him go, hating himself for not coming clean sooner. Now he'd only made Kris angry, with him and with the nightwolf.

I'm sorry, Attcha, he told the nightwolf. *I got you in trouble with Kris.*

Attcha released a small whine and nudged Ivy's palm with his large muzzle. *Strong one mad. Yes. But soft one need help. Black fur help.*

The nightwolf's kindness reminded Ivy of Shuri's words. *Attcha, was it true? What Shuri said?*

Kris had confirmed it, but Ivy wanted to hear a different perspective. Kris tended to be overprotective of him, as evidenced by his outburst. Attcha, on the other hand, would likely tell him about it.

Attcha eyed him with sharp, gold eyes. *Not lie, but not truth,* he said.

Ivy hadn't expected that response. *What do you mean? The previous Morai wasn't killed by his nightwolf?*

Nightwolf no hurt pack. Never. Brown fur black fur friend. Brown fur dead.

Brown fur? That was probably the previous Morai's nightwolf. Shuri had told him the beast had been killed, but somehow Attcha made it sound different. *I don't understand. The Morai's nightwolf was your friend?*

Yes. Friend. But brown fur realize. See weak one fall. Die.

It was a little hard to reconcile the terms Attcha used to the people Ivy knew, but he took his best guess. *Weak one? That's Kris's father? The Morai?*

Yes. Strong one father. Weak. No keep promise. Attcha growled. *Nightwolf always keep promise.*

Ivy petted Attcha's fur, trying to get the conversation back on track. Seeing Attcha's loyalty began to unravel the threads of confusion in his mind. *Your friend died because he killed Kris's father?*

Yes. Brown fur mourn. Die. But brown fur not to blame. Lying one.

Lying one? Who was lying one? *Is that Shuri? Are you talking about Shuri?*

That didn't feel right, even with all the resentment Shuri had displayed toward his family. So Ivy felt relieved when Attcha replied, *No. Lying one hurt one mother.*

Ivy was becoming quite adept at understanding Attcha's speech, so he figured out what Attcha meant. Hurt one. That fit Shuri perfectly, and it made the lying one Shuri's dead mother. *Shuri's mother was to blame? Why? Did she poison your friend somehow?*

Yes. Brown fur fooled. But lying one kill. Not brown fur. Attcha nuzzled Ivy's cheek. *Soft one believe black fur? Nightwolf never harm pack. Black fur never hurt soft one. Believe.*

Ivy's heart clenched at the surprising show of vulnerability. *Oh, Attcha. Of course I believe you.* It was strange how much Attcha reminded Ivy of Kris. Nightwolves truly did follow the call of the Nikari's soul.

Did you tell Kris about this? he asked.

Yes. Strong one know. Strong one believe. Black fur want revenge for brown fur. But lying one die.

Ivy knew he probably shouldn't prod further. Kris had practically told him as much. But something kept him from letting the issue go.

How did she die, Attcha? Do you know?

Attcha didn't reply, and just like that, Ivy knew it was unwise of him to use divination when it came to the imperial family. There were secrets buried here, dangerous secrets. What would Ivy do now that he'd gotten a glimpse of them?

It also occurred to Ivy that Kris had been gone a long time. Kris had told him to stay here, but he must have gone to meet up with Shuri. Ivy couldn't just wait while Kris and Shuri argued. He needed to do something about it, to explain.

I won't ask any more questions, Attcha. But can you help get me to the throne room quickly?

Attcha released a disapproving huff. *Strong one talk hurt one. But strong one mad. Need stay here.*

That didn't seem very reassuring. Attcha probably had a point, and Ivy might be making things worse if he went after Kris. But it just wasn't in his nature to sit around, twiddling his thumbs. If Attcha wouldn't help him, he'd just walk and hope for the best.

WHEN KRIS stalked into the throne room, the first thing he did was to send everyone away. "Leave us," he ordered, "and don't disturb us unless Nikaret is on fire."

The soldiers scattered in the face of his anger, and the large doors closed with a satisfying bang.

Shuri didn't even blink at the display. He just stood there, his arms crossed over his chest, his spine ramrod straight. "You do realize this is entirely unnecessary. There's nothing between me and Ivy, and—"

Hearing the shortened form of Ivy's name on Shuri's lips made Kris see red. He shot forward and picked his brother up, lifting him by the shirt and effortlessly holding him aloft. "For you, his name is Behnivyr," he said, cutting the other Nikari off. "And you're quite right. There isn't anything between the two of you, and there never will be."

To his credit, Shuri didn't seem too taken aback by Kris's loss of temper. "Even if I wasn't honor bound to you, it's you he wants, not me. Or are you worried that he'll see he has options, even after you took his innocence?"

Anger reared inside Kris, hot and bright. He tossed Shuri aside with all his might, but frustratingly, Shuri flipped in midair and landed on his feet. Kris took a deep breath and forced himself to gather a measure of control. "You don't know anything about Ivy and me."

"Perhaps," Shuri replied, watching him with shrewd but careful eyes. "But I seem to have hit a nerve."

And he had. That was one of Kris's greatest uncertainties. He'd known exactly what he was doing when he'd taken Ivy's virginity, and he'd gone through with it anyway because he'd wanted Ivy for himself. Ivy loved him and accepted him, so why did it matter? It shouldn't matter. But it did.

"What are you afraid of, brother?" Shuri continued, pursuing his advantage. "That he'll see you're not as selfless and welcoming as you make it seem? That he's in love with a lie?"

"Shuri, you're crossing the line," Kris said between gritted teeth.

"I'm not telling you anything you don't already know, brother," Shuri commented idly. "In the end, the truth is I'm not the one you should fear with regard to your relationship with Ivy. It's you. You know you're not good enough for him. Creator, you can't protect him from your own nightwolf."

Normally, Shuri's insistence concerning the dangers of Attcha's nature would have toned down Kris's temper because he knew his brother was mistaken. Now the comment reminded him of the strongest reason behind his anger.

No doubt about it, he'd been furious when he'd seen Shuri touch Ivy, but what had him out of control was fear. For the past weeks, Ivy had gone through brutal mental training, and he'd managed to keep it from Kris. Attcha hadn't told him about it either. It was too easy to imagine the two of them going too far and Ivy losing his mind within the chaotic power of the rift.

"Mind your own business, Shuri," he told his brother. "Ivy is mine. I'm perfectly capable of taking care of him."

The lie tasted bitter on his tongue, and Shuri sneered. "Our father was just as trusting with nightwolves. We both remember how that turned out. When I saw him there, sitting next to the den, the only thing I could think of was the way he'd look in the jaws of a nightwolf."

Kris couldn't resent his brother for his concern, since he was partially responsible for Shuri's enduring hatred of nightwolves. Even if he'd known Shuri's mother, Yoroshi, had been guilty of murdering their father, he'd kept her secret. One of the reasons had been his wish to keep his brother out of the whole matter.

The words were waiting on his lips now, sharper than any darach, ready to mortally injure Shuri. He might have actually uttered them, but a knock sounded at the large doors. "What is it? I asked not to be disturbed."

A Nikari guard slipped inside, bowing so lowly Kris didn't know how he didn't fall over. "Your Imperial Majesty, I apologize for the interruption, but your moraistele insists on seeing you. He says it's very urgent."

Kris scowled. "See him in," he ordered sharply.

The guard scuttled out of the throne room, allowing Ivy inside. Ivy bowed as well, kneeling in front of Kris like he usually did on a formal occasion.

As a rule, the position aroused Kris. Now it just seemed alienating, reminding him of Shuri's words. Pushing aside the thoughts, he said, "I told you to wait for me at the dens."

In spite of Kris's biting tone, Ivy took the phrase as his cue to get up. "Yes," he said softly, meeting Kris's eyes, "but I was worried. You were so angry. I wanted to apologize. I should have told you about what I was doing."

Ivy's emerald eyes begged for Kris to understand, and Kris was one step away from throwing all caution to the wind and just dismissing the entire matter. But Ivy still didn't regret going through with those ridiculous lessons. He just regretted getting caught. "You should have never done any of it in the first place. I don't know what Attcha was thinking to allow it, no, to encourage it."

He remained more than aware of Shuri standing there watching them, his brother's presence conspicuous in spite of his silence. Still, he couldn't let this mistake slide. "Ivy, what you did was very dangerous. Rifts are not something you can play with."

"I know," Ivy argued. "I never went too far, and Attcha helped me throughout it."

Shuri made a choked noise. "You went into a dimensional rift? Without Kris?"

Kris didn't even allow Ivy to reply. "That might well be, but even with Attcha there, it was too risky. Listen closely, Ivy, because I'll only say this once. I forbid you from doing such a thing ever again. Starting today, I'll give the den guards specific instructions. You are not allowed to see Attcha unless you're with my mother or me."

Ivy's eyes widened. "But... Attcha is my friend. You can't do this."

This was familiar territory. Ivy's parents had said something similar the night of the ball. "I can. You're my moraistele, Ivy. You belong to me. You have to do what I say."

Ivy's breath caught. For a few seconds, he didn't say anything. He just stared at Kris, his deep green eyes practically begging for Kris to say something else. And Kris wanted to do it because he knew how horrible and dismissive his words had sounded, and Ivy was so much more to him than just his concubine. But his anger made him hesitate, and he lost his chance.

Ivy clenched his teeth and exhaled deeply, very deliberately. "I understand, Your Majesty," he said. "I won't go see your nightwolf again." He paused, and for a few moments, Kris thought that would be that. But then, Ivy spoke again. "Perhaps I was mistaken. Perhaps your mother was right all along, and I don't know you as well as I thought. Who are you really?"

A single tear trickled down Ivy's cheek, and then Ivy turned away. Kris opened his mouth to say something, anything, but Ivy had already run out. Kris was left standing there, reeling from Ivy's final words, feeling like the floor had just been pulled out from under him.

The sound of clapping hands snapped him out his trance. He turned toward Shuri, only to find the other Nikari arching a brow at him in sarcasm. "Well done, brother. That went well. I didn't expect you to confirm my words quite so soon."

Kris ached to punch Shuri, but he held back. He had to admit he'd messed up. Even if Ivy had been rash in his actions, dismissing his identity and will had been cruel and disrespectful of what they shared.

He was trying to figure out a way to apologize to Ivy when a guard hesitantly entered the throne room through the still open door.

"Your Imperial Majesty, there's a message for you."

Creator. If anything that demanded his attention had happened, Kris was liable to just say "fuck it" and focus on his own personal life for once.

He took the letter the guard offered him and noticed in surprise that the seal bore the mark of the empire's borderlands region, the coastal province of Darach. So called because the shape of the province resembled the traditional Nikari weapon, Darach had always been one of the least problematic regions. Originally it hadn't even formed an actual country like Anderra or Tarkquin, so there was no nationalistic sentiment. People in the coastal towns were among the most loyal to the empire.

Disturbed, Kris opened the letter and scanned its contents. After the first few phrases, he cursed the timing of the one land that still dared to stand against them. "What is it?" Shuri inquired. "What's wrong?"

"Nothing," Kris replied. "Just the Aranken king stretching his muscles. I have to handle this, Shuri. Don't you even dare approach Ivy in my absence, or you'll truly learn the meaning of my wrath."

Shuri didn't answer. He just nodded, obviously realizing that, under the circumstances, further opposition or sarcasm would be a bad idea. In the end, Shuri, like most Nikari, knew that a threat from A'rankin couldn't be taken lightly.

Kris's ancestors had fought hard for their independence from their native land. A thousand years ago, when their species had been in its incipience, the first Fezenda had chosen what was now Nikaret as the haven for a group of escaping Aranken citizens. After selective breeding with the local populace—the Ndara—the Nikari had emerged as a race.

And now the Aranken seemed to be trying to gain control of Kris's people. It wasn't the first time the Nikari received communications from the Eastern Realm. What made it more suspicious was the fact that this time, the Aranken had tried to contact the governor of Darach behind Kris's back.

Kris wouldn't allow anyone, and especially not the Aranken king, to disrespect them and the history of his dynasty. As much as he wanted to go to Ivy, their reconciliation would have to wait.

CHAPTER NINE
DECEPTION

THE MORNING after his argument with Kris, Ivy woke up feeling strangely lightheaded. He thought he must have dreamed something during the night, but if he had, he couldn't remember it.

He combed his hair absently, all the while staring at Kris's side of the bed, where his lover usually slept. Kris hadn't come to see him the night before. He hadn't even been at dinner.

This was the first time they'd argued, and Ivy wished he'd done things differently. He would have regretted his words, but then he remembered Kris's, and his hold on his hairbrush tightened.

The role of moraistele had felt like a humiliating brand. He wanted to believe Kris had only said such things because he'd been angry, but he needed to clarify the situation with his lover.

Ivy might belong to Kris, but he had his own will, his own heart and goals. He wasn't a thing. If Kris didn't understand that… Sweet Reysen, Ivy didn't even want to consider it.

He picked an outfit from his wardrobe and dressed quickly, paying close attention to looking perfect this morning. He didn't want to further feed the unavoidable rumors at court. His fingers lingered for a few moments on the nightwolf hairpin he'd always been so proud of. The lines of the beautiful jewel seemed to burn him now. Nevertheless, he forced himself to bind his hair back, accepting his role for another day.

He felt tempted to leave the nightwolf cloak behind, but that would just be spiteful and foolish, and Ivy still hoped he could reconcile with Kris. It was merely an argument. All couples had arguments, and most came out of them just fine.

Ivy forced himself to find encouragement in that thought and wrapped the cloak around his shoulders. As he left his quarters, he debated heading down to the dining room where everyone usually ate, but decided against it. Knowing Kris, the Nikari might have had breakfast early and was already starting on his daily tasks.

It would be easy enough to find out. As always, there were guards posted outside Kris's door, and Ivy headed their way. The Nikari saluted when they saw him approach. Ivy smiled at them. "Excuse me, have you seen His Majesty?"

The guards shared a look, and instantly Ivy knew he wouldn't like what he was about to hear. "What is it?" he asked.

One of the Nikari cleared his throat awkwardly. "His Majesty left late yesterday. As far as I know, there were some problems that required his attention."

Ivy deflated. He'd hoped that he could speak with Kris today, but apparently that wouldn't be possible, at least not yet. It also embarrassed and saddened him that Kris hadn't let him know about his departure. The guards wouldn't even tell him where Kris had gone. Did Kris not care about Ivy's feelings?

Before Ivy could well and truly fall into depression, a harried-looking servant appeared in the corridor. He stopped in front of Ivy and bowed. "Your Lordship, we've just received a message for you," the servant said, offering Ivy an envelope.

Ivy practically snatched the piece of paper from the servant's grip. All he could think about was that Kris had decided to leave him a message after all. He only realized how stupid that thought had been when he saw the handwriting. The letter was from his sire—as the seal on it should have indicated if he'd been paying attention.

> *My dear son,*
>
> *We arrived in Nikaret late last night. We planned to surprise you at the palace, but apparently, it's nigh impossible to get an audience with you without prior notification. In any case, we'd like to see you at your convenience. We currently reside in downtown Nikaret, next to the Imperial Academy.*

The message went on to give detailed instructions on how to reach the lodgings in question. It didn't say much else, but then that didn't surprise Ivy. If his sire wanted to tell him anything specifically, he would say it when they could be together in private.

Perhaps it wouldn't hurt to see a familiar face. Besides, the neutral tone of the message revealed very little. For all he knew, something might have happened to his parents that required his immediate attention. Ivy's heart told him they were safe, but he'd been wrong before.

"Thank you," he told the servant. Turning toward the guards, he added, "Should His Majesty return, notify him that I received an urgent communication from my parents. I will come back as soon as possible."

One of the guards opened his mouth, perhaps intending to prevent Ivy from departing. Ivy didn't wait for the Nikari to act. He just turned on his heel and took his leave, heading toward the palace exit. He didn't even bother to stop by the dining room to have breakfast. If his actions stirred additional rumors, well, so be it. At the very least, his parents would provide a much needed distraction.

The stable boys prepared him a carriage without too much fuss, and Ivy slid inside. He leaned against the padded cushions, his mind divided between his argument with Kris and his parents' reasons to come to see him.

As the carriage started to move, Ivy realized that in all the time he'd spent in Nikaret, he hadn't seen much of the city. When he'd first arrived here, he'd been distracted by the impending ball, and after that, he'd tried to improve his skills. It was the only thing he knew, the only thing he'd ever done when he'd been in Seanda. He'd gone out very little and had sort of accepted it as natural.

Even now, as Ivy left the palace, Nikari mounted on large nightwolves trailed his carriage. While Ivy understood their presence, he couldn't help but be uncomfortable. Had he simply exchanged one cage for another? Yes, his bond with Kris made him happy, but he could be so much more than this. He would not give up his lessons in divination, but neither would he hide behind the walls of the palace.

Reassured by his resolve, Ivy watched the display of color and life that was the capital of the Nikari. The homes were built in the precise and minimalistic yet elegant style Ivy recognized from the palace. Businesses drew the eye with brighter colors and clear signs. In the distance loomed the fabled Imperial Academy where all the nobles in the empire trained. Ivy had heard a lot of stories about it from his sire and had caught glimpses of it during his previous visits. Could it be the reason his parents were in Nikaret?

It seemed like he'd finally get the answers to his questions. The carriage stopped in front of a medium-sized townhome done in tones of blue and black, the colors of the Academy. Torn between anxiety and anticipation, Ivy descended from the vehicle.

Almost at once, the door of the townhome opened, revealing his father standing in the doorway. Ivy acknowledged his father's presence with a polite Andari bow. "Greetings, Father."

The older Andari ushered him into the house. "Greetings, Behnivyr."

As Ivy stepped inside, his sire came down the winding staircase of the building. "Behnivyr! We didn't expect you to come quite so early. You look a little pale."

Ivy forced a smile and busied himself with removing his cloak. "I assure you I'm quite all right."

Predictably, his sire's shrewd eyes saw right through him. "Something's wrong. What did the Morai do?"

Ivy sighed, resigning himself to having to answer. "We merely had an argument yesterday. It's nothing. He's away now, but I'm sure that when he returns, we'll set everything in order."

He expected his parents would take advantage of the occasion to point out Ivy's previous insistence regarding Kris's qualities. He didn't think he could withstand a session of "I told you so," and took the initiative. "What brings you to Nikaret?" His father took his arm and guided him toward the back garden, where a table had already been lain for breakfast. "You, of course," he answered in the matter-of-fact tone Ivy recognized from many an argument.

Ivy blinked, taken aback by the statement. As they all sat down, his sire elaborated on his father's words. "It occurred to me that you might be feeling a little culture shock after being thrust in a society so different from ours. I made some arrangements and managed to secure a post at the Imperial Academy."

"Sire, that's excellent news," Ivy replied with undisguised enthusiasm. "Congratulations." For all his dislike of the Nikari, his sire truly respected the Academy, and Ivy was happy for the older Andari's achievement.

In response, his sire offered him a small smile. "Thank you, Behnivyr, but you know I never would have bothered if you hadn't come to live here. You know I think we Full Bloods belong in Anderra." He waved his hand, dismissing his own words. "In any case, you have to tell us what you've been doing throughout our separation."

Even if Ivy had never been very close to his parents, seeing them here soothed him. The blow of Kris's rejection had shaken him a great deal, but just like he'd told his parents, he and Kris would clarify their problem. In the long run, it might even make them stronger.

And in the meantime, until Kris returned, perhaps he could build a stronger relationship with his parents. After all, he'd never thought they'd accept his decision to forgo the ways of his people so he could be with Kris.

Ivy reminded himself not to lose caution in his enthusiasm. They weren't exactly the most ardent supporters of the Nikari. But they were his parents, and he loved them. What could be the harm of a chat over breakfast?

As the servants brought in plates and cutlery for him, Ivy replied, "On the whole, I've been well. The A'Mora has shown me great kindness and has been giving me lessons on the mental arts. I've made friends with Kris's nightwolf."

"I remember," his father said. "The beast seemed very attached to you ever since you first moved there."

Ivy nodded, although remembering Attcha also brought a flashback of Kris's words to his mind. He hesitated and knew his parents would have noticed if not for the fact that the staff began bringing the meal in.

Among them, Ivy recognized Akolo. A wave of relief filled him, since he'd feared what his parents would do to his former manservant if they realized he and Kris had met the night of the solstice. Akolo's skills in magic were limited, and unlike other Half Bloods, he didn't have the benefit of an important bloodline to support him if he lost his employment. And knowing Ivy's sire, that was the least threatening thing he'd come up with.

"Greetings, Akolo," Ivy said to his manservant. "You look well."

"Thank you, Your Lordship." The Half Blood smiled slightly. "I must admit it's very nice to see you again. Tea?"

Ivy accepted the offer, all the while musing over how to approach the question that had been bothering him for a while now. "What happened with Marquis Torildy? Was he very angry?"

His father grimaced. "You can imagine he wasn't happy. But the Morai turned out to be very convincing, and we settled our affairs with the marquis in a mutually satisfactory agreement."

"Thank Reysen." Kris had assured him everything was in order, but it felt nice to hear it from his parents too. "I feared our people might suffer because of my choices."

"I wonder about that, sometimes," his sire commented. "Was it really your choice? Did you dislike Torildy that much? To choose the Morai in his stead.... It seems like such an extreme decision."

How could Ivy explain his train of thought without revealing too much? Just mentioning his heat would be embarrassing for all of them. The night of the solstice needed to remain a secret if they hadn't already figured it out—which seemed to be the case.

"I don't think I can really make you understand," he said at last. "You don't know him like I do. You see him as the Morai, but for me, he's more than that."

Even with what he'd told Kris the night before, he realized that at the very core of his being, he'd never stopped believing in Kris. He added cream and sugar to his tea and stirred, smiling. He was sure now that he'd make Kris understand that he'd meant well. Kris had merely lost his temper, but that happened to everyone from time to time.

He stayed for a while longer with his parents, finishing the delicious Andari breakfast. The rest of their chat revolved around small things, and while Ivy told them a few tidbits about the palace, they steered clear of any sensitive topic.

"I do hope you're happy here, Ivy," his sire said at last.

That was the first time Ivy had ever heard the older Andari say his name in its shortened form. He beamed at his sire. "Yes," he replied. "I am."

He got up from the table and enthusiastically hugged both of his parents. "The hour grows late. Thank you for coming to Nikaret."

"You don't need to thank us," his father said. "We are your parents, after all."

The two older Andari led him to the door, whereupon Akolo proceeded to help him into his cloak. "Good luck, Your Lordship," the manservant said.

Ivy thanked Akolo, already wanting very much to return to the palace. Spending the morning with his parents had been great, but now, he wanted to be by Kris's side, to kiss his lover and show Kris just how good they were together. They might have their differences, but that didn't make them incompatible. On the contrary, they complemented each other.

The trip to the palace lasted far too long, and Ivy's impatience was such that he couldn't even focus on the stern beauty of Nikaret. Finally, the carriage rolled into the courtyard. No sooner had the vehicle come to a stop than Ivy leaped out of it. He tried to reach out to Kris through telepathic communication, but while he felt Kris on the grounds, he couldn't contact the Morai.

Well, it didn't matter, because Ivy could still track Kris down. He ran past several Nikari courtiers, some of whom gave Ivy wide-eyed looks. Ivy didn't care about what they thought. The frantic need rising within him guided his steps and his actions.

He found Kris in the interior garden, staring out into the distance. Ivy rushed to his lover's side and hugged Kris's back. "I missed you," he said.

Kris tensed and turned in his embrace. "Ivy," he started to reply.

Ivy looked up at the familiar face of his lover and cupped Kris's cheek. The gesture silenced Kris. Taking advantage of the opening, Ivy added, "I'm sorry about earlier. I realize my actions must have upset you, but I want you to know something. No matter how things might seem at a certain time, I'll always love you."

Kris's hands landed on his waist, although it was unclear whether he wanted to pull Ivy close or push him away. Ivy made the decision for him and pressed their mouths together.

Kris groaned into their kiss and flipped them around, pinning Ivy against a hard marble column. Ivy wrapped his arms around Kris's neck, reveling in the feel of the other man's body against him.

As Kris thrust his tongue into Ivy's mouth, Ivy did have a moment when he wondered…. What exactly? He didn't know. This was Kris, his lover, the man who'd claimed him. They might have argued, but the two of them would always be right together.

Just as Ivy surrendered to the kiss, however, Kris's body disappeared from on top of him. Ivy gasped, confused by the sudden development. Who would have dared to separate the Morai from his concubine? He wanted to jump in to help Kris somehow, but froze when he realized the attacker was… Kris.

Ivy blinked, staring at the two men in front of him, trying to make sense of what he was seeing. The only difference between them was their clothing, at least at first. But then, the Kris Ivy had been kissing appeared to… shrink. His body grew more slender, his face morphing under Ivy's very eyes. No, it wasn't possible. Shuri.

The other Kris—which Ivy now identified as the real one—turned furious eyes toward them. "I can't believe I trusted you," he said angrily. "Here I was, musing over how to apologize, and I find you in my brother's arms. So much for your love for me."

"No," Ivy said weakly, "it's not like that. You don't understand. I…."

"I understand, all right," Kris cut him off. "I understand Shuri broke his word toward me. You know what happens to honor-bound Nikari who lie? No? Well, perhaps I should show you."

A ball of electricity appeared in Kris's hand. As Kris readied himself to throw the spell at Shuri, the other Nikari just stood there, his fists clenched, seeming to have no intention of defending himself. "Do what you will to me, Kris," he said, "but if Ivy doesn't love you, you need to let him go."

Ivy already knew the words wouldn't help, not with Kris like this. The anger and the pain were practically radiating off him in waves. Ivy had to buy some time to explain, to tell Kris it had all been a huge mistake.

He didn't even know how he did it. When Kris threw the spell at Shuri, the floor opened, and an earth golem emerged from within. Easily twice Kris's height and surpassing Attcha's considerable bulk, the mindless creature formed a barrier between Kris and Shuri. It lifted its dirt-brown hands in the exact same way Ivy did. Naturally the gesture had no real effect, and the bolt of electricity struck it instead of Shuri.

Ivy felt the power of the spell all the way to his core. He'd never been very skilled at summoning—perhaps because of his shaky relationship with his father—but he did remember that the golems weren't actually alive, just extensions of the summoner's will, a physical manifestation of his magic. His golem looked humanoid, but that was only because that shape was easiest for Ivy to understand. For that reason, when Kris hit the summoned creature, he actually hit Ivy.

And as the golem crumbled in individual, lifeless pieces of dirt, Ivy swayed, staggering at the pain that rushed over him. He leaned against the column, narrowly managing not to slide to the floor. "Don't, Kris," he tried to say. "He's your brother. You don't want to hurt him."

Kris pinned Ivy with piercing eyes gone completely gold. "Stay out of this, Ivy. He'll regret the moment he deemed it wise to touch someone he doesn't deserve."

Ivy tried to come up with an explanation, but his head was spinning, and his brain couldn't find with the right words. It didn't help that Shuri decided it was a good idea to pour fuel over the fire. "You started this, brother, not me," he said. "You're the one who doesn't deserve Ivy."

As if making a sudden decision, he faced Kris, his stance now challenging, aggressive. Flame danced over his fingers, and Ivy saw what little chance he had of clarifying the situation crumbling to dust like his golem.

Kris didn't seem inclined to further conversation anyway. Without another word, he tossed a second spell toward his brother. At the last moment, Ivy gathered his wits and put up a shield between the two men. However, the attack on his golem must have weakened him more than he'd thought. Instead of dissipating when it struck the shield, Kris's energy bolt bounced off it, and straight into Ivy.

Ivy's shield neutralized most of the magic, but the force of the blow still sent him flying back through the air. A heartbeat later, pain exploded over him and the world went black.

CHAPTER TEN
GUILT

KRIS REALIZED what he'd done a moment too late. He turned away from Shuri just in time to see Ivy hit the thick column of marble with a nauseating crack. His body slid to the floor like a puppet with its strings cut, leaving a trail of blood from the point his body had made impact with the column.

In seconds, Kris dropped to his knees by Ivy's side. There was so much blood everywhere. Kris had no real medical talents, and what knowledge of first aid he did have flew straight out of his head at the sight of the Ivy's injuries.

Distantly, he heard Shuri call for the palace medic. He could only be thankful that, at the very least, his brother had maintained a measure of calm. Then again, if Shuri had kept his hands to himself, this never would have happened.

No. He couldn't blame Shuri for this. The responsibility for Ivy's injury lay solely on Kris, Ivy's blood on his hands. If Ivy died, Kris didn't think he could live with himself.

It seemed to take forever before help showed up. Kris had never felt more powerless in his entire life, but still, when the medic manifested by his side, he lingered there, holding Ivy's far-too-cold hand. "Your Majesty, you need to move back," the medic told him carefully. "I need space to work."

With great reluctance, Kris forced himself to comply and stepped aside. The medic and his assistants gently turned Ivy around, and Kris's stomach roiled at the sight.

The back of Ivy's skull had taken the worst of the blow, his white-blond hair now crimson with blood. In a strikingly gruesome yet fitting image, the nightwolf hairpin had shattered into shards that had pierced Ivy's neck. Fortunately, he'd been wearing his nightwolf cloak, which had kept his back from suffering the same treatment. It also seemed to have protected him at least in part from the shock of the electricity bolt. However, the situation remained dire.

"I can treat this, but there's no guarantee he'll survive through Nikari medicine," the doctor said. "We need an Andari healer."

Kris could work with that. He knew how to locate the best Andari healers, one of whom had a strong incentive for Ivy to live. "I'll go," he said.

Even as he spoke, a dimensional rift opened by Kris's side, and Attcha emerged from inside.

His mental voice drifted into Kris's mind. *Soft one? Hurt?*

Kris didn't even know what to say to soothe his nightwolf's obvious pain. He himself couldn't think because of the crushing guilt and fear. *Yes, Attcha,* he replied. *He's hurt.*

Attcha growled, and the medic's assistants fidgeted, apparently uncomfortable with a nightwolf's anger. The smell of Ivy's blood permeated the air, and if it seemed almost suffocating for Kris, he could only imagine how it must be for Attcha.

It was an accident, Kris tried to tell his nightwolf. He couldn't say much more, because the thought of his role in it sickened him to the core, and there was no time for conversation anyway.

Attcha's arrival was fortunate because this way Kris could leave knowing Ivy had one trustworthy friend by his side. In spite of his behavior yesterday, Kris knew Attcha was nothing if not loyal to Ivy and would protect him to the death. *Stay with him. Let the doctors do their job, but keep an eye on Ivy.*

Attcha's big head bobbed in an almost human nod. *Protect soft one. Black fur understand.*

He didn't ask any further questions, and Kris wondered if his nightwolf realized Kris himself was the culprit behind Ivy's injury. For the moment, he couldn't worry about that. He had a healer to find.

Kris walked away from the scene, giving the medic space to care for Ivy. He summoned a rift and stepped through, directing it to the imperial treasury. The actual treasury room was warded against rifts or any kind of portal, but Kris quickly dismissed the guards and retrieved the Moris's cloak from inside. He couldn't exactly remove Ivy's, and his mother had taken hers to Darach when Kris had asked her to stay there temporarily and make sure the Aranken king didn't go through with his threats. He needed the garment to bring the Andari healer through the rift.

With the precious item in his possession, he created another portal. This time, the chaotic energies carried him much further, so far, in fact, that in Kris's less than focused mental state, he actually felt the pain.

Even so, his Nikari resilience won out, and he emerged on the other side unscathed. The moment he stepped out of the rift, he found himself surrounded by dozens of female soldiers armed to the teeth.

"Males are not allowed within the sanctum of the temple," one of them told him. "You must—"

"Shut your mouth." Kris cut her off. "I am the Morai Kristelien Fezenda, and I'm here to see Sister Anfarasha. Stand in my way, and you will suffer the consequences."

Thankfully, his forceful voice and entrance must have convinced them, as they all dropped to their knees. "We'll summon her at once," one guard said.

"Please do so," Kris said, not bothering to disguise his displeasure. "I'm not a patient man."

The woman in question shot to her feet and retreated within the premises of the temple. This particular building hosted the largest number of female nuns dedicated to the service of Reysen. One of the oldest temples in Anderra, it dated from before the Nikari had even appeared as a species. In some areas, the structure showed its age, the engravings on the walls faded with time. Even so, the courtyard of the temple inner sanctum, where Kris currently waited, boasted a myriad of colorful, well-tended flowers. Kris knew that the outer part of the building, where visitors were allowed, was just as beautiful.

But not even the marvels of the Andari temple could distract him from his urgency. Thankfully, his quarry didn't delay in making her appearance. Both she and the guard who'd gone to look for her returned to the courtyard in minutes.

Like all the other women, Anfarasha was completely bald, a sign that she'd abandoned her sexuality and her willingness to commit to any worldly relationship. Just like Ivy's hair style emphasized the fact that he belonged to Kris, Anfarasha's pointed out she'd chosen to dedicate her life to the Creator. Kris's heart clenched when her too-familiar green eyes fixed on him.

"Greetings, Your Majesty," she said. "What can I do for you?"

"I'm sure you are aware of my connection to your son," Kris replied without preamble. "Well, Ivy has suffered a serious injury, and he needs your help."

Anfarasha's face drained of all color. "Yes, of course. I'll go at once."

"Sister, you need the permission of the Holy Mother to leave the temple," one of the female guards reminded her.

"This cannot wait for formalities," Kris said between gritted teeth.

"Make my apologies to the Holy Mother," Ivy's mother said. "I will go with His Majesty."

Satisfied at the response, Kris wrapped the cloak around her shoulders. "Back away," he told the guards. "I wouldn't want any of you to get sucked into the rift."

They hastily complied, although Kris felt little pleasure at their behavior. He slashed his hand through the air and called up a rift. Taking hold of Anfarasha, he dragged her into the portal.

They emerged seconds later in the rift room in the Nikaret palace. Anfarasha was breathing hard, but, like Ivy, she'd been protected by the nightwolf cloak. Not even her face—the only thing the cloak didn't quite cover—could be harmed when the hood was on.

By some kind of miracle—or perhaps through the strength of motherly love—Anfarasha recovered very quickly. She steadied her breath, slid the cloak from her shoulders, and faced him without hesitation. "Take me to my son," she said.

Guided by his instincts, Kris led the Andari woman to the healer wing of the palace. He found Ivy's room with ease. Shuri paced outside, while several guards lingered in front of it, their faces pale.

Kris couldn't have been gone more than five minutes, but anything might have happened during that time. "How's Ivy?" he asked his brother.

"I don't know," Shuri replied. "The doctor ordered for him to be moved inside, but he seemed skeptical about Ivy's recovery. And your nightwolf isn't happy about it at all."

Kris could only imagine. He himself was hanging on to his sanity by a very thin thread—the hope that Ivy's mother could do what Kris's medics could not.

As Kris guided her to the door, Anfarasha asked, "Was Ivy attacked by the nightwolf?"

"No," Kris replied. "It was an accident." He took a deep breath, knowing he couldn't hide behind that excuse forever. "He got in the way in a fight between me and my brother."

Anfarasha's jaw tightened. "I see."

She said nothing else, but Kris could hear the barely veiled hatred. Without another word, she slid into the room. Kris followed, and his gaze instantly zeroed in on the bed, where a motionless Ivy lay, his head carefully positioned to allow him to breathe without putting strain on his injuries. His long beautiful hair had been severed to allow the doctors access to the wound. Attcha waited in the far right corner of the room, giving the medics space to work.

Anfarasha didn't acknowledge any of them, not even the nightwolf whose presence she couldn't have missed. She simply knelt at Ivy's side and took her son's hand. Kris held his breath, waiting, hoping for a miracle.

When it came, Kris almost thought he was imagining it. He'd heard a great deal about Andari healers and had even witnessed the occasional healing process in the past. But it hadn't been like this. The point of contact between the two Andari began to glow, softly at first, but brighter and brighter by the second. The medics present reeled away from the luminescent power, but Kris approached, hypnotized by its beauty. It reminded him of Ivy's warmth, of Ivy's acceptance and kindness. What had happened to bring them to this point? Why had he driven Ivy away?

He stood behind Anfarasha, careful not to approach more so that he wouldn't distract her. Under his very eyes, Anfarasha's hair started to grow, white-blond locks falling down her back. Over her shoulder, Kris studied what he could see of Ivy's face.

His lover's pallor had already been replaced by a healthier, rosy complexion, and as far as Kris could tell, the bleeding had stopped. As Kris watched, minute pieces of crystal emerged from Ivy's skin with minimal damage, and the wounds they'd left behind sealed. Like in his mother's case, his hair began to grow back, shielding the previously injured area.

At last, Anfarasha pulled away, the glow of her hands fading. She knelt next to the bed, whispering what sounded like an Andari prayer under her breath. After kissing Ivy's hand, she struggled to her feet.

She was swaying so badly that Kris reached out to steady her. However, she shied away from him like his touch repulsed her—which was probably true.

He allowed her to catch her breath, waiting for her report of Ivy's condition. Anfarasha didn't disappoint. "We were lucky," she said, flipping her hair back as if she was unaccustomed to its length. "It seems that the cloak he's wearing shielded him from the spell and the impact."

"You could tell what happened?" Kris couldn't help but ask.

Anfarasha's glacial glare could have frozen a fire nova. "Of course. I could see it quite clearly in his injuries. It seems that in the process of arguing with your sibling, you somehow managed to crush my son's skull. He must have had some sort of jewel in his hair, because bits and pieces of it embedded themselves in his spine."

Kris felt sick. "Will he…."

He trailed off, unable to finish the phrase. The Andari healer's fists tightened, and Kris suspected that if he'd been anyone else, she would have slapped him or worse. "As I was saying, it is probably just the cloak that prevented a tragedy. Without it, he could have easily suffered a serious spinal injury. Not even my powers can heal everything." She cleared her throat and shook her head, having apparently frightened herself with her own words. "In any case, I managed to remove the jewel pieces, and the spinal damage is minimal. Ivy's own healing powers should take care of any lingering problems in that regard. It's the blow to the head that's the problem."

"What do you mean?" Kris inquired, surprised his voice came out so steady.

"I have no way of knowing how it might have affected him," she said. "His injuries were quite severe, and while I managed to heal them, I can't say for certain when he will wake. Some things I'll only be able to detect at that time. For example, he might have trouble with his vision, or he may experience problems in the balance and coordination of his limbs. Memory loss is also quite common in such cases."

Kris closed his eyes, struggling between relief and sorrow. Knowing how much he'd hurt Ivy and how close he'd come to killing him burned like his own personal brand of torture. In all likelihood, Ivy's parents and even Shuri had been right all along, and he never should have claimed Ivy. With that realization came another layer of pain, but the agony was tempered by the promise of Ivy's recovery.

"But he will feel better," he said, seeking reassurance that he wasn't just fooling himself into being more optimistic than the situation warranted.

"Yes," Anfarasha replied. "It will take time, but with the right amount of rest, care, and attention, he should be able to make a complete recovery. In the meantime, Your Majesty, I'd like to request the permission to remain here for however long it takes."

"Naturally," Kris replied. "I'll have quarters readied for you—"

"No," Anfarasha interrupted him. "I'll sleep in this room. The floor is fine if need be. I have to watch over my son. I'll also require clean water and a strong meal for me. The taste is irrelevant—it just needs the maximum amount of nutrients."

"Of course. Everything can be arranged. Do you require anything else?"

"Actually, yes," Anfarasha said. "I'll need access to my herb garden in Anderra or any apothecary who might have certain herbs I need. But not right now. Perhaps tomorrow."

"If you make a list with what you need, I can send my people to procure it," Kris offered. Even if his medics didn't have healing magic, they were quite skilled in herbalism.

Anfarasha eyed the Nikari doctors with an unimpressed look. Then she stole a look at the motionless Ivy. She must have decided it wasn't worth leaving her son's side just to dig her heels in because she said, "Yes. That will be fine. Thank you, Your Majesty. It would also be for the best if we were granted some privacy."

Kris had dismissed enough people to realize when he himself was being sent away. Anfarasha didn't even try to hide the hatred in her voice. Then again, Kris couldn't blame her. He nodded wordlessly and gestured for all of his staff to exit the room. He probably should have followed, but he didn't do so. Instead, he dared to touch the silky softness of Ivy's cheek.

"I know you loathe me," he told Anfarasha, "but thank you."

"I didn't do it for you, Morai. Surely you must realize that."

Kris could tell she was glaring at him even if his gaze remained fixed on Ivy. So warm. So fragile. How easily Kris could have lost him. "Yes," he told Anfarasha. "I realize it. But that doesn't mean I'm not thankful." He paused and turned to look at the former odale. "You know, Ivy loves you a great deal. I first sought you out because he mentioned you and said he wished he could see you again."

Anfarasha released a pained noise. "And yet, you didn't tell him. Why?"

Why, indeed. Kris would have liked to say that he'd wanted to respect Ivy's wish and his fear that his mother would reject him, but at this point, he couldn't really deceive himself. It had been easy for him to track down the odale Titexe had hired, as despite the privacy laws of the guilds, no one could really deny the Morai the information he sought. Ever since he'd learned that she had joined the Sisterhood of Reysen, he'd known Ivy's fears were probably unjustified. He could have shared the knowledge with Ivy, but he'd been worried he'd lose Ivy's affection to his mother. Selfish. Undeserving of Ivy. No wonder Ivy had turned to someone else.

However, he refused to open his heart to a woman who already hated him. "My motives are of no import. I can tell you that when I first offered to track you down, he said no. He feared that, upon meeting you, you'd deny his affection."

"Why are you telling me this?" the Andari woman asked softly.

"Perhaps because I want you to care for him better than I ever did." Kris pressed a kiss to Ivy's temple. "But then, that's not very hard, is it?"

Without another word, Kris forced himself to pull away from Ivy and left the room, his nightwolf trailing sadly behind him.

"I KNEW something like this would happen," Titexe Erethe exploded the moment he stepped into the throne room. "I should have never allowed you to take him. I realized from the very beginning you would be his downfall."

By Titexe's side, Rasami Erethe gave Kris a furious look that seemed out of place on the face of the usually cold Andari. From behind them, Sai arched an inquiring brow at Kris. Kris could tell his underlings were disturbed by the show of disrespect he'd allowed, but he shook his head. *Go,* he whispered mentally. *This is a conversation I need to have with them on my own.*

Sai saluted and left the throne room. Now alone with Ivy's parents, Kris didn't delay in approaching the matter at hand. "As I wrote to you in the message, Ivy has suffered a serious injury. I won't deny my own involvement in it, although I will say that the last thing I wanted was to hurt him."

"Like we'd believe you now." Rasami laughed bitterly. "I'm sure you know he came to visit us this morning. He was upset that you'd argued, but he said that everything would work out. And I asked him if he was happy, and he told me yes." Rasami clenched his fists, and his bond mate gripped his shoulder in a show of support. "I was never a good parent. I can admit to that. But I thought that maybe I could change that. He seemed happy. In the end, what did it matter if it was the Morai who made it so? I should have known better than to trust what he said. Ivy was always too kind for his own good. I'd seen the truth. Reysen, why did I let him go back to you?"

Kris didn't know what to make of Rasami's words. He didn't trust Ivy's parents, but for once, Rasami seemed honest. Kris wanted it to not matter, because he knew Rasami would be prone to lying in anything he told Kris. Even so, the words still hurt. They reminded him too much of the way Ivy used to smile at him and the fact that he no longer deserved that expression, if he ever had.

Gritting his teeth, Kris did his best to focus on practicalities. "I contacted his mother and she is with him now."

"Anfarasha?" Titexe asked. "Thank Reysen. She healed him."

"Yes," Kris replied. "At this time, she remains in his chambers, and she requested privacy. I believe she would allow you two to see Ivy."

Both men nodded, and Kris gestured the two Andari nobles toward a side door. He guided them out of the throne room and toward the medical area.

As they walked through the corridors, Kris couldn't help but notice the expressions other Nikari threw toward him. They were all discreet and respectful, but far more sedate and frightened than usual. By now, rumor of what had happened had reached most of the palace inhabitants. Even among the Nikari, something like this couldn't be contained. Kris hadn't even tried, since he'd been more focused on making sure Ivy survived. To a certain extent, it was better this way. At least no one seemed to have figured out the reason why Kris and Shuri had argued. What was left of Ivy's reputation would be intact.

No one spoke until they reached Ivy's sick room. Kris knocked at the door and waited for a few moments. He heard shuffling inside, signaling that Anfarasha must be watchful of Ivy's condition. Indeed, seconds later, the door opened, and a frowning Anfarasha appeared in the entryway. Undoubtedly, she wasn't too happy about having Kris intrude on Ivy's space so soon.

When she saw Titexe and Rasami standing next to Kris, her frown faded into a shocked, wide-eyed look. Her breath caught, and she stared from Titexe to his bond mate like she'd seen a ghost—or two.

Kris didn't know much about Anfarasha's relationship with the two men. Ivy's mother had been, on all accounts, a regular odale. Born from the union of two members of the odale guild—like all odale, in fact—she had received her first contract from Titexe Erethe and his bond mate.

The unusual thing was that Anfarasha had stayed with her son longer than odale usually did. When she'd finally left, she'd abandoned her life in the guild and had become a member of the Sisterhood of Reysen.

The reunion between the three lovers was quite awkward, but their mutual concern for their son won out. Anfarasha spoke first. "Ivy is still unconscious," she whispered, "but I have faith he'll recover soon. Come in. You can see him."

Kris knew he wasn't welcome with Ivy's parents, so he didn't linger. As Titexe and Rasami entered Ivy's room, he said, "Let my people know if you need anything else."

Much to his surprise, Anfarasha caught his arm, keeping him from leaving. "Wait. I need a word with you, Your Majesty."

Instantly, panic stirred inside Kris. The only thing he could come up to explain Anfarasha's sudden desire for his company was a worsening of Ivy's condition. She'd said Ivy would be fine, but still…. What else could she want to discuss? His heart hammering, he nodded wordlessly and followed the three Andari into the room.

At first, no one addressed him. They completely ignored him, like he wasn't even there. It almost amused him, or would have if not for the circumstances and the causes of their behavior.

Titexe and Rasami walked to Ivy's bedside, whereupon Anfarasha explained his condition. Her words were a little more gentle and reassuring than they'd been with him, but undoubtedly, the two Andari lords realized the seriousness of Ivy's condition. Not for the first time, Kris wondered how Titexe and Rasami truly felt about their son. In the past, they'd treated him like a political tool, and the impressions Kris had gotten from Ivy hadn't convinced him to change his opinion. However, today they seemed genuinely distraught. Could it be an elaborate deception? If so, Kris couldn't see the point.

It was a long while later when Ivy's parents turned toward him. Anfarasha's eyes, so much like Ivy's, begged for an answer. "At least, tell us what happened. We deserve to know that much. He's your moraistele. Why didn't you keep him safe? Why would you hurt him?"

How could Kris explain? It was true that he'd been in a poor mood when he'd returned from Darach, but he'd hoped he could reconcile with Ivy and turn his disastrous day around. But, of course, that would never happen now. In fact, Kris's existence would forever be haunted by those horrifying moments.

His acknowledgment of his role in the near tragedy made him reluctant to confess what he'd seen. "That's between Ivy and me," he said.

"That isn't an answer," Rasami replied coolly. "Come now, Your Majesty. What are you afraid of? It's not like we can actually do anything to you."

The bitter words didn't affect Kris, and he had told Anfarasha bits and pieces of what had happened. But in truth, it didn't really matter, because they wouldn't believe him anyway. "I saw Ivy confessing his love to another man," he explained at last. "I lost it and attacked the man in question. Ivy got in the way."

Titexe gaped at him. "Are you telling me…? Am I hearing this right? You're claiming that Ivy cheated on you?"

Rasami was already shaking his head. "You're mistaken. It's not possible. Ivy threw aside everything he knew for you. If this is some sort of deception designed to justify your deeds, I won't allow it."

"Believe what you will, but I didn't bring him here to harm him." *I love him*, he wanted to say, but under the circumstances, the words would have little meaning. Besides, he hadn't even said them to Ivy and probably never would.

"Perhaps you didn't mean to," Anfarasha said, "but the fact remains that you did." She toyed with the ends of her long hair without seeming to realize it. "I will be the first to admit that I don't know my son very well. I was absent from most of his life due to my odale contract. But…. My heart tells me that he would have never agreed to come here in the first place if he'd planned on any deception." Her piercing eyes fixed him again like twin emerald flames. "Unless you forced him from the very beginning, in which case you have no right to judge, and you're even more despicable than I thought."

Kris wasn't about to go into such debates with Ivy's parents. "Your opinion matters little to me," he said. "You aren't here for me but for him. Do your job, heal him, and we won't have any problems."

He planned to leave the room and hopefully bury himself in some documents he'd be unable to read, but Anfarasha stopped him. "After all this is over, after he recovers…. Will you let him go when the time comes?"

So that was her concern. She probably feared that once Ivy felt better, Kris would usher her out, leaving Ivy still in his clutches.

Kris would have loved to have a reply ready, but he didn't. He couldn't imagine an existence without Ivy, but was it truly his choice now? If he'd ever had any right to Ivy, he'd certainly forfeited it now.

In spite of this knowledge, he didn't answer the Andari healer's question. He just walked out of Ivy's sick room, his heart breaking a little more with every step he took.

LIKE HE always did when in a bad mood, Kris turned to his nightwolf. His mother was still away, which might have been for the best since Kris couldn't imagine she'd take the news of Ivy's relationship with Shuri well. For that matter, neither would Attcha. But Attcha knew Ivy and had connected to him in a way Kris's mother never had. The nightwolf might be able to give Kris another, more neutral opinion on the topic.

As soon as he related the events, Attcha released a low growl. *Soft one not like weak one. Soft one nightwolf soul. Keep promise.*

I saw him, Attcha, Kris said, leaning against his nightwolf's big body. *He was kissing Shuri. He said he loved Shuri. I trusted him. If someone had told me about it…. But I saw it with my own eyes.*

For the longest time Attcha said nothing. He stared up at the sky, in an expression Kris recognized as Attcha's deep-in-thought look. In the other dens, other nightwolves howled and growled, as if they felt Attcha's distress.

Kris could understand his nightwolf's confusion, since he himself couldn't figure out when he and Ivy had grown apart. Creator, he'd seen Ivy's soul when he'd claimed the young Andari, and he'd found just love for him, so much love. Things like that didn't just disappear overnight.

Kris suspected his own actions must have caused Ivy to have a change of heart, much like Shuri had said. But nothing fit. It was like being faced with a puzzle and ardently trying to put the pieces together, only to find that no matter how hard he tried, the corners wouldn't slide into place.

When Attcha finally spoke, however, his words shocked Kris. *Strong one…. Black fur remember. This like brown fur and weak one.*

Like what happened to my father? Kris asked with a frown. *How? I don't understand.*

Soft one nightwolf soul. Keep promise, Attcha said again. *But lying ones deceive. Soft one kind. Not see lies.*

Slowly, Kris began to understand. Could it be? Could the story truly repeat itself? The thought left Kris reeling, his mind working furiously as he tried to figure out the answer to those questions.

To this day, Kris wasn't exactly sure what had happened back then. After his father's gruesome demise, he'd never believed Spatha's nightwolf could have lost it quite like that without any reason. He'd tracked down the true cause and the murderer, following clues given by Attcha, who'd spoken to his friend before the other nightwolf had died. The details of the conversation remained solely in Attcha's memory, as did those of the death of the beast in question, but what Attcha had shared with Kris had forced that puzzle to make sense. Alas, by the time he'd figured out where the trail ended, Shuri's mother had already died, and, for obvious reasons, Kris had found it smarter to bury the whole thing.

The downside of this was that he'd never tracked down the real reason why his father's nightwolf had run amok. Yoroshi had clearly used some kind of poison, and Attcha had confirmed it, but the Nikari had no knowledge of any substance that could affect all manner of living beings this way.

Without a doubt, though, it existed, since a nightwolf killing pack made about as much sense as Ivy cheating on Kris did. Leaving aside his own guilt and anger, Kris could see that very clearly. And if Kris had been thinking when he'd seen Ivy and Shuri together, if he'd listened to whatever Ivy had been trying to say, he might have realized it before he'd nearly killed the man he loved.

Anger swelled through him, hot and bright. The possibility of Ivy's innocence didn't change a thing when it came to Kris's guilt, but it did give him something to hate other than himself, a focus. This attack had clearly been aimed at Kris. Since his father's death, Kris had instituted a rule of checking every member of his staff through his mental skills for treasonous behavior, and while many considered the method harsh, it now eliminated potential involvement on their part—or at least made the chances of it very small.

If this was indeed the case, he told Attcha, *there are only a handful of options. The substance could have been smuggled in by palace staff without my knowledge—unlikely at best—or it could be outside interference.* Even as he spoke, he remembered his conversation with Ivy's parents. Of course. Ivy had been with them this morning. His guards had told Kris all about it upon his return from Darach.

"Ivy's parents," he said out loud, to himself or to Attcha. "Anfarasha has amazing herbalism skills. While she wouldn't have gotten involved in this, some of it must have passed on to those two. Especially Rasami. He's a notoriously fast learner."

Then again, that didn't mean anything. Nikari were also skilled in herbalism. Since they didn't have healing magic, they used potions to treat their injuries. After his father's death, Kris had looked into everything he could get his hands on without making too much of a fuss but had found no answers.

Attcha, on the other hand, seemed pretty convinced of the guilt of Ivy's parents. He snarled, his sharp fangs glinting threateningly in the dim light of the evening. *Black fur hunt. Kill lying ones.*

Kris got up and shook his head. *No,* he told his nightwolf. *I understand your anger, but we need to avoid any rash actions.*

Lying ones hurt black fur pack, Attcha said. *Black fur avenge.*

Kris buried his hand in Attcha's thick fur. *I was the one to harm Ivy, Attcha,* he whispered. *Whether he cheated on me or not is irrelevant. I almost killed him. No matter the cause, it was me, and that's unacceptable.*

Attcha whined, nudging Kris with his muzzle. *Strong one not to blame. Strong one like brown fur. Not hurt soft one.*

No, Kris had never wanted to hurt Ivy. In his heart, he'd meant to treasure and protect the Andari. But that hadn't gone over well, had it?

Kris frowned. He'd never been one to feel sorry for himself and wallow in despair, but he hadn't truly felt love before he'd met Ivy. Was that why Ivy had been targeted? The first method wouldn't have worked for Kris. Nightwolves had ridiculously good memories and tended to keep a grudge, so Attcha was extra careful and only allowed certain people to approach him. Ivy had been the exception for both of them.

Someone must have figured out what would happen if Kris saw Ivy and Shuri together. Shuri. How did he fit into all of this? What had been the goal to begin with?

Kris imagined the worst possible consequences of him having a jealous fit. It wasn't very hard, since he'd come quite close to it. *I could have killed both of them,* he said. *I was supposed to.*

Without Ivy, he would have lost his mind. Right now, the knowledge that the Andari would be all right tempered the guilt crushing Kris's soul. But if that hadn't been the case? If Kris had been forced to face Ivy's death? Yes, he'd have definitely lost it.

It was an attack against the dynasty, he told Attcha. As the nightwolf rumbled in agreement, Kris asked himself, *But who? Who did it?*

Had it truly been Ivy's parents or someone else entirely? Kris didn't know, but he planned to find out. And whoever had dared to implicate Ivy in their own private war would pay the price for their transgression.

Even as Kris made the decision, something stirred at the back of his mind. He couldn't quite put a finger on it. The touch felt distant, like a memory more than anything else, and Kris might have missed it altogether if not for the familiar glow of its source.

Attcha realized it the moment Kris did. *Soft one. Recovering.*

Kris didn't even wait to confirm that for his nightwolf. He shot to his feet and rushed into the rift that hid inside Attcha's den. Ivy was waiting.

CHAPTER ELEVEN
RIFT

WHEN IVY stirred on the bed, the first thing he became aware of was the pain. It exploded in his skull, pulsing like a living thing, making him groan in agony.

A soft hand landed on his shoulder, and instantly Ivy's pain started to fade into something more manageable. Ivy melted against the mattress, allowing the magic to do its job. When he could think without having to scream, Ivy turned, pursuing a feeling in his heart that simply wouldn't let up. His guess turned out to be correct, and he gasped as he came face-to-face with his mother. "Mother? How? Why…."

She hadn't changed in the slightest since the last time Ivy had seen her. Ivy couldn't quite recall when that had been. Still, the same feeling of warmth and affection invaded him when he saw her kind smile. "It's all right, Ivy," she said. "Don't worry about the reasons. The important thing is that I'm here with you now."

Ivy frowned, unsure what to make of the reply. "But I thought the odale contract didn't allow you to come close to me."

A brief flash of pain passed through her eyes before it quickly faded. Ivy just noticed it due to the fact that he had been watching her so closely. He didn't even get the chance to attempt to provide some reassurance because she squeezed his hand tightly. "I spoke with your father and your sire. The provisions of the contract have been temporarily dismissed."

Ivy couldn't imagine what kind of conversation would make his parents agree to a change. They'd always put so much value in tradition, as evidenced by them signing Ivy's betrothal agreement with Lord Torildy.

He couldn't help a grimace at the thought of the Andari marquis, but he quickly forced it out of his mind. Oh well. At least Ivy had his mother back. He'd worry about the marquis later.

As he looked around the room, he experienced a vague sensation of déjà-vu. The place seemed familiar but at the same time strange to him. It definitely didn't look like his home in Seanda.

What had happened? Ivy frowned, trying to remember. However, his efforts just made the headache worse, and he fell back on the bed, panting. "Shh," his mother said, her hands returning to rub his temples. "Don't strain yourself. You were in a pretty bad condition when I arrived."

"I don't recall anything," Ivy confessed. "It's.... It's a little frightening."

"Give it time," his mother advised him. "I assure you it's normal for these things to happen in head injuries, but you're already on the mend. In the meantime, I'm here to take care of you, and so are your father and your sire."

Indeed, when he looked past his mother's shoulder, Ivy caught sight of the two Andari lords standing there with uncharacteristic expressions of concern on their faces. Ivy's mother gestured for them to approach, and both of them did.

For a few moments, no one said anything. In the heavy silence, Ivy wondered yet again just how serious his injury had been to warrant such attentions. His parents weren't dismissive of his illnesses, but courtesy of his own healing magic, Ivy always recovered easily from whatever ailed him.

Titexe cleared his throat awkwardly and squeezed Ivy's shoulder. "How are you feeling, son?"

"I'm.... Well, I'm not very sure," Ivy admitted. "Mostly confused."

His sire smiled slightly, which served to add to Ivy's puzzlement. "I believe he meant how you're feeling healthwise, Ivy," he said.

Ivy. How strange. His sire had only ever called him Behnivyr. He frowned, feeling once more like he was missing something very important, something he had to remember at all costs.

Before he could figure out the answer to his dilemma, a knock sounded at the door. His parents tensed, and Ivy shot them a curious look. "Is anything wrong?"

"Not at all," his mother said, patting his hand. "Just relax. Let us worry about the rest."

Without giving Ivy further explanation, she went to get the door. She only opened it ever so slightly, but whoever was on the other side forced it wider. Ivy took advantage of this to sate his natural curiosity. He peeked past his sire and caught a glimpse of a muscular stranger.

The dusky tone of the man's skin identified him as a Nikari, a warrior judging by the braids in his midnight black hair. He towered over Ivy's mother, so even if she attempted to block his path, Ivy still managed to meet the stranger's gaze.

Gold-rimmed dark eyes fixed on him with an intensity that made Ivy's breath catch. The stranger easily dodged Ivy's mother and stepped into the room. "Ivy," the man said simply. "How are you?"

Ivy blinked in surprise. It was strange enough that his parents had even allowed a Nikari in his room, but that wasn't the only peculiar fact about the situation. Taking into account the Nikari's usage of the short form of Ivy's name, Ivy must have met him at some point, and they'd obviously become pretty close. However, for the life of him, Ivy couldn't remember the Nikari's identity.

In that moment, Ivy became aware that the heavy braid he'd used for the better part of his life seemed loose. Alarmed, he reached for his hair, only to realize it wasn't bound as usual. Somewhere at the corner of his mind, Ivy realized it was perfectly acceptable to wear his hair like this in his sick room and in front of his parents but not when a man not related to him was there.

He looked at his sire desperately, trying to convey his desire to fix the problem. For once, his sire didn't seem to understand. "Are you unwell?" he asked with a frown. "Do you need to lie down?"

Ivy was tempted to claim he felt sick, because that would remove him from the embarrassing situation. However, his mother's efforts had made the pain go away, and the lie would only make them all more worried than they already seemed.

The strange Nikari appeared just as concerned. "Ivy?" the man repeated.

Ivy couldn't stay silent forever. His parents' reactions didn't give him any cues, other than confirming the obvious fact that he had some sort of relationship with the Nikari.

A fist clenched around Ivy's heart. He didn't want to reveal his lack of recognition to the stranger. It felt... off. Perhaps he could disguise it until he got a chance to figure out the man's identity. "Yes," he said, forcing a smile. "I feel much better. I was in a little pain earlier, but my mother's power helped."

The Nikari's full lips twisted in a small smile that made him even more devastatingly handsome than he'd already been. Ivy's body heated in a way that was entirely inappropriate, and he struggled to bury the odd, confusing feeling. He tried to focus on the Nikari's words, but the stranger's voice, like velvet on steel, didn't help in the slightest.

"That's a relief," the man said. "We were all very worried about you."

He approached the bed and went around Ivy's parents, who tensed visibly. In spite of their obvious displeasure, however, they didn't do anything about the Nikari's proximity.

The stranger sat down on the edge of the bed, slowly, as if Ivy were a skittish animal he was trying not to startle. "Do you think you're well enough to talk about what happened?" he asked carefully.

"I don't remember it, I'm afraid," Ivy admitted.

Was it Ivy's impression, or did a hint of relief sweep through those far too beautiful gold-rimmed eyes? Whatever he'd seen faded away, melting into a frown. "Nothing?" the Nikari repeated inquiringly. "What about this morning? Your breakfast with your parents? Do you remember that?"

"Don't force him," his mother piped up. "He just woke up. I warned you that he was liable to experience some memory loss."

The Nikari released a heavy sigh. "You're right, of course. You have my apologies, Ivy." His hand landed on Ivy's, and Ivy froze, shocked at how familiar the touch felt.

His parents didn't seem to notice his predicament. "Perhaps we could start at what you remember without forcing yourself," his father suggested. "If your mother thinks it's all right."

After a small hesitation, Ivy's mother nodded. "Yes. It would help assess Ivy's condition." She sat on the other side of the bed and kissed his cheek. "Just relax and tell us, Ivy. The first thing you remember. Don't force it if it hurts."

Hypnotized by the warmth of the Nikari's hand on his own, Ivy complied without protest. Still looking into the stranger's eyes, he tried to figure out when he'd seen them the first time. When that memory didn't come, he sought the first memory that emerged in his mind. "I remember... I was with Akolo, the morning before the summer solstice. There was a party in Seanda that night. I wanted to go even if Father had locked up the manse." He scowled fiercely. "Did I go and something happened to me there? Is that how I was injured?"

The Nikari went pale. It was a remarkable thing to notice, especially due to the man's dark complexion, but Ivy knew he'd said something he shouldn't have. He bit the inside of his cheek so hard it bled. Damn it. He should have kept to his resolve to remain discreet.

Slowly, the stranger released his hand. "You don't remember me at all, do you?" he asked in a voice so low Ivy almost didn't hear him.

There was no point in trying to hide things now. Ivy shook his head and offered the man an apologetic smile. "I'm sorry. No."

The Nikari reeled back as if Ivy had physically struck him. At once, Ivy wanted to reach for him, to soothe whatever ache he'd caused with his words. Maybe he'd have actually done that, but then the Nikari's expression shut down. He got up, pulling away from Ivy. "Then I must apologize. I must have scared you with the unjustified intimacy."

"Not scared, per se," Ivy replied. "I was merely surprised and a bit embarrassed."

"Because you don't have your hair tied back," his sire muttered under his breath, just now realizing what Ivy had tried to convey earlier.

"Yes," Ivy said. The entire conversation made him very uncomfortable, and he wanted nothing more than to feel the warmth of the Nikari's hand again. That desire reminded him that he still didn't know who the other man could be.

The Nikari almost seemed to guess his thoughts. "I'm forgetting my manners. Introductions are in order. I am Kristelien Fezenda. Again,

I welcome you, Behnivyr, in my home, and I must apologize for the harm that came to you while here."

The information provided in those phrases had Ivy gaping in shock. The Morai. When had he met the Morai? How much time had passed since the solstice and the last thing he remembered? Why was he even in the Morai's home—in Nikaret?

Once more, the Morai appeared to figure out his dilemmas, although that couldn't have been too hard. "Roughly two months have now passed since the solstice," the Morai elaborated. "I invited you and your parents for a ball here. Later, we became friends, but unfortunately, during your stay, you suffered a serious accident."

Ivy didn't know what to address first. How could an Andari Full Blood befriend the Nikari Morai? It was like something out of a fairy tale. However, he couldn't doubt the truth of the other man's words. It even felt odd to hear the Nikari call him Behnivyr.

It also occurred to him that given the time frame the Morai spoke of, his bonding ceremony to the marquis should have happened long ago. "Wait.... Does this mean I'm bonded now?"

A chill swept over Ivy's spine, and his stomach roiled as he realized there might be another reason for his loose hair. Had he been forced to give his innocence to the horrible man? He'd always hoped he'd find a way to avoid it, but it obviously hadn't happened. Ivy didn't want to remember, but at the same time, he felt even more violated because he didn't.

"No, darling," his mother said. "You aren't."

Ivy didn't try to hide his relief, although if he wanted to be perfectly honest, his question had been a rhetorical one more than anything else. "Really? But how?"

The betrothal agreement had included fierce penalties if either party didn't go through with it. Had Ivy refused to bond with Torildy, his parents could have lost whole sections of their land.

"You expressed your distress over the unwanted union to me when you visited for the ball," the Morai explained. "I convinced Marquis Torildy that it would be in his best interest to renounce his claim to you."

There was something in the Nikari's tone and expression that made Ivy shiver, and not in distress. He still felt so confused, and he didn't know what to make of all these emotions bubbling inside him.

He wanted to ask why the Morai would go to so much trouble just for him, but before he could do so, the Nikari cupped his cheek with striking gentleness. "Don't think about it too much," he said with a slight smile. "Just worry about recovering. Slowly, your memories will come back, and it's not good for you to try to assimilate too much information at the same time."

"It's worse to not know," Ivy argued. "I can handle it, Kris. I'm not afraid."

Kris. Why did the nickname feel so natural in his mouth? Had he called the Morai this? He must have, because the other man didn't seem offended.

"Get some sleep," he told Ivy, "and be patient. Sometimes, you need to slow down to make progress."

Kris had a point. His mother's powers might have helped him, but he was in no way completely healed. His head was already starting to hurt again, and with Kris's help, he lay back down on the bed.

"All right," he said in reply. "But I want to know everything when I wake."

If his parents or Kris replied, he didn't hear it. No sooner had he closed his eyes than exhaustion overcame him, and he surrendered to restless sleep.

KRIS HAD thought he would be prepared for Ivy's every reaction. After the terror he'd experienced upon seeing him injured, he had almost deemed himself immune to any shock that could come from the situation.

He had definitely not been ready for Ivy to forget him altogether. To see everything he and Ivy had shared wiped away, just like that, was a devastating blow.

Then again, in a way, this rift between them seemed suitable. He himself had made the mistake of forgetting the extent of Ivy's dedication to him. He'd allowed appearances to fool him, and if not for

Attcha's insistence, he might have continued to believe Ivy had cheated on him. He didn't deserve Ivy's affection.

Ivy's parents appeared to be quite pleased with this development. "This is a stroke of luck," Rasami said. "With Ivy forgetting about his time here, we can start over, give him a chance to recover without the burden of the role he forcibly assumed."

"Ivy will feel something is not right," his mother said. "However, if we work together, we might be able to satisfy his curiosity with the bare bones of what occurred—along the line of what we've already told him."

Kris had indeed given Ivy only bits and pieces of the events. He couldn't say that at the time it had occurred to him to keep Ivy in the dark. He'd just done so instinctively, perhaps because of his enduring guilt.

He found it somewhat amusing that Ivy's parents seemed to have forgotten altogether about his presence. "And what, pray tell, do you think you're going to do after that?" he asked with a bitter smile. "How long do you think you'll be able to hide the truth? After all, Ivy is still my moraistele. That hasn't changed."

Anfarasha eyed him with undisguised horror. "You can't mean to continue this liaison given what happened."

Kris was thankful to Anfarasha for having saved Ivy, and he acknowledged her love for her son, but he had no intention of letting her rule his actions. Furthermore, his earlier conversation with Attcha brought him to the conclusion that Ivy's father and sire had been behind the entire thing in the first place. In this case, they definitely didn't have Ivy's best interests at heart.

"Even if I were willing to let him go," he said, "it would not be safe for him to leave Nikaret."

"Safe?" Anfarasha repeated, the blazing hatred in her eyes hot enough to flay Kris's skin. "How is Nikaret in any way safe?"

"Fara, keep your voice down," Titexe warned her. "We don't want to wake Ivy."

Anfarasha took a deep breath and paused for a few moments. When she spoke again, her voice held a chilly calm that somehow managed to convey as much disdain as her previous anger. "I think my son is safer anywhere else but here."

"I care nothing of your opinion, woman," Kris said with an unpleasant smirk. "Ivy still belongs to me, and that won't ever change. Now that he's awake, it is my decision whether I even allow you to stay here, or I send you back to the temple you chose over him."

Anfarasha took a threatening step forward. "You…. You monster."

Rasami grabbed her arm before she could lunge at him. "Don't," he whispered simply.

Anfarasha gave Rasami a pleading look. "But… Ivy needs us. We can't let this man do whatever he wants to our son."

"You speak as if you have a choice," Kris said. "Haven't you told your odale, Your Lordship, that I always win?"

As Rasami gave him a venomous look, Titexe said, "I thought Ivy might have softened your heart, Morai, but apparently, I was mistaken. I have no doubt now that you hurt him on purpose. Somehow, you will pay for it."

Kris didn't bother with further threats. At this point, they'd just be repetitive and petty. He had nothing to prove because they already knew he was more than capable of going through with what he'd said so far.

His mistake had been to lower his guard and allow people to see how much Ivy meant to him. If he hadn't done so, Ivy might not have been targeted. With a bitter smile, he studied Ivy's sleeping face. Sometimes, no matter how much he wanted to remain Kris, he needed to be solely the Morai.

"Rooms have been already prepared for you," he told Ivy's parents. "You're free to go now."

The three Andari didn't seem very eager to leave their son with Kris, but Kris didn't care about that. "Guards," he called out. As three Nikari responded to his call and entered Ivy's sick room, Kris ordered, "See Their Lordship and Sister Anfarasha to their quarters." Using his mental skills, he added, *And make sure they stay there until I give further instructions. The only exception is if my moraistele needs medical attention, in which case Anfarasha should be brought in at once.*

The soldiers saluted and surrounded the three Andari. Kris watched them go, scanning the expressions on their faces, wondering which of them had been cruel enough to involve Ivy in their own vendetta.

Unfortunately, unless he broke through all of their mental shields, he couldn't know for sure. That sort of thing could also tear apart their minds, and Ivy would never forgive him for it. Not to mention that in the process of finding the culprit he could seriously hurt an innocent.

It seemed clearer and clearer that to solve the problem in his present he needed to dig up the past. He had to talk to Shuri since he must have been the last one to have a coherent conversation with Ivy. But first, he needed to contact his mother. He needed to find out if Yoroshi had told Katara anything before Katara had killed her.

AFTER INSTRUCTING Attcha—who wasn't at all happy at the news of Ivy's amnesia—to discreetly watch over Ivy and telling Sai to keep an eye on Shuri and Ivy's parents, Kris traveled to Darach. He still hadn't notified his mother about Ivy's injury—there just hadn't been time, and the distance between Darach and Nikaret made telepathic communication impossible even for them.

When he stepped into the rift room of the Darach governor's manse, he ran straight into his mother. She blinked at him, her hand still hovering in midair as if she'd been in the process of summoning a rift. Since she was wearing her nightwolf cloak, she'd obviously been planning to return to Nikaret.

His expression must have been more telling than he'd hoped, because her eyes widened. "Kris, what's happened? I had a feeling something was amiss. Did you argue with Ivy again?"

Kris had mentioned his clash with Ivy just before he'd asked her to take his place in handling the issues in Darach. His mother had advised him not to stifle Ivy's bid for independence and instead to encourage and help him. Her words had given Kris hope at the time. How funny. It seemed like that particular conversation had happened a lifetime ago.

He realized he hadn't answered to her question when his mother pulled him aside, squeezing his arm so hard it hurt. "Kris?" she prodded.

"When I went back to Nikaret, I found Ivy kissing Shuri," Kris blurted out. "I heard him tell Shuri 'I love you.'"

Katara gasped. "What? No…. There must be some mistake. Ivy wouldn't cheat on you unless…." Her expression grew vicious, twisting with a dark anger that reminded Kris of a time in his life he'd have preferred not to remember. "It's that man. Shuri. I always knew blood would talk eventually. I knew he'd stab you in the back. He must have seduced Ivy, just like his mother did with Spatha."

Kris found it humbling that his mother trusted Ivy more than he himself had. True, her reasons might not have been ideal, but the fact remained that she hadn't immediately condemned Ivy. Meanwhile, for all his words of affection and devotion, Kris had rushed into judging Ivy. He'd have never even considered the situation might be similar to that of his father if Attcha hadn't pointed it out.

His enduring silence must have alerted his mother that something else was wrong.

"Creator… Kris, what did you do? Don't tell me…. Did you hurt him? Did you hurt Ivy?"

Kris nodded, barely managing to squelch the urge to bury himself in her warm embrace like he had when he'd been but a child. "I got angry. I was going to kill Shuri for breaking his vow. Ivy stopped me, but when he got in the way, he was harmed in Shuri's stead."

"How bad is it?" his mother asked quietly.

"I brought in a healer for him," Kris replied as he slid to the floor of the empty room, suddenly drained of strength. "I told you about her before, Ivy's mother."

"The odale who turned to the Sisterhood of Reysen." Katara nodded. "I remember. Did it work?"

"Yes," Kris replied. "Ivy is fine. He's already opened his eyes, and he seems to be on track for a speedy recovery. But the blow to his head induced amnesia, and he's forgotten all about me."

"And about Shuri and whatever occurred when you saw them together," his mother pointed out. "Convenient."

Without meaning to, Kris bristled. "I thought you didn't blame Ivy for what happened."

His mother snorted. "I like Ivy," she said, "but you are my son. I can't bear seeing you like this, looking so defeated, so lost. Whether Shuri did initiate the entire thing or not, it doesn't make it forgivable on Ivy's side. It just seems so... out of character."

Kris took the opening and plunged straight into the conversation he'd wanted to approach with his mother in the first place. He got up and shook off his depressed mood. Taking his mother's hand, he summoned a dimensional rift.

She arched a brow at him but didn't comment when he pulled her into the portal. They emerged a mere instant later on a distant beach at the very edge of Darach.

This particular beach didn't have a name, and indeed there was nothing all that special about it. However, the reason it held meaning was that it represented the closest point to the Eastern Realm, to A'rankin.

The actual location where Kris's ancestors had first landed in the Western Realm—what was now the Nikari Empire—wasn't very far from here, but Kris didn't particularly like it there. A great many people lingered in the area, seeking answers to their own dilemmas in the actions of a man who'd formed a nation. As much as Kris admired the first Nikari leader, he was his own man and would make his own decisions.

Of course, his mother knew all this, because she frowned at him. "Kris? Why did you bring me here?"

"I wanted to make sure we were in private," Kris replied.

"We could have used telepathy for that," she pointed out, just like Kris had known she would.

Yes, except Kris didn't want to be in her mind right now, when he approached the issue he'd been avoiding for decades. "I'd prefer it if we spoke out loud this time around."

"Kris, you're scaring me," his mother said. "Simply tell me what's on your mind."

Kris looked out into the distance, in the general direction of A'rankin and the Eastern Realm. The waves lapped at the shore, the light of the moon dancing on the liquid surface. Kris didn't know why, but the glow reminded him of Ivy's smile. "Attcha suggested that Ivy suffered from the same thing that happened to father's nightwolf," he said without looking at his mother. "A poison of some sort, to change perception."

Even if he was trying to ignore her reactions, Kris could still feel her shock and tension. "That... Creator, it makes so much sense. They targeted Ivy so that they could get to you."

"And to Shuri, most likely," Kris replied. After all, Shuri remained a prince of the Nikari. If something happened to Kris—such as, him losing his mind due to guilt—Shuri would have to step up. It would be a problematic situation, but most people at court knew the truth about Shuri's identity, even if it wasn't something anyone brought up in polite conversation.

"But if that's the case, who could have done it?" his mother inquired, sounding as bewildered as Kris felt.

Kris turned and faced her again. "I was hoping you could tell me that. Back then, when Father died.... Did you manage to learn anything from Yoroshi?"

She arched a puzzled brow at him. "How could I possibly do that, Kris? I'm not a necromancer. You know as well as I do that by the time we reached her, she was already dead."

"By the time *I* reached her," Kris corrected. "You arrived there before me, remember?"

Much to his surprise, his mother burst into laughter, genuine hearty chuckles. "You think I killed her."

Kris crossed his arms over his chest and narrowed his eyes at her. "Didn't you?"

"No, Kris, I didn't," she said, shaking her head. Her laughter suddenly stopped, and she wiped her eyes. "I admit I was going to. I don't think I ever told you this, but right before he died, Spatha used his mental powers to learn which of us—me or Yoroshi—had planned the whole thing. He never thought his nightwolf was guilty. He trusted the beast as much as we trust our own nightwolves—and rightly so, I might add."

This was indeed news to Kris. "What did he see?" he asked.

"I'm not sure," his mother replied. "I could only manage to get a glimpse of a barely there memory—Yoroshi sliding some sort of powder in the nightwolf's meal. I think Spatha wanted to tell you about it, but he never got the chance."

"He must have told his nightwolf, though, who revealed it to Attcha before he died," Kris mused. Even if Attcha had kept the details of that conversation from him, it now made far more sense than it had before.

"Probably, yes," his mother replied. "In any case, if you remember, Yoroshi left Nikaret immediately after he was declared dead. She didn't even wait for the funeral."

At the time, Kris had been tied up in formalities of succession, and his mother had managed to slip away first. When he'd tracked her down in Tarkquin, he'd found his uncle mourning his wife who'd inexplicably decided to throw herself off a cliff.

"I saw it, you know," she said. "I saw her jump. I stepped out of the rift in the forest outside their home, and there she was, right above me. She stared straight down at me." Katara smiled bitterly. "I think a part of me wanted to try to save her, but I simply couldn't move. I just stood there and watched. I wonder.... Does that mean I killed her?"

Kris couldn't answer that question. Their past held too many secrets for him to hope to navigate without tearing apart the tenuous balance between all of them. "Did you see anything else? Anyone?"

His mother shook her head. If she truly felt any guilt over Yoroshi's death, it didn't show. "There was no one on the cliff, not that I could see, at least. But.... There is something else. Well, two things."

Kris didn't like the sound of that. "What?"

"First of all, from the glimpses I got of your father's memories, I figured out her motives. Your father had found out something about her. She was in contact with someone very dangerous. Although I couldn't quite grasp who it was, he seemed to be debating whether he should reveal the information or not. In any case, I don't know why she threw herself off the cliff after Spatha's death, but your uncle arrived just as her body hit the rocks below. He saw me standing there, and as you can imagine, he pretty much drew the same conclusion you did. I didn't want any further trouble, so I wiped his memory."

Another piece of the puzzle slid into place. "That was why you didn't want Ivy to track him with divination. You were afraid his power would nudge his recollections."

She nodded. "The last thing I wanted was to stir that old story again." Her lips twisted into a small smile. "Although I never imagined you thought I'd killed her."

"Why else would I bury the whole thing, Mother? You know as well as I do that if not for my suspicions, I would have pursued the matter and found out what Yoroshi used on Father's nightwolf."

"To be honest, I thought you were doing it for Shuri," she answered with a sigh. "You always showed such affection toward him, even if he never appreciated it. I knew you wouldn't have wanted him to know that his mother had killed Spatha."

"That's true," Kris admitted, "but I wouldn't have chosen it over the benefit of learning who'd killed Father. In any case, it's a moot point now." He frowned, a thought niggling at his consciousness. He remembered his uncle's weird behavior a while back, and something clicked in his mind. "With both Shuri and me out of the way, the Morai's role would have fallen to Uncle Phura."

All the blood drained out of his mother's face. "But…. How could he have remembered? If Ivy didn't push for it…."

"Ivy's parents," Kris said. "I was already suspecting them of being involved. Ivy went to see them this morning for breakfast. Either of them could have easily slipped him something. And Rasami Erethe has considerable mental skills. He could have nudged Uncle Phura's memories."

Things did seem to fit, and at this point, Kris wouldn't be surprised if his uncle's hatred of Kris surpassed his dislike for the Andari. He couldn't be sure things had truly happened this way, but he needed to check out this possibility.

Following that train of thought, Kris summoned a rift to take him and his mother to his uncle's home in Quintera. As they stepped into the portal, though, Kris immediately felt something was wrong. He attempted to control the energies, just like he always did, but the threads of the rift escaped his grip. No, that wasn't right. They were tangled with something else, with another portal.

Kris cursed and tightened his hold on his mother. The chances of a double rift opening were one in a million. Much like what had happened earlier with Kris and his mother, Nikari always saw a dimensional rift summoned by another person. To cause a double rift, one would have to slice reality for a second time, in the exact instant before the original rift was used to transport its summoner.

Such a thing would be insane, however, since it had the potential of unbalancing not just the double rift, but all others opened at that exact instant—such as the nightwolf rifts. Not to mention that it could reduce all of its users to indistinguishable pieces of stray matter dissipating into nothingness.

Kris felt the assault of the rift pulling at his flesh, trying to destroy his very core. The furious power of the dimensional portal clawed at him, mere moments away from disintegrating the foolish creature who'd dared to attempt taming pure chaos. He heard his mother screaming his name, but he knew that the nightwolf cloak she wore would keep her alive—maybe not unscathed, but definitely alive.

Still, just to be safe, Kris wrapped every drop of his power around her, keeping her safe. His mother's magic tried to reach for him, but he'd opened the portal, not her, and she couldn't help.

Kris thought about Ivy, about the way Ivy had looked earlier at him, completely ignorant of what they'd shared. He thought about Ivy's blood on his hands, the shards of his gift embedded in Ivy's spine.

It would be so easy to let go now, to surrender to the rift and to oblivion. Easier and better for everyone. After all, once Kris was gone, there would be no reason for anyone to target Ivy. His mother would be hurt, of course, but she was a Nikari. She would survive and grow stronger, in time.

And then Ivy's voice drifted into his memory, his treacherous mind summoning one of the most treasured moments he'd shared with the young Andari.

"The empire itself is only as good or as bad as the people who live in it and who lead it. You can make it so much greater than just a union of territories. I know you can."

Kris could remember those words so well, like Ivy had just said them. They echoed into the darkness around him, within his torn heart and mind. *"Ivy, why do you always show such faith in me?"* he had asked then.

Ivy's reply still haunted him. *"Perhaps I just see something in you that no one else does. Then again, it's easy to trust a person when you love them."*

Ivy had loved Kris. That was the one truth Kris could cling to, the truth that both tortured him and soothed his wounded soul. In that moment, when Kris had claimed Ivy, he'd felt it, like he could feel his own despair now.

Perhaps Ivy didn't love him anymore. Kris had lost the chance to even hope to earn that love back. But those feelings had been real and had echoed the emotions inside Kris's own heart. Kris needed to honor it.

Running away wasn't the solution. Embracing death might seem like an easy way out, but it was simply cowardice. That wasn't something the Kris Ivy trusted would do.

This time, Kris would not fail Ivy. Not again, never again. He couldn't abandon Ivy to the ill intentions of people who cared little for him. A double rift didn't appear out of nowhere. Someone had created it, someone who planned to unbalance or perhaps destroy the entire empire. But Kris wouldn't let them get away with it. He wouldn't let them get away with using him to hurt Ivy. Oh, he'd never skirt or forget his own part of the blame. He would pay the price for it, but so would the culprits behind this crime.

Somewhere deep inside, he felt an energy not his own reaching out to him. He embraced it, feeding on it, learning from it. With its help, he willed the portal into compliance. The rift swirled wildly around them, and for the first time, Kris could truly register the beauty of the chaotic energies. So many colors, so much power. Was this what Ivy had seen when he'd mentally followed Attcha through the rift? It must have been. For some reason, the thought encouraged him.

It only lasted for a few moments, and then the portal spat them out in a large clearing. Kris stared up at the sky, trying to read their location in the stars, but his head was still spinning, and he felt like he'd had an unpleasant meeting with a throng of manticores.

Just as he managed to shake off most of the dizziness, a familiar figure landed on top of him, sending him back to the ground. His mother peppered his face with kisses, tears trailing down her cheeks. Kris hugged her back, distantly wondering how he'd thought, even for a moment that he could leave her just like that. "It's all right, Mother," he said. "I'm fine."

His words didn't seem to convince her since she kept poking and prodding at every part of him. "We need to get you some medical attention at once," she breathed out. "Creator.... Where are you injured, Kris? Can you tell me?"

"I'm not injured," Kris said, breathing hard, shocked to realize that he wasn't just saying that to comfort his mother. The pain was fading away already, like would normally happen with a regular rift.

His mother freed herself from his embrace and squeezed his shoulders. "Focus, son. Kris, you're not fine. You're covered in blood."

Kris stared down at his clothes, only to realize she was completely correct. Of course, out of that crazy impulse that made people not process some obvious facts until they checked them for themselves, he palmed his garments and stared at his hand when it came out tainted crimson.

"It's... I don't think it's mine."

He wasn't familiar with its scent either, but it did remind him of something—or rather, of someone. He looked beyond his mother's shoulder to a dark lump curled just a few feet away from them. As his naturally acute senses took in what he was seeing, he shot to his feet and rushed toward his target.

His mother soon joined him, having obviously realized what was happening as well. With eyes glazed by agony, Phura stared up at them. "Curse you. Murderers."

CHAPTER TWELVE
CONSPIRACY

IVY DIDN'T know what woke him from his sleep. He was quite comfortable under the sheets, and returning to the real world seemed like too much trouble. But something wet insistently nudged him, and Ivy had to abandon the warm arms of slumber.

As he struggled to return to consciousness, the first thing he faced was a pair of bright golden eyes. After that, a lupine face came into view. A black wolf hovered over Ivy, and his tongue came out to lick Ivy's cheek.

Ivy wasn't afraid in the slightest. Rather, he felt... frustrated. It seemed to him that this scene—or something similar to it—had happen to him more than once throughout the past few months, but he couldn't remember it.

Even as he mused over this, a voice drifted into his mind, startling him. *Soft one wake,* it said. *Soft one not safe.*

Ivy looked around the room, trying to determine who could have contacted him telepathically. The black wolf nudged his cheek again. *Black fur want protect soft one. But black fur weak. Soft one hide.*

Comprehension dawned in Ivy's mind. It was the wolf. The wolf was talking to him. *I don't understand,* Ivy said, trying to make sense of the creature's words. *I should hide?*

Even if Ivy hadn't been very experienced in telepathic speech, it came to him so naturally that Ivy felt shaken. However, the black wolf didn't allow him to dwell too much on his befuddlement. He took hold of the material of Ivy's robes and pulled. *Yes. Soft one hide.*

Ivy's heart told him the black wolf meant well, so he followed the creature out of the bed. As he pulled on his sandals, he gave the beast an inquiring look. *But where should we go? Why?*

Strong one room, the black wolf said. *Has spell. Quickly. Black fur explain later.*

In spite of the peculiar speech of the creature, Ivy understood that his odd friend planned to guide him to a warded room. Kris's room. Yes, Kris was "strong one." Ivy didn't know how he remembered that but he did.

That recollection made him all the more aware of how much he didn't understand, of the nigh innumerable gaps in his memory. He swayed and leaned against the wall to keep himself from falling. The black wolf released a distressed whine. *Soft one hurt?*

I... I'm sorry, Ivy said. *I just don't remember anything, and it feels like there's a hole inside of me. Inside my heart. Do you understand?*

The wolf bobbed his head up and down in a strikingly human gesture. *Black fur understand. Black fur know soft one forget. But soft one not worry. Soft one nightwolf soul. Pack for black fur. Remember.*

Encouraged, Ivy steadied himself and smiled at the wolf. *Yes, you're right. I'll remember eventually. Come. Lead the way.*

The wolf guided him to the window, which Ivy proceeded to open. They were two floors up, and unlike Nikari, Andari were never all that athletic. However, Ivy was fairly certain that if he tried hard enough he could summon an earth golem who could act as his staircase. That was another thing that confused him and another skill he hadn't been good at, but he decided to worry about it later.

Why can't we just use the door? he asked dubiously.

Not all Nikari nightwolf soul, the black wolf explained. *Try use soft one against strong one.* He growled threateningly. *Black fur not allow.*

To use him against Kris? But why? Had he truly been so important to Kris? If so, why had Kris left, just like that? Damn it, Ivy hated the fact that he couldn't remember.

The black wolf pulled his robes again, and Ivy temporarily pushed his thoughts aside in favor of focusing on the ground beneath them. His head started to ache a bit, but nonetheless, a humanoid earth golem manifested below. The sight of the hulking brown creature prodded at something at the back of Ivy's mind, but for the moment, he ignored it in favor of more practical considerations.

Just as Ivy stepped out of the window, and his wolf friend followed him on the golem's shoulders, the doors of the room burst open. Ivy ducked aside just in time and surreptitiously closed the window.

A curse sounded in the quarters he'd just left. "What?" a male voice Ivy didn't recognize inquired. "This cannot be. He was here mere minutes ago. Where could they have gone, Sai? That beast cannot be trusted."

"With all due respect, Highness, his Majesty's nightwolf has never hurt Lord Behnivyr," another answered. "I doubt he'd start now."

"Do you know that for a fact? You've seen how the other nightwolves are acting."

A small moment of hesitance, and then the second man replied once more, "They're probably headed toward the dens, so there might be a degree of risk. You are correct in saying His Imperial Majesty's moraistele must be protected at all cost."

"Don't call him that," the first man snarled. "Ivy is a victim in all of this, just like my uncle. Kris should have never been allowed to touch him."

"Your Highness, remember your position. Such words can be considered seditious."

"I don't care. Go ahead and arrest me, Sai. I won't allow anyone to hurt Ivy ever again."

The words puzzled Ivy and did nothing to calm the racing of his heart. He willed the golem to lower him and the wolf down, and it complied, albeit a bit more abruptly than Ivy had intended.

He winced, hoping no one had heard the sound of the golem made when stomping around. Apparently, Reysen was with him, because no one peered out the window. Even the black wolf exhaled a sigh of relief as they started to walk away. Ivy was forced to send the golem away, since the creature drew far too much attention, and he still hadn't recovered enough from his injury to control it for too long.

Can you tell me what's going on now? he asked the wolf. In the distance, angry howls sounded, sending shivers down Ivy's spine.

Strong one ambushed, the beast explained. *Black fur help, but now weak.*

What about the man in the room? What did he want with me?

The wolf snarled. *Hurt one betray. Want take soft one. But soft one pack. Black fur protect.*

That didn't really help Ivy. But then, what more did he need to know? He'd heard it quite clearly from the men in the room. They'd called Ivy a moraistele. The Morai's concubine.

No wonder Kris had felt entitled to touch Ivy like that. No wonder he'd been hurt when Ivy had owned up to his amnesia. And the worst thing was that Ivy suspected there had been far more between them than simple sex. Ivy had felt it even then, when Kris had come to see him. His mind might not remember, but his body and his heart did. The Morai definitely had the power to force Ivy into his bed, but there had been no forcefulness involved. Ivy had wanted Kris. He still did.

Concern rose within him as the full extent of the wolf's words sank into his consciousness. His own confusion aside, someone was obviously trying to hurt Kris. *Is Kris all right?* he asked the wolf.

Yes, the beast replied. *Strong one fine. But still danger.*

Ivy didn't even know whether to feel relieved or more worried than ever. In the end, he didn't get the chance to decide because he ran into someone he hadn't expected to see here.

"Your Lordship," Akolo said with a gasp. "We've been looking everywhere for you."

Ivy released a sigh of relief at the sight of his manservant. "Akolo, thank Reysen. I need you to help me. Something suspicious is going on. I… I don't understand anything anymore."

Akolo nodded, a sympathetic smile on his familiar face. "I know, Your Lordship. I realize how difficult things have been for you. But you don't have to worry about that any longer. Your sire is here, and he can take you back to Seanda, where you'll be safe."

It wasn't a bad idea, per se. In fact, it made sense in that Kris could easily come and find him in Seanda after he put his affairs in order. But Ivy didn't want that. In fact, just the thought of abandoning Kris repulsed him.

"No, that's not what I need to do," he whispered. "I need to get to Kris. Now."

"Your Lordship… I'm not sure how to tell you this, but the Morai…." Akolo rubbed his eyes like he didn't know how to approach the matter. "He compromised you. He… forced himself on you."

The black wolf got between Ivy and Akolo and bared his fangs at the Half Blood. *Lying one,* he whispered in Ivy's mind. *Soft one trust strong one. Lying one enemy.*

Ivy would have never thought that one day he might see Akolo as a potential enemy. And maybe Akolo truly didn't have any ill intentions. Perhaps he did indeed believe Kris had hurt Ivy. It didn't matter, because Ivy planned to make it clear that Kris was his lover not his abuser. "No, he didn't. I might not remember everything, but my heart does, and I know how I feel."

"Your emotions have been twisted by the Morai and his nightwolf," Akolo said, pointing at Ivy's companion. "You can't trust them, Your Lordship."

So the black wolf was Kris's nightwolf. That seemed strange, since Ivy's memories of his lessons told him such beasts boasted a far greater size and fiercer nature. Perhaps something had happened to the beast when he'd helped Kris. The realization solidified Ivy's decision. The nightwolf was his friend and had protected him many times before. It was Ivy's turn to stand by his side.

"I do trust them, Akolo. This is where I belong now. If you are as loyal to me as you say, tell me where my parents are. I will speak with them myself."

Akolo's expression changed so quickly Ivy almost wouldn't have believed it if he hadn't seen it himself. "How unfortunate," Akolo said. "I always did like you, Your Lordship, and I would have preferred it if I could have at least fucked you once before you died. Ah well. We must all live with our regrets."

A ball of fire formed in Akolo's palm, and before Ivy could act, his manservant launched the projectile at him. It all happened so fast that Ivy couldn't even put a shield up. He couldn't process that the man he'd known for the better part of his life would want to kill him.

His shock and weakness might have ended up killing him, but before the fire spell could hit him, Kris's nightwolf threw himself between Ivy and Akolo. The impact was so strong that it propelled the beast's body past Ivy, into the bush beneath his window. At the same time, though, the magic also recoiled against Akolo, and the Half Blood crumbled to the ground, screaming and moaning.

The smell of scorched flesh and fur filled the air, nauseating Ivy. He rushed to the nightwolf's side and dropped to his knees next to the beast. As he pet the creature's head, the same voice drifted into his mind, now barely a whisper, *Soft one run. Go to... strong one.*

If Ivy left now, he might be able to make it to safety. With Akolo distracted by the injury he had caused himself, Ivy could put a good distance between them before the Half Blood managed to gather his wits or use potential healing skills.

However, in that situation, Ivy would have to abandon the nightwolf to his fate. The beast was too heavy for Ivy to carry—even when he'd been at full strength, he couldn't have done it. He could summon a golem for that purpose, but in his condition, he doubted he could control it long enough to make a difference. And Akolo.... It was strange, but Ivy had always thought his abilities as a Half Blood were far weaker. If he'd had to guess, he wouldn't have deemed Akolo capable of summoning a firebolt capable of harming a nightwolf, even a weakened one like Ivy's friend. Clearly, Ivy had underestimated him.

All things considered, it didn't take long for Ivy to decide. Sending a prayer to Reysen, Ivy lowered his hands over the nightwolf's injury. The beast tried to push him away. *Strong one need soft one more than black fur. Soft one go.*

Ivy had no intention of abandoning his friend. He could feel it now, so close, the cold hand of death. Before his very eyes, the nightwolf's figure grew smaller, dimmer. With no hesitation, Ivy gripped the beast's paw and closed his eyes. He focused his magic, summoning his healing abilities, willing them to mend the hurt to his friend's body.

This part of his power had always felt very close to Ivy's heart, perhaps because he'd inherited it from his mother. In spite of his previous injury, his energies responded to him, flowing over the nightwolf. The shadow of death faded away, and Ivy opened his eyes, satisfied with the result.

It was only then that he realized the paw in his hand had significantly shrunk. Instead of the fully-grown wolf who'd come to lead him from his room, a wolf pup now lay on the ground.

The pup struggled to his feet and bit Ivy's ear, as if to chastise him for his recklessness. *Black fur tell soft one run. Soft one not listen.*

Apparently, even if the nightwolf's form had become younger, he'd preserved his previous mental state. Thank Reysen for that, because Ivy was confused and weakened enough to need his guidance.

There was nothing he wanted more than to find Kris and bury himself in the other man's embrace—an impulse that should have been alarming but felt completely natural. Akolo hadn't recovered, so maybe Ivy actually had a chance to achieve this.

As he got up, though, he found himself facing a new obstacle. A man who looked a lot like Kris approached him in a rush and wrapped his arms around him. "What happened to you, Ivy?" the man asked.

Judging by the stranger's voice, the man was the same Nikari who'd come after him in his sick room. He hadn't displayed any inclination to hurt Ivy, so maybe Ivy could play along for a bit while he figured out how to escape and reunite with Kris.

He hugged the man back, awkwardly and weakly, pretending to be more drained than he felt. All the while, Ivy shielded the wolf pup's body with his own form. It worked, because the man in front of him seemed too focused on him to care about a random, harmless animal.

"I was attacked by my manservant," Ivy explained, pointing to Akolo. "I narrowly managed to escape with my life."

His would-be savior turned toward Akolo, who was only now trying to get up. A second Nikari, who Ivy guessed must be the first man's companion from earlier—Sai, if Ivy remembered correctly— grabbed Akolo's arm before the Half Blood could flee. "I don't think so," he said. "You're not going anywhere. Why did you attack His Lordship?"

"Fool," Akolo spat. "You don't understand anything. You don't even realize how unimportant you are in the big picture."

Even if his burn injuries still hadn't healed, Akolo didn't seem to want to go down without a fight. Ivy didn't think the Half Blood could do anything against two well-trained Nikari, and more people were gathering around as they spoke.

Indeed, Ivy's parents soon made their appearance, followed by a host of Nikari soldiers. "Ivy!" Ivy's sire exclaimed. "Thank Reysen. We were so worried about you."

That seemed to be a widespread sentiment, so widespread, in fact, that Ivy couldn't tell if any of it was genuine. He forced a smile he didn't feel. "I'm fine, Sire. Just confused. What's happening?"

"The nightwolves suddenly went insane," his mother explained. "We knew the Morai had left that beast of his with you. We feared the creature would harm you."

Ivy didn't know what was safe to say. He could no longer tell friend from foe. Were his parents aware of Akolo's intentions? He didn't want to think that, but it was all too suspicious. The nightwolf they were accusing had saved his life from a man he'd deemed if not a friend, then a member of his household, for the better part of his life. What should he make of that?

"I want to see Kris," he blurted out, knowing how needy that sounded but unable to help it.

"I'm not sure if that will be possible right now," the man who looked like Kris said. "We've just received word that there's been an altercation between His Imperial Majesty and my father. I am told my father was seriously injured, and His Imperial Majesty is handling the matter. I don't know much, as the Morai has forbidden the use of rifts until further notice."

Ivy frowned. Apparently, whatever plans this man had of using Ivy weren't common knowledge amongst most Nikari. It took more to shake their loyalty than hearsay and appearances.

That comforted Ivy, and it must have reassured the nightwolf as well. He nudged Ivy's leg with his muzzle. Ivy picked the black wolf pup up in his arms or at least tried to. He settled for petting the beast's head, since even now, the nightwolf wasn't exactly small.

"Kris never does anything unnecessary," he said, surprised at his own certainty. "For the moment, you cannot be sure of anything until you're able to travel there yourself."

It might have been a tactless thing of him to say, but his loyalty lay with Kris. He was tired, so tired of lies, of pretending, of hiding. Was it truly so much to ask to understand his own life, his own emotions and past? Didn't he have the right to decide for himself what he wanted?

His parents probably didn't think so, because his father took this cue to pipe up. "Well, this might be a sign that we need to return home. Wavewayfaring remains safe, and once we're in Seanda, we can start over."

"This isn't a good place for us, Ivy," his mother offered. "Just look at how they're treating your manservant."

Ivy almost burst into laughter at her words. "I don't think Seanda is safe for me at all," he said. "As for Akolo, he tried to kill me. I'm still waiting for an explanation to that."

Akolo just grinned at him, and Ivy had a very bad feeling. "You talk too much, Your Lordship. Thank you for that."

In that moment, Ivy realized that in his zeal to defend Kris from accusations, he'd yet again underestimated Akolo. Something burned in the manservant's eyes, something Ivy had never seen before in any Andari, Half Blood or otherwise. A surge of divination magic awoke inside him, and he looked at Akolo, perhaps for the first time in his life.

As much as Ivy hated to admit it, the privileges that came with being a Full-Blood Andari unavoidably brought on consequences. No one was immune, not even Ivy, who preferred to carve his own path in life and judge others according to his own standards, not the arbitrary bias of others. In spite of his efforts, his perception unavoidably became colored by public opinion.

For that reason, it had been easy to dismiss Akolo as just another Half Blood. Ivy might have claimed Akolo belonged to his household, but he hadn't truly considered the other man worthy of much attention. Even if he'd known a few things about Akolo, in the end the manservant had been peripheral to his own desires.

It had been a mistake; he realized that now. Perhaps Akolo had been planning something all along. Then again, Akolo might have gone bitter over time, and Ivy could have prevented this if he'd paid attention.

Regrets didn't matter right now, though. Because beyond Akolo, someone else existed, another person who'd found it easy to use Ivy's former manservant for his own interests. Ivy couldn't quite see his face, not yet. But a little further, just a little further.... Ivy caught a glimpse of a huge, transparent wall, glittering in all the colors of the rainbow. His vision shifted closer to his target. Finally, he found himself in what looked like a large sunroom.

The architecture and decorations were unlike any Ivy had ever seen, but at the same time they had a familiar feel, something Ivy couldn't quite put his finger on. Similarly, the plants growing all around were completely alien to him.

A settee lay in the center of the room, and on it, a tall, slender man lounged, his eyes closed. Judging by his elaborate garb, the man must be someone important. Confirming that guess, an elegantly dressed woman approached and bowed lowly. "Prince Tynare, are you well?" the woman asked.

The man rubbed his temples as if trying to chase away a migraine. "Yes," he said. His eyes shot open, and his gaze fixed straight on Ivy. "I just have a feeling.... A feeling that someone is watching me."

That was Ivy's cue to retreat, and he did so as quickly as possible, stumbling back into his own body with such a dizzying speed that for a few moments, he couldn't even see straight. When he did manage to focus his vision, he found himself lying on the ground with his parents gathered around him. "What is it, Ivy?" his father asked. "What did you see?"

Ivy cleared his throat and blinked, struggling to gather his thoughts. "A man." What had his name been? Ivy had heard it when the woman had addressed him. "Prince Tynare."

By his side, his sire cursed. "Tynare'Or'Therar? The heir of A'rankin? Reysen...."

Ivy didn't get to confirm that one way or another, because all of a sudden, a large burst of mental energy struck him. Pain exploded through him from every direction. It followed the same path Ivy had taken through his divination abilities but, of course, in reverse. Ivy gasped as the power attempted to suck in his consciousness. Ivy knew that if he surrendered to this, if he lost the battle, he would become a shell, a mindless husk with no will of his own. He knew it even if he'd never experienced a magic quite like this before.

But what hope did he have of fighting something so powerful? His lessons in divination hadn't prepared him for such a mental battle.

His desires, his hopes, his dreams, they meant nothing compared to the overwhelming force.

No, that wasn't right. Ivy might have forgotten the events of these past few months, but he couldn't forget his feelings. He had something to live for, something stronger than the emptiness trying to destroy his very sense of self.

Kris. Ivy writhed against the magic assaulting him, blindly reaching out to Kris. Something cracked in his mind, and memories flooded him, images of a solstice night spent in the arms of a mysterious Nikari, of stolen kisses and the moment when he'd loosened his hair for Kris. Trust, passion, love, pain—Ivy didn't know how he could have forgotten it all, but it returned to him now. In it, Ivy found strength, the same resolve that had urged him to take a chance and train his divination skills with Attcha.

Using every ounce of his newfound power, Ivy pushed the peculiar magic away from him, all the while trying to rebuild his damaged mental shields. The person behind the spell must have been taken aback by Ivy's counterattack because for an instant the ruthless assault faltered. Ivy found the opening and made his retreat, coming to once again.

His mother hovered over him, tears flowing down her cheeks. His father was trying to shake him awake, but he obviously hadn't expected a result, because he gasped when Ivy opened his eyes. "Ivy.... Thank Reysen!"

His sire said nothing. He knelt at Ivy's side, staring at him with an alarmingly blank expression. Ivy instinctively wanted to reach out to him, but his attention was drawn to the battle taking place around them. Shuri guided the Nikari forces to surround Akolo, but no one could quite approach him. A dark swell of energy rippled around the so-called manservant, keeping the Nikari from attacking.

Akolo's gaze zeroed in on Ivy. "Impressive," Akolo said. "But you won't live to tell the tale, Your Lordship."

"I CAN'T believe this," Kris's mother said as the medics struggled to stabilize Phura's condition. "This is all my fault."

"Stop blaming yourself," Kris told her. "You couldn't have known what would happen."

"I should have monitored his memories more vigilantly," she argued. "I got careless, and this is the result."

Kris couldn't argue against that, although neither did he think the fault truly lay with her. There were so many things that didn't fit. In Darach, he'd thought he'd finally figured it out, but he'd obviously been mistaken. The double rift might not have torn him apart, but it had shaken his theories. It didn't make sense that his uncle would risk killing himself with a double rift if he'd planned to take over the empire.

Besides, the whole sequence of events seemed off. When exactly could his uncle have started plotting with Ivy's parents? To what extent were they all involved in the matter? It was all too convoluted and confusing.

To top it off, Kris couldn't help but feel a measure of guilt too. In a strange twist of fate, the accident had caused Phura to lose his arm, just like Kris's father during the nightwolf attack. Kris had a moment during which he found it somewhat fitting.

The thought nauseated him, and it did absolutely nothing to soothe the strange ache in his heart. Kris turned away from the bed and stalked out of the room. He couldn't stay here. He might have ordered all the rifts to be closed, but something told him he was needed in Nikaret. Attcha had helped him when Kris had been trapped in the double rift. Kris realized that now. But the kind of assistance Attcha had provided him with didn't come without a price. Attcha couldn't have died, but he must be at the very least incapacitated—which left Ivy with very little protection. By now, Shuri would have learned of the accident, since Kris had felt a rift opening as soon as he and his mother brought Phura in for medical treatment. There was no telling how Shuri would react to the news.

His mother followed him into the corridor of his uncle's home. "Kris? What is it? Where are you going?"

"To Nikaret," he replied. "You stay here, Mother. Keep an eye on Uncle Phura. If he wakes, we must learn who put him up to...."

He trailed off when a familiar mental touch reached out to him. His heart just about stopped. It couldn't be. Not even close family could use telepathic communication over long distances. And yet, Kris could never mistake Ivy's presence for anyone else's.

Had Ivy somehow made his way here? No, the mental connection was too distant for that. But there was no doubt in Kris's mind that Ivy needed him.

The call grew more frantic, more urgent, almost desperate. The intensity of it was such that, for a few seconds, Kris couldn't even breathe, let alone act. But when Ivy's fear and pain became too strong for him to endure, Kris's anger solidified into resolve.

He slashed his hand through the air, creating a rift just like he always did. His mother made a noise, obviously still not over what had happened earlier, but Kris ignored her. He stepped through the portal, bracing himself for whatever ploy waited for him once he reached his destination. The interdimensional space through which Kris usually cut his path bore the traces of the double rift, like a wound that hadn't quite turned into a scar yet. Kris found it a little more difficult to tame the chaotic energies than he regularly would have, but he did it just the same.

An instant later, he emerged in the gardens of the imperial palace in Nikaret. He hadn't actually willed himself there, but he'd followed Ivy's call, and he'd obviously made the right decision.

No sooner had he stepped out of the rift than he was struck by the chaos that seemed to have followed him out of the portal and into his reality. Ivy's manservant—the same one Kris had met the night of the solstice—faced Kris's forces in battle, a whirlpool of dark power swirling around him.

His rift had left Kris some distance from the battle. As he rushed there, he took in the situation. Ivy lay on the ground, his parents huddled around him in a protective wall. Anfarasha threw a shield around them while Titexe shouted at Rasami, "Get us out of here, Sam."

Kris guessed Titexe wanted Rasami to open a wave that would take them to safety, although he doubted Rasami could actually do it. As a rule, wave-wayfaring provided safer traveling than dimensional rifts, but it took time for them to form, and under such circumstances, the summoner of the wave would have great difficulty focusing on keeping it from collapsing.

It was a moot point, since Rasami didn't react to Titexe's words. He just stared at Ivy and showed no sign of having heard his bond mate. The power emanating from Ivy's manservant burst out toward them, somehow absorbing the ground beneath their feet. Anfarasha screamed, but Titexe managed to summon an air elemental that kept them all from being swallowed by the nothingness. The winds themselves came to life, and the figure of a woman manifested from within. White hair flaring wildly, her nude form surrounded in the raging force of the storm, she kept Ivy and his parents aloft, her transparent body a barrier between them and certain death.

Sadly, the air elemental couldn't resist the power sucking them in. Before she could turn her power onto Akolo, she screamed and dissipated. The four Andari might have been killed had Kris not reached them in time. It all happened in the blink of an eye and yet exactly as Kris planned it.

As he ran, Kris zeroed in on his nightwolf. Right now, Attcha had been turned into a mere pup, the same form he'd had the moment he'd come out of Kris's very first rift. Kris reached for him and passed a hand through Attcha's fur. Instantly, his nightwolf returned to his mature form and shot forward, catching Ivy and Titexe. In turn Kris managed to take hold of Rasami and Anfarasha. All the while, he summoned a strong wind that carried them past the point of danger.

Sai jogged to his side, dodging a bolt of magic from the supposed manservant as he did so. "Your Imperial Majesty, all evidence shows that neither your cousin nor Lord Behnivyr's parents are involved in this coup, at least not directly. How do you want us to proceed?"

"For the moment, stay with Ivy," Kris said. "I'll be waiting for a more detailed report later, but right now, I have a little matter to deal with."

Attcha padded to his side, and Kris mounted his nightwolf. For the first time in what seemed like forever, he felt like he was going to war. A sense of calm flowed over him. This battle had become personal. These people—because he doubted Ivy's manservant was the only one involved in this conspiracy—had committed a serious mistake by targeting Ivy.

As he readied himself to attack, however, a gentle hand landed on his shoulder. Kris turned to see Ivy looking at him with earnest eyes. "Kris," Ivy whispered, "be careful."

Kris wondered if Ivy would say that if he remembered what Kris had done. Now was not the time to ask such questions or discuss their personal problems. Ivy must have known that too, because he brushed his lips over Kris's cheek.

During that moment when they touched, a wave of soothing power flowed over Kris. He recognized it as healing magic—Ivy's energy, shielding him, supporting him. Ivy must have still been weak from his injury, because he went pale and leaned against his father for support. Even as he did so, though, two simple phrases echoed in Kris's mind, *Remember what you told me. Don't do anything rash.*

Kris couldn't believe it. Ivy must have regained his memory. His words and actions couldn't be explained otherwise. And yet he didn't seem to resent Kris for what he had done. Even after everything that had happened, he showed no fear.

Someone like him, someone so beautiful and purehearted should have never been pulled into Kris's world. But once again, Ivy proved to Kris that he was stronger than Kris had ever believed. *I saw something through divination,* he whispered in Kris's mind. *A man. Father said he was the Aranken prince. I couldn't get a better glimpse of his motivations or of whether or not there's someone else involved. But this power.... Be careful, Kris.*

In that moment, Kris finally understood. He should have seen it before. He didn't believe in coincidences, and the recent behavior of the Aranken crown should have warned him to expect something more.

Well, Kris might have his own goals separate from the ones of his predecessors, but he'd die before he let politics destroy what he shared with Ivy. Beyond the importance of the empire, beyond the duty of the Morai toward the rest of the Nikari, Kris fought for Ivy. Even if he'd already decided he had no right to claim Ivy anymore, he would make sure Ivy was safe, no matter what he needed to do.

As he guided Attcha forward toward the Half-Blood attacker, Kris assessed the situation. Ivy had been right in warning him about his foe's power. No Half Blood, no matter how strong, could keep three dozen Nikari in check. The fact that he'd managed to take out the air elemental so quickly was a feat in itself. Whether this was because of the Aranken royals or not, Kris needed to be careful.

Nikari didn't have many defensive spells. Kris's own powers mostly rotated around the elements of air and water, like those of an Aranken Storm Caller. However, after centuries of exploring the unique qualities of their nature, Nikari also had affinity with other elements. In Kris's case, this element was earth. He didn't use it nearly enough, but it still obeyed him when he summoned it. He surrounded himself and Attcha with a strong barrier of stone. His precautions didn't really help, though, at least not significantly. No sooner had he come into contact with the circle of magic than his painstakingly built armor crumbled like dust. Kris groaned as the darkness touched him, his very sense of self sucked in by the strange power.

Oddly, the feel of it reminded him a little of a rift, while at the same time contrasting with it. Anomalous occurrences aside, long-distance traveling through such a portal made him, at worst, feel like he had needles pushing through his skin. It could have been comparable to the double rift that had nearly killed him, at least in intensity. But whereas the double rift had been unleashed chaos, this... this nothingness was unlike anything Kris had ever experienced before.

Nevertheless, the assessment gave him an idea that he didn't delay putting it into practice. He guided Attcha away from the main power surge. *Get ready, Attcha,* he told the nightwolf.

Yes, strong one. Black fur understand.

Together Kris and Attcha opened a rift right then and there, at the edge of the whirlpool of darkness. Tendrils of power snaked after them but couldn't reach them. Kris escaped within the dimensional portal, only to emerge seconds later, right behind his opponent.

This close to the source of the enchantment, Kris felt like his skin was being flayed off his bones. But he didn't need long. In fact, he didn't need to do much at all. This wasn't solely his revenge, after all.

Before the Half Blood could try to attack them directly, Attcha landed on him. Burying his fangs in their foe's shoulder, he bit off chunks of flesh, clawing at their opponent's body. *Black fur avenge,* he said. *Lying ones hurt black fur pack. Must pay.*

Kris felt exactly the same way, to the extent that he hated being the one to stop Attcha's fun. In fact, he'd have preferred to get his turn at his opponent, but no sooner had Attcha started to rip at the Half

Blood's flesh than the power around them dimmed. The man collapsed facedown on the ground, completely at the nightwolf's mercy.

Attcha would have probably enjoyed himself quite a bit with tearing the Half Blood apart, but Kris pulled the nightwolf's fur, gesturing for his friend to stop. With a reluctant growl, Attcha complied.

Kris dismounted and took a deep breath so he wouldn't be tempted to destroy what was left of his opponent. In his heart, he wanted nothing more, but he needed some answers, and only this man had them.

Much to his dismay, however, as he turned the man over, he realized he was too late. The Half Blood's eyes were already blank, his body slowly going cooler in death. Kris could only curse in disgruntled dismay. What now?

CHAPTER THIRTEEN
ANSWERS

THE BATTLE ended faster than Ivy would have expected. At one point, Ivy's heart nearly stopped when Kris and Attcha simply disappeared, but then he realized they'd merely used a rift to transport themselves behind Akolo.

After that…. Well, Ivy didn't like seeing that particular event, but at the same time, he couldn't ignore it either. He didn't even think he wanted to, because, like he'd told Kris once upon a time, he refused to pretend his lover wasn't the Nikari Morai.

Still, it was sobering to watch Attcha attack Akolo. It wasn't that he didn't understand it or had expected anything different, but the fact remained that this was the first time he'd seen Attcha do anything violent, and it was against someone Ivy had once been close to.

When Kris turned Akolo over and cursed, Ivy knew without being told that his former manservant was beyond help. Ivy experienced a pang of grief, not only at Akolo's death, but also at the thought that maybe some interest from his part could have prevented this.

But not even that bite of guilt could keep him from what he needed to do. His mental struggle with Akolo's mysterious power had brought back his memories, including those of the events that had led up to his injury. There were still bits and pieces missing, but what he did remember made him struggle to his feet and stagger toward Kris.

Using his abilities several times after a potentially life-threatening injury had him weak as a newborn babe, and he already resented that because of it he hadn't been able to help Kris more. Ignoring his mother's gasp of protest, he made his way to Kris's side.

Kris's attention immediately turned toward him. As their eyes met, Ivy took a deep breath and said, "I'm sorry. I'm sorry about earlier. I.... It wasn't Shuri I saw when we went to the interior garden. I thought he was you."

"I know," Kris replied. "I... I figured it out." He laughed bitterly. "Well, to be fair, Attcha made me see it. I truly had no right to treat you the way I did."

Kris cleared his throat, and Ivy became aware of all the eyes now focused on them. He bit his lower lip uncertainly. Perhaps he shouldn't have approached such a delicate, personal matter in public. For all he knew, most of the people here weren't privy to Kris's private affairs. Not to mention that it wasn't in the least bit tactful to mention it with Shuri there.

Ivy winced at his own behavior, wondering how he'd managed to drive such a huge rift between the brothers. *It wasn't Shuri's fault,* he said through his mental skills.

I know. The fault was solely mine. He reached for Ivy's cheek but pulled back before he could touch Ivy. *I have no right to you anymore.*

Ivy didn't like the sound of that. He'd expected some guilt on Kris's part, and to be fair, his injury had been pretty serious. Nonetheless, Ivy saw it as an unfortunate accident. He didn't want to give up on a relationship so precious to him because of it. He still believed in Kris. They just needed to do more adapting to each other so that in the future they'd never get to that point.

Attcha nudged Ivy with his muzzle. Even if he'd just seen the nightwolf maul Akolo—and Akolo's blood lingered on his black fur—it didn't scare or disgust Ivy. *Soft one?* Attcha asked. *Soft one climb.*

Kris must have heard that too, because he picked Ivy up and settled him on Attcha's back. *Go rest. We'll talk more about this later.*

Right now, Kris had to be the Morai. Ivy understood. But even if he hadn't been able to support Kris in battle, he wanted to do so with his presence and whatever knowledge he'd managed to gather from his divination.

"I want answers as much as you do," he said, shaking his head. His gaze went to his parents, specifically to his sire. He didn't know why, but he had a feeling the older Andari knew something about this.

He guided the nightwolf to his sire and pressed his hand to Rasami's shoulder. "Sire? Are you well?"

The older Andari seemed to snap out of a strange trance. His glazed eyes fixed on Ivy's face. "Ivy? You're.... You're alive. But how? No.... It can't be."

"Why? What do you know about all this, Sire? What made you come here in the first place?"

It couldn't be a coincidence that his parents had suddenly decided to like him. The strangeness of their behavior—from their concern, to their willingness to forget about Ivy breaking the betrothal promise to the marquis, and his sire's abrupt decision to use the short form of Ivy's name—should have alerted him to it.

His sire stared at Ivy's face without replying. At last, ignoring the fact that Ivy remained on the nightwolf's back, he embraced Ivy tightly. "You're alive. Reysen, thank you. This truly is a miracle."

Over Rasami's shoulder, Ivy threw his father a look. The Andari lord's bereft gaze shocked him beyond measure. His mother seemed just as lost and shaken. Ivy didn't know how to react, so he just hugged his sire back.

The gesture felt awkward to Ivy, too different from anything he'd known his sire to do. It relieved him greatly when Kris intervened. "We should take this inside," he said. "Sai, Shuri, come with us. The rest of you, make sure the body is taken care of and patrol the palace. I want to know who exactly let this man in."

"What about the nightwolves, Your Majesty?" a Nikari guard asked. "They grew exceedingly restless, almost maddened not long before you showed up."

"Do not approach them under any circumstances," Kris said. "Attcha and I will deal with it personally, once they've calmed down a bit."

Ivy's sire released him with obvious reluctance, and together they made their way inside. Kris didn't take them to the throne room or any of the potential meeting areas available. Instead, they entered the imperial wing and headed straight for Kris's personal chambers.

"These rooms are shielded," Kris explained as soon as the door closed behind them. "We'll be able to talk here without fear of anyone overhearing."

Ivy had innumerable questions, but most of all, he wanted to know what he could do to help mend an impossibly shattered family. He was torn between his own parents, Kris, and Shuri. Before he could find some way to vocalize his thoughts, though, Shuri turned to glare at Kris. "What happened in Tarkquin, Kris?" he asked. "Why did I receive news that Uncle is dying?"

"That's a good question," Kris replied steadily. "Perhaps you could tell me when exactly Phura decided to open a double rift."

Shuri paled. "A double rift? Creator…. That's why the nightwolves were acting the way they did. But why? Why would he do such a thing?"

Ivy already had his suspicions, and Kris confirmed them moments later. "It all goes back to Father's death at your mother's hands. Uncle Phura was led to believe that my mother was behind her death, which caused him to set that suicidal trap."

Shuri stared at him. "You can't be serious. My mother would never…."

He trailed off, stopping before he could finish the phrase. Ivy wondered if Shuri himself had suspected something. It was almost unbearable to think. "Did she truly do it?" Shuri finally asked.

"I have it confirmed from several sources," Kris replied. "My mother said that before he died, my father revealed this truth to her, and the nightwolves were aware of it."

"And you would have me believe Katara did nothing to avenge her husband?" Shuri scoffed. "I am not a fool, Kris."

This was an issue that would forever separate the two brothers, and something Ivy couldn't do anything about. Thankfully, Shuri must have known throwing accusations at Katara would not help, since he focused on the other part of Kris's revelations. "How can this sort of thing even be possible?"

"Father's nightwolf was poisoned with a substance similar to what Ivy ingested. As far as we can tell, in Ivy's case, it was aimed at his perception, leading him to mistake you for me."

Even if Ivy had said that himself in the garden, his heart still clenched when the corner of Shuri's mouth tightened. "I see," Shuri said. "It's all starting to make sense now."

"I'm sorry," Ivy piped up before things could get any worse. "It was my fault. If I'd been stronger, if I'd fought it...."

"If there's anyone innocent in this whole affair, it's you, Ivy," his mother interrupted him. "I believe that all of us here can agree on that much. You just ended up in the middle of a conflict you didn't actually cause."

His father nodded. "Whatever happened in the past to shake the imperial family, you have nothing to do with it, Ivy. You can still come home."

Ivy didn't know what to believe anymore. "I thought you hated me, Father. I disappointed you by choosing Kris."

His sire took his hand, squeezing it tightly. "You asked me why I came here. Shortly after you became His Imperial Majesty's moraistele and we returned to Seanda, I started having dreams. At first, I couldn't remember too much of them, but I knew that they were in some way connected to you. I didn't grow too alarmed in the beginning, since at the time, your father and I were discussing how to control the aftermath of your actions."

Rasami took a deep breath, as if bracing himself for something very difficult. "The dreams grew more vivid. In every single one, I saw you dying. I became increasingly restless, and while I tried to tell myself it was simply uncertainty playing tricks on me, I couldn't let it go. Both your father and I agreed it would be best if we moved to Nikaret and kept an eye on you. Our move was pushed forward when the dreams turned into visions and followed me even outside slumber." Rasami sighed heavily. "I feared the worst. I realize now that part of it must have been manipulation on Akolo's part. In my desperate concern, I gave him the perfect opening to reach you."

"It's not your fault," Ivy said. "You couldn't have known he was behind it."

"I could have if I'd given him more than a cursory glance," his sire argued, pretty much exactly the way Ivy had berated himself. "But that's beside the point. I'm so proud of you, son. You have no idea.... When I saw you fall, I thought this was it. I'd failed. The vision had come true, and you were gone forever. But you surpassed any expectation I might have had. You did fight it, and you were stronger than I ever was."

"So I take it Ivy was supposed to die," Kris said darkly, interrupting the exchange. "Since I didn't kill him, the Aranken decided to take matters into their own hands, or rather Akolo's."

Ivy hesitated, looking at all the expectant faces in the room. His situation already seemed quite frustrating. Kris's earlier words scared him a little. Still, he couldn't stay quiet, not with the conversation rapidly escalating to a possible declaration of war.

"I'm not so sure it was them, Kris," he said. "I saw the Aranken prince, yes. But I know your magic. It's elemental. Nikari have Aranken ancestors, right? Their magic should be similar. What I experienced then felt entirely different."

"I would be inclined to agree," Kris said, "but we don't know enough about the Aranken anymore. In the past, they have made attempts to approach us, but it's the policy of the Nikari crown to ignore such actions and turn them away."

He threw a glance Shuri's way, obviously noticing the lingering tension in the other Nikari. "We will make a decision later. For the moment, I think my brother would like to see Uncle Phura."

He didn't even wait for a reply on Shuri's part, but then, it didn't seem necessary. Ivy could read the relief on Shuri's face as well as he could see Kris's frustration. To top it off, since Katara wasn't by her son's side, Ivy could only imagine she'd stayed behind to keep an eye on Kris's injured uncle. If Shuri already blamed her for his mother's death, having Phura die in her presence would be a recipe for disaster.

"Anfarasha, I'd like to enlist your assistance in healing my uncle. I worry there's not much time left."

Fortunately, in spite of whatever misgivings Ivy's mother might have had with regard to Ivy's stay in Nikaret, she remained above all else, a healer. "I'd be happy to help," she said, "as long as Ivy is safe."

Ivy opened his mouth to argue that he wanted to go as well, but Kris kept him from even trying to do so. "Don't worry, Anfarasha. I assure you that Ivy's safety is my priority as well. He will remain here, in my quarters, until the two of us can reach a satisfying conclusion to this situation."

Ivy highly doubted the end result of whatever conversation they might have would be satisfying for either of them. Even so, he nodded.

At the end of the day, as much as he loved Kris, he had to admit that the things Kris had said and done hurt him. He'd wanted to believe Kris could see him as something more than a concubine, but perhaps he'd been wrong to hope that all along.

As silence fell over the room, Ivy climbed off Attcha and walked into the bedroom. He didn't want to watch Kris go. Perhaps if he didn't, he could still deceive himself that there might be a way for him and Kris to be together.

Curling on the same bed they'd first made love in, Ivy closed his eyes and half wished he'd never remembered anything at all.

THE RIFT obediently carried Kris and his two companions back to Tarkquin. He found his mother waiting for him outside Phura's room. "Thank the Creator," she said. "I was worried sick. What happened?"

"We were attacked in Nikaret," Kris replied. "The situation is contained for the moment, but we still have to learn the root causes." He paused and looked at the door. "How is he?"

"Not well," his mother replied. "It's a good thing that you brought Shuri here."

On cue, Shuri walked past her and entered the room, dragging the Andari healer along. Kris settled down to wait, giving the two of them privacy. He could have followed, but if he wanted to be perfectly honest, his thoughts were consumed by other matters.

A part of him wanted to jump at the chance Ivy had given him, to make use of Ivy's kindness, but he couldn't do that. He'd had one chance to build something that might have helped him to become more than he was, the man Ivy saw in him. But he'd lost the right to Ivy's love, and he could be brave enough to admit Ivy deserved better.

He had told Ivy's parents that he wouldn't allow them to take Ivy out of Nikaret, and at the time, it would have indeed been a bad idea. Proof in point, the fact that Ivy's manservant had attacked him.

Ivy couldn't return to Seanda anyway. What would he do there? Suffer the shame of accepting the position of moraistele and then being cast aside?

As if guessing his thoughts, his mother took his hand and asked, "What are you going to do, Kris?"

It was a good question. The brother whose affection he had hoped to earn had turned against him and stabbed him in the back. He'd broken an honor bond—and all because he wanted Kris's lover.

Kris had been furious, and a part of him still was. At the same time, though, he acknowledged that in a way, his enduring jealousy had partially been caused by the realization that Shuri might be better for Ivy than Kris.

Could he truly blame Shuri for wanting Ivy? No, of course not. He himself had witnessed firsthand the pull of Ivy's sweet strength. He didn't even have the right to be possessive anymore, not after what he'd done to Ivy.

So where did that leave him? He'd already decided he would not pursue any further punishment for Shuri breaking his honor bond. It might make sense to free Ivy from his duty as a moraistele and allow Shuri to pursue him.

However, Ivy wasn't truly in love with Shuri, and Kris couldn't lie to himself and claim that didn't relieve him. Yes, those feelings made him even more of a bastard, but knowing that didn't change any of it.

His mother pressed her hand to his shoulder, and Kris realized he still hadn't answered. "I'm sorry," he told her with a strained smile. "It seems I just can't decide."

"What exactly happened?" his mother asked him.

As Kris explained, her eyes grew progressively wider. She'd known about the first part, but the attack on Ivy changed things. "The immediate threat might be gone," he told her, "but what is to say it won't happen again?" He rubbed his eyes tiredly. "Guessing by what he said earlier, he probably still wants us to be together. But I don't deserve him, Mother. I never have."

It occurred to him that his mother might not be the ideal person to explain his insecurities to since she was liable to be biased in his favor. "I know what you're going to say," he quickly added, "but the fact remains that I hurt him. I should have protected him, and I didn't. I should have trusted him—Creator, I saw his soul when I claimed him—

but I didn't. I can't forgive myself for any of it, and I can't expect Ivy to do so, even if he might want to."

His mother sighed heavily. "Are you sure you can leave behind what the two of you shared?"

"I don't have much choice, do I?"

As he looked at her, an idea sparked in his mind. He owed Ivy for everything that had happened between them, and in his heart, he didn't want to lose Ivy. There was a way, a selfish way, perhaps, but one that would keep Ivy safe and give him the chance to shine like he was meant to.

For the first time since this entire ordeal had started, Kris smiled. His relationship with Ivy might be shattered beyond repair, but that didn't mean Kris couldn't remain by his side.

"I'm going to ask him to bond with me," he said. "I'm going to ask him to be my Moris."

He'd expected his mother to be surprised or argue with him, but she didn't. Instead, she just smiled. "The two of you do make a wonderful couple."

Before Kris could figure out exactly what she believed of his new plan, the door opened. Shuri stood in the entryway, stone-faced. "What is it?" Kris asked, immediately alarmed.

"Uncle Phura wants to see you," Shuri replied, but not to Kris—to his mother.

"Me?" Katara blinked in surprise. "Are you sure?"

Shuri just stepped back and gestured for her to enter the room. Kris went with her, automatically suspicious. Not that Phura could do anything to his mother. Even under normal circumstances, she could have protected herself from him. But whatever Phura wanted to tell Kris's mother couldn't be good. At the very least, Kris needed to hear it too, and maybe in the process, he'd figure out if there had been more to Phura's attack than him remembering things best left forgotten.

The moment he and his mother stepped in view of the injured Nikari, Kris couldn't help but notice how much better Phura looked. He might not have recovered his arm, but his coloring had drastically improved. Against all odds, Ivy's mother had saved his life.

"Your Imperial Majesty," he said coldly, "I see you are well."

Kris wanted to offer a scathing reply, like "no thanks to you", but it would just be petty and wouldn't supply him with the answers he sought. "Yes, I am. Thank you. I can only hope you'll recover as well."

Phura grimaced, obviously aware that he would never be the same again. "Perhaps it would be best if we didn't play games," he said. "I might have lost a limb, but my only regret is that I didn't take at least one of you with me."

Everyone in the room—with the exception of Kris—gaped at the older Nikari. For Kris's part, he'd known his uncle wouldn't try to utter any apologies. The situation had escalated too much for such things to have any value. And because Phura likely didn't care who heard what, Kris ushered the medics out. Once they were in private, he addressed his uncle once again. "How unfortunate for you," he said. "But I believe it's my mother you wished to speak with."

"Indeed. Tell me, why did you wait so long to murder them? I always knew you hated my wife, but I didn't expect you to turn against your husband, as well."

"Is that truly what you think?" Katara chuckled, although the laugh held no humor. "I hate to disappoint you, but she was the one who killed him. I came here that day to punish her for it, but I never got the chance to do it. Someone else got to her first."

"Someone?" Phura snorted. "And who would that be?"

"Perhaps the same person who convinced you to do something as stupid as a double rift," Kris prodded. "The same person who gave your wife the substance she needed to poison Father's nightwolf. Come now, Uncle. You can't possible believe in her so blindly."

"What about you?" Phura shot back. "You trust your mother's words just like that, without wondering why she found it necessary to destroy my memories."

"This is a pointless conversation," Kris answered, not in the least bit shaken. "My mother is not on trial here. Once you fully recover, you will be incarcerated for treason. I might be persuaded to soften your punishment if you cooperate and tell me what I want to know. Otherwise, I can just take the information from your mind, and I'm sure you realize that won't be pleasant."

"Do what you like." Phura shrugged. "While I love to listen to your conspiracy theories, there is absolutely no one else involved in my decision—just like there's no one but your mother involved in the death of my wife and my brother."

"So was it you who attacked my son, then?" Anfarasha glared at the Nikari. "If I'd known, I never would have healed you."

"Your son?" Phura stared at her as if he'd completely forgotten about her presence.

"Ivy," Kris elaborated. "My moraistele."

"I haven't touched him," Phura replied, still sounding gobsmacked. "What interest would I possibly have in an idiotic Andari whore?"

Anfarasha released an outraged gasp, and Kris couldn't blame her for her anger. He narrowed his eyes at his uncle. "You'd better watch your tongue, Uncle. I hardly think you're in any position to call other people idiotic, and you'll find that crossing me further is not a good idea."

"That might be the case, nephew," Phura said, "but it doesn't change any of the truths I told you."

Kris had grown weary of playing games. Ironically, he believed his uncle, and he didn't intend to follow through with his threat once Phura recovered enough. But, of course, he wouldn't tell them that. Sometimes it paid to be feared. "Shuri, come with me. The two of us have a conversation pending."

Phura suddenly paled and tried to get up. "I told you everything I know. Leave Shuri out of this."

Kris had never understood Phura's attachment to Shuri. At one point, he'd believed it might be just for show. The fact that Shuri had offered to honor bind to Kris for his uncle's sake canceled that possibility.

Kris ignored his uncle and left the room. Shuri followed shortly after that. "Do you truly plan to break his mind?"

"I'm certainly entitled to it," Kris replied, "as I am to punish you, but I have no intention of discussing that. I have one question for you. Do you want to help Ivy?"

"Yes, of course," Shuri replied. "I've only ever wanted what was best for him."

The implication seemed to be that Kris didn't want that, but Kris ignored it. "Then tell me something. What connection did your mother have with A'rankin? What did Father learn that caused her to kill him? You didn't seem very surprised when I mentioned it, so I gather you must have some idea."

Shuri shook his head. "I hate to disappoint you, but I don't know anything specific. I just remembered that around the time of her death, she and I spoke extensively about the change in Father's attitude toward me. She was very angry, and she mentioned at one point that he wanted to separate me from her."

"That isn't good enough," Kris replied. "Start looking into it. If you don't provide me with the answers I seek, I'll start making more forceful inquiries, in your mind and Phura's."

"And you'd trust my word, even if I broke my honor bond to you?"

A different time, Kris might have said that the two of them were brothers, and things like honor bonds didn't apply between them, at least not like that. Now, however, Kris had resigned himself to the fact that they would never have a real sibling relationship. And so Kris said, "It's not your loyalty to me that I trust, but your affection toward your future Moris."

He left his brother standing there, speechless, while he plotted his next move. He could only hope Ivy wouldn't refuse his proposal.

EVEN IF he felt more exhausted than he ever remembered being, Ivy couldn't sleep a wink. Attcha had left for the dens, likely to help control the other nightwolves. His parents had given him privacy, and he was thankful for that, but right now, he would have welcomed a distraction from his thoughts.

Would Kris leave him? Ivy couldn't be sure, not really. Kris hadn't told him that outright. But Ivy knew Kris well enough to read between the lines. So what did it mean? Ivy hated this uncertainty, and he hated it even more that he was worrying about himself when the current status quo involved possible war.

For that reason, when Kris appeared in the room, Ivy got up so fast he nearly fell out of the bed. His lover shot him a concerned look. "Are you all right?"

"Fine," Ivy replied automatically. "Just a bit unsettled."

Kris arched a brow. "A bit?"

"Well, maybe more than a bit," Ivy admitted. And wasn't it ironic that Akolo's attack on him and subsequent death didn't seem to be the main cause of that anxiety?

Kris sat on the edge of the bed next to Ivy and reached for Ivy's hand. "I need to talk to you about something."

Ivy licked his suddenly dry lips. A part of him wanted to push Kris into giving them another chance, but something told him he needed to stay quiet and listen.

Apparently encouraged by Ivy's attitude, Kris fixed him with a steady, piercing look. "Behnivyr Erethe, I would be honored if you agreed to be my Moris."

For a few moments, the words didn't even process. Ivy blinked, wondering if he'd heard wrong. He waited for Kris to say something else, but when the Nikari remained silent, he finally asked, "You want me to be your official consort?"

That was the exact opposite of the separation Ivy had expected. Ivy should have been ecstatic. He'd always hoped to be more than a concubine to Kris. But for some reason, Kris's words made his stomach roil and his heart clench. "Why?"

"Because you deserve it," Kris replied. He released Ivy's hands and looked away. "Rest assured, you'd have all the freedom you want. You'd be entitled to take your own *stele* if you so desire, and I would not demand any intimacies from you."

Ivy frowned. He didn't understand. "So you don't want us to be intimate. But you're still asking me to bond with you."

Kris nodded but didn't elaborate. Perhaps it was better that way, since any further explanations might have made things worse. Ivy wanted to cry. This twisted empty offer wasn't his idea of his future with Kris.

But when he looked at Kris's face and saw the pain in Kris's eyes, he couldn't say no. He couldn't say yes either. "Can I think about it?" he asked quietly.

"Yes, of course," Kris replied, getting off the bed. "You can take as much time as you need. I won't pressure you into anything."

It seemed strange to see Kris so... sedate, if that was even the appropriate word under such circumstances. Ivy instinctively wanted to reach out to Kris, but he realized now that a different kind of rift existed between them. Ivy had followed Kris to Nikaret based on nothing more than what his heart had told him. And while he didn't regret what he and Kris had shared, he wondered now if two people who were so different could truly be happy together.

Still, when Kris left the room, Ivy felt the Nikari's absence like a physical blow. He buried his face in his palms, more torn than ever. What now? He didn't want to leave Kris, but could he truly accept Kris's conditions?

A female voice snapped him out of his depressed musings. "He asked you, didn't he?"

Ivy looked up, only to see the A'Mora standing there a few feet away from him. It was disconcerting to see her appear out of nowhere in the exact place Kris had been. Katara must have walked in through the door—using a dimensional portal would have had effects that Ivy would have noticed—and Ivy had just been too distracted to notice.

"Yes, he did," Ivy replied. "I… I'm not sure what I should reply."

Katara sat on the bed, once more in an eerie echo of what Kris had done. Ivy wondered what she wanted to tell him. Whatever it was, it couldn't help him decide. He wanted to tell her he needed some time alone to think, but Katara didn't give him the chance. "Do you remember that night when we first met? I asked you if you could carry the burden of the Morai's affection."

Yes, she had, and Ivy had reeled at the phrasing. "I remember," he said.

"I won't ask you the same thing now," the A'Mora told him. "However, I will tell you a little secret. Perhaps I should have warned you then, but the truth is we Nikari feel things very intensely. You probably understand since it's just like with your heat. Our problems stem from the mix of the Aranken bloodline with your distant cousins, the Ndara. We might be a very powerful species, but that doesn't come without a price."

Ivy scowled. "What exactly are you saying, Your Majesty?"

Katara continued to speak like he hadn't asked anything at all. "Do you know how the very first Morai died? He was Aranken, the Fezenda lord who set the basis of our civilization. He was killed by his own son, the half-breed he had with a Ndara woman."

Ivy hadn't known that. How odd that such a vital piece of information in the history of a nation would be kept secret.

"Things have improved somewhat since then," Katara added. "Like the Andari, we strive to contain our impulses. But whereas with you, these urges are largely sexual, ours can be violent in nature. You yourself said it once. Nikari are like nightwolves. Dangerous."

"I realize that," Ivy replied. "I thought I knew before, and maybe I did, but only at an intellectual level. Now I've seen it with my own eyes."

"Indeed," Katara replied. "Under those circumstances, do you think you can be what my son needs? Are you strong enough to give him what he can no longer ask for?"

"I don't know," Ivy admitted. "I want to be, but… I'm not sure anymore."

"Then you know what answer you should give him." To Ivy's surprise, Katara smiled. "Just be honest with yourself and with him. In the long run, it will be the best thing for both of you."

The knot in Ivy's gut tightened. "But I… I still love him."

"Do you? Is love what you feel, or is it merely lust? How much time did you two have together to begin with?" Katara's gaze seemed to pierce his soul. "How long had you known him when you first told him 'I love you'?"

Ivy gaped at Katara. Her words held no accusation, but they still struck Ivy like a torrent of ice water.

He had told himself that being in heat hadn't influenced his decision to become Kris's concubine. That had, of course, been foolish of him. It was far nobler to speak of making his choices based on emotion than to say that he'd been thinking with his dick when he'd spread his legs for Kris.

Something inside Ivy rebelled at the thought. He might be naïve, but his feelings were real. Clenching his fists, he took a deep breath and straightened his back. "It's not like that. Yes, we might have had a little of a whirlwind romance, but that doesn't change the fact that what I feel is true. I think that goes for Kris too. Otherwise, he wouldn't have asked me to be his Moris to begin with."

"I see." Katara finally left the bed and headed toward the door. With her hand hovering over the doorknob, she threw one last comment over her shoulder. "In that case, it seems there's no reason for me to be here. You know exactly what to do."

Much to his surprise, Ivy realized that he did know. "Thank you," he told the A'Mora.

"Just don't fail me, Ivy," she said. "Take care of him. His heart is frailer than other people might think."

When Katara finally left, Ivy jumped out of bed with renewed energy. He had a plan now, and he would not let go of Kris, not just yet.

KRIS STARED at the map of A'rankin without really seeing it. His mind remained focused on his earlier conversation with Ivy. In hindsight, he should have expected refusal on Ivy's part, but that didn't mean the prospect terrified him any less.

When the knock came, he instantly knew who it announced. He forced himself to get a good grip on his emotions. If Ivy said no, Kris had to let him go, and that was that. No more excuses, no more futile attempts to rebuild a simulacrum of a relationship that could never exist. There were other ways—giving Ivy a second nobility title, for example. Ivy didn't necessarily have to rebuild his life with an Andari. There were plenty of people who would give just about anything to have the chance Kris had wasted. Never mind that the thought made Kris want to scream. This wasn't about him, and he needed to remember that.

That resolve had him rushing to the door and lasted until he opened it. When he saw Ivy standing there, with his beautiful green eyes a little wide and his lips a little swollen—he must have been biting them in concern—Kris wanted nothing more than to pull Ivy into his embrace and forget any of this had ever happened.

But he couldn't do that, so to keep himself from reaching for Ivy, he crossed his arms over his chest. "Do you have an answer for me?" he asked.

"Yes." Kris's treacherous heart started to beat faster before he realized Ivy's "yes" was in reply to this latter inquiry, not to his offer.

"And?" he prodded.

Much to his surprise, Ivy bowed lowly, just like he had the very first time they'd met. "Your Imperial Majesty, you honor me through your proposal. I do feel, however, that our relationship hasn't yet reached that point in which we can bond, so I would prefer it if we got to know each other more before we took any further steps."

The formal address startled Kris, and for a few seconds the reply didn't process. When it finally did, he was torn between shock, dismay, and reluctant enthusiasm.

Ivy had not refused Kris's offer, but neither had he accepted. He'd suggested an alternative—a clean slate for both of them. Ivy might not have said so outright, but Kris heard it regardless.

At some level, he knew he shouldn't agree. It would be like taking advantage of Ivy, and he'd already decided that, above all else, he couldn't do that. But in spite of knowing this, he could not refuse.

"I find that to be an excellent idea," he heard himself say.

His reward came moments later, when Ivy shot him a blinding smile. "Good. I look forward to spending more time with you, Your Imperial Majesty. In the meantime, as your betrothed, I can no longer stay in the palace. I have already spoken with my parents, and starting tomorrow, I will move to their home, here in Nikaret."

Kris wasn't so thrilled about that, but at the same time, he also deemed the change necessary. If Ivy continued to live in the palace, things would just go on as before. "Very well," Kris said. "It will be as you wish it."

"Thank you," Ivy replied. "You are, as always, too kind."

Kris wanted to say something in turn, anything that would keep Ivy here. But the new formality between them threw him, and he couldn't come up with anything that would feel right.

What did regular Nikari do when they wooed their bond mates? What had his father done with his mother? Kris realized in dismay he didn't have a clue. He'd taken Ivy for granted so much that it hadn't even occurred to him to ask.

Not knowing what else to say, he offered, "With your permission, I will join you tomorrow and provide you with an escort to your new accommodations."

"I would not presume to take you away from your important affairs," Ivy replied.

Ivy had never made such demands before either, and Kris had always allowed his oh-so-important affairs to come first, neglecting the young Andari who'd thrown everything to the wind just because of him. Not again. Never again. "Nothing's more important than you."

For a split second, Ivy gave him a look of such want that it nearly shattered Kris's control. Kris's entire body went taut, his cock hardening as he imagined dragging Ivy into his quarters and ravishing him. Then Ivy looked away, and the spell was broken.

"I should go," he said softly. "I look forward to seeing you tomorrow, Your Imperial Majesty."

"And I, you," Kris murmured back.

As he watched Ivy go, Kris realized not for the first time how madly in love he was with Ivy. He'd never felt more ill-prepared for anything in his life.

Chapter Fourteen
Again

Ivy's PROVERBIAL first date with Kris happened on a beautiful summer morning, one week after he had approached Kris with his plan. Up until then, they'd shared several meals, sometimes at the palace, other times in Nikari restaurants, and once even in the home of Ivy's parents. However, they'd always had company, with Ivy's father or sire hovering nearby.

Today, however, they would finally be alone. Kris had asked Ivy to a walk in a nearby forest, at which point Ivy had realized he'd never gone on such trips with Kris, only with Katara.

Therefore, Ivy had readily agreed. Kris came to pick him up, not in a carriage, but on his nightwolf. It was really nice to see Attcha. Because of this new situation, Ivy's visits to the nightwolf dens had been restricted, and he'd missed the nightwolf. Besides, it helped distract Ivy from his nerves.

Right before he left, Ivy's sire pulled him aside. "Don't let him pressure you into anything. Remember your position."

Ivy refrained from pointing out he and Kris had already made love countless times before, because that was beside the point. "I know, Sire," he said. "I will remember."

He knew why his sire had chosen to emphasize this particular fact. After the time he'd spent at Kris's side, his body had grown accustomed to regular sexual activity. He'd already started to feel the incipient signs of a heat approaching.

But this time around, he would not let lust get in the way of finding the right path for the two of them. He clung to that decision as he turned toward Kris. "Greetings, Your Imperial Majesty."

"Good morning, Your Lordship," Kris replied in turn. "I take it you're ready to go?"

"Yes, thank you," Ivy answered. Kris offered him his hand and pulled him on top of Attcha.

At the back of his mind, Ivy heard Attcha's contended rumble. *Soft one. Black fur welcomes back.*

Ivy patted Attcha's fur, smiling softly. In the process, he realized this was the first time ever he'd ridden Attcha with Kris. Leaning against Kris's wide back appealed to him in such a natural way that Ivy forced himself to resist the urge. He did need to wrap his arms around Kris's waist, but he did so as demurely as possible.

Kris made no comment on Ivy's posture. Since Ivy didn't have the nightwolf fur cloak anymore—he'd returned it upon leaving the palace—they proceeded down the main road of Nikaret.

Ivy had to admit he felt a little embarrassed. Their passage naturally drew the eye, and although Nikari were too pragmatic to stand there gawking at their Morai, he still sensed the scrutiny acutely. But then he often felt that wherever he went. People wondered what had changed between the Morai and his concubine, why Kris catered to Ivy so much when appearances suggested Ivy had been kicked out of the palace in disgrace.

Gradually, Ivy got used to the looks, and he allowed himself to enjoy the walk. There was a message in the fact that Kris so blatantly displayed himself with Ivy. Not only that, but Kris didn't head directly toward the city gates. Instead, he took them on to meandering streets, small alleys through which Attcha's bulk barely even fit, hidden bazaars that somehow widened into a large bustling marketplace. Like most things in Nikari civilization, it all seemed very organized, the grid-like structure of Nikaret assigning each building to a particular zone in the city. And then there was the occasional establishment that challenged the rule, breaking the norms, giving the city a mysterious air, full of exciting possibilities.

"I remember a time when I would run through these streets, playing hide and seek," Kris said at one point. "Of course, no one would really play with the future Morai, so I always forced my mother to do it, whether she wanted to or not."

Ivy chuckled. He could definitely imagine that. "You're describing yourself as quite a naughty child."

"Maybe I was," Kris answered. "And then I found Attcha, and he just encouraged me. Damn beast."

Attcha released a self-satisfied rumble, perhaps confirming Kris's words. "How old were you when you summoned your first rift?" Ivy asked. He knew from his lessons that Kris had hit his one hundred and third birthday a few weeks prior to the summer solstice, but he had no idea about more private information, even if by now, he should have.

"Oh, I was a little over fifteen," Kris replied.

"That's very early, isn't it?" Ivy asked. At fifteen, Nikari were still considered children, unlike Andari, who matured faster in the first years of life, only to slow down after they came of age.

"Yes, it is, but sometimes, you just know. You just feel the soul calling out to yours."

Ivy's stomach started doing somersaults, and his face flamed. He had a feeling Kris wasn't solely talking about Attcha. "I agree," he replied, unable to control the tremor in his voice. "We just have to find our way there."

And sadly, Ivy and Kris hadn't done so, not yet, at least. His injury had been an accident, and Ivy didn't blame Kris for it, but even before that, their relationship had lacked a certain level of emotional intimacy. Now, however, they were making progress. Simply talking about things brought them closer. In a way, it reminded Ivy of the night they'd spent together on the summer solstice. They might have worn masks that day, but oddly, they'd been more open with each other than after those masks had fallen.

As Kris finally guided Attcha toward the city gates, it occurred to Ivy that the two of them must have already spent a good couple of hours exploring Nikaret. Since he'd left the palace, he didn't know what had happened with the investigation on Aranken involvement in the conspiracy that had targeted them. Could Kris really set it all aside just for Ivy's sake?

Ivy waited until Attcha entered the forest, ensuring they had privacy from anyone who might want to listen in. "Your Imperial Majesty…. About what happened a week ago…."

Kris tensed. "Which part?"

It was a delicate thing to discuss, because they'd been doing a lot of dancing around the topic. In some ways, the "starting over" plan had disadvantages, because there were things in their shared past that couldn't and shouldn't be forgotten.

"I was wondering if your forces managed to uncover more information on the attack and the foreign influence on it," Ivy replied.

Kris stopped the nightwolf in the shade of a humongous tree. He dismounted and offered Ivy his hand. Ivy didn't necessarily need the help, but he took it regardless. As he joined Kris on the grassy forest floor, Kris's fingers tangled with his for a few moments, and their bodies brushed.

Ivy bit his lower lip to smother a whimper, more than ever aware of his blood heating and his face flushing. Fortunately—or unfortunately—Kris pulled away, taking away at least part of the temptation.

"I had Shuri look into it," he said. "He has the incentive of helping you and earning my forgiveness for Uncle Phura, if not for himself."

Ivy blinked, realizing he'd completely forgotten about his own question. After a few moments of hesitation, the answer finally processed. "I don't think you ever told me the details of what happened with your uncle."

They were falling into their old habits of familiarity, and it was a dangerous ground to tread, but it couldn't be helped. Kris wrapped an arm around Ivy's waist and guided Ivy through the foliage. "That's right," he mused. "I didn't."

He proceeded to fix that, and Ivy's eyes widened as he took in the seriousness of the facts Kris presented. "Oh my," he said. "This might be worse than I thought."

"Quite," Kris agreed. "And the danger isn't over yet, since we don't know who ran the entire scheme in the first place. Uncle Phura claims that he remembered everything on his own, and I believe he thinks he's telling the truth. But he's never been that powerful in the mental arts, and someone could have manipulated him without him realizing it." He chuckled without humor. "In a way, it's all my fault. I should have known better than to bury the entire affair because I thought my mother was behind Yoroshi's death."

"I also believed she'd been the one to kill Shuri's mother," Ivy confessed. "Attcha only told me bits and pieces of what happened back then, but I kind of drew that conclusion."

"The irony is that she didn't even have any reason to hide it. As the A'Mora, she was entitled to enact revenge on the Morai's killer. But Shuri's existence made the entire matter more complicated, largely because I cared for him so much."

"Perhaps she did it for you, yes," Ivy said, "but you can't carry the burden for other people's actions."

Kris released Ivy's waist, staring straight ahead. "I have enough with my own, don't I?" he mused.

Ivy took Kris's hand, squeezing the other man's palm. This time, the touch held little sensuality, since they were both focused on other things. "Stop thinking about that. We can't let the past lead us."

Kris freed his hand from Ivy's and faced him. "I don't know if I can do this, Ivy," he said. "I'm trying, and I… I have to admit that it makes me… happy, I suppose."

The words seemed to be coming out in a staccato rhythm, as if Kris had trouble saying them. A knot formed in Ivy's throat when he realized how difficult it was for Kris to utter the simple word "happy." "But?" he prodded.

"You've made me happy from the moment I met you," Kris answered. "That didn't keep me from hurting you. I'm afraid, Ivy. I'm afraid I'll just hurt you again."

Kris's answer almost shattered Ivy inside. As the Morai, Kris probably saw the admittance of fear as an unforgivable show of vulnerability. Ivy couldn't dismiss Kris's concerns. It would be cruel and dishonest. "We made a mistake," he told the Nikari. "We jumped into something without understanding what it entailed. But if we take our time, if we truly learn everything there is to know about each other, we can fix that. A real relationship is based on trust, and we just didn't have that, but that doesn't mean we can't earn it."

Kris's torn expression melted into a fond smile. "You're fearless, aren't you? How did I ever miss how strong you are?"

"I don't think I'm that strong," Ivy protested. "I just think that what we have is too precious to discard without trying one more time."

"And what does my beautiful future Moris suggest?" Kris asked, still smiling. "I'm all ears, since he seems so much better at this than me."

That was something Ivy hadn't considered too closely. "Let's just start at the beginning. You told me about when you first summoned Attcha. But what about now? What do you like to do?"

Kris leaned against a tree trunk and eyed him in disbelief. "What I like to do? To be with you, of course."

Ivy suppressed the swell of pleasure building up inside him. "But before me. What did you do for your own enjoyment, in your free time?"

"I'm the Morai," Kris replied steadily. "I don't have much free time, and the moments I did steal away, I regularly spent with Attcha."

Oh. Ivy should have guessed, since Kris and Katara had hinted at it more than once. He himself had witnessed the fact that even in a period of relative peace, displeased nobles always showed up with their complaints, or small rebellions appeared out of the woodwork. Leaving aside all that, the regular affairs of the Morai—administrative issues such as monitoring the individual policies of each province, making changes in taxation, monitoring trade routes, and so on and so forth— occupied a lot of time.

Ivy wanted to change that, but he couldn't realistically expect Kris to skirt his duties on a regular basis. It wasn't even something to be desired. However, Ivy now saw the true depth of being a Morai's consort. When Kris had asked him to be his Moris, Ivy had been so focused on the romantic implications that he'd ignored the political ones.

Oblivious to Ivy's fretting, Kris went on to say, "My apologies. I suppose that I don't have any real hobbies or likes when it comes to private time."

"I see," Ivy replied. "Well, that's understandable. It occurs to me that I've been remiss in considering something very important. Given my future potential role as Moris, I should start taking lessons. I believe that Her Imperial Majesty assisted your father when he was alive?"

Kris nodded. "Yes, the Mora or the Moris are like the right hand of the Morai. I think you'd be amazing at it, Ivy. I'll bring it up with my mother. She will teach you everything you need to know, and of course, so will I."

As Attcha rested in the shade, Kris and Ivy sat together on the ground. Ivy leaned against Kris's chest. As he petted Ivy's hair, Kris added, "For the moment, let's not think about that. Tell me about your life in Seanda."

"I will, if you tell me more about yourself."

And so they began a sort of game. Ivy would share something about himself that he'd never told Kris before, and Kris would reciprocate. Ivy thus learned a variety of information about his lover, from his favorite color—green—to his relationship with Shuri. In turn, Kris listened carefully as Ivy spoke of his lonely childhood in Seanda, of his parents, and his fear of having to marry Marquis Torildy. They spoke of their respective mothers, at which point Ivy finally got the chance to thank Kris for tracking Anfarasha down.

"It's been amazing to get to know her again now that I'm an adult," he said. "I should have never been wary about it to begin with."

"I'm sure she doesn't begrudge you that," Kris replied. "Will she be staying with your parents from now on?"

Ivy nodded. "She doesn't want to leave my side again, and my father agreed to forgo the original contract. I'm told that the Sisterhood of Reysen understood and accepted her choice. I don't know if anything will ever happen between her, my father, and my sire, but it's just nice to be together, to be… a family."

Titexe and Rasami were definitely doing their best, and while in some respects their relationship with Ivy remained somewhat awkward, they were steadily growing more comfortable together.

"I'm happy to hear that," Kris said. "If there's anyone who deserves to be wholly loved, it's you."

"I think everyone deserves love, Kris," Ivy whispered, "as long as they are capable of appreciating that love and giving it back. Love makes us better people, if we're open to it."

In reply, Kris pulled him close and kissed his temple. "Of that I'm quite certain," he murmured. "After all, I have firsthand experience."

Ivy's heart did a funny leap at the emotion in Kris's voice. Their gazes met and locked, and in that moment, Ivy wanted nothing more than to bury himself in Kris's embrace, to throw his resolve to the wind, forget about all his self-imposed rules, and allow Kris to claim him. Kris's lips were just so close, too close for Ivy to keep himself from kissing them. Perhaps he'd have done exactly that, but Kris pulled away at the very last moment.

"We should go," he said. "I think we've been away for quite some time, and your parents are bound to be worried."

As Kris helped Ivy up, Ivy took a deep breath to steady himself and control his raging libido. In spite of the need now burning through his veins, he managed to smile at Kris. "You're probably right, but before we leave, I just want to say one thing. This…. This was really nice."

"Yes, it was," Kris replied, sounding almost surprised at his own words.

Encouraged, Ivy mounted Attcha without further comment. His relationship with Kris would work out. Their first steps might have caused them to stumble, but they were on the right path now. Ivy just knew it.

KRIS'S CONVERSATION with Ivy had an unexpected and not wholly welcome effect. Kris's mother welcomed the chance to teach Ivy everything he needed to know about being a Morai's consort. Since a Mora and a Moris were essentially the same thing, with the only difference being that of gender, she was the perfect person to do so. While Kris liked to see the two of them grow closer, Ivy ended up spending more time with her than he did with Kris.

A few weeks after Kris's proposal to Ivy, Kris found himself sitting in his private office, browsing a report from Sai on Aranken activity—or rather, the lack of it—and Shuri's progress in terms of learning his mother's connection to A'rankin. It was important, especially since, according to Sai, Shuri had managed to unearth an old journal of his mother's that mentioned a new acquaintance. But everything still remained sketchy, and the only real clue Kris had was Ivy's vision during his attack.

Kris sighed and rubbed his eyes. No matter how much he tried to focus on something else, his thoughts always returned to Ivy. Ivy was right here, in the palace, and Kris couldn't be with him. They were supposed to meet for lunch, but Ivy had apologetically begged off at the last minute, explaining Kris's mother still had something important to show him.

In a way, it was a lesson for Kris too, since he imagined that this must be how Ivy had felt before, when Kris set him aside for Morai business without really thinking about his wants and needs. Kris wouldn't be surprised if he learned his mother was doing it on purpose. Still, it irked him that he'd reached a point in his life when he was jealous of his mother. His mother, for Creator's sake.

With a huff, Kris set the papers aside and shot to his feet. This was so ridiculous. The whole point of them starting their relationship anew was to get to know each other all over again, but they couldn't do that if they were apart.

As he headed to the door, Kris reminded himself that he needed to respect Ivy's desires. This was important for Ivy, for their shared future. Kris might still have moments when he doubted himself, but he'd made a promise to Ivy to try again, and this time he would not fail.

Therefore, when he reached his mother's quarters, he knocked politely. A few moments later, she opened the door, a knowing smirk on his face. "Kris. How nice of you to join us."

Just like that, Kris knew he'd been correct in his original assessment. "Are your lessons for the day finished?"

"Not just yet," Katara replied.

Her words would have annoyed Kris, but at the same time, Ivy appeared behind her and beamed at him. "Greetings, Your Imperial Majesty. I thought I wouldn't get to see you today."

"Well, we did promise ourselves that such a thing wouldn't happen," Kris replied. "Might it be possible to cut the lesson short?"

"I suppose that, just this once, it wouldn't hurt." His mother smiled. "Go on ahead. We've covered enough ground today as it is."

"Thank you, Your Majesty," Ivy replied. "I am, as always, exceedingly grateful for your generous assistance."

Kris's mother just waved them both off. Kris wasn't about to waste this opportunity. He offered Ivy his arm, experiencing a strong jolt of arousal when Ivy took it. A pretty blush covered Ivy's face, and Kris had the urge to peel off Ivy's Andari garments and see just how far it went. But, of course, he did no such thing. Instead, he guided Ivy into the corridor, in the general direction of the gardens.

"I trust my mother hasn't been working you too hard," he commented.

"Not at all," Ivy assured him. "In fact, it's been very interesting to see what you do on a daily basis."

Kris arched a brow in disbelief. "Interesting?" he repeated. "I would call bureaucracy many things, but interesting isn't one of them."

Ivy chuckled. "It's not the bureaucracy, per se. It's learning more about all the provinces that make up the Empire. I've actually been thinking. I've always wanted to travel, and I never got the chance before I moved here. I believe that, as a Moris, it would benefit me to see the lands I am supposed to govern."

Pride swelled in Kris's chest. Even if his motives for choosing Ivy as his Moris had mostly been selfish, he could see now that his heart had not led him astray. Ivy had set a goal for himself and would not be deterred until he achieved it.

Naturally, the situation wasn't ideal, and Kris would have preferred to have Ivy for his own. But that hadn't worked out too well before. Beyond his physical beauty, Ivy had too much potential to be restrained to the role of concubine.

"I can't say I'm wholly happy with the idea of you leaving my side," he confessed, "but I'll support it. I know that you'll always want to decide what is best for everyone in the empire."

Ivy's smile was so bright it seemed blinding, and Kris knew he'd said the right thing. "No matter what happens," he said, "I'll always return to you."

Whenever Ivy spoke like this, Kris was reminded of how much he'd hurt the young Andari and the exact extent of what he could have lost. Ivy must have noticed Kris's change in mood, but he didn't acknowledge it like before. Instead, he squeezed Kris's hand where it lay on his arm and said, "Let's do something new today. Something we've never done before."

"Like what?" Kris asked, bemused.

Ivy thought for a few seconds, then released a victorious sound. "Like seeing Attcha's world."

Kris gaped at his lover. "Are you crazy? We can't do that. Even during regular travel, rifts are dangerous. You know what happened to Uncle Phura when he attempted to manipulate them for his own purposes."

"Yes, I know. Just trust me on this, all right?" Ivy gave him a pleading look. "I want to try something."

Kris had doubted Ivy before, and it had led them to an argument that had eventually contributed to that near tragedy. Saying no outright wasn't the answer. He should have learned that by now. Besides, it would have taken a man stronger than him to resist those beautiful green eyes. "Very well," he said. "But if there's any danger to you, you have to promise me we won't take it further."

"I promise," Ivy replied. Taking Kris's hand, Ivy pulled him in the direction of the exit. "Come. We're going to need Attcha for this."

Kris obediently complied, swept away in the whirlwind of Ivy's enthusiasm. Seeing Ivy like this, so joyful, made him realize the mistakes he'd committed in trying to curtail Ivy's freedom. Was it possible to fall in love with Ivy just a little more every day? It certainly seemed so.

Ivy led him by the hand right up to the nightwolf dens, as if Kris hadn't known the way for the better part of a century. Kris enjoyed the warmth of Ivy's palm too much to care, and he even ignored the confused looks the occasional courtier shot them. When they finally reached Attcha's den, they found the nightwolf already waiting for them.

Attcha released a satisfied growl when he saw them holding hands. *Strong one. Tame soft one.*

Kris couldn't be sure who had tamed whom in their relationship, so he just arched a brow at his longtime friend. *Ivy wanted you to show us your world.*

Just like we did it last time, Ivy added.

Attcha eyed Kris with obvious skepticism. *Strong one, yes?*

Yes, it's fine with me, as long as there's no risk to Ivy, Kris replied.

"There isn't," Ivy assured him, this time speaking out loud. "My sire's been giving me lessons on divination. He was furious when he found out what I'd been doing with Attcha, but he decided to teach me the art in more detail, since I wasn't liable to stop."

In other words, Ivy had his parents right where he wanted them. Kris would have been intimidated if he hadn't been so happy for Ivy. Just like he'd told Ivy a few weeks ago, the young Andari deserved to be loved.

Ivy sat down at the edge of the den and patted the spot next to him. Kris complied, settling down onto the ground. Ivy leaned against his shoulder and took his hand, threading their fingers together.

"Relax," he whispered. "I've done this before, although never quite like this. I'll need your strength."

Kris tightened his hold on Ivy's hand. "You have it," he replied as he closed his eyes.

He wanted to say more, to tell Ivy that Kris would be willing to give him the sun and stars if he'd had them. But then those very same stars exploded in his vision in a bright array of colors. Kris gasped as the dazzling kaleidoscope engulfed his entire sense of self. He'd caught a glimpse of it before, when he'd been in the double rift, but now it was so different.

Kris felt Ivy's presence with him, and his vision cleared, settling the chaos around them into something tamer. He saw Attcha moving through the portal, supporting himself on the sway of colors that seemed far more solid than Kris knew them to be.

All of a sudden, Kris himself was within the rift, with Ivy by his side. Ivy's eyes were very wide, and he held Kris's hand so tightly Kris thought he might lose all feeling in the limb. Not that he cared. In fact, that couldn't be further from his mind.

I've never felt like I was actually here before, Ivy confessed, *not quite to this extent. This is amazing.*

Kris agreed. He would have thought himself truly here, but that couldn't be, because Ivy didn't have any physical protection against the energies of the rift. Confirming that guess, Ivy explained, *Our bodies are still outside, next to the den. Our minds are anchored to Attcha's, and so we're seeing what he is.*

As Ivy spoke, their forms floated after Attcha, navigating through the rift. Up ahead, Kris spotted a bright light, and he realized that must be their destination. Indeed, Attcha disappeared within the light, and a few seconds later—or maybe a few hours, since time had no meaning here—so did Kris and Ivy.

The blinding whiteness seemed to be a barrier of sorts, and maybe it would have held Kris back normally. But now he wasn't an errant rift-traveling Nikari. His spirit was the one following Attcha, and it bypassed the barrier with ease.

Once upon a time, Kris had asked Attcha about his home. As was his way, Attcha had growled at him and replied, *Home with strong one.* But Kris had insisted, and Attcha had eventually told him that his birthplace wasn't something Attcha could describe. Kris would have to see it to understand.

Kris had accepted his friend's reply and hadn't asked again. But he realized now that Attcha had been completely honest. *Creator,* he whispered. *Where are we?*

I'm not sure, Ivy replied. *I've never actually been this far before.*

The area where Attcha had led them didn't seem to have any beginning or any ending. It stretched as far as the eye could see, in every angle possible. When Kris turned—and wasn't it miraculous that he could even do that?—he found that the white barrier had disappeared, and he couldn't see any sign that it had ever been there.

He would have called that white doorway a dimensional rift, except this wasn't a separate dimension. For lack of a better description, it seemed to be an endless space where bits and pieces of individual worlds had been absorbed. Kris recognized a place that looked alarmingly like a Nikari forest, and not a few feet away—if the distance here could even be measured like that—a stripe of beach floated, waves lazily licking across the sand. Further, he caught sight of grassy plains and a barren, arid desert that drove shivers down Kris's spine. There were even buildings, a strikingly well-preserved mansion with the exact shape of the Nikari palace. At the back of Kris's mind, a memory stirred, and he recognized it as the Aranken home of the very first Fezenda, as it had been depicted in ancient journals.

Is this... our world? he asked, although he didn't even know who to address the question to.

Nevertheless, Attcha answered. *Our world, yes. Pieces. Dead pieces.*

Dead pieces of our world? Kris repeated. *How so?*

Attcha tossed his head and threw him that look Kris recognized as his "rolling-his-eyes" expression. *Things vanish. People forget. But nightwolves always remember. The rift always remembers.*

Kris had countless questions, and he could tell Ivy did too. *So does that mean there are other worlds here?* he asked Attcha. *Can we see them?*

Attcha shook his head. *Strong one anchored to own world. Not allowed to see. Too risky.*

It could make us doubt our sense of reality, right? Ivy guessed.

Yes. And other creatures here. Dangerous. Must stay here to be safe.

Kris took the warning to heart. Attcha's world was fascinating of its own accord, and he didn't want to tempt fate by asking for too much. He would have liked to know what other creatures inhabited this place, but Ivy's well-being remained his priority.

Still holding Ivy's hand, he willed himself to float in the general direction of the beach. To his surprise it worked, and soon they were lying down together on the sand, watching the waves disappear into nothing as Attcha quietly lay by their side.

You were right, he told Ivy. *This is... I have no words.*

To be fair, I wasn't sure it would work either. Ivy chuckled. *The last time I tried this was.... Well, that day when we argued. Shuri interrupted the divination.*

Kris remembered it all too well, the way he'd ranted at Ivy for the foolish risks he'd taken. *I'm sorry,* he said for what seemed like the millionth time.

Don't be, Ivy replied, *not about that. I was pushing myself too much. I can see that now. I just wish we hadn't fought about it.*

Let's make an oath, Kris said, peering into Ivy's emerald eyes. *Even when we disagree, we'll do things differently. I'll stop being such a domineering bastard, and you can be more open with me in turn.*

I don't know. Ivy hesitated, his green gaze dancing with mirth as he pretended to think about it. *I happen to like it when you get a little domineering.* His faux-serious expression melted into a luminous smile, and he cupped Kris's cheek with his free hand. *I swear.*

Kris couldn't help himself. Ivy was so close, and his lips so rosy and full, begging to be kissed. He buried his fingers in Ivy's hair, distantly noting that Ivy still wore it in the same style he'd adopted after he'd given his virginity to Kris.

Yes, some things that had happened between them couldn't be forgotten, but that didn't only apply to the bad part. They'd shared so many beautiful moments—stolen, and not as regular as they should have been, but still there—and Kris valued those memories too much to discard them.

They could build something just as beautiful from now on, but with the solidity that came from trust. And maybe Kris could even learn to believe in himself, if only because Ivy constantly displayed such faith in him.

He'd have undoubtedly kissed Ivy, but through the corner of his eye, he caught sight of a white blur rushing his way. His instincts kicked in, and he pushed Ivy down, covering his lover's body with his own.

He almost laughed at his own precautions when he identified the cause of all the commotion as a white nightwolf pup bounding their way. The small beast seemed to have been hiding in the floating forest and had emerged upon seeing Attcha. It—Kris couldn't guess the pup's gender yet—made a beeline for Kris's friend, growling playfully. Attcha grabbed the pup by the scruff and tossed him in the air, much like a parent would do with a child.

Kris's analogy must have occurred to Ivy, too, because he asked, *Is that Attcha's pup?*

I don't think so, Kris replied as he got off Ivy and helped his lover up. *He'd have told me about it.*

Then again, he also hadn't thought the pup could hear them, but the moment Attcha set him down, the nightwolf made his way to Kris's side. It was pretty much the same size Attcha had been when Kris had gotten him, maybe a little bigger. The pup eyed them with curious, wide gold-green eyes. It quickly lost interest in Kris, but kept sniffing around Ivy, whining softly.

I think... he wants me to touch him, Ivy said, sounding completely taken aback.

Kris hadn't expected this either, but then if anyone other than a Nikari could tame a nightwolf, it was Ivy. *Do you want to? This is an unclaimed nightwolf. He might want you to be pack.*

Ivy bit his lower lip uncertainly. *I want to, but.... How does it work exactly? Can I be pack for two nightwolves?*

Even as Ivy asked this, the world around them started to swirl. They were both propelled back through the rift so fast that Kris didn't immediately register it had happened. One moment he was floating in the strange not-quite-world, and the next, he lay on his back in front of Attcha's den with Ivy draped over him. He guessed that Ivy's dismay must have caused him to lose focus, therefore separating them from their anchor.

His skin prickled strangely, like he should be in pain, but it hadn't quite processed. His head was spinning so much that by the time he had any dirty thoughts about their position, Ivy had already gotten up.

"Oh no," Ivy said as he struggled to get up on shaky legs. "What happened with the white nightwolf?"

"I imagine he's with Attcha in the rift." Since Ivy had identified the creature as male, Kris could be fairly certain that must be the white pup's gender. He was also pretty sure the nightwolf would follow Ivy out of the rift, just like nightwolves had been doing for Kris's people ever since his ancestors had found a way to bond with the intelligent interdimensional beasts.

His guess was proven correct seconds later when Attcha emerged from his den, followed by the small nightwolf. The white pup didn't pay much attention to his new environment. He just pounced on Ivy, his momentum making the young Andari fall back on his ass. Kris watched in bemusement as the nightwolf licked Ivy's face, his tail wagging so hard his entire lower side was shaking.

Did you know about this? he asked Attcha.

Soft one nightwolf soul, Attcha said calmly, sitting back and looking particularly satisfied with himself. *White fur see that. Feel soft one. But white fur could not come if soft one didn't want him to.*

Kris buried his fingers in his friend's fur and smiled. *You're just as scheming as my mother, you know that?*

Attcha seemed pleased with the comparison. His golden eyes fixed on Kris's face, and that was the only warning Kris got before Attcha licked him all over his face.

Kris wanted to be outraged, but he was too happy to be angry with his friend for getting slobber all over him. For the first time, he truly believed that maybe he hadn't ruined everything after all. He still didn't know if he deserved this second chance, but Creator help him, he'd make good use of it, and he'd never allow Ivy to regret it.

AT FIRST, the courtiers and the Nikari nobles were kept in the dark with regard to Ivy's future role. If anyone suspected, they didn't say it outright, perhaps because they deemed it an impossibility for the Nikari Empire to have an Andari Moris.

However, the secret could not be kept forever, and Kris seemed to plan to reveal it in style. One month after his proposal to Ivy, he announced throwing yet another ball. Of course, there were countless rumors with regard to Kris's reasons for this party. No one came out to ask Ivy outright, but judging by the occasional look Ivy got, he suspected that people were more likely to believe Kris would be choosing a substitute moraistele, not asking his current one to bond with him.

Ivy wasn't too worried about them. Or at least, he tried not to be. Still, the night of the ball, he found himself just as nervous as he'd been when he'd first come to Nikaret. While his sire fussed over his hair and outfit, Ivy fidgeted and worried, wondering if he could handle this after all.

"Stop fretting, Ivy," his sire chastised him. "You're more than capable of doing anything you set your mind to."

Ivy met Rasami's gaze in the mirror, biting his lip. "I just…. This is so important, Sire. Technically speaking, I just agreed to be the Moris for Kris. What if that's not enough?"

"Aren't you always telling your lover to stop doubting himself? You should take your own advice. You've earned this, Ivy, and the Morai trusts you. Personally, I'm still not very sure I should trust him, but since this is what you want…."

"It is," Ivy assured his sire. "I love him."

"Well then, let us speak no more of it. You have plenty of time to worry about it when your actual bonding day arrives."

Rasami would have probably launched into an elaborate description of what Ivy's bonding celebration would be like, but their conversation came to a grinding halt when Reisl appeared out of nowhere. Ivy's sire yelped, having yet to grow accustomed to living with a nightwolf, albeit a miniature one.

Ivy just chuckled and welcomed Reisl, petting the white nightwolf's head. *How do I look, Reisl?*

The white nightwolf gave him an approving growl. *Brave one beautiful. Mate will like.*

Ivy couldn't help but blush at Reisl's words. He liked how Reisl identified Kris as his mate, even if they weren't bonded yet. *I'm a bit nervous,* he admitted.

White fur know, Reisl replied. *But brave one not fear. White fur protect. Always.*

Even if he risked getting nightwolf fur all over his elaborate outfit, Ivy hugged Reisl, half to encourage himself and half to comfort the nightwolf. Throughout the time they'd spent together, he'd learned that Reisl had felt him when Ivy had first been training his divination abilities with Attcha. However, Reisl had been unable to come to Ivy.

Not only that, but he'd sensed Ivy's predicament when Ivy had been injured and had been very anxious, especially when Attcha had lost some of his power too.

I told you Kris wouldn't hurt me, he reminded his nightwolf.

White fur understand, Reisl replied. *Greedy one nightwolf soul. But white fur still protect.*

Ivy snickered at Reisl's description of Kris. While Reisl liked Kris and had accepted Kris in their extended pack, he still felt Kris hogged Ivy, which was why Ivy's lover had been deemed the "greedy one."

His sire released a long-suffering sigh at Ivy's antics. "Come on before that beast destroys all my hard work. And you, nightwolf. Make sure you keep an eye on Ivy if I'm not around."

Reisl snorted, like he was wordlessly telling Rasami "of course I will." To Ivy, he said, *Clever one strange. Not understand white fur.*

Not everyone is privileged enough to understand nightwolves like I do, Ivy replied.

To his surprise, he realized his conversation with Reisl had soothed his nervousness. "All right," he told his sire. "Let's go."

His father and his mother were already waiting for them, decked out in finery that must have cost as much as the entire Seanda manse. Ivy offered his mother his arm, while his father did the same for his sire.

Together, they left the townhome they shared and got onto the carriage Kris had sent beforehand. Even Reisl joined them, and Ivy distantly thought it was a good thing his nightwolf hadn't yet grown into his full bulk like Attcha.

The trip to the palace took forever. When the carriage finally came to a halt in front of the entrance of the majestic building, a liveried Nikari footman opened its door. Ivy's father and sire first left the vehicle, then helped his mother out. Ivy came last, followed by his nightwolf.

Predictably, some of the Nikari stared at Reisl. Perhaps they'd thought the rumors of Ivy having a nightwolf were just that, rumors. Ivy ignored the discreet gaping and nodded in acquiescence of the guards' presence and assistance.

Inside, Ivy expected more of the same, but Sai greeted them at the doorway, pulling them aside. As Sai guided them through both familiar and unfamiliar corridors, Ivy marveled at the way the palace had been decorated. The blue crystals that were the Nikari trademark adorned every individual stone at a perfectly equal distance. Given the fact that they were arranged in a geometric pattern, Ivy couldn't imagine how much concentrated effort that had taken.

Sai stopped in front of the majestic doors of the ballroom. No, these weren't the regular doors but the side entrance, the one Kris and Katara used. This was it. The moment when everyone would learn the truth had finally arrived.

Reisl nudged him with his muzzle. *Brave one go to mate,* he said.

Ivy pet Reisl's head and smiled. *Thank you.*

Reisl sat aside, since he wouldn't follow Ivy in the ballroom. A pup he might be, but he remained a nightwolf. However, he'd assured Ivy that if he was needed, he'd rush to Ivy's side, and Ivy believed him.

At last, Sai opened the doors. A gong sounded, and Ivy heard his name and those of his parents being announced. Like a man in a dream, he stepped past the entryway and into the glittering ballroom.

He had a small moment during which he almost thought he'd accidentally ended up in Attcha's not-quite-world. The light of the blue crystals danced over the masked figures of the guests, creating a surreal atmosphere. Here, the geometric pattern of the crystals seemed splashed in a wild array, like the stars had decided to leave the sky and pay the Nikari Empire a visit. No lighting other than the crystals existed, but their luminescence was such that additional torches would have been superfluous and possibly ruined the effect. Ivy's breath caught when he realized the blue lights were placed in the exact position the stars had been on the night of the solstice. He couldn't be sure how he knew that, but it still made his heart flip.

His parents seemed pretty impressed too. "His Imperial Majesty went all out today, didn't he?" his father murmured.

"Good," his sire said. "I want everyone to realize how important our son is for the Morai."

Sometimes, it still took Ivy aback to see his sire so protective of him, but he guessed that he would never truly know the extent to which the older Andari had been shaken by the visions he'd had of Ivy's demise. But Ivy couldn't think about that now. He was too busy remembering a different night, when he'd escaped his parents' scrutiny and sneaked out to enjoy a masquerade ball. And then there had been the party when he'd officially met the Morai and realized the identity of his Kris.

Seeing the elegant masked nobles everywhere around him had a peculiar, hypnotizing effect, as if those two distinct memories had come together to form this one. It threw him so much that he froze right there, breathless as images of past and present piled on top of one another. It certainly didn't help that everyone was staring at him.

And then the crowd parted, revealing Kris heading their way. Kris smiled at him, and just like that, Ivy snapped out of his trance. He stepped forward, meeting Kris halfway.

Kris made no attempt to hide his satisfaction at having Ivy here or his appreciation at the efforts Rasami had put into his outfit. *I've been waiting for you,* he said, kissing Ivy's hand. *You're beautiful.*

He whispered the simple words in Ivy's mind, a sign of their increased intimacy. However, out loud, he offered a more formal address, "Greetings, Your Lordships. You honor my home through your presence."

In turn, Ivy and his parents bowed in front of the Morai. It was already unusual that Kris hadn't waited for them to come to him, but breaches of protocol could be accepted on Kris's part—not so much when they came from Ivy and his family.

"On the contrary, Your Imperial Majesty," his father said. "You are the one who honors us through this invitation."

"The doors of the palace are always open to the Erethe," Kris replied in turn.

The exchange made Ivy remember yet another night, the one when he'd first become known as the moraistele. But that day, he'd knelt in front of Kris. He'd only been a concubine, succumbing to the power of the Morai.

Kris smiled at him, and as his fingers entwined with Ivy's, the familiar notes of the *awaye* echoed through the room. Ivy would have thought his lover had done it on purpose, but Kris went tense. He turned in the direction of the minstrels, and Ivy followed his lover's gaze, only to see the A'Mora standing next to the first performer. She waved and winked at him, and Ivy took that as a seal of approval. Kris shook his head in obvious bemusement, then directed his attention toward Ivy once more. "Can I have this dance?"

Ivy didn't hesitate in the slightest. He nodded, allowing Kris to pull him onto the dance floor. The melodious sway of the *awaye* fell over him as he and Kris began to move in tandem. Given the dance's Andari origin, he and Kris had only danced it once, during the solstice, but it still felt so natural.

At first, the soft notes reminded Ivy of the way Kris liked to comb his fingers through his hair, of the nearly worshipful look in his eyes as he gazed at Ivy—that look he wore now. When Ivy lifted his leg to Kris's hip, the Nikari's hand landed on his thigh, so gentle, lingering in a clear display of yearning. As the dance exploded in a volcano of passion, Ivy lost himself in the sensuality of each motion. After all, how could he not? When he ground against Kris, he could feel the other man's erection against his ass. When Kris flipped him through the air, he unavoidably landed in Kris's arms. Kris's scent, his warmth and strength were everywhere. Ivy felt more certain than ever that he was doing the right thing.

This dance was reminiscent of the two of them, of the relationship they were building. The passion didn't clash with the gentleness. They complemented each other. The trust that came with knowledge that Kris would catch him felt somewhat symbolic, although tonight things seemed the other way around. Kris was taking his own leap of faith, entrusting his empire to a non-Nikari. Perhaps they had finally come full circle.

Kris appeared to guess his thoughts. As the last notes of the *awaye* faded, Kris didn't immediately release Ivy from his arms. He held Ivy close as his voice echoed clearly through the ballroom. "I have an announcement to make. In two months' time, His Lordship Behnivyr Erethe, son of Their Lordships, Earl Titexe Erethe and Earl Rasami Erethe, and Her Ladyship Anfarasha Terneal, will become my Moris."

The formal phrases solidified the reality of Ivy's situation, but it was the words drifting into Ivy's mind that made him melt against Kris. *I love you, Ivy.*

It was the first time Kris had actually confessed his emotions to Ivy, and Ivy's eyes filled with tears. He pushed them back and smiled up at Kris. *I love you, too.*

Yes, they had come full circle. This time, they'd done things right, and no rift, dimensional or otherwise, would separate them ever again.

EPILOGUE
DEPARTURE

SHURI CLENCHED his hands into fists as he watched his brother unashamedly paw Ivy. Since he'd made his announcement, Kris hadn't left Ivy's side for a second, and Shuri hadn't dared to approach out of the fear that he'd punch the bastard and make his situation worse than it already was.

All of the guests had already started the regular process of assuring themselves of the future Moris's favor. It disgusted Shuri to see them all fawn over Ivy, when most of them had displayed only scorn for the young Andari when Ivy had been a concubine. But then, Ivy had a way of worming into people's hearts. Shuri was the first to know that.

Ivy would probably never understand how Shuri had fallen in love with him. He'd been attracted to Ivy from the moment the man had first stepped through the doors of the ballroom. Later, at the first breakfast they'd shared, he'd been intrigued by the young Andari. But when Ivy had approached him of his own accord, he'd fallen captive to the purity of Ivy's smile and the strength of his soul. He'd realized then what a treasure his brother had uncovered. Ivy's beautiful face hid an iron will and a strength Kris would never truly appreciate.

Shuri took a deep breath and looked away from the sight. If only he'd been braver, he might have managed to stop this. But no, he'd told himself he needed to keep his word to his brother. He'd forced himself to simply watch as Ivy was caught deeper in the snare of the Morai and his murderous mother.

Why hadn't he approached Ivy differently? Why had he remained a distant friend and nothing more? After all, an honor bond hardly mattered when it involved someone as honorless as the Morai. But it was far too late for regrets now.

The wedding between the Morai Kristelien Fezenda and his Andari bond mate would undoubtedly be the event of the century, but Shuri had no intention of being here to see it. He turned on his heel and stalked out of the ballroom through the glass doors that led into the garden.

It didn't take long for him to realize he was being followed. "What do you want?" he asked his pursuer as he turned to face her. "To gloat?"

"Actually, I was merely checking why you hadn't come to congratulate your brother on his upcoming nuptials." The A'Mora arched a brow at him. "Or do you still believe Ivy will ever look at you like he looks at my son?"

Shuri glowered at the woman who'd killed his mother. "You bitch. Haven't you taken enough from me already? What more do you want?"

"I want my son to be safe and happy, of course." Katara narrowed her eyes at him. "If I had it my way, I would lock you in the first available dungeon and throw away the key. You're a menace, just like your uncle and your mother."

"And I'm sure you're so satisfied that you got rid of them, aren't you?" Shuri sneered. "Kris is a fool. I have no idea how he doesn't see you for the murderer that you are."

Katara didn't flinch at the accusation. "Your mother deserved to die for what she did to Spatha. She was a traitor before she even killed my husband. But then you know that, don't you, Shuri? You might tell Kris only bits and pieces of what you've uncovered, and you can even get away with it because Kris is focusing on Ivy. But once Ivy becomes the Moris, you might find yourself in a very unpleasant situation."

"I'm not afraid of your son," Shuri shot back. "And for the record, I don't plan to be here when that happens."

"Oh? And where will you go? Will you run from Nikari justice, abandon your uncle to the fate he chose for himself?"

Leaving his uncle would be among the hardest things that Shuri's choice involved. The older Nikari might have recovered from his injury, but he didn't have anyone else other than Shuri. Still, Shuri needed to do this, for himself, for Ivy, and his dead parents.

"I'll be departing for A'rankin," Shuri replied. "I'll investigate the matter myself and find out who tried to kill Ivy." And who his mother had been in contact with, too, but he wasn't about to tell Katara that.

Katara burst into laughter. "You must either be suicidal or a fool. Do you think the Aranken are a pleasant people? If you go there, you do so at your own risk."

"I do everything at my own risk." He paused as he processed her words. "So you won't try to stop me?"

The A'Mora shrugged. "We do need the information. I was going to suggest to Kris to send a spy there since it seems unlikely that we'd find out what's going on through your dubious efforts. Personally, I don't trust you not to join forces with the Aranken if you think it will benefit you, but no, I won't stop you."

"Of course you won't." Shuri smirked. "If they kill me, I'll be out of your hair."

Much to his surprise, Katara's expression sobered. "Shuri," she said, her voice now serious, "don't do anything stupid. Whether you like it or not, Kris does love you."

"He has a funny way of showing it," Shuri shot back.

Katara released a heavy sigh. "If you truly want to do this, do it right. Speak to Kris and become the representative of your people with the Aranken. He'll give you the support you need for this task you've decided on."

Shuri opened his mouth to tell her where she could shove that support, but at the last moment, he decided against it. "Very well." He experienced a moment of satisfaction when Katara's eyes widened. Perhaps she had expected him to refuse, something she could have pointed out later should Kris ask about it. But as much as it irked Shuri to admit it, Katara was right about one thing. This endeavor would be too risky to chance without official backup. He had too many plans to throw all cautiousness to the wind.

Even as he thought this, Kris and Ivy appeared in the garden. "Is everything all right, Mother?" Kris asked with a frown.

"Everything is fine," Katara replied, smiling at her son. "Shuri was just explaining his plan to find out more information on our predicament."

Kris knew both of them too well to actually believe their conversation had been that harmless, but he let it slide—just like he always did when it came to any suspicious matter his mother was involved in. For the moment, that might work in Shuri's favor.

"I think it's necessary for me to go to A'rankin," he said.

Ivy gasped. "That's far too risky. No, absolutely not. There has to be another way."

Shuri's heart clenched at Ivy's honest concern. His resolve faltered, and he wondered if he should be leaving after all. Ivy needed him here. How could Shuri simply abandon the innocent beauty to his fate?

And then Kris wrapped an arm around Ivy's waist and kissed his temple. "I agree with Ivy. While I will be the first to admit we need the information, we can't chance such an incursion, not when we know them to be hostile to us. You would be risking your life."

Shuri swallowed around the knot in his throat, knowing that he had no choice now but to go forward.

"This is what I want," he said. "The matter cannot be left hanging forever. I can take care of myself. Besides, I doubt the Aranken will want to start an outright war. It's more likely they have a rebel force with an agenda of their own. We need to find out who's targeting you, Ivy. The immediate threat might be over, but that doesn't mean we are in any way safe."

"That's another argument why you shouldn't go there," Ivy said stubbornly.

Shuri forced himself to smile. "I'll be fine. I promise."

For the longest time, Kris just looked at him. Shuri met his brother's gaze without flinching. This was for Ivy. They had that in common—concern for Ivy. Or so Shuri hoped. He hoped Ivy meant something to Kris, and, at the very least, Kris wouldn't hurt him again.

Of course, Kris's skepticism reared its ugly head. "If I trust you with this," he said, "you could easily cause an international incident. Can I rely on you to do what's right?"

"I will go with him," the A'Mora offered. "Between me and my nightwolf, there's very little we can't handle."

Shuri clenched his jaw, wondering if the blasted A'Mora existed solely to antagonize him. He hoped his brother would refuse outright, but Kris did no such thing. "Are you sure, Mother?"

"Positive," Katara replied. "Trust me, Kris. I might be the A'Mora, but once you bond with Ivy, I won't have any official position. It's perfect."

Shuri tried to say this entire arrangement seemed unnecessary, and he could handle this mission just fine. However, before he could protest, Ivy took his hand and smiled at him. "Promise me you'll be careful?"

Shuri melted. "I promise," he said, knowing he'd already lost the battle before he'd even fought it. Turning toward the A'Mora, he reluctantly added, "I appreciate your generous offer, Your Majesty."

"I will allow it," Kris said, "but at the first sign of anything going wrong, you're coming back—both of you. That's an order."

"Yes, Kris," Katara replied. "You don't have to worry about that. I have to live long enough to see you and Ivy give me grandchildren."

Ivy's face flamed as he stammered, "W-We haven't discussed that yet."

The A'Mora just laughed, while Kris brushed his lips over Ivy's. "We have time. Maybe one day we'll think about finding an odale, but right now I want you all to myself."

Ivy still looked concerned. "I suppose this is where I tell you I have no interest in women whatsoever."

Kris kissed his cheek. "Don't worry about it. We'll find a solution."

Shuri watched the exchange in silence, and his decision solidified even more. *Wait for me Ivy,* he thought. *I'll make you mine yet. I won't let them decide your future.*

Whether Kris and Katara knew it or not, Shuri would find a way to avenge his mother and rescue Ivy. The alternative was unthinkable.

Fractured Souls

By Alana Ankh

Sequel to Beyond the Rift
Elemental Lovers series

Centuries ago, a group of Aranken mages left their homeland and became the ancestors of the Nikari. Now a Nikari prince will return, seeking truth and finding far more than he expected.

Shuri Fezenda has one goal in mind when he departs for A'rankin—to identify the culprit behind the conspiracy targeting Ivy, his brother's consort and a man Shuri cares for deeply. But when he meets Prince Tynare'Or'Therar, Shuri's world is turned upside down.

Beautiful and mysterious, Tynare draws Shuri like no other. The secrets he whispers taunt and tease, but Shuri's treacherous heart races and his body responds when Tynare shoots him a knowing smile. And then Shuri meets Tynare's twin brother, Nari, and in Nari's kindness and blind eyes, he finds refuge and a love beyond anything he thought he could feel.

Torn between duty and confused emotions, Shuri faces an A'rankin on the brink of civil war and a foe he didn't count on—the neighboring land of Shyrn. At the heart of the conflict, one question remains. Who is Tynare really, and who is Nari? Shuri is almost afraid to learn the answer.

ALANA ANKH is a hopeless romantic. Once upon a time—no, not in the Stone Ages, but when Alana was a nosy teenager—she lived and breathed mainstream romance, but after she discovered m/m…. Well, her fate was sealed.

Regardless of the genre, Alana thinks love can be painful, heartbreaking, but also fun, corny, and a little silly. Love is different for everyone and anyone—and in her books, she tries to celebrate that.

Alana also loves sci-fi, fantasy and paranormal. But even if her boys have scales, fur, claws, fangs—or whatever else occurs to her—they're really very nice people. Most of the time. Well…. Most of them are nice, but all of them deserve love and a HEA.

When Alana isn't feeding her addiction to happily-ever-afters and hot men, she's randomly slaying monsters in MMORPGs or thinking up the next idea to share with readers.

You can find Alana at http://alanaankh.wordpress.com/ or on Facebook (which she does try to monitor) at
https://www.facebook.com/alana.ankh.

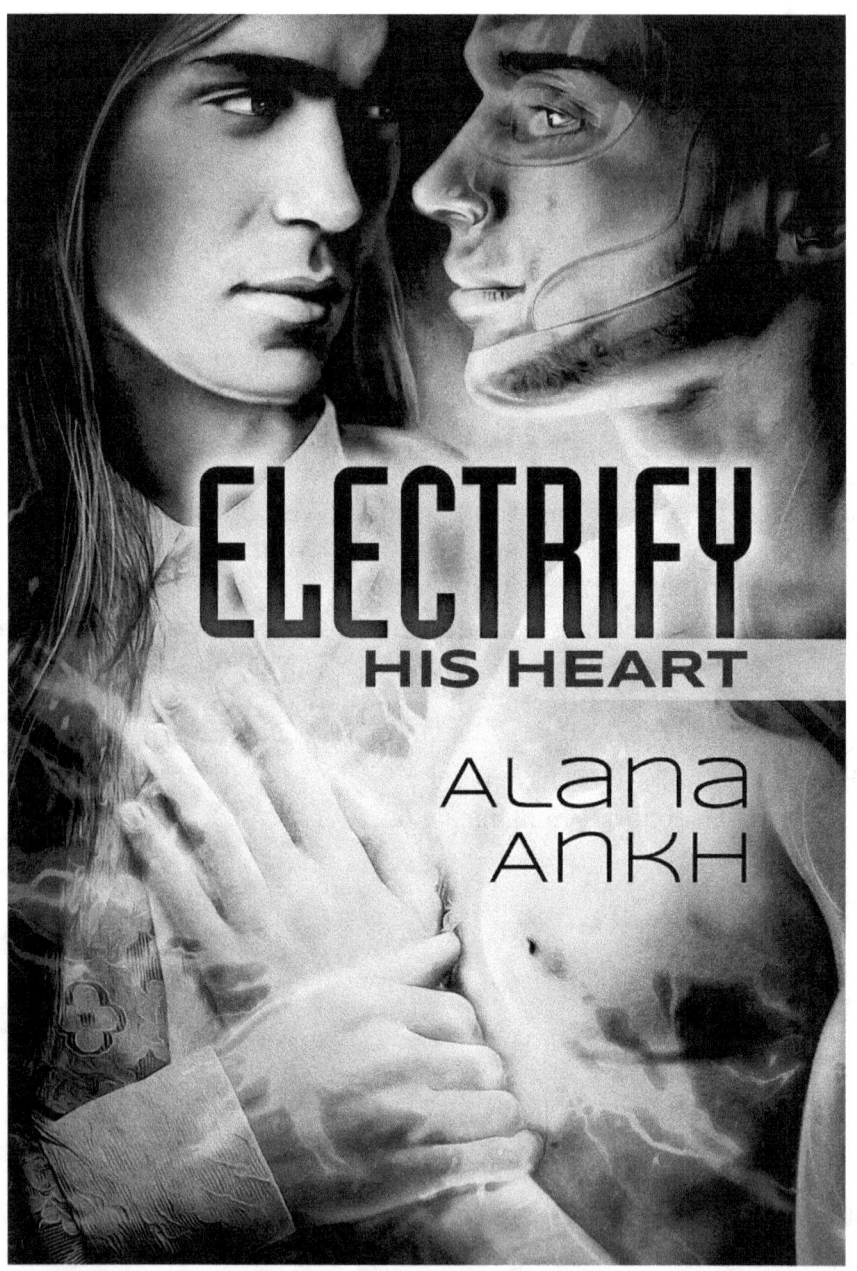

ELECTRIFY
HIS HEART

Alana Ankh

http://www.dreamspinnerpress.com

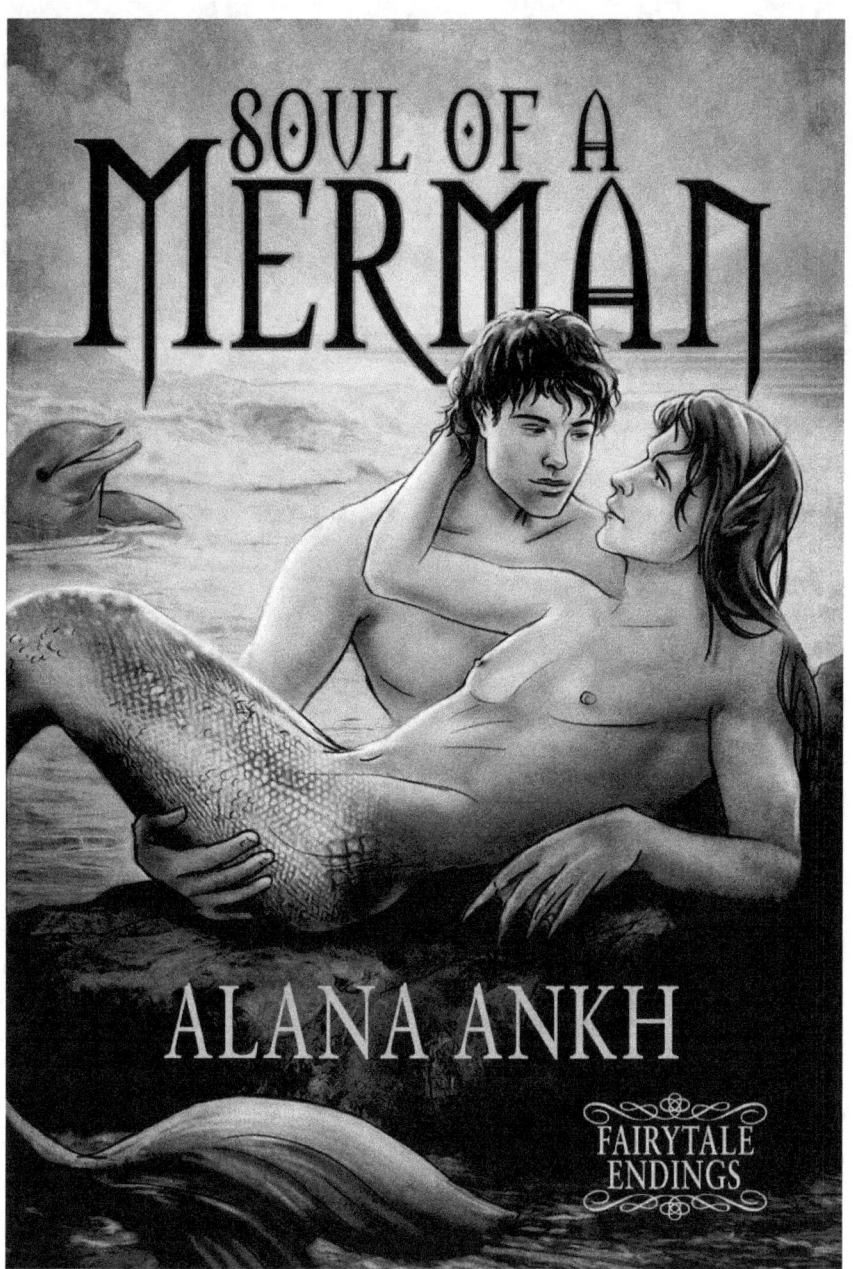

SOUL OF A MERMAN

ALANA ANKH

FAIRYTALE
ENDINGS

http://www.dreamspinnerpress.com

SUI LYNN

ADEL'S
PURR

http://www.dreamspinnerpress.com

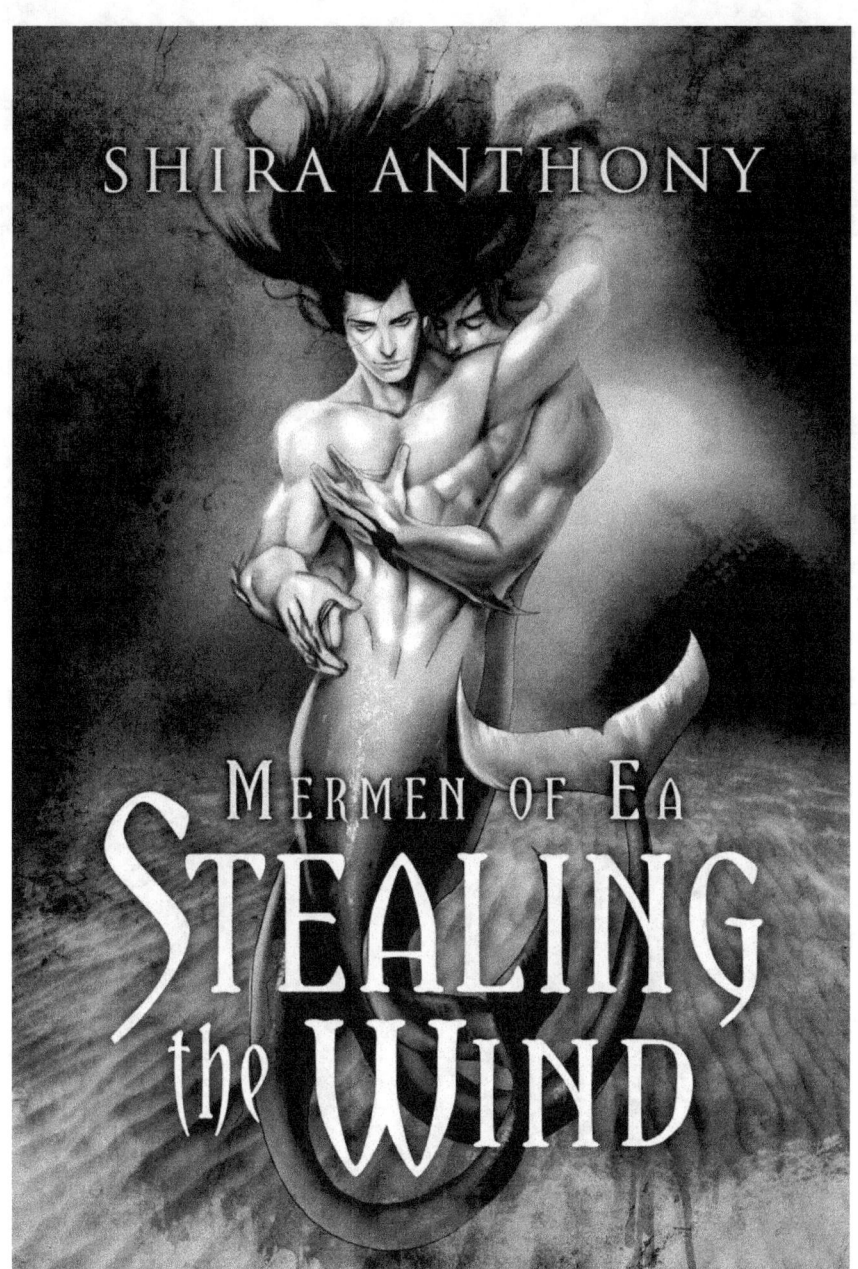

SHIRA ANTHONY

MERMEN OF EA

STEALING
the WIND

http://www.dreamspinnerpress.com

www.ingramcontent.com/pod-product-compliance
Lightning Source LLC
Chambersburg PA
CBHW051631260626
47170CB00004B/1133